BLIND ITEMS

Also by Matthew Rettenmund

Encyclopedia Madonnica
Boy Culture
Totally Awesome 80s

BLIND ITEMS
A (LOVE) STORY

Matthew Rettenmund

St. Martin's Press ♏ New York

Design by James Sinclair

Library of Congress Cataloging-in-Publication Data

Rettenmund, Matthew.
    Blind items : a love story / by Matthew Rettenmund.
       p.   cm.
   ISBN 0-312-19242-8
   I. Title.
   PS3568.E774B55   1998
   813'.54—dc21   98-34222
                                    CIP

First Edition: October 1998

10 9 8 7 6 5 4 3 2 1

For José Vélez,
who helps me see things clearly.

Acknowledgments

Special thanks to Dana Albarella, Jane Jordan Browne, Linda Rettenmund and Melissa Rettenmund.

The author would like to acknowledge the following books for their
wealth of information on the subject of film history:

The Celluloid Closet (HarperCollins, 1987) by Vito Russo
Dark Star: The Meteoric Rise and Eclipse of John Gilbert (St. Martin's
Press, 1985) by Leatrice Gilbert Fountain with John R. Maxim
The Film Encyclopedia (HarperCollins, 1994) by Ephraim Katz;
Melinda Corey and George Ochoa, editors
The Gay Book of Days (The Main Street Press, 1982) by Martin Greif
Hollywood Babylon (Dell, 1975) by Kenneth Anger*
Lost Films: Important Movies that Disappeared (Citadel Press, 1996)
by Frank Thompson
Our Movie Heritage (Rutgers University Press, 1997) by Tom Mc-
Greevey and Joanne L. Yeck
VideoHound's Golden Movie Retriever (Visible Ink, 1998), Martin Con-
nors and Jim Craddock, editors

*The "excerpt" from *Hollywood Babylon* that appears in *Blind Items* is
completely fictional.

Chief among the many magazines and newspapers that proved invalu-
able in researching the art of the blind item and celebrity reportage were:

Entertainment Weekly
The Globe
Movieline

The National Enquirer
The New York Daily News
The New York Post
People
The Star
Vanity Fair
The Village Voice
Weekly World News

BLIND ITEMS

OFF THE LIST

BY WARREN JUNIOR

THEY "DO" . . . BUT THEY DEFINITELY DON'T

Wedding bells have rung for Mr. and Mrs. Fuck-Me-Raw, those two physically delicious (if suspiciously smooth) soft-sex stars I was telling you about three months back. You remember: "Meet The Inverts"?

He's *big* in R-rated potboilers and she has graced more than her fair share of "tasteful" made-for-video *exploitatifs*. We've seen these two fucking half of Hollywood in their grimy movies, which makes their flicks semiautobiographical.

Only "semi" because these two have never done same-sexploitation movies: In real life, he's a gay sex addict and she's a tortured high-society dyke. Who says gays and lesbians can't get along?

To throw off the hounds, these two B⁺-list stars had been shacked up since practically before I was born. But I treed 'em.

After my column's I-thought-heavily-veiled reference to these longtime live-in co-conspirators, the crazy kids (he's 41, she's officially 37) tied the knot in a charming ceremony that took place in the great outdoors—that's as much as I can say, due to the highly "unique" (a.k.a. identifying) nature of the spot they chose for their nuptials. I'd say more, but I don't like court. Except for when the jury is, well— you know the rest.

Memo to Tinseltown re the shotgun marriage of Mr. and Mrs. F-M-R: I wasn't aware that I wielded such power! I've never made those Hot 100 lists in *Entertainment Weekly* or *Premiere*—perhaps I'm just bubbling under?

Regardless, don't you think it's a tad déclassé that even though my column caused—er, *inspired*—their marital bond, they failed to so much as *invite* me to the "I do"s? Maybe they didn't want to sweat out that part where the guests are encouraged to volunteer info on why the lovebirds at hand should not be married.

How about the fact that this bride and groom have never gone further than holding hands—and have only done *that* when cameras were around? Kiss the bride? *That's* a first!

I guess Mr. and Mrs. Fuck-Me-Raw, née The Inverts, were wise to leave me—as always—"Off the List."

CHAPTER 1

Guess Who? Don't Sue!

David Greer — It's startling to learn this about myself, but I can walk through a crowded Manhattan apartment sale and notice a plastic Farrah Fawcett-Majors head circa 1977 in mint condition under a table near the back, even if the box is partially covered by a trash bag.

I'd just done that earlier in the day, amazed that the head—a toy I'd coveted as a boy, but which had been restricted to girls' Christmas lists—still had the soft hair attached and came with a few intact vials of gooey makeup that could be painted onto Farrah's grinny skull. It had to be worth seventy-five dollars, and I'd gotten it for ten dollars, on the major cheap.

Farrah's head was resting in an old brown Bloomie's bag at my feet. I glanced down to check on it and shuddered a little at the barely life-like scalp with its enormous hairplugs.

When Warren saw my find, he rolled his eyes and sneered out an unenthusiastic *"Faaabulous."* Warren, despite his rep as a somewhat flamboyant queen, didn't comprehend camp the way the average gay man (like me) did. Or maybe it was just that Warren could appreciate the camp of a Farrah head but couldn't get over the idea that someone would pay ten dollars for it, let alone feel that he'd gotten a bargain.

Warren was hunched at his cramped desk, a smorgasbord of work in progress. He was mechanically dashing off a letter to someone, either thanking them for an invitation proffered or berating them for having "forgotten" to put him on the list. Warren Junior was, after all, the most famous gossip columnist in town, and the town in question was the most famous one on the planet. No, not Hollywood. Hollywood's not a town, it's a concept. *New York City.* Snap, snap.

Indisputably, fame is devalued in the nineties. A man whose opinions occasionally hobbled careers, a man who appeared almost daily on just about every talk show as an outspoken panelist, a man who had interviewed everyone from Kristy McNichol (big mistake, "Buddy") to Red Buttons . . . that man, Warren Junior, wasn't even knocking down six figures for his weekly column at *Island Rage.* He worked in a homely office space in midtown Manhattan, and sometimes walked to work to avoid wasting his MetroCard. He liked to say that he had an office with a view—of Port Authority.

I sat on the corner of Warren's massively overcluttered desktop, gagging on decades of recirculated cigarette smoke, and idly paged through letters and invitations. We often spent our lunch hours together, killing time in solidarity, even though I worked a world away—downtown. Warren would work straight through any conversations we had, banging out column ideas as I ticked off the bad TV I'd watched the night before or offered my take on the current state of Faye Dunaway's face. I always marveled at Warren's industry—he worked nonstop, never needing motivation or having to fend off sloth.

I found a jumbled set of contact sheets, millions of tiny black-and-white images of Warren smirking in borrowed Versace for an updated author's photo to accompany his column, "Off the List." After eight years on the job, the same photo he'd used since his debut was more like a before photo in one of those infomercials. The proposed replacement that he'd circled in red was a competent enough photograph, a decent Meisel knockoff, but I thought that Warren should have either tried to do something funny or used trick photography to package himself as a sex bomb, anything high concept instead of . . . *this.* He just looked like a smug, shaved, black queen. I held up the contact sheet and looked across the desk at Warren. *Oh.*

As my Farrah find proved, I had the kind of eyes that caught absolutely everything that could possibly be of interest to me. I had programmed them to ferret out certain insignias, colors, shapes.

"Here's something," I said, my fail-safe eyes having caught a famous name while scanning one of a hundred or so bastard documents. The name didn't immediately attach itself to a face, it was so big. *Alan Dillinger.* Visions of a gun-toting gangster. No, wait, it was the name of the cute guy from that lousy TV show about lifeguards, *Lifesavers.* He was the overexposed guy who caused young girls to scream much harder than anyone on *Baywatch* ever had, even if *Lifesavers* was never quite as popular. Still a ratings bonanza, it was so bad even *I* couldn't watch it, not even to laugh.

"What is it?" Warren asked. "Because if it's a benefit, I don't have the time. *You* go, David. I'm tired of giving. I can't afford to have a heart anymore." He was unconsciously lapsing into his legendary Della Reese impersonation, his head already swaying with each word. It was such a skillful read on Della I could almost see the skunk on top of his head.

"It's this . . ." quickly reading the raised gold letters on the heavy invite, "bash. It sounds like an all-out bash. A network celebration for *Lifesavers.* Tonight."

Warren grimaced, stuck his tongue out while typing, and reserved comment.

"I'm not saying I'm an Alan Dillinger groupie, but it'd be kind of cool to say I went to a party for him and was in the same room with him." I needed some excitement and wasn't above such an admittedly cheap thrill.

"Honestly, David. Would you French-kiss Nicole just to say your tongue was *thisclose* to Tom's cock?" Warren saturated each word with venom from a reservoir of the stuff he might've kept in one of his unstylishly chubby cheeks. "This boy is just like toilet paper. Popular, yes, but nothing to shout about and you can always find it in the closet. And did you see him on Letterman last week? Seems like the—" smacking the crook of his arm loudly— "rumors might be true." He was referring to a blind item written by Janet Charlton which had alluded to an unnamed TV hunk's drug of choice under the headline "Hero's Heroin." I hadn't interpreted Alan Dillinger as a sloppy addict on Letterman, more as surprised prey.

But really, the main reason Warren disapproved of my push to go to the party was that he just didn't relate to why I would be attracted to the idea of seeing any particular star in person, let alone one who broke the cardinal rule: gay but in denial. The idea of Alan Dillinger on heroin was a stretch, but every gay man alive seemed to know someone who knew someone who *knew* for a fact that Alan Dillinger sucked dick. For queers, it wasn't in dispute anymore, it was an accepted, unwritten, faithfully repeated fact. Straight women across the world continued to believe in the myth of Alan Dillinger as potent, insatiable, heterosexual lover, but then the masses used to think Eva Gabor and Merv Griffin were a red-hot couple.

With Warren and me, our game was that we were supposed to be well versed on every celebrity's entire life and oeuvre, and yet above actually being wowed by any of them. Informed, but jaded.

I refused to be discouraged. It reminded me of the time Warren had acted like a pig eating cake at the prospect of going to a crummy party thrown by Demi Moore for some air-brained New Age self-help queen, even though Warren hated Demi Moore more than her ex-nanny did, and had trashed her in his column more than once. He'd claimed he was just buzzed over being considered important enough to invite, over finally being on a list and not having to gate-crash.

The party had become a minievent because Demi had given the authoress a peck on the cheek, a demure kiss that the media had inflated into a hot lesbian smooch. No photos of the moment existed, so some of the tabloids had whipped up convincing, computerized artist's interpretations, "still reenactments" of what Demi *might* look like with her tongue down some chick's throat.

It was ironic. Warren Junior was the writer most ideologically interested in exposing someone thought or known to be queer, but he had pooh-poohed that rumor since he'd known it was just wishful thinking. "It's typical," he'd grumped, "that the *Post* and the *News* and all the rest will imply that Demi Moore has some lesbian thing going on when it's a complete hoax, and yet how many of them will ask David Hyde-Pierce about his roommate? Or at least write that Alan Dillinger is *rumored* to be gay? Disgusting."

Instead, Warren Junior's column the next day had ignored the faux lesbian angle. It had been titled "The Hostess Has Two Implants" and had, in 1,500 words, savaged Bruce Willis's unsinkable wife with such notorious zeal he'd earned a denouncement from the Willises and had been penned onto an unspoken blacklist that had kept him away from all the major celeb parties of the year. To Warren, it had been worth it: It had raised his profile, punctured the pride of an actress he found reprehensible, and had given him a slew of uninvitations to bitch about.

The Demi debacle had inadvertently led to Warren's favorite pastime, daydreaming fitting titles for his future autobiography; *Blacklisted Like Me* was a front-runner.

"I know there are cooler things to do than to show up and stargaze," I continued, already tucking the *Lifesavers* invite into my pocket. I had always been the little kid who, when presented with a playmate's toy, could be relied upon to proclaim it *mine*. "But won't you run the risk of not getting invited to parties if you don't say yes to *some?*"

"*That's* not my problem," Warren replied drily, leaning toward me. "I get *all* the shitty invites like this. It's the really *big* ones I fight for. But if *you* want to rub shoulders with beefcake, RSVP as me and add your name as my guest. Then go alone. They won't let you bring anyone."

Who would I bring?

"And don't let your inner schoolgirl giggle too loud just yet. If they're inviting *me*, chances are Dillinger won't even *be* there. The stars usually skip promotional bullshit like this. That twelve-year-old who plays the towel boy is the only *Lifesaver* you might see. I don't know why you'd care about a closet queen like Dillinger anyway, David. Mercenary faggots like him are dime a dozen." Warren clucked his tongue disapprovingly, but he was too reabsorbed by his Mac to work up any righteous indignation. "Just go and have fun."

"Deal." I knew it was pathetic to care. I felt like one of those homely, fat-faced women who sleeps out for three days to get Manilow tickets at Radio City. But I *did* care, and I got a kick out of imagining the *Lifesavers* party as much grander than it probably ever would be—the story of my life.

As I fondled the coveted invitation in my pocket, I felt another piece of paper, one I'd unearthed that morning and had been carrying around all day for no good reason. It was from the early years of my friendship with Warren, and it was bittersweet.

Warren and me, we went way back, *way* back. Back to the hellish shifts we worked at Crazy Kerry's Copy Shoppe on Twelfth in the eighties. These were the days when everyone was doing experimental Xerox art, color copiers took a full five minutes to generate a single splotchy page, and professors couldn't imagine a time when copyright holders would turn course packets into multimillion-dollar settlements.

We worked the single worst job in New York City, feeding paper into machines and copying precious documents for lunatics twenty-four hours a day. Actually, our shifts were usually only eight hours, but eight hours working on photocopiers could not be compared to eight hours behind a desk or at a cash register or even slinging burgers. The mind-numbing hum of the machines, the sickly sweet stench of the fresh ink, the repressive heat generated by thirty trays sliding back and forth as images were copied, copied, copied; it was enough to make you want to dive naked into a snowdrift after work, even one of those funky Manhattan snowdrifts that have an inch of soot and car crud on the top and three months' worth of dog crud two inches down.

Warren and I had bonded over syllabi and flyers, résumés and religious tracts, he the unflinching New York native and I the Iowa transplant, unwittingly high on toner.

The first mystery about Warren had been his name. We'd been working side by side for weeks before I'd noticed that the schedules listed everyone's first and last names—except for Warren's. His schedule always said simply "Warren." I'd asked him what the deal was, and Warren smiled slyly, like he'd been waiting for the pleasure of explaining.

"Wellll," he'd said, "I'm a junior. My father is also named Warren. I think my mother named him after me." I'd stared at him. He'd only been *half* joking. "Anyway, I hate him. He's not a good person, not at all. He used to beat my mother around like she was motherfucking Bluto. Me, too."

That admission had killed my amusement, had cut short our verbal tetherball. It had made me squirm, contemplating someone being beaten as a child. To me, it was something on the news or in an afterschool special, but impossible to attach to reality. I couldn't picture my athletic, dumb-joking father backhanding my elegant, witty mom for any reason, any more than I could envision her taking it. I think I disbelieved things like spousal battery existed in the Midwest until my late teens, when liquor had induced some of my friends to start blabbing about the duality of their home lives.

"He did us both like that my whole life. Until I got old enough to beat him back. I wasn't very good at it, but it got under his skin. It annoyed him to get hit back. So he left us alone. And when I booked, I decided I didn't want his name because it was nothing to be proud of. I didn't want her last name because it's ugly, it's Johnson, it's plain, and it's depressing because she's such a doormat. I decided I'd just be Warren. You know, like Prince."

"Well, I'm sure Prince would be flattered." I'd meant it as a compliment, even if it had sounded sarcastic. Like Prince? Also like Charo. I couldn't relate to the hubris (one of my first New York words) it would take to change your birthname—it seemed radical and I wasn't raised to rock boats. Moving to the East Coast at twenty-one had been the ultimate breach of the expected for me. Prior to that, my life had been a succession of perfect-attendance certificates and junior-achievement medals. I had been living on a line of neatly connected dots.

My fellow copyhound and I were very comfortable discussing TV, music, and movie stars, and I'd been surprised to find a black gay man my age who'd had almost exactly the same pop cultural experiences. We'd watched all the same reruns of sixties TV, had listened to and liked most of the same disco and cheesy pop music, and had seemed to retain the same useless but funny tidbits about celebrities, gleaned from dubious sources like *People, Us,* the *National Enquirer,* and Rona Barrett's facehole.

Putting his encyclopedic pop knowledge to use, Warren had started writing bitchy newsletters on the sly, name-dropping all the power-hungry pretty people he encountered in the clubs, opining on the careers of living legends, drawing and quartering deserving buffoons. He would dash off six or seven hundred free flyers and distribute them at Private

Eyes, The Mudd Club, The Roxy, The Funhouse. He'd known his free flyers were attracting attention the day Leona Helmsley had called him at Crazy Kerry's and threatened to rip off his nuts. He'd told her he'd rip off *hers* first.

Warren and I were always like interracial twins in the arena of pop culture. But in other ways, we were different.

I fingered the list in my pocket as I watched Warren juggle three frantic phone calls, one from Danny Pintauro, who seemed actually to be kissing up to Warren for an interview. A first. Warren usually had to trick subjects into a Q&A since he had a penchant for turning alleged puff pieces into verbal S&M.

I'd written the silly list one day during the Crazy Kerry's years while trapped on the E between Port Authority and Thirty-fourth. The train had stopped due to smoke on the tracks, a meaningless phrase to most New Yorkers that never fails to strike fear into the hearts of former Iowans. The way I'd seen it, smoke usually came from fire. I'd envisioned a slow death by roasting, remembering a movie about people trapped in a subway during an earthquake, one with Lynda Day George (very pretty).

I'd also remembered that nightmarish subway movie where the young thugs terrorized everyone. *The Incident.* I'd rather take my chances with smoke than put up with verbal harassment. I never feared violence on the mean streets of New York Fuckin' City, I was just always desperately scared that a Dominican child would yell out that I was a fag or that a group of Italian Jersey guys would start making fun of my hair or some black teenagers would start rapping in my face to underscore my Iowaness. It wasn't that I was a racist, just that I neurotically feared being pegged as one because I was so white I disappeared in winter. I guess white guilt wound up making a passive racist out of me against my will. But I swear to God I always voted Dinkins.

The subway had been crowded, stewing in sharp human smells and simmering with tension as a load of New Yorkers was forced to wait out a stall. It had been close to nine in the morning, so I'd known most of those people—and myself—had no chance in hell of arriving to work on time. Kerry eventually fired me for tardiness. It was hard getting to work in the Village at nine when you lived in another state—I cringed at the Smell-O-Vision memory of those first three years living in Jersey City, having to commute to work and play.

The car's silvered interior was streaked with ugly neon graffiti in spirals and lightning bolts, the unreadable signature of the artist blackening one of the windows. In the eighties, every New York vandal with a can of spray paint thought he was Keith Haring. Only one of them was.

As the train sat motionless, I'd been slumped in a coveted corner seat, avoiding the inquisitive stares of the men in jeans whose crotches were at eye level. I was busy writing because, you see, I was always under the impression that that's what I was, a *writer*.

Ways I Am Different

Using an erasable blue ballpoint, I'd jotted the list onto a raggedy page torn from a spiral notebook. I hadn't intended for the list to be about how I was different from my new city friend Warren—Warren, Jr.—it had just turned out that way.

(1) I don't like being swishy.

I had spent high school avoiding any behavior that would have identified me as a raging queer. I'd feared that even one fey moment would have been like a flashlight shining on my mouth wrapped around some Village People–guy's cummy boner. By the time I'd come out to myself and the world around me, it had been too late—the aversion to "acting gay" had stuck.

Warren, on the other hand, had come out to his mother and father when he was eleven, even experimenting with drag before it was time to learn to shave. I can't comment on that because I literally can't picture it. As this piece of information suggests, there was something superhuman about Warren. He was a sort of homosexual prodigy.

(2) I don't like one-night stands.

This wasn't exactly the truth. I really got off on the regulated one-nighters I had. There was something adventurous about trusting a stranger, about picking him up in some club where everyone in the city could see what you were gonna do, going back to his place (which could house an arsenal, a faggot kennel, a carefully concealed chainsaw, or possibly just a stack of condoms and some lube), and trading hand jobs, blow jobs, face fucks, ass fucks—oh, God, going all the way without an ounce of love involved always felt pretty groovy.

AIDS had always been a concern—by the time I'd lost my virginity at nineteen, AIDS was already in the headlines. I've never experienced sex without some degree of paranoia.

Medical angst, yes, but I never had guilt over sex. I was raised Protestant.

Scary pleasures aside, I *preferred* to wait for a man who would be a little more substantial than Stanley-with-grapefruit-biceps-and-accommodating-ass or that incredible Corey Hart-ish guy with the animalistic thrusting mechanism and absolute orgasm control. I wanted good sex, required it at least once every half year, but my goal was togetherhood.

Warren had attended circle jerks, spanking parties (he'd said he enjoyed safe violence), and had gone to back rooms, making no bones about it. "It's just sex," he'd always said, and meant it. I'd disagreed, but had always admired his certainty.

(3) I can't dress myself.

No fashion sense. Jeans, T-shirts, more T-shirts. An antique sweater too new to be retro and too old to be passable at even a burrito palace.

Warren would have looked chic, if unappetizing, in salami casing. I'd learned early on that the idea that most gay guys were into fashion wasn't just a stereotype. I'd figured that out when I'd dated a starving artist who would bum hamburgers off me, but who always managed to conjure up seventy-five dollars if a good shirt went on clearance at Barney's.

(4) I like girls.

For as long as I could remember, I had been fascinated by and enchanted with women. I had always felt excluded in school, never from jock society but from the snooty cheerleaders, the girls. I'd observed the girl packs with so much interest I could always provide informed sympathy to the unpopularettes who came to me to complain about their own outcast status. I would tell them to cheer up while secretly coveting their ponytail holders and long, silky hair. Of course, I wasn't a frustrated transsexual or drag queen, I just wasn't afraid to embrace girls. Figuratively, of course.

No, not all the gay men I'd encountered since the first one I'd met at a college party had been woman-haters. Actually, almost none would call themselves that, or would ever say out loud, "God, women suck," but I'd always felt a silent credo veining through a lot of gay male culture that excluded women except as far-off entertainments. I'd been traumatized the first time the upstairs section of the Limelight had tried to prevent my female guest from entering with me, and to this day I hate picking up gay and lesbian magazines to find them dripping with male-male sex ads and articles about Keanu Reeves-Geffen.

I wanted women around, all the time if possible. In fact, my buddy Carol, a straight chick with razorblade insight, was easily my closest friend, even if I rarely saw her and spoke to her far less frequently than I did Warren. I loved Carol like a sister, a sister who owned a store called Gods & Goddesses, a movie memorabilia warehouse bursting with magazines, posters, glossies, costumes, and kitsch. I had wandered into her store one day on the cusp of the nineties, had become emotional over a set of *Julia* paper dolls, and a friendship had been born. Carol wasn't into the stuff she sold, but she'd told me she'd known that anyone unembarrassed to cry with joy over Diahann Carroll had to be worth knowing.

Warren was no misogynist, at least not on purpose. But I would have been curious to know if he'd ever stopped to wonder how he'd lived almost thirty years with Carol as the only woman with whom he'd ever been more than passingly acquainted.

There was one item on the list that I knew didn't differentiate me from Warren. In fact, it was a characteristic that we shared—I'd thought at the time—wholeheartedly. It was a principle.

(5) I hate Donna Summer's fucking guts.

A lame reason to be different from most other gay men? No, like most pop culture relics, Donna Summer has underlying significance. Obviously, I liked her music, disco music. Fluff. But most gay guys forgave Donna Summer's ongoing born-again Christianity. I disliked religion and refused to accept any dogma that condemned me to hell whether it was spoken aloud or was simply acknowledged within a diva's own head as she sang about the love of Jesus at an AIDS benefit. I cynically believed that the mind of a Christian diva worked that way, and sometimes thought I could see their contempt for their gay admirers written all over their shining, lip-syncing faces. This item is really more about loyalty and liberalism than "Love to Love You Baby."

At the time I'd written number five, dismissing antigay divas, I hadn't felt there was any hypocrisy in being neutral toward male movie stars who were secretly gay but renounced it. After all, they *were* cute.

When I'd dug the list out from a box of old letters that morning, eight years after I'd written it, I'd wondered if my writing the list had been an example of internalized homophobia, but then laughed when I remembered I'd pulled that phrase from an old Charles Perez show. Or was it Jenny Jones?

No, the list wasn't antigay, it was just anti–status quo, with Warren standing in as all gay men. I thought how ironic it was that I'd spent my entire life up until age twenty-one desperately trying to assimilate in order to blend into Iowa, and ever since then seemed determined to push away anything too mainstream in order to stick out in New York. Once the entire gay planet discovered something I'd privately cherished, my ardor cooled. RuPaul was more fun before his recording contract. Don't Panic! T-shirts were more hilarious when they were mail-order. AIDS ribbons—well, those were always kind of queer.

I didn't want to be like all the other gay guys in the world, certainly didn't want to mimic the straights. What then? One thing was for sure: Making a list of reasons why I was different from the prototypical queer wasn't going to make me unique.

It wasn't long after the day I'd written the list that Warren had left a wetly enthusiastic message on my machine, a frantic series of words explaining that he had been offered a column at *Island Rage,* one of New York's biggest weeklies. All those Xeroxed manifestos had paid off—they'd given him local notoriety and street cred, and his voice was the talk of the Village. Billed as an outsider-insider, he called his column "Off the List," successfully predicting the reception he'd get from publicists who never missed reading each installment but who would rather die than feed him any clients to shred. He was called "the chocolate Musto," though never to his face, and immediately acquired a venomous and one-sided hatred for Michael Musto and *The Village Voice* that was so intense it bordered on psychotic love.

Warren became Warren Junior, an affectation selected to remind his still-living father that his son was a published faggot. Another way in which Warren and I were different: I wasn't bitter. I wasn't damaged.

After writing it, I'd tucked the list into my jeans as the train lurched ahead, no sign of smoke and no startling rise in temperature from unseen, uncontrollable flames. Something had made me save the list, hiding it so well I'd lost it, then had forgotten it was missing until I'd found it.

I thanked Warren for the invite, picked up my Farrah à la carte and took off, heading back to my office before I'd doubled my forty-five minute lunch break. At the end of my subway ride, I discarded the Ways I Am Different list, leaving it on the seat next to mine just like straphangers do with newspapers they've finished reading.

CHAPTER 2

Missing

John Dewey, 1981 — The first time John Dewey saw Gil Romano, he thought he was looking at his father.

The old photograph looked as though it had been dipped in vinegar and left outside for the sun to sizzle away its surface. As he handled it, it threatened to crack under John's tentative touch. It had been torn from someone's scrapbook, its sharp edges resembling shark's teeth. John owned a shark's tooth on a choker, an alien artifact he had found by the side of the road the previous summer, someone's Florida souvenir discarded.

The man in the photograph was handsome. John knew that because of the way the man was standing. It was a full-body shot of a strapping guy posed with his sprawling shoulders straightened and his face turned to the side in arresting profile. Despite the man appearing to be tall and substantially built, unusually muscled for the olden days, there was something . . . womanish in his looks. Gelled hair (but did they have gel back in the fifties and sixties?) capped his head, with a few rakish strands drooping down artistically, almost to his finely pointed nose. He had thick eyebrows, the kind John always secretly wished he himself had. John realized he was rubbing his fingertips over his own thin, flossy brows, scratching at them. He stopped.

There was something else effeminate about the man in the photo— he looked like he could be wearing makeup. That disturbed John deeply, the perfectly smooth skin, the too-dark and too-long eyelashes. He even looked like he was wearing *lipstick,* but it was hard to tell in black-and-white, except that his lips looked large and dark and prominent, unreal.

Covering the photo with his damp palm, John cracked a space between his middle and pointer finger, just enough to see the suspicious lips. Yes, they had to be painted. Out of context, they looked like a woman's. John wondered if he could trick some older boys into thinking the picture was of a sexy woman just by showing them the lips, then humiliate them by taking his hand away and showing them it was a man. Maybe, but who would he trick?

John was twelve years old and had no friends around his neighborhood or at school. He wasn't a Cub Scout or in student council, didn't play sports. He sometimes felt like none of the other kids in the fifth grade even knew he was in their class.

Refocusing on the photograph, he wondered: *If he's my real dad, why is my dad wearing makeup?*

There was a small and quiet space in John's chest that made chilling suggestions. *See? Your father was a homo. That's why Granny won't tell you about him. She's ashamed. She feels sorry for you.*

Worse: *Like father, like son.*

John had been told his real father had been queer for as long as he could remember. His classmates knew John's father had been absent all his life, so as an impersonal way of ribbing him, a syndicate of boys had taken to calling his father a homo. They'd never meant for John to actually *believe* it, their intention had been to wound. But you can hear something only so many times before it starts to seem real.

John felt his head clog with snot and the veins in his temples throb with an instant, familiar ache. Migraine. He had battled them since before he was old enough to articulate what was happening to him. As a toddler, he'd cried like a dying animal for hours, sometimes falling spontaneously asleep, overwhelmed by the pounding behind his eyes. Eventually, Granny had figured he was having headaches and had taken him to a free clinic to see if they could get him to straighten up and behave. The doctors had given him a prescription for pills that would bring relatively fast relief to the blinding agony.

John fished for one in his pocket but came up with only a stubby pencil he must've accidentally shoplifted from school that day. He'd forgotten to put a pill in his pocket that morning. That realization caused a spirited pang to spurt through his eyeballs.

Before dashing inside to swallow a dose of normalcy, John's gaze was drawn back to the photograph. There was the name of what he figured to be a photographer's studio at the bottom. It said "Gil Romano." A weird name, it sounded made up. Then John flipped the photo over and was shocked to find writing. Granny hadn't taken any pictures with her clunky camera for a long time, but all the pictures John *had* found in her chaotic albums were mysteriously unlabeled. It was like Granny didn't care if anyone ever knew who those faces belonged to. She could die and John would never know who any of them were. He didn't ask her who they were anymore because whenever he brought it up, she'd snort and say, "You don't care about them people," and hobble over to the fridge for a Fresca or to the phone to call someone and give them hell. Her tone was both dismissive and accusatory. She was always accusing him. She never *had* liked the idea of him rummaging through her memory books, as she called them.

But John wanted to know more about his family and their friends, parties they'd attended, vacations taken. With Granny's habit of leaving photos blank, John had tried in vain to identify her in them to put things in context, to try to figure out which, if any, of the people was her daughter—his mother—and which, if any, might be his father. Except for the most recent ones, from the seventies, when Granny looked about the same except with darker hair and a less prominent stomach, he hadn't been able to find any of her as a younger woman. Without more information, her photo collection was just a sea of possibilities. The beautiful high school girl might have gone on to become his mother, the grinning football player might have been his father. Or they could be an aunt and an uncle. Or strangers. There was no telling with Granny—she claimed they had no living relatives.

But here, out in the storage unit beside their trailer, toward the bottom of a chest he'd always assumed to be full of tax papers and receipts, he'd found this photo of a handsome man, a photo with some clues. On the back, in desperately faded red penmanship, was the inscription, "Loveing you always, Jim." Next to it was a shakily sketched heart shape with playful loops at the two points. It wasn't the right way to spell—that much John knew. But it made him smile a little. It was sort of like a valentine, like the ones other kids gave out and received in school each year. It was a valentine from a boy named Jim.

Was his father's name Jim?

John turned the photo over again and admired the man. He really was handsome. He could have been a movie star. The girls in John's class would think this guy was cute. If they could get over the black-and-white.

John wondered what the wind had felt like the day the photo was taken, if it had been a warm or brisk day (it looked like the sun was out), what the man's cologne had smelled like. Maybe makeup was an old-fashioned custom or something. Whatever, if that man was John's father, he couldn't have had a better-looking dad. Shocking, considering how . . . John felt like such an ugly dork.

John knew that all the girls found him intensely ugly, like a visual migraine. Most of them avoided looking at him, perhaps disgusted by his shapeless form, his admittedly unhip clothes courtesy of Granny's infrequent forays into the secondhand store, or even his face, his sheet-white, blankly serious face. Having thick glasses was bad enough, but on top of everything else, John felt they just functioned as reverse binoculars, magnifying his inescapable unappeal to all who saw him.

He hated *himself* when he looked in the mirror—how could he expect *girls* to like him? To want to go with him? He was pretty much resigned to never getting kissed or having a girlfriend or going to a dance or any parties. But at least the girls were politely if firmly repulsed by him. The boys were much more verbal. Much more.

In truth, he wasn't ugly, just plain, normal. Unlike beautiful children, whose greatest popularity in life occurs before age sixteen, John was pale and minor. He wasn't monstrous. But he felt with utter conviction that he might be some new kind of monster, human enough to live in society but too horrible for affection.

"What in hell?" Granny was startling even when you knew she was in the room with you. Since she'd snuck up on John, her crispy, shrill voice made him choke on air. Her question had started as a forceful yell and faded into a seething whisper.

He looked back over his shoulder at the crippled woman who had raised him. She was already all the way inside the room, so John knew he must have been doing what he called zoning. It was this weird time when he would blank out for a bit even though he never fell asleep or anything, just drifted off while he was awake and thinking.

"Well? Digging around?" Her pinched face was always moving, in contrast to her rigid left leg, which had been fused since before John could remember. She was wearing her bright yellow tank top and the same black slacks she wore most of the time. She looked so filthy to him, as always. He was ashamed of her and hated her for refusing to tell him more about his parents, even when she got roaring drunk every night before sundown.

Just then, with the sunlit doorway behind her making her wispy white hair look fried and floaty, he imagined the paper running a story on her as being the oldest woman alive. He had no concept of real ages, so he would've been shocked to know she was merely a badly preserved sixty-two—she looked like a ghost someone had seen. John hoped maybe she was dying.

They stared each other down for a while and then Granny showed a little skill at reading minds and said, "Oh, no, you thought—? Oh, no, that's not him. Are you kidding me? That man could have been *my* daddy, he's so far gone." She laughed her sour little laugh and waved her cane over his head like she was knighting him. But she was really just gesturing at the photograph. She hated him almost as much as he hated her. He was her lodestone, a product of her whoring daughter and some man. She had no idea where they were, or if they were alive. For saddling her with this moody, insolent boy, she wished them the worst.

"That man in the picture is an old-time movie star. You found the only good thing I own anymore. That's a real collector's item by now, I bet. It's an autograph of a movie star called Ji—er, Gil Romano." She said the name like it was fancy but funny, like she was saying "ooh-la-la."

So it wasn't a photographer's studio, it was a name. "He was our big movie star for the twenties. That picture is from when I was just a baby girl. He came from my neighborhood and my aunt Elisabeth knew him personally. She got that picture from a dime store and sent it away for him to sign it after he got famous and he did it, too. He signed it for her."

"It says 'Jim,' " John mumbled, surprised that Granny would waste her breath telling a story he actually wanted to hear. Maybe since it wasn't important, wasn't about his parents or anything, she didn't care as much.

"That's his *real* name, stupe. Jim something, I forget. But Gil Romano was more of his—whaddayacall?—acting name. Nobody named Jim whatshisname ever got famous then. Then, they all had real flowery names. Them were the silent days." She seemed about to give examples, but stalled.

John hadn't really been following her. He'd tuned her out, zoning again, looking at the precious photograph. So it wasn't from the fifties or sixties, it was from the *twenties*. He couldn't *believe* something would have survived that long in Granny's care. He wondered if he could sell it for a million dollars or something so he could run away. But he doubted it was as valuable as Granny said or else she would've gotten rid of it already and spent the money on the tabloids and wine. But even if it was a *little* valuable, he suddenly felt like he didn't want to get rid of it. John stared at the man and fantasized that he had been next to him the day the picture had been taken. He thought about them being friends and about the two of them doing things like fathers and sons did.

There isn't any hair poking out from under his collar. He looks like those swimmers. John had spent long afternoons lazily watching a televised series of sleek, graceful, hairless swimmers competing in some foreign country. He'd felt nervous at how they were almost completely undressed right there on TV, and at how naked his attention to them was.

John flushed hot red and fingered the photo and noticed that his migraine had eased, even without a pill.

CHAPTER 3

Would You Be Caught *Dead* in This Outfit?!

David Greer — Less than twenty minutes after retreating from Warren's office with the coveted party invitation tucked into my pocket, I was seated at what passed for a desk in a windowless cubicle deep in the heart of a shoddy building in NoHo. In my cube, I felt like a sightless worm, wriggling with life but never able to escape, to really *live,* to do anything but produce heartbeats and squirm in place. My eyes ached from staring endlessly at my buzzing, blue-gray computer screen. I had been annoyed one day when I'd realized that years in front of that computer had generated a persistent tiredness under the eyes that never left me, even if I took a couple of days off and did nothing but sleep. My first no-bullshit wrinkles were those fucking eyebags produced by too much unblinking data processing.

I was aware that someone was standing over my left shoulder, watching the obscene words bleeding from my fingertips to the keyboard and finally, jerkily, onto the blinding screen. Someone observed me as I punched the final word: "ballsac."

Normally, when you're caught at work typing a thought that contains the word *ballsac,* you're either reprimanded, fired, or propositioned, and a lengthy harassment battle ensues. But in the offices of two dozen gay and straight sex magazines, "ballsac" was one of the softer terms familiar to the spellcheck. It was also one of my wild peeves—much less tolerable than a pet peeve. Yes, when writing dirty words, there are bound to be many with no predetermined proper spelling. But the arbitrariness of the company's style sheet never ceased to irk: "ballsac," "buttcheeks" (but "ass cheeks"), "fuck-hole" (but "fuckpole"), "precum" (but "prespunk").

I turned and felt my heart fall screaming into the abyss—it was the office manager, who everyone agreed had probably never held a job before and so was unused to things like logic and humans.

"I'm looking for the Suck My Dick," she said plaintively, as if asking me to pass the sugar. She was asking for the color mechanical for a 900 phone line ad that had been the back cover of *Pumped* for the past two years. How it could be missing was just another of the many Big Questions around the office.

I waved her off. "I don't have it. You had it last month, you should have it this month." Larajane Meredith was the only human being I was comfortable treating like dirt.

"I only have a Xerox of it," she insisted. The folks at Xerox would flip if they knew their product's good name was being linked to the crappy, barely postditto quality of the photocopies in Whole Man's offices. Whole Man was the parent of such diverse publications as *Grade A* and *Buddy*, *Princess* and *Lapdance*. From all the magazines combined, the company made well into the tens of millions each year. I knocked down about $25K of that to write copy for their best-selling gay title, *Pumped*, and to edit every word in every single magazine.

"Sorry," I said, but I wasn't. I was sorry to *be* there, sorry to be typing "ballsac," sorry to have made the decision to take such a mindless job as editing a bunch of gay porn magazines, sorry that Whitney and Bobby had been allowed to reproduce—but not *sorry*, never truly *sorry* for Larajane. Larajane was typical of the chronically flustered office workers at Whole Man, an uptight spinster who seemed completely out of place surrounded by glistening cocks and shaved pussies. Her hair was always a mess, she owned exactly five suits, and she spoke like each word was an effort. It was possible to nod off in the middle of one of her winded queries. And. And. And.

Larajane had only two redeeming features: her extraordinarily shapely legs. When sitting in her office, she kept her gorgeous gams crossed and tightly locked together from knee to tiptoe, draped to one side of her chair as if they were the magnificent train of an uncommonly elegant gown. She received people like this, always at attention, always painfully posed, always aware of the eyes that would invariably be drawn to her showy stalks.

Imagine every heady excess, tawdry moment, and liberal work policy that you would associate with working for a porn conglomerate. Now think of the *exact opposite,* and you have a clear image of the environment at Whole Man. Whole Man's mysterious publisher, Eddie Beck, had been MIA for over fourteen years, his sagging empire incompetently managed by his grieving widow ever since. Although Sandra Beck was alleged to have had firsthand experience in the sex industry prior to her drug-induced nuptials to the self-appointed Sultan of Sleaze, she didn't seem to have what it takes to run a business. No matter how sexy you are—or how sexy you *think* you are—the sex business boils down to business, not sex.

Sandra Beck was just lucky that the magazines *sold* every month. It certainly had nothing to do with her input.

The magazines had started out pretty raw, so wild that even Larry Flynt had originally balked at distributing them, but they'd quickly toned down to achieve wider distribution and to accommodate the increasingly strict obscenity laws that swept America starting in the eighties. By 1998, *Pumped* had ceased to show penetration, masturbation, bodily fluids, duos, or groups—even logos, although Calvin Klein couldn't have *bought* better publicity than having the studs of *Pumped* seductively peeling his distinctive undies off each other. The lawyers had cautioned that almost anything could lead to a lawsuit of some sort, and Sandra Beck was so petrified that she'd banned the use of the term *boy,* even in such clearly nonpedophiliac phrases as "frat boy," "boy-toy," "boyfriend," and "cowboy."

"After all, this company is Whole *Man,* not Whole *Boy,*" her memo had reasoned.

Sandra may not have had much to do with Whole Man's daily operations, but she had once flown into a rage and stopped copies of *Pumped* at the Canadian border when she realized that one of the dirty stories inside—which nobody but I bothered to read, anyway—contained the phrase "Oh, boy!" In the end, she'd relented and the issue had passed muster and had sold better than average (probably *not* due to the "Oh, boy!") without incident.

Whole Man's bucketful of gay porn mags had always led the industry, mostly because they'd been among the first of their kind and they had unbeatable product recognition. Poll any gay man on the street from preacher to porn star and every last one will have heard of *Pumped* magazine. Children across America stumbled upon rain-soaked copies hastily discarded along highways every day, repressed college boys (and men) rented out P.O. boxes to subscribe every semester like magic, and old-timers bragged of mint-condition issues (worth only about twice the current cover price) that they'd had squirreled away since before Leonardo DiCaprio was in nursery school. Scores of competitors had surfaced and sunk since *Pumped* hit the stands in the good-time era of 1978, and although the latest batch was biting starved chunks out of the market, it seemed *Pumped* and its brother publications would be printed as long as there were men with nice cocks and other men who'd pay for the privilege of looking at them.

Whole Man was the last place I had pictured myself when I had been onstage accepting my high school diploma as class valedictorian. I'd made a sweat-soaked speech about self-actualization that had seemed plausible at eighteen but which seemed far-fetched at thirty-two. *What if I have self-actualized?* I thought in a panic, a splay-legged centerfold's unmentionables tacked to a bulletin board above my desk. *What if this is my destiny? My peak? My personal high?*

When I had taken the job, I'd thought it would be a lark and a way of supporting my vaguely leftist, anticensorship/pro-porn views along with my rent—or at least part of it. I'd thought all my friends would be enthusiastic, too, since everyone knows that gay men view porn much as they view Bette Midler—necessary and respectable. But I was in for a shocker. First of all, not all of my friends were gay, so regardless of how seminal porn is to the life of a gay man, many of the straight women I knew seemed visibly repulsed by my life choice. One of them had phased me out of her social circle entirely after a conversation we'd had which she'd ended by saying, "I don't see why you'd waste your life on this. But good luck."

Even the gay men had been less than universally cheery about the prospect of my employment. I knew for a fact that every one of them had purchased porn over the years, and knew from bugging the subscriptions lady that two of them were longtime subscribers to *Pumped*. Still, while some of them did congratulate me and seem genuinely interested, the rest were uncharacteristically uptight. Embarrassed? I knew that part of the discomfort was their vision of me as basically a "nice guy" who didn't even sleep around much, and this was being challenged by the idea that I was sitting around dreaming up kinky sex fantasies all day long, interviewing porn actors, and leafing through nude photos of various exhibitionistic gym queens and homeless studmuffins.

"Who . . . who would even want to be *in* one of those?" asked Donald, a muscular body zealot I barely knew, certainly not well enough for such an offense. Donald regularly wore sweats with no underwear and could be found shirtless outdoors if the temperature was above 50 degrees Fahrenheit, so the answer to his question, I knew, was, "Oh . . . *you.*"

But if half my friends had been grossed out by my job, the other half had been so into it they'd grossed *me* out. Some of these guys showed visible tumescence at the assumption my office would be jam-packed with porn stars. One had asked me to get him Ryan Idol's autograph. "I don't think he can spell his name, let alone write in cursive," I'd laughed, and the guy who'd asked had seemed deeply wounded.

Everyone's estimation of the porn *industry* was skewed to the negative, but—perversely—their vision of porn stars was beyond fantasy. In fact, all you had to do was fuck on video *once* to be called a porn star. Is our society *that* taken with the recorded image? You'd think after a hundred or so years, the novelty would've worn off. But in fact, the definition of star has steadily loosened, kind of like some of the guys in *Pumped.*

"The way gay guys think of porn stars," I had told Warren over lunch my first week on the job, "is just like all the masses viewed movie stars in the thirties and forties. Joan Crawford must have seemed so much more . . . *awesome* then, you know? I mean, she's still loved by a lot of people, but we know how many times she throttled Christina and we know she wasn't really sick when she accepted her Oscar at home and all that. She's still larger than life, but we know *why*. Back then, people must have thought she was some sort of goddess."

"They did," Warren said, aggressively grinding his Caesar before swallowing. "There *were* intelligent people around in the old days who realized that movie stars were just a hoax, of course, but the hardcore fans were just absolutely blind. They still are, to an extent, they're just less common now. That's why it's so expensive to go to the movies. There aren't enough blind followers like there used to be. More people go for the story or the action or the nudity than for whoever's in it. Mel Gibson sells a lot of tickets, but can you imagine a Mel Gibson fan club? *Please*."

If movie idols had been demystified, porn stars—about whom I myself had been mildly naïve before starting at Whole Man—still seemed to fascinate gay men beyond all reason. On the surface, they were stunningly beautiful men with perfect bodies, smooth skin, nice smiles, and dicks of death that shot gallons of thick, white semen. But once I had spoken with the human beings who embodied the over-the-top names (JEFF STRYKER! KEN RYKER!), as well as dozens of those whose names weren't famous yet, and once I had seen how the process worked, I'd been savagely unimpressed:

Pumped. "How did you like, um, *working* with Derk Dangle in *Sunset Breach?*"

Elijah Pitt: "Uhhh . . . was I *in* that?"

Porn stars were just prostitutes. Porno movies made millions for a few greedy, soulless fucks who lived in mansions and leeched off imbeciles, and for the stars themselves they functioned only as rewindable calling cards, advertisements for "private parties."

Actors got paid on average a grand per scene to sign away some very lucrative rights to royalties, and yet they risked their lives with just about every shoot. Condoms weren't even allowed until the late eighties, and some gay porn videos were made sans rubber well into the nineties. Straight fuck flicks *still* don't use condoms, for the most part.

White Girls Who Eat Black Cum was a real title I ran across in a catalog. It made me hope it was an interracial video and not a physiological freak show.

In theory, porn was wonderful and I loved it, was unshakably attracted to it. But in practice, it was so much more exploitative than all the antiporn crusaders realized or genuinely cared about. It wasn't immoral because people were fucking, it was immoral because people were getting fucked. And even though I was on the magazine end, even though I only wrote and edited fiction, words—had nothing to do with videos—I couldn't help feeling sometimes like a seedy pimp, just itching to bitch-slap his whores.

As offended as I was by the people who snootily disdained my career, I guess that deep down I related to them more than to the ones whose pupils engorged as they gushed, "Cool!"

Warren was more than supportive of my sleazy job since it gave him an entrée into the world of triple X, which led to some occasionally spicy stories for "Off the List." Of course, all stories linked to gay porn had to be blind items. Except for that *Dr. Quinn: Medicine Woman* guy who'd been photographed at the Probie Awards and, later, trading spit with a guy in a hot tub. But all the powerful moguls and big names who—just like their straight counterparts—enjoyed hiring deluded pieces of ass for kicks, they were left to steam in silence as they recognized themselves in one of Warren Junior's vicious blind items:

ORDERING OUT

Mr. Retro Superstar and his ambitious wife aren't sending any Christmas cards to the X-rated gay video performers— male only, please—who help him take off the edge during his long, long movie shoots. In fact, 10 minutes after one of those camera-ready boys made him see Jesus on the set of his next hit-or-miss, he pretended not to know who the guy was when security nabbed the "intruder" exiting a restricted area. When it became clear who the porno superstar really was (the security guard knew him from those funny magazines he keeps in his underwear drawer), the movie's director made sure he was released, though it's unlikely the stud-for-hire will ever be welcomed back. Don't knock the porn star for making house calls—just another way of staying alive in Hollywood.

Even though tens of thousands of gay men across the globe fantasized about working in porn, I wanted out. The first week had been a thrill, a hard on every day. The second week had represented a wind-down period, where things had become slightly boring. For the next three years, it had been strictly flat-line.

Worst of all, as I slaved away on purple prose, transcribed the profoundly uninteresting thoughts of sex icons, and corrected grammar in slogans printed across lurid color photos of male breasts, I could see on my computer a file containing a rough outline of the novel I'd always wanted to write, the first big project that would lead me to bestsellerdom. It was to be a coming-of-age novel called *My Parents Deserved Me,* based solely on make-believe since my childhood had been so disappointingly idyllic.

The last time I'd touched the file, according to the accusatory date listed on the screen, had been *nineteen months* earlier.

Larajane shifted away, out of my cubicle, on a search for the missing ad. She'd find a couple of wild geese before she found that ad, which I was betting someone in the art department had accidentally thrown away with a newspaper he'd been reading.

Facing a stack of new stories to proof—the top one boldly featured a glaring typo in the *title*—my heart skipped a beat when I realized I had the Alan Dillinger party to look forward to. I had dozens of naked men to stare at all day, but imagining Alan Dillinger in his famous electric-blue *Lifesavers* Speedo was much more exciting. Something about unavailability.

Prior to getting the invite from Warren, if you'd stopped me on the street or sidled up to me at the A&P and asked me to tell you what I thought of Alan Dillinger, I would have screwed up my face and said, "Not much. He's cute, but he's just another Hollywood closet case." But faced with the privilege of mixing and mingling with him, I had allowed my attitude to soften.

In just a few short hours, I'd be in the same room with Dillinger, could even try to flirt with him to see if all those rumors were true. What if Dillinger *flirted back?*

"Oh, boy . . ." I mouthed to my computer screen, smiling inside.

On impulse, I decided to throw caution to the wind and invite someone despite Warren's seasoned advice not to. I punched Carol's work number at Gods & Goddesses.

"Gods," she answered, lazy.

"Hiii," I breathed, cheered to be talking with my bestest bud.

"Hiii," Carol replied. "What, are you already *bored* over there? Must be a bad day if you're calling me right after lunch." I could tell by her voice that she was wearing a headband. We had that sort of a bond.

"No, not bored. Any more than usual. What about you? Has the Raymond Burr lady been in today?" One of Carol's regular customers was a hag with a Raymond Burr fetish whose insistence that Carol stock up on *Perry Mason* merchandise had dogged her for months.

"Nope. Not since I sold her that *Ironside* lunchbox."

I couldn't tell if she was serious, but enjoyed the image of a frightened six-year-old in 1968 eating lunch alone from a metal box with a garish cartoon of *Ironside* on it. Unappetizing. "I was actually calling to see if you were interested in crashing a party with me."

She laughed and I noticed the noise of her cash register. She must have been in the middle of a sale, probably selling a Marilyn Monroe poster to a tourist. She had some truly warped memorabilia, but made most of her money on common stuff. "I don't exactly feature gate-crashing, David," she said warily. "How *worth it* is it?"

"Very. It's a celebrity party. Supposedly Allan Dillinger will be there."

She whistled between her teeth sarcastically. "I'm sure he'll be coming out of a big old cake, huh?"

"I'm surprised Warren didn't already call you and tell you he gave me the ticket. You know, to make you jealous."

"He *would* do that, wouldn't he? If this was B.S., you would have given up by now. Tell me more about this party. Why do we need to crash it if you have tickets?" Carol's knowing voice was always such a teasing indictment. I knew better than ever to attempt deception.

"*Et.* Tick*et.* I only have an invite for one and Warren claims they won't let me bring a guest, but I have a feeling that they'd cave if it was a matter of a man bringing his lovely date."

"Where do I come in?" Our banter was so well-worn it sometimes ran together. If our conversation were converted to a more literal transcript, parts would be blackened by overlapping words, as if produced by a malfunctioning manual typewriter. "I have to admit it would be fun to see if he shows up," Carol said, "but I have about fifty customers who would happily hand me their gizzards for that ticket. Why don't I sell it and we'll go have a nice meal?"

"I'm not interested in fifty gizzards," I said, through with the tease. "I want to go and see a movie star."

"Or a TV star will do, right?" Carol sounded distracted. I could tell she was glancing around her store, satisfying herself that no fan-types were lurking about, taking advantage of her phone conversation by stuffing postcards or 8 × 10s into their parkas. She spent every day evaluating the worth of movie and TV stars and the silly artifacts manufactured with their likenesses, and yet she was agreeing to risk the old "but we're on the list!" scene to get a glimpse of Alan Dillinger. She decided she'd do it, but only for me, her favorite. "Okay, I'll put on something revealing and we can meet at your place, right? Is the party closer to your place?"

"Mm-hmm."

"Then let's do it. It isn't black tie, though?"

"Nn-nn." I couldn't wait to see how we were going to con her way in. "But I may wear my tux just for kicks."

"Sounds like a lark. I'll bring my camera and maybe we can get him to pose next to you."

I glanced over my shoulder and noticed I'd been leaning on my keyboard, filling my monitor with backslashes. "Oh—uh, no, okay, don't bring a camera because I don't think it's open to outside photographers or anything and I don't want to get booted. Meet me at my place by around seven-thirty and we'll get there in plenty of time."

"Sounds tremendous."

"It will be, I'm sure."

We good-byed and I set about trying to delete the offending back-slashes but wound up losing half of the porn story I'd been editing. I rewrote it from memory and accidentally improved it.

CHAPTER 4

Unattainable

John Dewey, 1986 — John was methodically suctioning away a popsicle, taking comfort in the cold sting on the roof of his mouth as he devoured the cherry-red tube. Sometimes when he ate popsicles, he had quick flashes of blow jobs, a weird-sounding thing he could picture only within the widely varying descriptions of the act that he'd heard at school. He basically understood, he thought, that the idea was for the girl to put the guy's dick in her mouth, except that homos did it, too. He couldn't really figure out what blowing had to do with it, or how the whole thing was done, and frequently masturbated trying to picture it.

He would lick his salty palm and seal it over his rigid penis and then force it up and down, imagining someone's mouth swallowing him. It was exciting, but never led to anything. He knew guys were supposed to explode when they had sex, that semen was alleged to come flying out. But at seventeen, John had no idea how to make that occur. He loved playing with himself, did it so much he knew it was a sickness, but he could never go so far as to make himself erupt. That was for his dreams to take care of, leaving his shorts sticky and squalid in the mornings.

In the john, he had been masturbating with a *People* from Granny's pile next to the commode. He'd selected that particular issue because it showed pictures of a guy he remembered was in *Top Gun*, Tom Cruise. His name was supposed to be a dirty joke but John didn't really get it if it was.

Tom Cruise was such a handsome guy, so built and with a gleaming, inviting smile. John hated *Top Gun* (even though he'd never seen it) and hated everything about the latest stars, but he liked Tom Cruise's face and body so much. He rarely allowed himself a male image for his eyes while his hand jacked his cock, instead forcing himself to try to get excited by pictures of sexy babes like Phoebe Cates or the MTV one. But he knew he really liked the pictures of guys more. He got hard either way, but he could get hard just looking at photos of men, whereas his hand probably had more to do with his boners when he was staring at Madonna.

He didn't have to think of specific sex acts when he fantasized about Tom Cruise or John F. Kennedy, Jr., or Tony Danza on *Who's the Boss?* He just thought about their naked bodies, their arms over their heads with their armpit hair showing, their butts and what their dicks looked like. He wondered if they had big, hairy dicks and balls like the ugly but undeniably sexual guys who fucked dishrag girls in the old porno movies he'd once seen at a neighbor kid's house. Joey's dad had been a stoner in the sixties and a real pervert, judging by the old videos he'd amassed. When Joey had moved away, John had regretted the loss of those movies even more than the loss of the only guy his own age he'd ever had any sort of relationship with, however symbiotic.

I'd love to spend an hour alone with Tom Cruise and . . . And what? John drew a blank when he tried to picture the sex acts. He couldn't really picture himself sucking Tom Cruise's penis, definitely didn't see Tom Cruise sucking his. Anal sex seemed really sick and alien. Kissing?

John knew he'd never come jerking off anyway, so he gave up when he turned the page in search of more Tom photos and instead found a one-page article titled "Finally Ready for Its Closeup."

The article was about an old movie being found, a movie called *A Midsummer Night's Dream,* about the Shakespeare play. This, not contemporary phenomena like *Top Gun,* was in John's realm of knowledge—he knew a lot about old movies. The article said the movie got made in 1912 and everyone thought it was lost until this old guy— "Truitt Connor, 81, of Seattle"—had donated it to the American Film Institute. It had been fully restored and they were going to have a screening soon, almost seventy-five years after it had first played. The geezer was a retired projectionist from around the silent movie days and he said he had wanted to donate *A Midsummer Night's Dream* once he realized it was the last surviving copy.

John felt funny reading something serious with his penis flaccid and damp in his clammy palm. He washed his hands and awkwardly soaped and rinsed his dick in the sink before pulling up his pants and straightening his shirt. Carefully, so that Granny wouldn't suspect, John removed the page of interest from the magazine and folded it into his cramped jeans pocket for safekeeping.

John emerged slowly, making sure Granny wasn't nearby to quiz him on why he'd been in the john for over twenty minutes. She wasn't around. Probably watching TV. He thought he could hear one of her soaps buzzing in the front room. He crept down the hall to his room and shut the door, annoyed with the odor that never went away. It was like his space always smelled bad, the scent originating somewhere in his dark, cluttered lair. Sometimes he feared that the smell leaked from his own pores.

His room was always a mess, a carpeted cube with an unmade bed whose sheets rarely saw the washer. John had a lot of old comics and back issues of *Boys' Life* from his scouting days, some seventies rock records he'd gotten for ten cents at rummage sales, some newspapers. He had a stack of homework in one corner, and all the grades were passing. He threw the F grades away but kept anything above that for the future, in case Granny called him stupid again. The older she lived to be, the more cutthroat she got.

He had some posters on the fake-wood walls that had been there almost since childhood, just some NFL things and one of the Fonz that he'd put up to impress Joey, years ago. The poster had been cool then, but John knew he'd have to tear it down if anyone besides Granny was about to come into the place.

He had another poster on the wall, too, a large, cheap, black-and-white face shot of his idol, Gil Romano. It was a rare item, probably the last ever marketed, already a disappointing seller when it was done by some celebrity bootlegger in the sixties. John had tracked down a warehouse full of them, discarded leftovers moldering in the heat and humidity. This one had been the closest to mint, and he'd liked the pose, very classical and proper, Romano's devilish smile looking less forced than usual. It was from a film called *Il Bandito,* which despite coming from later in Romano's career was considered permanently lost, like thousands of movies from the twenties.

John knew it was easier idolizing someone dead, and that it was even easier when that person's body of work existed largely in fragments. It made his fandom more an act of imagination, he thought, giving him things to wonder about, allowing his own mind to fill in the blanks. He'd only ever seen one or two complete Gil Romano films, on a PBS show that aired original silents with piano accompaniment, and lots of clips on a TV special he'd stumbled upon which documented the history of film. He drank in the arresting images, unable to save them with no video cassette recorder, a rich kid's toy he was unlikely ever to possess.

The most important things John owned he kept in sturdy, white, cardboard boxes under the bed, away from possible spills or careless garbage-hunting trips by Granny. He had six huge boxes full of plastic-wrapped magazines, photos, advertisements, postcards, lobby cards, folded posters, vintage fan letters, and even one original contract bearing a bona fide signature. All of the boxes were full of Gil Romano memorabilia. He had more treasures than anyone in the informal and lifeless Romano Fan Club, more than anyone else he'd ever encountered.

John knew some of his finds were one-of-a-kind, like the 1919 program from Romano's only foray into the theater, a wildly successful light comedy called *Delightful* that had run for only thirteen performances at a house in Trenton before movie scouts had lured the lead to Hollywood. Once he'd read of the play in the Katz *Film Encyclopedia*'s spotty bio on Romano, John had been electrified to realize that the play had been staged nearby. He'd made a day trip to Trenton, over twenty miles away, and had found the program in the local historical library's attic. He'd signed a phony name and had said he was doing a research paper for high school, promising to return the fragile booklet within a week. That had been a year earlier, and ever since it had been wrapped in plastic and logged into his collection, valued at about $250. ZEKE IS PLAYED BY JIM STEPPS, it said, the name that would be replaced by the more assertive Gil Romano.

John sat on his bed and again examined the *People* article about the rediscovered film. He reread every detail, noting the elderly man's name and the city in which he lived so he could dial information and get his number and call him, ask him if his personal film library might also contain any of a number of lost Gil Romano movies. This was how he'd become such a successful collector: playing hunches, being resourceful, tricky. He'd written hundreds of letters in search of Romano items, and though most turned up zilch, the rest had resulted in a series of finds, a series of petty larcenies, stacks of treasure under his bed.

But even though John Dewey would have been thrilled to have discovered lost masterpieces like *Il Bandito* or *Used and Abandoned,* or even one of the missing films that had Romano in small roles, like *Having a Good Time* (one original review declared that Gil's performance as a peeping Tom was the film's saving grace), there was really only one film he was desperate to discover. It was a film that had taken an entire year to make, and had destroyed a decade-long career in approximately seventy-five minutes. It had never been shown to anyone but studio brass, not even to its star. Despite such undistinguished details, it was a film that had survived as a legend in the world of the cinema for sixty years, and was probably more well known in 1986 than its star, a man who had been a household name in the twenties.

Of Gil Romano, it was said that the silent-screen romeo's speaking voice had damned him in *Gay Was the Hero,* his widely anticipated talkie debut. Legend held that after a first screening in 1928 for the head of Romano's longtime studio, inappropriate laughter over what was described as Romano's "feminine" speech had led the studio's maverick honcho to demand that the negative and sole print be burned and Romano bought out of his contract. Instead of protecting its million-dollar baby, the studio had maliciously publicized the failure of the film—John had a sheath of photocopies from crumbling trade papers.

Immediately, Romano went from international acclaim as a dashing icon of romance to the frigid reality of being a punchline. He'd never worked again, though the film's director had gone on to make quite a name for himself: Frank Capra.

Eventually, it was as an early Capra effort that the loss of *Gay Was the Hero* had been mourned, not as the potentially illuminating, fatal climax of Gil Romano's glittering career. With memories of most of his movies dissolving along with their original nitrate stock, lost in fires, misplaced, damaged, held from public showing, his legacy was known only to scholars and a handful of fans.

Dogged research by film historians had led to the belief that *Gay Was the Hero* might not have been such a cinematic abortion, that its star had probably not had a fey voice at all—no one who'd ever met Gil Romano could confirm that he sounded any less of a man than the actors who rose to fame during the early years of sound: Clark Gable, Gary Cooper, John Wayne. After all, he'd been discovered on the stage, where his delivery had been cited as "booming" and "majestic." The studio had, more likely, simply grown tired of its star's posse of perks and escalating salary demands and had seized the moment to make a clean break, ruining a man in the process. Romano's name would elicit blank stares from the average person sixty years later, but his story had survived as a popular cliché—the silent actor who should have remained so.

John had read of Gil's postcareer life in Kenneth Anger's hateful *Hollywood Babylon* book. Gil had bucked the odds, had managed to keep some of his money and to invest it and to live like a king, a deposed king, in a palatial home in Bel Air. He'd lived there until 1958 when, a few months before turning sixty, he had taken his own life by firing a bullet into his face. Legend had connected the shooting to the young men Romano was said to have hired to be his constant companions, his "playmates," Anger wrote. According to *Hollywood Babylon*, Gil Romano had been a homosexual, and everyone in the industry had known about it, even though his adoring public would never have dreamed such a thing:

ROMANO VENTS, RAMON'S LAST LUNCH

. . . or take the grisly case of The Other Pink Powder Puff of the silents, Rudy's raging rival Gil Romano, the kid from Joisey who conquered the silver screen with his pretty looks and macho poses. His career was wrecked when he opened his mouth and a girlish whisper emerged. His last movie, *Gay Was the Hero,* was said to be so bad even the fire that consumed the only copy thought twice about licking the reel with its inescapable flames. Or had the movie been A-okay, and Romano the victim of his studio's corporate greed?

Unlike Rudy, Romano survived shame to live a life of luxury not all that far away from his old buddy Ramon Novarro. Romano checked out in 1958, ventilating his still-handsome noggin with a carefully aimed .38. Hollywood insiders, the ones who even *remembered* Romano 30 years after the scene of his prime, have whispered ever since that someone besides Romano had a hand in his self-snuff.

Possibly it was one of the endless Lust Parade of playmates, down-on-their-luck male hustlers he paid to keep him company in the twilight, a lifetime devotee of Priapus. He balled half of Tinsel Town, and only half because the other half was *female.* Homosexuality was not a hush-hush subject for this silent ham.

Never an innovator, Novarro also met his fate at the hands of two hustlers, bludgeoned with a lead dildo in '68, a toy that had been given to him by Rudy. Death at the hands of two brothers-for-rent, the family that slays together . . .

John felt *Hollywood Babylon* and other books just made things up. Judging by studio portraits of the actor dressed as everything from sheik to jewel thief, Gil Romano had been too much of a man to have been homosexual.

Maybe film scholars had given up on ever finding a print of *Gay Was the Hero,* but John Dewey had never felt *closer* to finding it. He'd canvassed every known possible resting place for a print, had a stack of negative replies from the American Film Institute and many other prestigious societies. But it seemed that every few weeks he made another important discovery for his collection, and he felt confident that his crowning glory would be the unearthing of that fatal film. He fantasized hosting a screening that would prove that Romano's career had come to an end not as the result of his girlish voice, but because of a vindictive studio head. Gil had not been homosexual, had not spoken like a woman, but had been a man, perfect.

It was all about the recovery, whether of something as unimaginable as a pristine print of a sixty-year-old movie or of something as banal as an old issue of a magazine in fair to good condition with a feature on Romano, or even—on a deeper level—of Gil Romano's good name.

Sitting on his bed, knowing that every square inch underneath was blanketed several layers deep with memorabilia, items he'd hunted down and captured even with his meager resources over the past several years—sometimes that knowledge was profoundly moving to John. It was an emotional experience, his preoccupation.

On the other hand, there were times when he'd wake up, eyes wide, in the middle of the night, and he'd almost feel as if his bed were absent, that he was stretched out on top of a heap of lucky magazines that had escaped the elements long past their life expectancies and were currently amassed in a paper zoo in an ugly dork's room. It was still an emotional experience, his collecting, on those uncomfortable nights, but instead of contentment, the emotion was fear. It was an oppressive fright that made him open his eyes and realize that he had fed his collection for too long to abandon it now, too long ever to abandon it.

CHAPTER 5

Behind-the-Scenes Exclusive!

David Greer — Lying on my bed, eyes up, I waited patiently while two Tylenol dissolved in my bloodstream.

Normally cheery and distracted, I was prone to sudden bouts of self-reflection that at their worst made me—if for only a lucid instant—feel so at odds with the rest of the world that I could finally grasp why a human being would stagger toward suicide. This didn't mean that I would ever end my own life, no matter the circumstances. It was just a strange sort of emotional catch-up my mind and body played on me, like how every hour a person can expect to take an extra-deep breath to compensate for sixty minutes' worth of involuntarily shallow respiration. My soul seemed to be gasping at these times, my mind preoccupied with how my life hadn't turned out exactly as expected, and how my expectations themselves seemed . . . alien. At best.

For instance, I would contemplate my place in society as a likable guy who never did anything too controversial outside of being homosexual and working as a pornographer. But these superficially outrageous things weren't particularly zingy to enlightened New Yorkers. In fact, I was the most *vanilla* variety of homosexual and pornographer. I was gay, not queer, never queer, not a radical or even a faux radical wearing ACT-UP T-shirts and no hair. As for the smut I peddled, it was so homogenized and shiny you could practically show it to your grandmother. I worked in an office. In a *cubicle,* for shit's sake. I corrected commas and presided over a series of "erotic" images plucked and

shaved and posed clear of any real sexual steam. I felt like Frank Pur-
due sometimes. Parts in plastic.

I'm thirty-two. What am I doing? Who am I?

Thankfully, these gasps didn't last for long or I would have suffo-
cated from unbearable self-absorption. Sad people are really just ego-
maniacs with shortcomings.

The phone rang just as I was sinking not into depression but sleep.
Soft medication always made me drift.

"Hullo?"

The voice on the other end of the line was familiar but distorted, like
when your mother eats a sandwich while updating you about the neighbors. It was Warren, sounding muted as always when he'd been smoking pot.

"What are you wearing?" Warren asked, giggling.

"Is this a . . ." I lost my place, spacing out the term *obscene phone
call.* "I'm not sure yet. You *do* mean to the party?"

"I don't mean to bed. At least I don't *think* I mean to bed. Who
knows? Maybe you'll get lucky with a TV mogul, y'all'll move in together. I'll never speak to you again." Warren's distaste for all moguls,
but especially young, closeted, gay ones, was well documented. It was
mostly out of disgust at their trashy values and vapid conversation and
laughable life choices, but a hefty percentage was also secretly out of
envy. He wouldn't have gone to any of their genuinely exclusive parties
anyway, but it would have been nice to have received invitations to
tear up.

"I'm not really looking," I lied. I *always* was.

"You?" Warren accused playfully. "You never met a man you didn't
lick."

"No, I'm just going for a little touch of star quality," I said lamely.

"Listen, I called because I wanted to warn you not to talk with a redheaded chick, a sort of baggy, nasty old thing. She'll be wearing something revealing, but you won't be able to figure out *why.* About fifty. Not
ancient, but looking like she missed all the warnings about suntans and
skin cancer."

I laughed. "Whatever. Who is she?"

"I'm not even sure she'll be there if Dillinger bags, but if he's there, she's there. His manager, Shara Quincy." Warren's lips wrapped around the name like he was blowing a spit bubble. The effect made me queasy. I'd heard of her. She was one of those manager/agent/publicists who was such a character that she got about half as much press as her over-hyped clients. Famous publicists were a rare breed: Chen Sam, Liz Rosenberg, Pat Kingsley. I recalled seeing the name *Shara Quincy* in bold print in the gossip columns several times in the past but I couldn't summon up an impression of her and couldn't remember what was being written about her. Probably just a bunch of crap.

"Why? Is she a bitch?"

"Hmm," Warren snorted. "Not mean and standoffish like me, but aggressively uninteresting and once she latches onto you she doesn't stop talking. I'm warning you, even though once she finds out you don't work for *TV Guide* or something she'll waltz right through you on her way to the next young man in a suit. You *are* going to wear a suit, aren't you?"

"No, I think I'll just wear some old jams and a tube top. Give me some credit. I clean up nice. I'm thinking: Tux."

Unnecessary laughter. "Very nice. Say hi to everyone for me," Warren said as he beeped his cordless off, "except Sha—"

I woke up an hour later feeling like I'd been sleeping under Luther Vandross—winded and sore and disoriented. I'd dozed after Warren's call and realized with a jolt that I needed to get showered, dressed, into a cab, and to the party immediately if I wanted to show up an hour late. Carol hadn't arrived yet, or perhaps she'd buzzed and I'd incorporated the noise into my dreams, her frantic plunging converted to nightmar-ish electroshock in slumberland.

It was okay. I always worked better under pressure. At least on the small scale.

In a groove, I caught myself "getting ready" for the Alan Dillinger party. I wasn't just showering, shaving, dressing; I was reverting to a form of behavior I thought I'd left behind with my early twenties. Get-ting ready was as much about psyching up as it was about cleaning up, dressing up. It was about playing just the right mixture of music to evoke a certain chemistry in my brain that would keep me sailing through the evening ahead. I would play power songs by eighties girl groups singing about sugar-coated sex, and feel like a vampire at a new neck, rejuvenated. Some people augment their getting-ready process with lots of liquor or a few lines. I prefer the Cover Girls.

I was blasting the stereo in my bedroom loud enough to hear it in the bathroom over the hiss of running water. "My heart goes bang-bang-bang-bang!" I sang, mimicking the hysterical basso of Dead or Alive, a group I'd once worshiped and which—suddenly?—qualified as a nostalgia act. It had been almost ten years since I had gotten ready that way, a ritual usually reserved for pre-bar-hopping when Manhattan had been new to me.

Oh, that explains why I haven't done this. I don't go out anymore.

Which wasn't true. I *did* go out occasionally, but over the years, my excursions had lost the element of fun, that Mardi Gras vibe. It was no longer about how excited I was over my new dancing shirt, doing and redoing (and then having to rewash and reredo) the hair, it was about looking talk-to-able. Presentable. Penetrable. Pretty grim, compared to the days when I would be giddy while getting ready to go dancing. I didn't even go out dancing anymore—I just went out. My acquired aversion to the nightlife was strong enough that Carol, no party animal herself, had once called me "lunarphobic."

Maybe I *did* fear the moon. A luminous full moon, like a spotlight, tended to make me icy and rigid, though anything but frigid. The lunar spotlight made me perform, catapulted me into a different, more aggressive and immodest personality, just the right combo for hitting on and picking up guys. I felt unfriendly and selfish when I was going out to meet men, just another asshole willing to buy you a drink in exchange for total intimacy on either side of a rubber. I didn't like myself much toward the end of my regular partying days. Sex had become less important to me *(How many times do I need to get laid until I'm convinced it's too easy to mean anything?),* and yet sex used to compel me to stay up past six in the morning, drink too much, fuck a guy I'd be embarrassed to introduce to my friends.

I was forgetting it was not 1988, but 1998. I also couldn't help feeling horny. My body was remembering what usually followed my getting-ready process, and was getting ready for its own expected party, a party that was not forthcoming.

My thirty-two-year-old hair was a challenge. I seemed to recall a time when I could do just about anything to it, *with* it. There seemed to have been a collaboration going on then, when I could slick it straight back for *Miami Vice* or crop it close and just with my fingers make it rise into a modified Morrissey. Or I always had the option of doing absolutely nothing to it and it would fall into place and look cute and natural. After a long, unhealthy relationship with a blow dryer, my hair had changed. I'd first noticed it about three years earlier when I'd attempted to go for the casual look and had wound up with a halo of straw and a collection of unintentionally rude comments on my new do. At least I was not, not, not balding.

It was distressing, after a long day of cavalierly criticizing virtually identical slides of gorgeous twenty-year-old *Pumped* hopefuls, to come home and deal with my own appearance. And it wasn't just the fact that the twenty-year-olds had better lighting, y'know?

Despite my preoccupation with the past and with the prospect of seeing Alan Dillinger in the flesh, I managed to make myself look pretty good. I'd gelled my hair up and away, except for a shank that dipped down on the left side of my face, softening my square features. It had taken so much effort to make it look so effortlessly in place that, for a brief second, I felt like a movie star. I knew they probably spent hours calculating which way a stray hair would fall at a premiere or during a filmed chat with Oprah or on MTV Europe.

With no one around to snicker, I indulged myself, staring at my head and shoulders in the mirror, scoping myself out objectively. I didn't feel cute anymore, not cute like that time when I'd been twenty-four and sitting at a bus stop. A car full of Latin girls had stopped for a red light in front of me. Out of reflex, I'd glanced at the car and had been faced with six girls ogling me, giggling and pointing and teasing each other. The decibel level in that car had probably been eardrum-taxing, but all the windows were rolled up so I heard nothing, only saw their wild, teenage expressions. It was a throwaway moment, but it had given me enough confidence to dump an unappreciative boyfriend whose name escapes me. I'd felt so incredibly *cute* that night. Valuable.

I didn't feel cute as I waited for Carol to show up as my Dillinger party escort. I *did* feel good-looking. Good *enough*. I wouldn't have been sick to my stomach with self-doubt on a blind date, at least not physical-features-wise. And with the right man, I could still, for a matter of minutes, have felt totally hot, sexual, and desirable. But cute was a stretch.

There wasn't a single feature about myself that I felt stood out. I had nice hazel eyes, a strong jaw, straight, broad shoulders, usually zitless skin, dark eyebrows, and brownish hair. All good things to have, but none singularly beguiling. My body was also fairly average, or rather, average among those with reasonably appealing bodies. I was too lazy to gym it up much, though I loved to jog in Central Park on sunny days because it felt so metropolitan and was how I envisioned a true New Yorker would spend his afternoons. I seemed never to get terrifically fat, even though the birth of my love handles had been eye-opening a few days after I'd hit 3-0.

In your midtwenties, you tend to forget your exact age. I mean, everyone knows when he's twenty-one. But twenty-two, twenty-three, and twenty-four all run together. Twenty-five is another milestone, but you won't recall your exact age again until twenty-nine, which might as well be branded on your shoulder because you're acutely aware that it means you're a burp away from thirty. After twenty-nine, you won't start forgetting your age again anytime soon—maybe once you get really old, like past ninety, when no amount of convincing can make you believe you're still a part of the game. But thirtysomethings especially are keenly aware of their exact ages. I wasn't thirty-two years, I was roughly a billion seconds old. Even if I didn't look a day over nine hundred million.

I lightened up and darted to the kitchen to pour myself a tall Diet Coke.

Carol arrived thirty minutes later, an hour late. We were going to be arriving when the thing was in full swing. She looked much better than I did, as always. She wasn't a great beauty and had no use for obsessing over appearance or style, but maybe it was her lack of concern that lent her a confidence that enabled her to pull off just about any look. Her straight brown hair spent most of its time hacked into arresting Bettie Page bangs and either pulled back into a ponytail or allowed to drag her shoulders. For the *Lifesavers* party, Carol had apparently tied her hair in a knot and pulled it up, carelessly pinning it in the middle of the back of her head. The effect was startlingly chic, I thought. Hadn't I just seen Lauren Hutton wearing her hair that way? Carol's bangs were curled under, making her narrow eyes appear larger and inescapably alert. She looked, at different moments, like a playful foreign princess, an unmarried, superhip East Village mom, or the biggest bitch of all time. I could see why most men and women she met decided they wanted her.

She was wearing a tight, deep blue silk dress that fell to midthigh, a vintage Halston that she'd been given for free while cleaning out someone's basement in search of salvageable goodies. She'd found the first issue of *Island Rage* that day, too, and had delighted Warren with it as a gift. All three of us had laughed at the paper's original incarnation in '72—as a men's fashion magazine with a strong emphasis on swimwear and enormous, fake-gold watches. It was dripping with cheesy women's lib cigarette ads. The paper had come a long way, baby. It had transformed into a powerful and widely read serious newsmagazine over the years, one nonetheless equally popular for Warren's infamous, unacademic, disemboweling column.

I was always impressed by Carol's resourcefulness, starting a business on her own in the eighties and making more and more money off it each year; she did most of the dirty work herself. She could look so appealing and so feminine, and yet she spent most of her time knee-deep in someone else's discards, ferreting out the good stuff. She had once found an original Andy Warhol silkscreen in a garbage dump, probably thrown away by someone who'd either thought it was a fake or that any so-so painting of some unrecognizable woman (Bianca Jagger) belonged in a landfill.

Carol wore a tight cluster of pearls that encased her throat, like some African beauty rite. I wondered if she'd found the pearls in someone's attic, or if they were even real. No one would be able to tell, and that's what counted.

Her regular customers saw Carol Terry as a pretty, serious thirty-eight-year-old businesswoman, but they probably wouldn't have recognized her with lipstick, let alone in party clothes.

"You look great. C'mon in."

We hugged warmly. I recalled that our shared, four-year-old secret—at least *I* kept it secret—had been started by a warm hug. That hug had grown old and comfortable, followed by my hands unexpectedly cupping Carol's small breasts, finding their nipples with my thumbs. We hadn't "gone all the way." I knew I would have lost my erection if I'd stopped to tug on a condom, and would possibly have chickened out if I'd examined the situation. Instead, we'd used our hands and mouths and each had reached orgasm before we'd had a chance to get too drastic. I'd never so much as kissed a woman before, but I'd kissed Carol that night, kissed her entire body. I'd been left with a numbness to my lips the next day, similar to how they felt when I made out with a guy with a mustache or goatee. Except the odd sensation hadn't been caused by abrasion but by Carol's foreign softness.

I'd been able to smell her body all over myself that next morning, and I'd felt I'd made a horrifying mistake, had committed a crime against (my) nature. It was like incest. But it was also like a betrayal. I'd been so proud to be one of the few gay men I knew who'd come out of the closet early on, who had recognized his sexuality and had kept it sacred by refusing to cave in and date girls in high school and beyond. Maybe that was at the root of my shock—perhaps I was just startled to find that all that "nonrestrictive gender and sexuality" B.S. of the nineties . . . might . . . be . . . valid?

I didn't like remembering that confusing encounter, but as far as I could tell, Carol had absorbed it cheerfully and continued on in our otherwise unromantic, close friendship. We'd never really discussed it much after the fact except when Carol had called and told me not to worry about it and had tried, for my sake, to make it into something lighter than it had been. Eventually, I'd come to think of it not as a revelation of latent bisexuality, but as moving proof of just how much I loved Carol, my best pal.

"Do you think I look good enough to compete with the Carolyn Bessettes and . . . whoever, Kate Mosses?" Carol asked with a tight, excited smile. She wrinkled her nose at herself.

"Definitely. You always manage to look one step ahead. I, on the other hand, feel like a reject from prom night '88."

Carol laughed and moved toward the fridge to get herself some soda. She knew I always had a sea of Diet Coke on hand at any given time. I drank so much my bloodstream was carbonated. She opened the door while I read the details from the invitation. The interior of the refrigerator looked like one gigantic sixty-pack.

"I think Diet Coke qualifies as your religion, David," she said, the sarcasm fitted over her tongue like a velvet opera glove.

"Like Scientology, except it's allowed in Germany."

She freed a can and closed the door, turning and leaning back against the plastic surface. Savoring her own words as they rolled out of her mouth, she said, "I wonder if Scientologists are allowed Diet Coke. Maybe it's too *powerful*, a *threat* . . . " She popped the can open and guzzled it like a trucker. Her thirst was incongruous with the independence of her presence. "Maybe it's too subversive, like a false idol."

"Nah, all the machines in the centers sell it at ten bucks a can." We loved razzing Scientology. Carol was a devout atheist and I, at best, was a shaky agnostic.

As we chatted, Carol had the same reaction to my apartment as always—she utterly ignored it. Most visitors found themselves wandering from shelf to shelf, examining my kitschy artifacts, looking to see what was new. Here's that *Room 222* coloring book you had when you were eight, here's an Earring Magic Ken Doll in the original box, over here we have a first-edition *Valley of the Dolls* signed by Jackie the year she croaked. I even had a vintage magazine carousel from an extinct Woolworth's carefully adorned with old gossip magazines, their hilarious cover lines reading everything from "Cook Makes Tallulah Fat!" to "Ali MacGraw—*Why?*"

The room was a veritable archive of useless fun, and yet Carol couldn't have cared less. To her, it was just a smaller, less complete version of her own store. I had very few objects that Gods & Goddesses didn't have or hadn't had and sold. To the untrained eye, I was sitting on a fortune, but Carol knew that as much of a kick as I got out of it, it was strictly amateur. Maybe if she'd been a used-car dealer she would have noticed my new Farrah Fawcett-Majors head, which was front-and-center on my coffee table. Instead, she almost set her drink down on top of it.

Carol *did* admire my attachment to objects, because even though she was in the business of hawking things, she'd never had strong feelings for any of it. She regularly, dispassionately, dug up collectibles that made enthusiasts come unglued. She'd once found a pitiful Sandy Dennis scrapbook that had reduced two rival fans to tears in front of her. After consoling them, she'd swiftly auctioned it to the richer of the two, the one who had money in his account since he hadn't paid his rent yet. Carol liked to joke that she'd sell her own soul if it were worth over a hundred dollars.

But I wasn't compulsive like many of her return customers. I had a more sentimental connection to objects.

Carol had first identified the depth of my feeling for objects when she'd noticed a tiny canister in my room. It had thrown her, trying to figure out what it was, then she'd determined that it was a tube for a filmstrip, those pre-VCR classroom novelties. She'd quizzed me about it.

"I found it outside that run-down flea market at Seventh and Twenty-fifth. It was in a pile of absolute junk that this homeless guy had. I couldn't believe he was trying to sell it, but I also couldn't believe how interesting it was to me, how much I wanted it. It reminded me that when I was little, we showed filmstrips in science class and I got chosen to be the one to run them.

"You had to listen for the beeps on the cassette and then plunge this little handle on the filmstrip machine and this picture would come up on the screen. I felt so important whenever I got to do it that I sort of fantasized I had actually *created* the filmstrip and I was screening it for the class. I never screwed it up." I had been gushing remembering my history in showbiz. "So I figured it was worth a quarter to get this little doohickey just as a symbol or something."

Carol told me many times she doubted she'd ever get all goose pimply over a valueless bit of plastic, but that she loved me for my ability to do so.

Carol used to be more interested in objects. She'd started out life as a pack rat of the first order, and at age thirty had still been able to lay her hands on a carefully preserved corsage from her seventh-grade Sadie Hawkins dance or the first 45 single she'd ever purchased. When her mother died unexpectedly, the cancer having crept up and surprised them both, Carol had called me in tears. I'd been out drinking with her the night before and suddenly she was a distant, whimpering voice on the phone, already transported back to her hometown in Maine. It had taken her two weeks to sort through her mother's horde: Lotto tickets bundled in spaghetti-soft rubberbands older than us both; paper and plastic shopping bags stacked as high as humans in narrow closets; empty prescription bottles dating back to the war (the second world one); nicety cards from friends and coworkers long forgotten.

Carol had spent those Maine days discarding, and her evenings appraising the items of value, the things that she didn't want but that somebody might: chairs, tables, frames, antiques. A Shirley Temple doll, badly decomposed. A perfectly preserved box of chocolates that had been hidden in a stack of forty-year-old correspondence (the mummified candies were pitched but the box itself found its way into the hands of a very pleased collector of ephemera). She wound up making very little money after the items were sold, even less considering the time she'd spent editing her mother's possessions.

When Carol got back, she was different. She was still fun and still warm and still picked up the phone with the same tone and still listened to me with a patient ear, but she was somehow more mercenary with details. Having thrown away everything that had ever mattered to her mother, she went through her own closets, returning the fifteen-year-old corsages back to the fields from whence they'd come, junking birthday cards and childhood scrapbooks and baby booties. She later told me that she'd always held on to everything, *everything,* so that once she'd started eliminating items that weren't essential, she'd found herself unable to draw a line. If her high school cheerleading outfit was no longer worth saving, what about the Bible she'd received at her first (and last) communion? Or her junior high diaries? Or photos of her family? In the end, Carol had excised precious items with which most of us feel we could never part, leaving her apartment bare except for day-to-day livingware. It had made her twice as good at her job: Since she didn't really have much use for any of the items she salvaged, she never regretted letting any of them go.

I was getting my coat. I didn't want to be later than we already were and risk missing interesting arrivals.

"Are we going or are we going?"

"Let's go," Carol breathed, having downed an entire can of fizz with graceless gusto. She walked past me out the door with an almost macho lurch.

That's why I slept with her once—I mistook her for a guy. I smiled at this idea and wished I would be able to remember it to tell Warren, except not even Warren knew that the thoroughly queer David Greer had once made love to a woman, to our pal Carol. Warren's standards were so high that probably all of his friends were traitors on some level.

We left the apartment, abandoning all my precious toys to the dark.

CHAPTER 6

Faces & Places!

David Greer — On the surface, the party was devised to promote and celebrate the upcoming fourth-season opener of *Lifesavers,* the little beach show that could, the numbingly dim-witted series that had become the fifth most-watched TV program on the planet.

Beyond that, the beach-themed party was an experience I'll never forget because it was the night I met a man who changed my life.

I remember the details of the evening with a bracing clarity, even infinitesimal things, like the way the carpet felt under my slick-soled shoes, the odd aftertaste when you downed one of the hot dogs that were being sold from a phony beach concession stand, the way the air smelled—heavy with artificial fragrance, sweat, and smoke. The beach motif had inspired several open bars made of faux driftwood sitting atop clusters of phony sand. Whose job is it to make phony sand?

The party wasn't exactly the stiff and formal event I'd nervously envisioned, it was a vulgar, splashy, old boy's network with some chicks thrown in for good measure, mostly small-faced women with grapefruit tits who hadn't married for love. Half the attendees were sun-kissed brown, since they'd flown in from the West Coast for this shindig. *Lifesavers* was taped in L.A., but the producers were also feting it in New York—the same party thrown twice, a week apart. This being the second staging, the energy level had understandably dimmed.

At the door, we had to spend a few minutes on queue with others whose faces were not instantly recognizable as TV bigwigs or welcome members of the press. The slouchy older woman with the guest list was brave in a glitzy designer frock meant for someone of her exact weight but three feet taller. I was prepared to hate her for giving us a hard time, but instead she glanced up and saw us and immediately waved us up to her. I loved line-jumping the dozen or so people ahead of us—it was like Studio 54 except without Calvin Klein. But I also felt guilty since Carol and I were undeserving of any sort of special treatment. *Lifesavers* was getting nothing out of being nice to us; we were just gawkers.

"Names?"

"Just one name," I said in a low voice, self-conscious and unwilling to give everyone a tragic show if we were booted. "Greer. David Greer. And guest."

She flipped through pages seemingly at random. You'd think they'd have gone with alphabetization. A little obvious, but always functional.

"You're in," she said under her breath, "and I'll be nice and let you take your friend in, too, since she's your date."

The ruse had worked much better than expected. Carol gave me a conspiratorial eye-batting and hooked her arm into mine. "See, honey? What would you do without me?"

It was fun, like sneaking into the movies, but in retrospect it was the first time I'd ever used a woman like that. Carol, my friend and my onetime lover, was reduced to being my beard, my ticket to passing for straight.

The room was a large, formal reception hall at the offices of the network at Forty-second and Lex, twenty floors above the unbroken sea of channel surfers who flooded the streets during summer reruns.

The people at the party were either looking indiscreetly about for anyone at all famous or were executive eyesores so rich they believed *they* were famous, the star attractions of the party. We did see Gregory Harrison with a leggy lovely, and also a guy who looked like Jack Scalia. Maxwell Caulfield was there with his mother-figure wife, Juliet Mills; we overheard that he was in town working on a featured role in yet another gay-themed play in which he was to strip naked and act his heart out. All of this into was carefully noted and discussed by us, so our stories would match later when we told Warren of our *Night of 100 Almost Stars.*

After one shuffling sweep of the room that saw me accidentally snagging a plastic starfish with my tux, we grabbed some fruity drinks and parked in a loveseat that was draped with colorful beach blankets. Bingo—we were bored. It was as unexciting as the beach was for me, except you didn't even get to work on your tan or check out how everyone else's was doing. I felt like my tux was shrinking on me as the night wore on, bonding with my skin.

Carol seemed to be holding up beautifully. She got smashed (well, as smashed as she gets) on mixed drinks and slouched next to me chewing a lime slice and giggling. She looked fantastic and I'm sure she featured in some executive dreams later that night from all the approving glances she received. I told her if she caused a scene it might land her her own TV show.

"Yes, like *Carol in the City,*" she cracked.

"Or maybe you could be Caroline's new love interest. Be a lot more believable than her crush on that flaming assistant."

For some reason, this made her laugh so hard she leaned forward and almost doffed the top of her dress.

When she leaned past me, I suddenly realized that our quarry had entered and was standing at the head of a large group of especially important-looking flunkies.

It always gave me a slight start to see a celebrity in a public setting, expected or not. Living in New York, you get used to seeing John-John tooling around town on his bike (pursued by sixty stalkerazzis), Deborah Harry walking her teacup doggie, and Ethan Hawke. Actually, you see Ethan Hawke at least once a week.

But if it's uncool to walk up to a star and ask for an autograph or to shriek when spotting Johnny Depp and to then chase him until he can't run anymore, New Yorkers *do* enjoy noting which celebrities they've spotted at the end of a long day:

"You know who I saw today?"

"Who?"

"Debbie Gibson."

"You mean *Deborah*. Sure it was her?"

"Absolutely."

"What was she doing?"

"She was in the MAC store in SoHo."

"How about that?"

No big whoop, and yet required conversation.

For me, I'd gone through several stages when it came to star attraction. As a kid, I'd learned from my mother to think of stars as a sign of intelligence. Knowing who stars were showed your celebrity IQ. If you couldn't provide the answer to such probing questions as "Wasn't Natalie Wood in *The Silver Chalice*?" then you were . . . lacking. Unaware. Six degrees of Kevin Bacon is for peewees. The free-form version I practiced with my mother was far more challenging. We'd sit at the coffee table with a cable movie on, passively absorbing it in the background while engaging in name associations that would get so intense my sisters would just stare at us, uncomprehending. They had no idea whether or not Natalie Wood was in *The Silver Chalice*. They had no idea who, exactly, Natalie Wood *was*.

Another pastime was my cataloguing. I would pass the long, dry Iowa summers on my bunk bed, which I shared with my upstairs brother Kenny, making lists—from scratch—of every famous person I could think of. It'd been hard the first time, when I was approximately ten. I hadn't known as many as I'd wanted to. I think I made it to about two hundred, with a heavy emphasis on TV-only actors, like Bert Convy or Marcia Wallace or Lynda Carter. I did the list another thirty or forty times over the years. I guess I had a lot of time on my hands, a lot of issues to avoid.

One time the list became a clue. I'd started to add more and more male names to my celebrity lists. I was very much aware of glamorous women, but suddenly the supposedly boring male stars started popping into my head just as quickly. It got so that male names would materialize from the moment I'd pick up my pad and my leaky blue felt-tip to start my list. Leif Garrett. Erik Estrada. Tom Wopat. Lee Horsley. Shawn Cassidy. I recognized the trend, but only on a purely superficial, factual level. *I'm getting better at naming boys.* I decided to do two lists, separating stars by sex. I would start with the male list. Robert Conrad. Richard Hatch. Grant Goodeve. Freddie Prinze. Andy Gibb.

I had no agenda when I was making those lists. The act of recording gave me intense satisfaction, even the act of writing, of making sure the lists were neat and that each name had a well-formed number before it: (1), (2), (3). . . . But little did I know that I was creating a document that could be used against me, interpreted (correctly) by an enemy in a way that would shed light on parts of myself that I wasn't hiding, but which were hiding inside me.

Kenny had found my list and was reading it when I came into our room. Our room was blue. It was a room for boys, so it was blue. Our bunk bed was a dark wood with a bar across the top bunk because Kenny, although two years older than I and considerably more athletic, had a freaky habit of rolling out of his bed and whizzing past me to the floor. He'd broken his collarbone and his nose the second time, which was the day when my mother had purchased and installed the somewhat undignified safety bar. Kenny had gotten so mean after that day, meaner than ever.

"Give it!" I'd shouted, making a swipe at my list. For although it was supposedly something dry and meaningless, I'd suddenly been filled with a desperate rage to recapture it.

Kenny had moved it easily out of my reach. "What is this, Davey? A list of your *boyfriends?*" He'd sneered the word with such relish it had eighteen syllables, each one damning me silent. I was flabbergasted. The concept wasn't really real to me, but I knew it was heinous, an act against God. "Boys don't marry boys," my Sunday School teacher had gently told us when we were little. Some dumb girl next to me had claimed they could. Even *I'd* known the answer to that one.

"Who do you think is cutest—David Cassidy or John Travolta?" Kenny was Satan at that time. When we learned about the devious ways of the devil in church each week, I had no problem envisioning the Prince of Darkness: He would look like Kenny with hooves.

I just started bawling my eyes out. I couldn't respond, I didn't know what he meant so I didn't know if it wasn't true. I cried so hard my legs flopped out and I sat down hard on my ass, helpless. Of course, that had led to a Mom Intervention and swift, crisply unconvincing apologies all around. I later made sure to leave a female star list laying around where Kenny would see it, but he never mentioned it if he did. Loni Anderson. Catherine Bach. Lydia Cornell. Adrienne Barbeau. The bombshell list, special edition. A terrible waste of a list for a twisted sibling.

Over time, as I got more and more interested in celebrities, I invested in exclamation-point magazines like *Teen Beat, Tiger Beat, 16,* and *Superteen.* They had bios and filmographies and personal interviews and pictures. I found myself eyeballing a Rick Springfield pullout poster, examining his jeans and his unbuttoned shirt and his eyes and hair, all under the guise of the prominent Cheryl Ladd cover—thank God for integrated magazines, integrated star lists.

Maybe it had taken Kenny to suggest something that made perfect, if secret, sense. I gave the whole boyfriends idea a lot of careful consideration and decided that maybe I *did* like boy stars more than girl stars.

The magazines were my first taste of adulation. I read letters sent in by other kids near my age: Becky, age 12, Springfield, Miss.; Andrew, age 9, Buffalo, NY. Their letters were drenched in adjectives, outlining fantasy meetings with their favorite stars. I came to realize that stars were like angels, superheroes. I figured out that most people, including adults, found stars irresistibly interesting, daunting. Even my aunts would speculate in hushed tones about the intricacies of being married to Elizabeth Taylor, and when I prodded them, they'd go into girlish stories about dormant crushes on Robert Walker, Sal Mineo, or Clifton Webb. One of my aunts confessed to still owning a pseudoauthentic George Gobel autograph, and my mother later mocked that admission behind her back so mercilessly I cried sugary tears of pity for the wayward aunt, the aunt who'd loved the wrong star.

Later, as an adult, I would spend hours fabricating letters to the porn magazines I worked for, and as I did so, I suddenly realized that the letter from Becky, age 12, in *16* magazine had probably been scripted by Joe, age 45, all those years ago. Another bubble burst.

As a teen, I made excursions to the Big Star Theatre in Des Moines to watch the touring company productions they boasted. I was the only unescorted patron and the only seventeen-year-old kid in orchestra seating for silly renditions of *Oklahoma!* or *Sugar Babies* and one-person shows starring Rita Moreno, Mitzi Gaynor, Phyllis George, or Anita Bryant (I didn't know any better, but I hated her act, anyway). I was razzle-dazzled when I got to meet Ann-Margret outside the theater. She was leaving after a performance and graciously signed a dozen or so autographs. I got one, and she seemed turned on by me, not sexually, but as if rendered alive by the flick of a switch triggered by my attentive eyes. I guess the older stars get, the more entranced they are to see that they still have underage fans, if only one or two. She pinched my chin and cooed, "Aren't you just a *dear?*" I had no reply for her. I just remember being overwhelmed by her cotton-candy redness and heavy, flowery scent as she nestled in close and signed her name on my program.

I was ecstatic! I'd just met *the* Ann-Margret. (I told my sisters and they asked, "Who?" like I'd just announced I had a disease.) I think the driving factor at that point was the idea of "the." There was something outrageously unique to me about meeting one-and-onlies, especially in Iowa. It meant that for twenty seconds, I was the only person on the planet being addressed by the legendary Ann-Margret.

Then I got over it.

I don't know, I guess that after meeting so many stars, I came to realize how common the thrill was and I started getting more discriminating. I mean, I went to see Sandy Duncan as Peter Pan and then afterwards I just took off. I felt weird about passing up my shot at meeting her, but did I really *want* to meet her? No. What would I have said? "I like Wheat Thins, too?"

I never stopped being interested in celebrity, but the percolation flattened out for me. I decided that *I* had what it took to be a star, and that's an idea no true fan can ever have. I had stopped being a fan, and was instead an observer, an aspirant even. I didn't know how I was going to get famous, but I knew I could if all those other losers could. I mean, what made Bo Derek famous? Her raging talent?

I had deprogrammed myself from the cult of personality.

In the meantime, I'd taken to writing poetry and short stories for my own amusement and for the amusement of my friends. I wrote mysteries, mostly, Alfred Hitchcock–style whodunits—real pedestrian material, but with untouchable grammar and spelling. My teachers, not to mention my parents, were bowled over. They decided I was gifted and predictions were made that I'd be the next Stephen King.

Fifteen years later, I would've settled for being Tabitha.

Seeing Alan Dillinger was kind of fun because he was one of the most currently popular celebrities I'd ever encountered. When Ann-Margret and I had interacted, she'd been way past her prime and the Big Star Theatre just one more stage for her to avoid plunging from. But Alan Dillinger was the boy of the moment, and I got a sly thrill from the fact that thirty million teenage girls would have done *anything* to have been in my place at the party.

Carol leaned back and followed my gaze and immediately perked up. "Hey, it's him. Get a load of that."

Alan looked dazzling, a shimmering object that could have been a perfect robot from a distance. But not one of those cold, metallic models, more like the hot, trashy feelgoods beamed up for your pleasure in *Logan's Run*. Sexy because they were available, with no games or begging or bagging necessary. He seemed to have an aura, but it was really because the people around him were staring at him, leaning slightly away to get a good look at the whole package, to commit him to memory for feverish reports to loved ones later. The effect was like visible radiation, a path clearing from all points around him.

Alan was a big enough star that he didn't have to arrive in a tuxedo or suit, just a carefully casual outfit probably dreamed up by a pair of charmingly starstruck queens named Dolce & Gabbana. His silky shirt was black and shiny, almost as if sequined, and his pants were thin, tan, and expertly tailored. He wore snug black sneakers on his feet and his bleached hair was short, styled, reflective, healthy-looking. You can always tell stars by their good hair. Even the ugly ones have good hair from expensive conditioners pushed on them by overenthusiastic hired stylists. I loved how his eyebrows stayed dark as mink even though his hair cheekily pretended to be Nordic—the contrast made his pale blue eyes stand out dramatically. His body was an instant hard-on, a perfectly proportioned wall of muscle, never overdone, not even in one spot. Okay, maybe his biceps were a little bee-stung, and that alone should have been proof-positive that all the hopeful gay rumors were true.

He was what they used to call beefcake. I never found that food-sounding term very appetizing, and yet any red-blooded queer would have to admit craving a mouthful of Alan Dillinger.

Carol ran her finger over my lower lip and pretended to flick away the drool. I hotly denied that I thought he was *that* cute. After all, don't you know it's uncool to lust after anyone popular, anyone who's *supposed* to be considered gorgeous? How many of your friends would even *admit* that someone like Rob Lowe is easy on the eyes?

"He's okay," I said, squirming. It's also hard to admit appreciation for someone who you don't think would return the favor.

" 'Okay?' He's sort of literally like a *god*." Carol groaned, twirling a strand of her hair around her fingertip, sampling its softness. "Not my type, exactly, but you've gotta give it up for him. He's what Joanie Cunningham would call a hunk."

Of course Alan didn't arrive stag. That would've been a little bold. It would have sent out the message that he couldn't get a date, or that he was a faggot. Both applied to me, but Carol and I were just there as friends, we weren't trying to fool our fans into thinking we were a couple. But then maybe that's what Jodie Foster says to herself as she's stepping into Armani two hours before she attends the Oscars with one of her favorite nells.

That's a great queer litmus test for stars, their dates. If he shows up with his mama, sister, or costar; if she shows up with both her husband and her single, female best friend; or if anyone shows up alone, there is a fighting chance that queerness is to blame. The best is when they show up with a child as their date, some needy kid. That way, the press is further blackmailed into shutting their traps—who would dare to criticize a big-hearted star for bringing a basket case to the Tonys?

Alan's date was an underwhelming knockout. You know, one of those beauty contestant types, the ones with a tendency to wear beaded low-plungers and lots and lots of hair and makeup. This particular chick (what else to call her? I don't think she'd be likely to object to "chick" on feminist grounds) had blond highlights all over her deep-brown tresses, hunks of hair here, hunks of hair there. She looked like a walking chocolate mousse, except I bet neither as smooth nor as creamy. She had that awful pink lipstick that when overused looks metallic, and which she'd carefully lined with a darker shade of rose. She looked like she was ready to mash her head onto a piece of paper and sell a face print.

She had her hairless arm locked around Alan, at his side as if she'd been born there, a 102-pound birthmark or an underdeveloped Siamese twin. I was eating my heart out, even though her true function was probably as an Elizabeth Taylor to his Malcolm Forbes.

Alan was laughing at something a squat, suited yes-man was saying to him when he scanned the room, seeming to avoid eye contact with any one person. It was like he was checking out the walls for mirrors, a sixties Bond knockoff, Austin Powers with a body. Or like a stage actor, playing to the space beyond the expectant faces. The bimbo he was escorting was similarly distracted, seemingly ensconced in a personal stupor. It must've been frustrating for the suit to be having a conversation that was playing more like a staged reading.

Then Alan seemed to see me on the couch, slouchy in my hours-old outfit, cozied up to my own semibeard; Carol wasn't a full beard, just stubble.

Alan's attention to me was like when you're eighteen and you go to a Wham! concert and you're about ten rows back but you manage to convince yourself that George Michael stared *right at you,* sang "I'm Your Man" *right to you.*

"Smile," Carol said, her lips immobile. "You're on *Alan Camera.*"

I refused to believe I was being stared at by the man *TV Guide* had voted Most Eligible Bachelor of '98. I'd never been voted anything at all. I didn't even *vote.*

"Wouldn't it be funny if he came over and picked me up?" I mumbled and we started laughing under our breath.

"What a notch in your lipstick case, David."

Alan seemed to excuse himself, tearing away from his beard. The girl looked mortified at the deviation in the schedule, deeply confused. *Why-he-leaving-me?* her guileless face implored to the air. Shrugging off his entourage, Alan made a beeline for us, the whites of my eyes sagging with fright. He was coming right towards me. I sat up a bit straighter and looked away, locked my knees and tried to feign that I was engrossed with something Carol wasn't saying. When I glanced back, it was because Carol was grinning excitedly upward. Alan Dillinger was standing right above us, right next to our loveseat, and I was hating every minute of it. I was being doused with hot oil. I was being asked to square dance in the seventh grade. All eyes on me.

"I'm glad you could come to the party," he said. I *think* that's what he said. I've forgotten parts of that one moment because I was so alarmed. His voice was very measured, almost practiced, like he'd gone to an elocution class—but not as bad as Kathleen Turner or anything. The falsity was more like he consciously had to trick your ears into thinking he sounded a little more forceful than he really did. Yes, there was a hint of what they call "butching it up." Like when I'm on the phone with my uncle Roy.

"Thanks!" Carol exclaimed. "I'm Carol Terry and this is my friend David Greer. You're fantastic on your show." I hated Carol for calling attention to the fact that we were little nobodies, but loved her for saying *something*, and for at least saying the only honest and reasonable thing either of us *could* say. Thank God she didn't try to pretend she was a TV critic or the actress who plays Helen Hunt's sister on *Mad About You*, like most best friends might be tempted to do.

Alan immediately snapped his head to Carol and quizzed her on some details, asking what she liked or didn't like about particular episodes, affording me an unselfconscious front-row seat for his profile. It says something that he cared about this stranger's opinion of his acting—something good and something bad. I'd had no idea she even *watched* the show and was sick that he would find out I'd only seen bits and pieces of his claim to fame, and that I'd found them to be as stiff and bright and uninteresting as old hard-rock candy.

I scanned him from head to toe, impressed at how steady I felt with his pelvis practically in my face. He had the air of one of those guys who'd been a star quarterback in high school, having developed Charles Atlas muscles overnight at age thirteen. He was one of the flawless ones, those specimens who either become actors, models, rent boys, or next-door neighbors who exist to drive the rest of us insane.

"What about you?" he asked, looking down at me. Up close, I could see that while his eyes were still pretty and blue, one of his contacts was slightly off the mark, leaving a crescent of brown at the outside of his left iris. For some perverse reason, this served to calm me.

"I'm also a big fan," I said, not altogether honestly. *I'm a big fag is what I am. Are you?*

"Really? That's nice of you to say. Are you guys reviewers or with one of the stations or . . ."

"No, we're just guests of a columnist," Carol said with a degree of misguided pride.

Alan's interest clicked off like a light bulb. "Oh. Well, I hope you have a good time."

Before he took off to work the party, Alan took my hand to shake it and looked at me very oddly, like he was forestalling his exit. I couldn't figure out what he was doing. Was he hitting on me? It seemed like he was staring at me with a real urgency, like he wanted to break down and tell me something. Or ask me something. But it was inconceivable that one of the world's most famous closet cases would be so brazen and take such a risk in public.

"Thank you for having us," Carol interjected. "It was nice of you to come over. Why us? There are so many important people here, why did you decide to come over to us?"

Was she losing her *mind?*

Alan smiled and blushed a bit around his open collar. "You're important," he insisted easily, his voice more relaxed.

"Yes," I said, "and among the only people in the room who can't answer the question, 'Where were you when President *McKinley* was assassinated?' "

Alan laughed loudly, and people standing near us watched him do it. "Besides," he continued, "I just wanted to come and talk to someone who looked normal and nice."

"I'm Normal, she's Nice," I offered. He seemed to be taken with me, but soon he was being drawn away by several corporate types.

"Nice meeting you, Normal," he said with a wink. "And, uh, normal meeting you, Nice."

He was looking more at me than he was at Carol or at both of us. Then he stopped looking at either of us, turned, and stalked into the crowd, extending various limbs to overdressed party-goers with weekly columns and thirty-second slots on *The Gossip Show.* Across the room, he turned to give me a last friendly glance.

He had said the perfect gracious things, the benevolent and humbly charming pronouncements destined for publication. But everything he'd said had seemed sincere.

"Well," Carol said, sucking in her cheeks, "I think you've answered the question that every gay man in America has been debating for the last few years. He *has* to be."

I was a little anesthetized by the surreal moment, but not too numb to fight off a case of suspension of disbelief. *"Please*—we all knew *that.* Or at least *thought* we knew it. But I don't think he was actually, well, coming *on* to me. He just looked preoccupied. Maybe he's on drugs or something, Warren says he's on drugs. Besides, he could have his pick of any man in the world. He could probably get Mark Wahlberg to swing."

Carol straightened and leaned in to me. "Maybe he's interested in finding someone—what did he say? —'normal and nice.' And do you really think he'd have to be on crack to find you sexy? You're very cute, David. I'm sure you could have your pick of men, too."

It was nice to receive genuine compliments, even if slightly uncomfy that they were coming from the only woman I'd ever gotten naked with.

"I think I'm cute enough," I lied, "but why would he pick *me?* You can't tell me there aren't a hundred million other gay guys swarming around him every second of the day. I could be a tipster, for all he knows, or a close pal of Warren Junior's—*hello.* If he's really so closeted, why would he be so reckless?"

Carol was actually quite an expert on the subject of tabloids, having sold back issues of them for over ten years. She always told me that when times were slow at the store, she'd dig into a *Star* from 1978 and read what scandalous things Dinah Shore was up to with Burt Reynolds or how Princess Grace was ashamed of her androgynous daughter. "He's smart, that's why. He knows that even though people in the press have made up their minds, and that gay guys and others with insight know he's probably gay, the tabloids won't out-and-out *out* him without a lot of juicy circumstantial evidence. With the possible exception of the *Globe*. Be that as it may, how convinced do you think Middle America would be by the headline 'Alan Dillinger Cruised Me at a Party!'? It's weak. He knows that his core audience, the trillions of teenyboppers and frustrated housewives out there, are never going to be convinced he's gay unless he says it or—or—I don't know, unless there were some very clear photographic proof."

I let that sink in.

"Keep in mind, David, that the majority of the world's citizens think that Michael Jackson had a baby boy out of paternal instinct and that he's morally superior to Goldie and Kurt because at *least* he and Debbie got *married.*"

"Shara Quincy, and you are?"

We were startled by the speed and vigor with which she had thrust herself into our conversation and pumped both our hands as kneejerk introductions were made. Warren had warned me to avoid her, but she'd launched a sneak attack in the wake of her golden client Alan Dillinger.

Shara was as Warren had described, a redheaded vixen well past her prime, likely to be harvested by Jackie Collins for a future novel. She was wearing a sheer blouse and severe black leather skirt, very stylish but not very flattering. I thought I detected an appendix scar smiling from behind the transparency. Her hair was pulled up but was fighting the glittery clips holding it in place. She had turkey-neck syndrome and a chestful of freckles that made her seem half leopard. She was one of those well-to-do women who don't have a reliable, objective self-sense of how they really look, and are too overbearing for any intimate girlfriends to advise them on fashion.

"Pleased to meet both of you, and Alan is, too. I saw him over here talking to you. He's a dazzler. Are you with TV or print?" she asked, eyes snapping from face to face.

I shrugged and smiled and tried to sound nonchalant as I made up something to avoid being booted. "Both, we're from a little TV slash print outfit, local. We run blurbs on new . . . movies, actors, you know, human interest."

"Called?" she accused.

"Flight . . . Night Flight," I bluffed. "We also do cabaret listings."

Satisfied that we were likely legit but small potatoes, Shara nonetheless seemed to be using us as a break between serious schmoozing. "Big company, small company, these things are murder on all involved. Only good thing about 'em is free food. And booze. Listen, kids, if either of you ever gets into showbiz, *don't.* But if you do, call me, we'll talk. We'll do a deal. I'll get you movies, TV, endorsements, the whole *Jerry Maguire.* I got Brooke Shields on the tube. I got George Clooney's name in lights. I got Fergie into plugging Weight Watchers. I'm a deal-maker, it's what I do, thirty-five years it's what I'm doing."

We were sort of glassy-eyed listening to her speak, watching the vertical creases in her lips mash together in lipsticky red while she laundry-listed her accomplishments and always, always the refrain, "We'll talk. We'll do a deal." That she would waste her time pitching herself to a couple of nobodies broadcasted her blanket approach to PR. This woman left no stone unturned. That, or she was so brainwashed by her own spiel that she couldn't hold a normal conversation. Her mouth was always on.

"I've always wanted to do commercials," Carol offered, the falsehood rendering her voice childlike.

"Commercials, you're not right for, but you come to me for something you're right for, you get your foot in the door, you're in. You're never too old, sweetie. I do everything. I get your nose done, I have that hair straightened, I get you some tits. I'll hold your hand for the audition. I'm your mother, your best friend, your agent, I'll be whatever. That's how I work. That's what I do."

It was kind of an outrage to hear such things discussed so indelicately. Shara Quincy was in dire need of a good personal(ity) trainer. We attempted to act as if everything were peachy.

"Your client Alan Dillinger is having a great year," I heard myself say, detached. The room felt like it was full of rolling steam, hot in patches and suffocating. I found myself wondering if Alan had already paraded through the kitchen and left the building.

"A great year? It's the best, the best." She skillfully slipped me her card from a small, zippered pocket in her skirt. It said: SHARA QUINCY — DEALMAKER.

The movement of her hand to her card and of her card to my hand mirrored the covert precision of a drug transaction.

She forged on. "It doesn't get any better than this. This is it, this is what they all want, even the ones who don't do TV don't have years this good. I'm right there with him every step of the way. Between you and me, I'm the brains. That kid has the body—all natural, body by God— but I have the brains. Brains by God. You have a card?"

"Um, huh? No. No, *Night Flight* is run by cheapskates. We're small. Practically nonprofit."

"What's your name, kid?" she asked me. She had a look on her face like she was trying to get across that I might be her long-lost biological son, given away for adoption in the disapproving past.

"David."

Impatiently, "You have a last name?"

"Greer."

"David Greer. Not bad for a stage name, no reason to ditch it. Nobody changes their names anymore, anyway. Big stars named Duchovny, Drescher, Degenerate. Jesus Christ! No reason to bother. I never forget a name, Mr. David Greer. I'm going to look you up if I need one of those whaddyacall *blurbs*. Or for you to recommend me some cabaret, maybe slip me some tickets." She stuck the tip of her tongue out like she'd tasted something hot. It made me think of her sex life, which in turn made my stomach lurch.

When someone called her name and Shara's head snapped left, I exchanged a wide-eyed glance with Carol, who was self-consciously stroking her hair, wondering how much straighter it could be, *should* be.

Shara trudged off like she was stomping through a cow pasture full of mud, clomping with an out-of-whack energy, as if a shoe could be sucked off her foot if she got careless.

"Hurricane Sharon," Carol muttered, recovering.

"Shara," I corrected. "She's Dillinger's agent, and Warren told me she was like that."

"I didn't think *anybody* was really like that," Carol whispered, amazed. We both agreed that while a lot of people would find Shara Quincy amusing and eccentric, we both found her revolting. Her existence was disturbing to us; we couldn't picture her as a little girl, a teenager, a young woman, couldn't piece together the home life or experiences that possibly could have shaped a living, breathing, two-dimensional object in the form of a woman, *that* woman.

Once we managed to get Shara out of our minds, the rest of the evening was taken up with my trying to get over my brush with fame. I was totally preoccupied, as would be expected, but I couldn't draw the line between the excitement that I had actually *met*—not just seen or been received by, but *met*—a superstar, and the fact that I had also had a possible romantic connection with an attractive man. It was like when a friend of a friend shows up unexpectedly at a gathering and you all see a movie but you and the new guy sit next to each other and press your thighs together and have a charged conversation. You feel like there's something going on, and you're keyed up to call him right away, and you start imagining what it would be like to be dating him.

Only in my case, that seemed impossible. No one with at least one foot in reality considers, *What if I date a celebrity?* It just doesn't seem like an option. But so many unknowns have been there and done that, all the Shoshannas who had become mildly famous in their own right after getting romantic with a superstar.

There had been a spark between Alan and me, but the spark had been limited, like a single bolt of fireworks. One blinding explosion and then clear-sky anticipation.

Still thinking of missed opportunities, I engaged in some rusty ballroom dancing with Carol that proved to be right up her alley. Waltzing with her pressed against me while the band played reminded me of an apocryphal story I'd once read about Tyrone Power forcing his date, Joan Blondell, to go dance with Clark Gable just so she could report back to him what Clark *felt* like. Sneaky.

The party actually became more fun when the orchestra took off and Junior Vasquez arrived to DJ. It was sort of a bad executive decision somewhere, with Junior spinning all these radically hip dance mixes and the majority of the crowd unaware that Fleetwood Mac had broken up, let alone had made a comeback. I guess it was a matter of making the event seem exclusive, but it was a monumental waste to have a hot DJ spinning for the Streisand and Manilow crowd. That's the way it always is, with the ones who'd really appreciate something being kept at arm's length by the ones who have no clue but who have clout.

We danced, working up an aerobic sweat in our fancy clothes. Carol whispered to me how gratifying it was that we'd overcome our initial outcast status at the party, winding up being the only "couple" able to keep up with techno and the only people there who didn't separate music by slow dance and fast dance. Also, we'd been seen chatting with Alan Dillinger, so we were obviously *somebodies.*

I still couldn't stop thinking about my close encounter. Alan Dillinger had more than lived up to the hype, looks-wise. He had been such a striking person, magnetic. Right from that first insubstantial exchange I'd started obsessing over when I'd see him next, if ever.

The party was in full swing, but Carol and I weren't, at least not anymore. After two hours of hoofing like we were mere children, we breathlessly retired to the sidelines. It would've helped if there had been anyone around we felt like talking with, but the other guests had BOR-ING scrawled across their foreheads in permanent ink. My shirt was soaked under my jacket, my body feeling supercooked. I wanted us to make a dash for a nearby roped-off terrace, but Carol's independent streak flared up, as it was sometimes prone to; she preferred to hover in a near-empty corner and survey the goings-on.

"You go," she encouraged. "I want to stand here and people-watch." Carol could read people like dimestore pulps.

As I left her, though, I thought she had the look of a bald eagle observing a field—lovely, but you better hope you're not a mouse. I wondered if she'd try to pocket some network ashtrays to market.

Hopping the rope and passing through an ornate arch leading to the terrace, I saw a man leaning against the heavy balustrade. From his clothes, I recognized right away that it was Alan Dillinger again. He must've come back around from outside on the walkway that surrounded the floor. It was eerie to see a star standing alone. I don't think I'd ever seen anybody recognizable without an entourage, bodyguard or histrionic crowd, least of all fanbait like Alan Dillinger.

I had a flash of nerves—*Should I talk to him? What should I say?*— just before the scene went Fellini.

A man literally fell from the sky, landing in a heap between myself and Alan, his body crashing to the marble with a sickening thud. I was on the defensive, hunching my shoulders against any further human rain. Alan spun around instantly, but his face betrayed no fear at all. In fact, he gave the impression that he might have just looked up from reading the Sunday *Times*.

I hurried over to the crumpled form and reflexively looked up to see where he'd fallen from. A higher floor? A passing plane? Then, a series of clues came to my attention that made me realize this guy was a photographer, a paparazzo after a good ambush shot of Alan. First, there was a small ledge above the arch on the outside where part of a creeping vine had been torn away. The "victim" had obviously been perched there. Second, there was a professional camera on top of him, where it had landed after the plunge. And third, Alan said calmly, "Hello, Chip. Still trying to get a good shot to crucify me with?"

I knelt to see if the fall guy was okay, simultaneously retrieving the delicate-looking camera. I ascertained almost immediately that the photographer was perfectly fine—a little rattled and snappish in the face of assistance, but fine.

I'm not a buff, so I don't know how I knew to do this, but I tugged on a lever at the side of the camera and out popped a roll of film. You didn't have to be an expert to know that the roll of film, like Pee Wee Herman, was destroyed when exposed. I committed this anarchic act without consideration, without any real emotion. I had just . . . reacted. And yet it seemed perfectly logical as I was doing it, and I didn't cower from the inevitable fallout either, so great was my conviction. I tugged the film sharply out of its spool.

There was something about Alan that triggered a protective urge in others, in me. It wasn't conscious at the time, but its effects were immediate and sensational.

"Whoops," I said, catching Alan's eye. He saw me holding the film and smiled broadly before laughing gleefully, like a spoiled child you can't help adoring. Meanwhile, the clumsy photographer staggered up and cursed me bitterly for screwing up his film.

"You did that on *purpose!*" he spat. "You *fuck*ing *fag*got asshole! What the *fuck!*" He shoved me in a short, staccato movement, his fingers outspread, like he was playing volleyball with my chest. It startled me, made me fear that I was about to get into a fistfight, my first ever. I knew I didn't stand much of a chance versus Chip the Stalkerazzi. He was a skinny, vicious little ferret in a cheap tuxedo, his thinning hair, slight form, and gray eyes making him seem like a visitor from another planet compared to his unwilling subject. It was a no-cameras event, so he'd probably conned or bribed his way in before ensconcing himself in a prime spot for a good shot. Caterers are notorious for collusion with paparazzi; caterers and restaurateurs and, of course, malignant publicists.

Why the photographer hadn't just stood on the terrace and stuck his camera in Dillinger's face, I had no idea. I could only surmise that he'd had run-ins with this hard-to-shoot actor before, and was perhaps in need of an edge. Or a ledge.

Security trundled onto the scene in the form of two big, sexy bullies of color getting paid to make people disappear from sight. They grabbed the loudmouth and dragged him away as my heart pounded with the excitement of it all, and with the suppressed rage of his insults.

"I'll sue your *ass,* you *fuck*ing *fag*got!"

"Don't let him get under your skin," Alan said, approaching me and patting my back like a true comrade. "He's a real shit. He gets paid to be. He's taken pictures of me for three years now, and he gets meaner every time I bump into him. Has insider info on where I'll be and gets me several times a week. I'm putting his kids through school. I'm like his Jackie O." He told me this in a self-dishy way that disarmed me.

"Nothing remotely like that's ever happened to me," I admitted, still daunted by Alan's aura. His legendary personal charm was like warmth in place of the sun that had disappeared behind the skyline. His blue eyes were headlights in the dusk. "I just emptied his camera on instinct."

"I really appreciate it," he said. "In the long run, it won't affect me whether or not he has some shots from tonight, but I really appreciate the gesture. My hero."

I turned and looked into his eyes and felt something electric pass between us, that first little shock when you both realize at once that the interest is mutual.

"I'm sorry, Alan, what's going on? What the *hell?* What the *hell?*" Shara came running up to us followed by some more security types, and within the space of a few minutes Alan was surrounded by thirty people, his chance for a private moment stolen by an infestation of shutterbug. "What the *hell?*" Shara continued like a barking terrier in need of corporal punishment.

It was awkward for me to stand there, still hoping to talk with Alan more to see what he was really like. Up until then, he'd seemed like an impossibly level-headed guy, someone eager to make a friend in me. I had the feeling that most celebrities would have brushed me off, but in this case, it was Alan's minders who'd brushed me off by their sheer volume. I started to slink away.

I looked back as I returned to the dance floor and saw Alan's blond head bobbing just above the throng of too-late supporters. He was looking at me, had been waiting to see if I'd turn back. When I did, he mouthed, *"Thank you."* I nodded and waved and dashed over to find Carol, my heart thumping so sternly it seemed like it was in my vest pocket.

CHAPTER 7

Contact

John Dewey —

November the 30th, 1986 (Remember Cary Grant? Another of the great ones returns to dust).

Dear Mister Dewey:

Many thanks for your de-lightful letter! I am always much amused to find that the younger set can still be fascinated with the stars of yester-day, the true Golden Age of Cinema.

I do indeed have a few films featuring your honorary "idol" Gil Romano. They are in finer shape than any circulating prints you may have en-countered, to say the least! I had not thought of Gil Romano in many years until receipt of your letter. Thank you for reminding me that he has always been a-mong my favourites as well!

Mister Dewey, I _do_ own rare pieces featuring Mr. Romano that I think you would find most interesting. Should you ever find your-self near Seattle, I would be happy to set up a meeting for you to view these "one-of-a-kind" items. They are un-seen by any eyes other than my own for at least 50 years or more, and I would love to re-experience them along-side a true fan, such as your-self, before de-ciding if they should go the way of my Mid-summer Night's Dream, the film to which you re-ferred in your query.

Please call on me at your leisure.

I am and will remain,

Very Truly Yours —
Truitt Connor

P.S. I would enjoy corresponding with you on "all matters silent" if you are interested in other silent films as well. I am a silent film buff with much to say! Cheers—

John hadn't called after all, he'd written, making it easier to withhold information; he hadn't told Mr. Connor his age, or the extent of his devotion to Gil Romano. As he'd guessed, a businesslike letter was more apt to get results than a gushing note scrawled and sent in a state.

He was reading the results of his request at the mailbox, unable to wait until he was safe inside his room, tucked away from Granny's antsting inquiries. She had set off for the QuikMart an hour before. He knew it took her twenty-five minutes to get there and another twenty-five to get back, plus no *way* was she going to be able to select, stand in line with, and pay for even a couple of items in under ten minutes. He figured he was safe.

The old man's writing was spidery and blue, like a document from the past. The Constitution. He felt a sickening pull at the pit of his stomach as he read and reread it, interpreting what the old cinemaniac was trying to say. What were the "one-of-a-kind" items? If he owned a copy of *Gay Was the Hero,* why didn't he say so flat out? And if he owned such unique items, why not donate them like he had the other one, the Shakespeare one?

John couldn't figure out why the old man would pen such a teasing letter, something that gave no information, just an invitation. How was he supposed to make it to Seattle in Washington State all the way from Jersey? Was the guy nuts? He had always managed to find ways of paying for the precious Romano artifacts he'd found and which could not be stolen, but theft had its limits considering John's own limits—he could never rob a bank or otherwise steal anything truly substantial, enough for a cross-country plane ticket. And he couldn't sneak onto a train or ride his bike there.

Maybe there is something worse, he thought, *than not having the movie I want—knowing it exists, but not having any way to see it.*

As the clandestine minutes collapsed into one another, Granny hobbled into view down the neat dirt road that wound through the trailer park. She was carrying a small bag of groceries that contained, John guessed, some liquor, probably something like hot dogs, and maybe some lottery tickets. She seemed lost in concentration, in the effort of making her estranged leg move in sync with her good one. She did not see her grandson at the mailbox, staring into a letter, a suspicious missive from a strange old retired movie projectionist.

John lingered from some uncontrollable, self-destructive urge, watching his grandmother's frustrating journey toward him, willing her to look up and get p.o.'d at him. When he'd pushed it far enough, to the point where she really might have looked up at any moment, he darted into the trailer and rocketed to his room. If she didn't buy very much, he knew she might not bother calling him in to help her put away the groceries.

John held the letter like it was a newborn baby in need of comfort. It represented something—a major breakthrough, he thought. He had the jittery nerves he got when he stumbled onto a good lead, a clue. It was the same when he'd found the play program, and the time he'd discovered the posters in the warehouse. And when he'd found that first photograph, the totally unique photograph that nobody else in the world owned, the one personally inscribed by Gil Romano to John's sort-of relative.

The old man in Seattle was sitting on something big.

John lay chest-down over the edge of his bed, swinging his arms under to retrieve the box closest to the edge. He'd rummaged through it just that week but it already had two clots of dust on top of it. He blew them away fearfully, convinced that dust was somehow connected to triggering his migraines at times, the way emotional stress could breed body aches or flu symptoms or, yes, even migraines.

The box was stuffed with paper; it was his clippings collection, and since Romano wasn't breaking news, most of these clippings were from the archives at various libraries, who would never miss the articles that had survived in their care for fifty or more years until John happened along. He didn't know what he was searching for when he rifled through that box. He was well acquainted with all the pages and with the details of each column: "ROMANO'S NEXT HIT!" "STAR BUTTS HEADS WITH STUDIO," "GIL ROMANO: MAN OF THE YEAR." But he sometimes sifted through them to indulge in the familiarity, to reassure himself that they were still there and in chronological order.

In every studio portrait, Gil Romano's eyes were fixed, brimming with emotion. Lust. There was an intensity that dared the camera to look away, that never failed to preoccupy John, to make him zone.

Imagining Granny's labored progress up the steep steps of the trailer, panting as if each breath would be her final act, John made himself focus on an article he'd read many times, an early piece from a movie magazine called *The Thrill of it All* which followed Romano's path from being an average joe named Jim Stepps to being a worldwide movie idol in a few short years. John found himself noticing a caption under one photo of Romano as if for the first time, a short sentence meant to sum up the star's journey from Jersey to Hollywood: "GO WEST, YOUNG MAN!" it blared. A cliché, an easy caption in the days before captions and titles in popular magazines were necessarily puns. And yet it seemed newly pregnant with meaning.

"Go west, young man . . ." John breathed, startling himself at the sound of his own voice. He realized he rarely spoke around the house, never at school. He sometimes fantasized that he had lost his voice forever; the longer he waited between utterings, the larger the illusion that he was a mute. He wondered if never speaking again might give him a tragic status, sympathy. *That over there is John. John Dewey. Can't speak a word. Good guy, though.* But it was unlikely, since Granny never took notice of the times he went for over a week without saying a word. If he gave up words forever, who would know it?

"Go west." With a realization that flowered in his mind with the suddenness and solemnity of religious awakening, John knew he was going to find a way to Seattle to see that movie, and that somehow it would be his ticket away from the trailer, his grandmother, his life. Seattle was going to be a new life, just like Hollywood had been for—

"*John!*" Granny's voice ricocheted through his room at the same time he heard a bottle of wine clink onto the kitchen counter, rested there after a long and halting walk. "I could use some *help.*"

CHAPTER 8

The Mysteries of Your Dreams: *Revealed!*

David Greer — That night, I had my first Alan Dillinger dream.

Psychologists say that there's a reason why we dream about celebrities; we use them to measure ourselves against, and so when we dream of stars as equals we are self-confident, and when we dream of them as gods we are self-*un*confident, possibly deranged.

I wonder what it means when you dream of having sex with a star? Probably that you're horny and have expensive taste.

In my cramped single bed with the striped sheets that needed a tumble at the laundromat, I closed my eyes and saw Alan Dillinger, blond icon, making my breakfast in our kitchenette. He was completely naked, basted brown, with sand clinging to his bare feet. His body looked like a classical sculpture or like it belonged on a porn star, smooth, molded, ideal. When he turned, he was smiling at me, then laughing. I didn't get the humor, then I noticed he had no penis and no testicles. Nor had they been removed—it's not like there were any telltale scars, no Heaven's Gate starchild. He was like a great big Malibu Ken doll.

Next, we were on the floor, and he was grinding into me. What he was grinding, I have no idea. It just felt like skin against skin. Then I had the exhilarating sensation of being penetrated, but I couldn't figure out how he was accomplishing that with his rounded mound. I looked into his face for an answer but he'd suddenly morphed into someone else I'd had sex with once, a long time ago. Someone who as a person had been utterly valueless to me. But apparently the sex had been memorable.

I always had sex fantasies about celebrities. Always reaching out, in one way or another, beyond my grasp.

I couldn't come the first few times I slept with a man without thinking of Jon-Erik Hexum. I *still* think about Jon-Erik Hexum when I come sometimes, when I'm going for distance and intensity; volume is beyond your control, it's all about what you've been eating and how recently you visited that well. Those long-distance Jon-Erik episodes are when I "accidentally" hit my own shoulder, face, hair. Tasting myself. I use him like an idol carved of jade, except instead of salvation I'm praying for the briefest and most irresistible of reliefs. And instead of jade, my idol is a figment.

Anyone who knows who Jon-Erik Hexum was would almost *have* to be my age, twentysomethings, thirtysomethings, our age groups distinguished by that vague and slightly evasive "-something." It's parallel to saying, "My name is Davidwhoever," that last nebulous suffix of self-consciousness.

We were addlebrained teenagers in the early eighties, when Jon-Erik was making it big. He was a pretty-boy actor and the most straightforward, no-bones-about-it hunk since Rock Hudson and the old Hollywood star system. He was an ex-football jock, I think. This much I know: He was definitely over six feet tall and weighed well over 220 pounds of solid muscle. He was meat. Usually had a shaggy chest to masculinize the startling beauty of true-blue eyes and feathered, curly brown hair. He starred in some idiotic TV shows about time traveling and spying, ending up costarring with Jennifer O'Neill, a fate worse than death. Well, not worse. Because this poor guy ended up dying for *real*.

Jon-Erik had a brother named Gunnar, one of the factoids I absorbed from *Tiger Beat* or maybe from my Norwegian pen pal whose address I'd gotten from the back of a record called "Friendship" by a one-hit wonder named D'Orado. "Blondie is a band," but "D'Orado is a singer." Bumper stickers seemed so much cooler at the time.

The gimmick was that D'Orado's record company had purchased thousands of pen pal addresses from a legitimate foreign service and plastered them on his debut record's shiny, happy sleeve. There's no telling how many transcontinental friends were manufactured in this way, friendships that long outlasted D'Orado's undercooked career. D'Orado, who sounded like a Latin lover on vinyl, was in reality a three-foot queen with Leo Sayer's hair and Agnes Moorehead's *Bewitched* sense of fashion. Caftans. Nefertiti earrings. Blue eyeshadow. Platforms. Yes, *he*. To my knowledge, D'Orado was not openly gay, but if he was closeted, then it was a drop in the bucket because he could've had his manhood challenged by Sylvester.

The first clue that D'Orado was not camera-friendly was the fact that his record company preferred to put pen pal ads on his record sleeve instead of his grinning face. Obviously, he'd never heard of using a stylist. In the eighties I longed to be able to afford a personal stylist. I had visions of handing over two thousand crisp dollar bills to a chic little woman who would tell me which jeans to wear and when it looked good to leave my shirt unbuttoned at the top. But for D'Orado, it would have been like being a hundred and getting an eye job. Wasted effort.

I'd written my "Friendship" pen pal Dieter, hands shaking, unsure. His address was the most clearly legible on the sleeve, dead-center with no lettering or edges to obscure the nonsensical Norwegian destination info.

I didn't know why, but I felt I needed to conceal my attempt at correspondence from my family, never saying a word and watching for the mail like a mother cat minding her litter. After eight weeks, Dieter replied. Thanks to D'Orado, the poor kid had been deluged with over six thousand cards and letters—and he wasn't even dying. Dieter said he'd chosen to reply to my (in truth pathetically unimaginative) one-pager because he'd liked my handwriting and said I'd seemed really fun and "open-minded" in my letter. My eyes burned when I read that phrase: "open-minded." I suddenly felt like I was on the beach in last year's too-small swimsuit, my cock hanging out for all my friends to see and criticize.

What else could open-minded mean but gay? Always decoding.

It took us three letters to discover a mutual, sexually sublimated fascination with Jon-Erik Hexum (who was second-generation Norwegian), an interest that was triggered accidentally when I'd asked what American TV shows they *got* over there. *Voyagers,* he'd replied, and I knew I had a live one. It was the dopey series starring Jon-Erik.

It took six letters before the tricky words got hot enough to jerk off to. Eight letters after our initial "Hello! I hope you understand my language," we were writing with an open, same-sex prurience, two-, three-, four-page letters written on translucent sheets of air-mail paper in garish black strokes, describing the kinds of sex we craved. They were confessions we made with blind confidence, admissions we had never made to another soul, barely to ourselves. I was diving into the volcano every time I wrote Dieter, diving and surviving, swimming in a molten core.

I think about Jon-Erik working out like he was in those pictures I sent you from Telemundo magazine. He is on his back, in shorts and no shirt. His hairy chest is soaked with sweat and his arms are lifting up so many weights. He has hairy underarms and his biceps are bigger than my legs. I'm standing at his feet, watching him strain to pump the iron. I can see into the loose flaps of his shorts. His cock is long and soft and hairy. I can see his balls, too, bigger than any I've seen, with sweat running off them. I can smell them. I go over to him, get between his legs so I'm kneeling there. He gets shocked and asks me what's happening but I tell him to be quiet and I bury my face in his hot, wet crotch, rubbing my mouth over him. He doesn't like guys, but he goes, "Shit, that feels great," and lets me. He stops lifting weights and lets me lick his cock until it gets too big and hard. It needs more than licking. I don't think I can take it all, but I try—I open up my mouth and swallow down his penis, sucking it and carefully avoiding my teeth. I then just suck my mouth over him, up and down, until he gets so aroused his balls pull up tight and he tells me he's going to come. He's not warning me, he's just stating the fact, and he holds my head down and Jon-Erik shoots hot come that I drink.

Thinking of those letters makes me blush even now. They were unfiltered lust, pure sex. Despite being so raw, they were also amazingly naïve. They were telling in what they objectified, in what their ideals were.

Why Jon-Erik Hexum? Because he was as masculine as it got while still seeming "nice," touchable and approachable, a good-natured air that I would years later interpret as having possibly been gayness. Even corpses are in danger of being outed. In fact, they're even more at risk since they can't issue denials. Franz Schubert was gay. This I know and accept as fact even though there are no candid photos of him at all-boy fuckfests. Walt Whitman, Ramon Novarro, Danny Kaye, Dag Hammarskjold, Monty Clift—outing requires faith. And intelligence. And common sense.

Jon-Erik Hexum's muscles were the absolute maleness we coveted. How many times did we trade raunchy stories about Jon-Erik's "hairy" body? The hair under his arms and across his broad chest, even on parts we'd never seen in promotional stills or magazine layouts, like his crotch and his ass. These parts we imagined in patchwork, stitching mental images of our own privates, what we'd seen of our fathers, the flashes in R-rated movies, diagrams in superthick school encyclopedias. If we'd learned that Jon-Erik had hair on the balls of his *feet* we'd have probably been even *more* turned on. Hair and sweat. He was the supreme male, and our own insecurity as future men made supremacy all the more important, something to bow down to, something commanding us to kneel and supplicate, to suck. To suck the hair, to drink the sweat, like a potion for getting older and becoming men.

I remember Dieter's letters fondly, but it's probably an exaggerated appreciation—he was no writer, and his mastery of English was as girlish as his taste in clothes, as evidenced by cheap photo-booth portrait strips he later sent of himself swathed in Ocean Pacific pastels with what looked like eyeliner around his crooked eyes, eyes like a flounder's, so close together toward one side. It was the eighties, though, so I didn't feel it was correct to disapprove of makeup, even on a sexual aesthetics level. To rule out my only gay friend as a sex object would have made me too guilty. Jon-Erik Hexum, unachievable, was okay to fetishize, and yet Dieter, impossible only due to geography, was *not.*

No, it wasn't Dieter's great writing that made me so aroused, that still makes me hard when in a weak moment I think back on those days. It was my own writing, whether or not it was particularly good. Just the act of writing literally unspeakably hot scenarios involving myself and another man, then stuffing the dreams into an envelope, pasting stamps in the corner and sending them away to a stranger—that whole process always left me wasted with a need to touch myself and to explore my body in private, where no asexual parents could catch me and scold, "What are you doing to yourself? What's wrong with you?"

If they knew I was squandering what they believed was my God-given talent for writing on gay pornography, they would've been paralyzed. There's no telling what would have happened to our relationship. *I still haven't even told them I'm writing porn now, as an adult.*

When I first started having sex, I'd close my eyes and imagine Jon-Erik Hexum in a towel, walking toward me, unwrapping the towel, showing me his hard cock and naked, supplely muscled body, giving me the cock to hold, fondle, operate. I'd let the fantasy snap into a blurred scene of kind-hearted, sweet-seeming Jon-Erik fucking me, punishing me with his body. No matter what sort of sex I was engaged in, whether on the bottom or the top or somewhere in between, a disjointed vision of Jon-Erik could always speed along an orgasm, and when two guys are having sex there is no great big deal made about stamina, eh? As long as it lasts fifteen minutes, they're happy. It's worse to take forever than it is to take a few passionate minutes. That empty space while they're waiting can take so long that the moment is lost and he may never try again with you.

Of course, after Jon-Erik Hexum accidentally killed himself with a prop gun on the set of his TV show on October 12, 1984, my fantasies were charged with pathos, a powerful aphrodisiac. But there was no way I could ever talk about my fantasies with any of my partners. Are you kidding? How creepy to open your mouth and tell someone you were envisioning a dead man while they were fucking, sucking, touching, being with you.

I'd had my first Alan Dillinger dream, but it wouldn't be my last. I still dream about him, a million emotional miles away from where I was the night we met.

CHAPTER 9

The Case of the Lavender Cadaver!

Carol Terry — *Transcript of a conversation at Gods & Goddesses between Carol Terry and Mary Felbin, the Raymond Burr lady.*

Carol Terry: Hello. I haven't seen you for a while—

Raymond Burr Lady: I'm very upset to see that you didn't take my advice and feature Raymond in your windows.

CT: Well, like I said, he isn't as big a draw as a Marilyn Monroe or a—

RBL: But you even have pictures of *Tab Hunter* in the window. Don't you think Raymond was a better actor than *Tab Hunter?*

CT: I don't know, Mary. I'm not the Academy of Motion Picture Arts and Sciences. I have a *small* photo of Tab Hunter in the corner of one of my windows because he's good-looking and has more of a following than Raymond Burr.

RBL: You really think so? Are you aware of the Nielsens for the Perry Mason TV movies Raymond was doing right up until the end?

CT: Not offhand, but I do know that in this neighborhood, young Tab Hunter is more of a draw into my store than young or old Raymond Burr. Now, I've told you that I'm sure Raymond Burr was a great star and I am *thrilled* to have you as a customer, I'm happy to pick up Raymond Burr magazines for you when I see them, but you really can't ask me to do something I don't want to do just because he's your favorite star.

RBL: It's not just for me.

CT: What?

RBL: It's not just for me, what I'm asking. It's for everyone. Raymond Burr is a great star who is someone . . . everyone should become familiar with.

CT: ?

RBL: I just feel that I have to ask you these things or I'm not doing everything I can since he passed away.

CT: Yes, but I . . . I just don't . . . I'm flustered [laughs]. Congratulations! You've got me *completely*— I'm almost . . . speechless!

RBL: I just wish I could have introduced you to Raymond. He was such an amazing *and* warm star; that's rare.

CT: Oh? I wasn't aware you'd ever met him.

RBL: Well, we weren't *close*. I did see him at a movie premiere once. It was a press-only screening for his first return to Perry Mason, *Perry Mason Returns*, back in '85. That was just about the greatest day of my life. I met Barbara Hale's son William Katt, who is so handsome in real life. I can remember his curly blond hair!

Barbara Hale. A classy lady, a real gem. She talked with me for over fifteen minutes, just like we were neighbors catching up. I saw her many times after that and she always seemed to recognize me from that day.

But the most wonderful thing was when Raymond arrived. He was just such a lovely man, so elegantly dressed. Barbara had told him I'd spent a long time waiting to see him, and he graciously came over and posed for a picture with me and asked me if I'd liked the movie. I hadn't seen it because I didn't have a ticket, but I assured him I would be just one of millions who would watch the movie once it debuted on TV the following week. It was the second-highest-rated telefilm of 1985.

CT: *[Pause]* Really?

RBL: Yes, it was one of the best days of my life. The worst was the day when the last regular episode, "The Case of the Final Fadeout," aired on September 4, 1966.

CT: *[Shrugging]* He's not making it into my window, but at least he never lost a case.

RBL: Oh, but he *did.* Those so-and-so's had him lose "The Case of the Deadly Verdict" in either 1963 or I want to say '64. That was just a shocker that I didn't need.

CT: I have to tell you that even though I like Raymond Burr—well, I mean, at least I don't *not* like him, I mean, no offense—I can't really feature him more prominently because he doesn't attract a large crowd of people like . . . yourself.

RBL: *[Bitterly]* You're just kowtowing to the gays.

CT: *[Alarmed]* Excuse me?

RBL: You're just putting up all these stars that the gays like. There are other stars to like *besides* Marilyn Monroe, who was really just a glorified streetwalker. Christopher Street was such a charming place to bring up a child once upon a time, and now it is just wall-to-wall gay, gay, gay.

CT: But why do you care? Raymond Burr was gay, wasn't he?

RBL: That's a lie started by Hollywood insiders who were jealous of him and who wanted him to fail.

CT: He never got married, right?

RBL: That's no proof! Are *you* married?

CT: No, and *I've* slept with lots of men, too.

RBL: !

CT: I'm sorry, I'm not trying to offend you, but Raymond Burr had a longtime lover who came out and talked about their relationship after he died. I'm sure I read that. In the papers, not just the supermarket tabloids.

RBL: *[Leaving]* I'm sure you *did* read it. And I'm twice as sure it was a lie! You people can't leave well enough alone. You people can't let a classy man rest in peace without dragging his name through the mud. You *gays* all stick together.

CT: But I'm not—*[Pause]*

[Door slams]

CHAPTER 10

Picks & Pans!

David Greer — I awoke abruptly, no tiredness to slough off me. It was only seven-thirty in the morning by my VCR's unreliable digital clock, but I believed it, I believed it.

I'd had a fitful night's sleep after returning from my night out with Carol. We'd subwayed to my neighborhood and had encountered a thuggish woman who obviously looked to Queen Latifah in *Set It Off* as her role model. She'd been a tank of strength, rough with no flourishes, no lip service to style, her hair pulled back without ceremony. She'd given Carol a sour string of insults and then had dared me to defend her. I hadn't.

We'd both just shrunk into the plastic seats as "Cleo" had ranted and raved how the white man was destroying her and her community, and how the Jews were stealing all her valuable resources, tapping all she had to offer, profiting off rap. Except not in those words. Two young black queens stifled laughter at the other end of the train, and an elderly black woman nearby tsked, clearly embarrassed. A white woman of thirty or so with a jeans jacket and expensive boots pretended to sleep to avoid the whole affair.

White guilt can be a powerful thing to tap into, but this run-in had been less about guilt than about shame. I'd been humiliated for the woman—she was so far out of the loop it was obvious she'd never amount to anything at all, by anyone's standards, her appearance too unpleasant, her speech strangled and inarticulate. It always moved me when I thought about a person chained to a bleak fate, a nine-to-five life—if even a minimum-wage job could be had. I didn't know if I could go on without the rather dubious hope that I might someday get famous, be known.

Carol and I had escaped the humid subway at Twenty-third Street, feeling not unfortunate to have survived. Carol was full of masturbatory debate for the absent woman's claims, reasons why she felt the woman's thesis had been flawed. I couldn't waste the energy after being exposed to white supremacy in Iowa and black retaliation in New York and every shade in between; race issues paralyzed me, made me unwilling to venture an opinion.

Less abstractly and more honestly, I'd still been buzzing on Alan.

Seven-thirty in the A.M. and still unable to sleep, can't forget about the night before. I'd had the bizarre Alan Dillinger dream, but the reality had been more intense. I've never had a sexual type, really—I liked regular guys, guys with hair in all the right places and love handles were all right by me. High foreheads, smelly feet, slight shoulders, fat asses—no reasonable flaw would be enough to repulse me if I connected with a man. I guess I couldn't have dated an idiot, but I'd have probably tried sleeping with him for a while just to give it a chance.

But I'm human. And Alan didn't quite seem human. He was just so precociously good-looking, like he should be on a poster above your bed and not pumping your hand at a party. In fact, he *was* on posters above beds. And on trading cards. And, undoubtedly, on notebooks and on a variety of other moneymaking objects. He was a good investment—he had the kind of magnetism that separates stars from personalities and the kind of undeniable looks that appeal to a broad cross section of the public. Your grandmother would think Flea was one ugly son of a bitch even if *you* would sacrifice a functioning testicle to lay with him as a man does with a woman, but she'd agree with you if you commented that Alan Dillinger was the sexiest man alive.

I always spent my Saturday mornings in a galloping coma, recovering from the fuzzy dullness of the week by pretending to read *The New York Times* and puttering around my pad, organizing documents and correspondence I would later dump unceremoniously. I had a nervous habit of needing to be busy, though I worked at a slow pace, sedentary and thorough. For years I'd interpreted my activity as industriousness, until I'd sat back and realized I'd never really accomplished *anything*. Hours and hours of organizing and filing and sorting had amounted to nothing. I had no projects to show for it, no finished work, God knows no novel. That's when I decided I was infected with a need to keep myself swamped, preoccupied, so that I would not have *time* to write, to create, to achieve.

But that Saturday I knew I wouldn't have the luxury of spinning my wheels. I'd promised Carol weeks earlier that I'd pitch in for her at a memorabilia show. Junk for sale at top prices. I sat at the edge of my bed in my underpants, wolfing down Raisin Bran, staring across the room at an oversized calendar I'd hung on the back of my door, the date circled in indelible red ink and clearly marked "CAROL/SHOW."

I didn't feel like participating, but I'd spoken too soon, promising my time so far in advance it hadn't felt like I was promising anything at all, like, "Oh, is *that* still on?"

Rich weirdos shelling out thirty thousand dollars for Audrey Hepburn's Oscar or Marilyn Monroe's tampon or for the late Claudette Colbert herself—how could they afford such luxuries?

I gotta do something really expensive. I need to do something for which I can get paid a lot, right now. If someone gave me twenty thousand dollars for some service rendered, I could pay off all my debts and buy a Milky Way for the trip home from the bank. But giving me four hundred dollars a week doesn't help me out. At all. Did I forget to mention I was living in New York?

I discarded the empty bowl at my feet and hugged my body, watching the extra fat bunch up. I was by no means fat, but I was by no means skinny. I had never really thought about weight much until the day I'd walked into my apartment and had felt my side brush the door handle. I had given myself *plenty* of clearance for getting through that door with no contact, and yet my *side* had somehow *touched*. It almost seemed like my love handles had popped out at that exact moment. Most people get fat slowly until it dawns on them that their clothes no longer fit and the neighbor kids are pointing. But I felt like my slight weight gain had happened instantaneously, all those Chinese and Mexican takeout nights having accumulated for one big, immediate expansion.

Of course, I had been gaining the weight an ounce at a time; I'd just been oblivious because I'd never had to watch what I ate and had figured I was just one of those people with a great metabolism. And yet I had gone from one hundred fifty lanky pounds to my current fuller, curvier one hundred seventy-five. I was still at least twenty-five pounds away from looking fat, but there was no denying it: I'd chubbed up.

I sort of liked my new body, but only sort of. I felt sexier in a weird way and enjoyed filling out my clothes. I'd always been hot for straight-seeming guys with overhang, so it was not a horrifying concept for me when I found myself becoming one. The down side was that I spent way too much time worrying whether I might be starting to sprout boobs, several of my friends had felt the need to observe that I looked like I was getting bigger, and I'd also noticed that some guys I looked at on the street seemed to scan me and then look away in disapproval, noses up. I no longer had the more desired slim build, had never had the most desired killer bod. I just had to make do with, well, with the much more common *okay* body, which was admittedly a far cry from the significantly less popular he's-got-a-gorgeous-face-and-a-great-sense-of-humor model.

I had the worst morning boner. Usually, I either ignored it till it gave up, or jerked off in a matter of minutes to get it over with. But the morning after my Alan dream, I felt so aroused sitting there on the bed, smelling my morning musk and touching my gut. I leaned back and started to play with my nipples at length, indulging in the kind of rare auto-foreplay that meant I might be willing to tease my body for up to an hour before a crashing release. I was thinking about all the usual stuff, but I had injected Alan Dillinger into my fantasy, Alan and his tight blue swimsuit with the treasure trail of hairs bisecting his perfect torso.

I always found jerking off to be easier than actually going out and having sex. And cleaner, too. And safe? The *safest.* They say the safest sex is no sex at all, but I say that's based on a very narrow view of what qualifies as sex. Though it seems strange to consider the idea of bragging, "Yeah, I got a piece last night," in reference to yourself, I think masturbation is usually just as good as two-ways. Sure, I've never jerked off while fantasizing about other times I've jerked off, but . . . well, I'm still working out the kinks in this theory.

It occurred to me as I rolled my nipples in my fingertips that I hadn't had any sex at all in probably over a year, the last time having been right after that stultifying house party.

That fateful night, I'd spent an excruciating evening watching *Valley of the Dolls* with a roomful of horse-faced queens from Michigan, friends of Warren's who'd felt the need to guffaw at every third sentence. You'd think they had invented camp from the dust of Adam. I was a Susann loyalist—a Jacquelinista—so they made me sick. The movie wasn't campy, it was just plain *bad,* but they were too ordinary to question its authority. Eager to display how much they got it, they accidentally showed that they not only didn't get it, but that they had no idea what "it" was in the first place. The whole experience had left me craving a doll for real. Or maybe just a guy.

That had been the last time I'd gone out looking for sex. Deliberately.

I'd left the apartment and headed over to Splash, wondering if I could luck out and find a really sexy guy who I could fuck and then date and then marry and be too wrapped up with ever to contemplate infidelity or to orchestrate a three-way. It's not asking much, but then perhaps it's a little unrealistic considering that Splash is a gay cruise bar in Manhattan where heterosexual musclemen take showers on stage and flaunt themselves in fluffy white towels. Husband material is in short supply.

It was steamy inside, damp-packed with bodies, and it had that classic gay-bar smell, that strange scent that always reminds me of the dry ice used in high school plays mixed with, maybe, Drakkar Noir. It was loud.

It wasn't hard to find a willing guy. It never is. Men aren't choosy. They don't take a lot of time deciding what to order from a menu and they don't fuss too much over which warm body they'll take home. Because they know it's all the same.

He was sweet-faced, brown hair and raisin eyes with a touch of rookie charm. He wore his baseball cap turned forward (a switch), the bill carefully rolled in a style I'd seen all over Eighth Avenue that month. In fashion, he also had the popular warm-up jacket and sleek running pants, black with double white stripes up the sides. Tennis shoes an afterthought.

He'd checked me out and I'd allowed my interest to show. We'd chatted about the rude porno on the screen above the bar, exchanged gropes, and resolved to go have sex after an amazingly clean negotiation.

"Live nearby?"

"Want to come over?"

"Great."

"Great, great."

We'd walked the all of two blocks to his cute studio, part-time doorman building, laundry, original fixtures, $1,200 rent. We'd chatted more and then started, him tugging my jeans down and me realizing with a jolt like an innoculation that I hadn't even *showered* that day—that's how seriously I took cruising at that point. It wasn't important, it was just a reflex, something to do. He'd started to blow me but then had slithered back up to make out. I could tell it was over already. I was mortified that I might smell bad, bad enough to have doused this horny Chelsea boy, a boy so available he took care to rent a fuckpad two giant leaps away from a foolproof pickup bar. I broke into a sweat, which probably didn't help my aroma, feigned a headache, and took off. He was listening to Garth Brooks by the time I was at the elevator. The doorman had stared at me as I'd left, like he was memorizing my shame.

I'd been accepted, rejected, then had rejected the evening's logical outcome by leaving. I could've pushed him to continue, could've jerked him and myself off and feigned satisfaction. But instead I'd called it quits. *Do I really want to be here right now?*

That abortive one-nighter had put an end to my infrequent hunting. I'd decided I was just going to have to kick back and wait for a guy to find *me*. And when he came, I'd smell good and be clean-shaven and do everything just right to make him stick around. I'd wear a baseball cap with the bill rolled and the right shoes and would grow sideburns or razor them off if necessary. I'd give up anal sex or accept it as a daily ritual, anything to please, to get, and to keep.

When I'd first gotten fucked back in the *forties,* I'd decided that sex was purely great and should be had as often as possible. Never say no. Why *would* you? After over a dozen years of having sex, off and on, I'd come to feel sort of the opposite. I could count on one hand the number of sexual encounters worth remembering, that had really transported me, made me forget everything else and wish it would never stop. I'd stopped counting partners by then. I'd probably had about . . . fifty. Fifty divided by thirteen is just about four. Four a year—is that a whole lot? I don't know. It could have been so much *higher.*

A kaleidoscope of fifty handsome faces tripped through my mind as I stroked myself on the bed, all attached to the various slutty things I'd enticed them to do for me, to me, with me. Who knows if it was true, but several had said I was their first, and one of them—the best time?— had told me he was engaged to a woman and had never so much as kissed another guy.

I added Alan Dillinger into that memory, his gleaming form hunched in the shadows, jerking off while he watched me instruct that straight man on how you insert your cock up an ass, coaching him on what to do and how hard to do it.

I suddenly came, choking down the urge to make noises, to talk myself through it—I didn't want my next-door neighbor waking up to that. Instead, I just whimpered as I ejaculated, the thickness heavy on my chest. I lay back, catching my breath, then stretched on the bed, trapped by ladybug-feet dribbles of semen down my sides.

The phone rang. It was Warren. I felt vaguely shy speaking with him in my state of postcrank saturation.

"Warren! What's up?" I fairly shouted, overcompensating.

"Listen, stop by and we'll have lunch. I'm in the office screwing around with my column—surprise, surprise. They have sandwiches."

I lay there, sopping and afraid. "Sure," I said. "I have to go help Carol by, like, one . . . but . . ."

"Okay, come over now and then you'll have time for Carol. Hafta go—here comes trouble." No doubt in my mind that he was referring to his boss, the E-in-C of *Island Rage,* Pamela Radclyffe. She was known to eat human heads for snacks and had laughed loudly, publicly, at Jules Feiffer when the cartoonist had come seeking employment after *The Voice* cut him loose. "But I wanna hear all about the party when you get here——" The sound of a finger snapping flat the phone's plunger, cutting me off. I could envision Warren sitting there with the receiver in his hand, his mouth held open as Pamela lifted her finger and paraded in front of his desk, offering him her complaints for the week. She usually made all her points by prefacing them with verbal bullets. "Bullet—your column needs more stars. Bullet—stop writing so much about Barbra Streisand, she is *over.* Bullet——" Like an editorial machine gun.

I hung up and reached blindly for the roll of paper towels I kept concealed next to the nightstand, tearing off too many sheets and soaking up my pleasure. I was already refocusing on reality, dreading my duties at the memorabilia show and wondering how untruthful I would be with Warren. I would have to tell him about Alan, tell him how Alan—according to Carol and to my disbelieving instinct—had flirted with me. I would have to tell him how I singlehandedly saved Alan Dillinger from an instance of unwilling photo documentation, and in the process had deprived a paparazzo of thousands of dollars in international sales.

Or *would* I have to tell him?

I plotted how I would deceive Warren, inventing excuses and a believable chain of comments to enmesh them.

"We didn't see him." "But Carol called and said she *did* see him." "I was in the bathroom." *Or:* "He was there but he looked just like you'd expect and the whole thing was boring." "But the *Post* had a dazzling paparazzi shot of him." "It was a file photo."

These were the rejects. *It's going to be a bitch of a day,* I thought, discarding the sticky toweling.

But at least I'd gotten laid.

CHAPTER 11

Kevin Spacey Has a Secret!

David Greer — "Do you realize that Matthew McConaughey lives with a 'film school buddy' and their dog, 'Miss Hud?' " Warren was talking shop while I was trying *not* to get a word in edgewise about my close encounter with Alan Dillinger.

"No," I said, "I wasn't aware of that. I've been avoiding him, socially." Dogs often attracted Warren's attention—I recalled reading in "Off the List" that the only longterm relationship Kevin Spacey would cop to was with his pooch, Legacy.

"It's fucking *in*teresting," Warren continued, "because for once this is *fac*tual information provided *by* Mr. McC for a puff piece, not just rumor or innuendo—not that those are *bad.*" We shared a conspiratorial laugh. What cynic can resist gossip? And what reasonably intelligent gay man isn't a cynic?

He raised an eyebrow and hoisted a stack of letterhead up to his desk, plopping it down on an 8 × 10 of Cindy Crawford, who I surmised was about to get thrashed in the column for some offense.

"Do you actually think Matthew McConaughey is queer? Is Sandra Bullock really Antonio Sabáto, Jr., in drag?" I offered.

"I'm not saying I know anything at this point. But you can believe that where there's smoke—or poodles named after Paul Newman movies, or bachelor pads—there's faggots."

I wondered if Matthew were really gay, and if he were scheduled to be anywhere *near* the set of *Lifesavers* in the near future. Hoped so and hoped not, respectively.

"How was the party?" Warren asked, switching gears, filing the McConaughey lead for later. "Heard that Alan Dillinger washed ashore after all."

"Yes, and—"

I was cut off by the harried entrance of Dot Hiawatha, one of Warren's fellow *Island Rage*rs. She had been a fundamentally funky performance artist in the late seventies, a respected but uncommercial painter in the eighties, and was spending the nineties working for a living. She had her own, off-kilter column in the magazine, wherein she recounted long evenings spent at her home with wacky dinner guests like Timothy Leary (*before* he died) and Lene Lovich. She was approximately fifty, which showed in the deep chasms that ran from her eyes to the corners of her mouth, but which she denied with her whipcord body that was usually painted with leather or vinyl. Her black hair was frequently uncoiffed, parts of it dyed a deep, subtle green color, for no apparent reason. I think it was the hair that made her seem tragically out of step as the millennium approached.

"Stop the *press!*" she husked. *Island Rage* was known for its cheapness, so employees always singularized the quintessential newspaper phrase. Dot teetered into the office. Platform tennis shoes? Didn't she recognize them as a solely 1993 phenomenon? The scent of patchouli she dragged with her was overpowering.

She held in her silver-ringed hands a small photograph that from my spot on the globe looked like a peach-colored blur.

Warren scanned the glossy square. "Looks like Andrew McCarthy."

She smiled smugly and nodded her head vigorously. "Going into *Champs!* Everyone is talking about it!"

Warren didn't start babbling, which was usually his signal that he had a verifiable scoop to go with. In this case, he just studied the photo, looking at the back to scrutinize the blue streak identifying the brand of film and date of development.

"Even if this is Andrew McCarthy, and I'm not saying it is or isn't," Warren said skeptically, "it's pretty useless when you can't see what's happening in the background. It just looks like *maybe* Andrew

McCarthy walking into—I don't know, a bakery?—caught by some fan with a disposable camera."

"Oh, come on, Warren," she whined. "You've been to Champs. You recognize this block!"

I took a closer look and couldn't see any details at all. It didn't even seem like Andrew McCarthy to me. More like Robert Sean Leonard. I'd been to Champs myself, oh, about thirteen thousand times, and I didn't really recognize the faux macho bar for athletically built and yet sports-phobic Chelsea boys.

"It's nada," Warren said, returning the photograph. "It's a blind item at best: 'which sensitive brat packer is also a fudge-packer?' "

"Isn't he pretty, pretty in pink," I sang, offkey.

Dot shrugged her shoulders and took off, barely acknowledging me. She was always trying to horn in on Warren's inglory, always digging for dirt he could peddle. The best thing she'd been able to provide was the scoop that Stephen Geoffreys, the dorky sidekick from *Fright Night,* had become a gay porn actor (really more of my bailiwick, but who can recognize ex–child stars with their legs in the air?). Warren had enjoyed that extremely minor piece of gossip since it was one of the first times his editors had been forced to allow him to out someone—he'd gotten ahold of commercial video footage of the actor having his horizons broadened.

Aside from that, Dot was better off just mining her own slender vein of celebrity. For example, she counted Simon Rex among her closest New York buddies and yet had not been able to find out that he'd done gay jerk-off movies two years before hitting MTV. She and Warren had read about that in an Associated Press story, the worst insult of all. Scooped by aging hippies with no interest in showbiz whatsoever.

"Simon Rex was choking chicken and riding his finger right in front of our noses and the Associated Mess figured it out before I did. Well, wake up and smell the semen." Warren had been beside himself that day.

The room, as always, seemed more bearable once it was Dot-less.

Hoping Dot's nonevent had been enough of a distraction, I quietly told Warren that Dillinger *had* been at the party and that he'd looked gorgeous and had worked the room like a pro.

"They say he once *was* a pro," Warren said grimly, "and if *they* ever come up with any sort of evidence I will drop to my knees and shout, 'Hallelujah!' "

I'd heard those whispers, too, and the heroin rumor dogged him more tirelessly than it had Julia Roberts. *If you end up looking like Alan or Julia by doing smack,* I thought, *where can I get some?*

I recounted for Warren the boring biz crowd, the underappreciated arrival of Junior Vasquez, Alan's flawless appearance, the demeanor of the crowd around him. I didn't tell him that we'd met Alan. I didn't tell him that I'd defused a paparazzo for Alan. Which were slight oversights in the story, don't you think? *I'll have to tell Carol to shut up about this if I'm really going to deceive Warren.*

Warren seemed not to give Alan a second thought, having already made up his mind that it was a minor event with no gossip potential. "Junior hates me because I printed his real age," he noted. "That man was around when they *invented* rhythm." He pounded his pencil haltingly on his keyboard to illustrate.

"Thanks again for getting us into the party, Warren," I chirped as I left. I was already half-late for Carol's show. Warren smiled and waved me off and swiveled back to his glowing computer, completely trusting. "You should come over to my place for dinner soon so we can talk about real life, too, okay?"

"Okay."

Even with no bombshell news or insider info—just my impressions of a flirtation, just the beginnings of a blind item—I knew that by keeping my mouth shut, I was protecting Alan Dillinger, a stranger, and in some way betraying Warren Junior, my friend.

CHAPTER 12

Headless Body in Topless Bar!

David Greer — I was semishocked to see Rock Hudson standing in line in front of me at the turnstile. *Gee, you look great for your age. And for being dead.* This guy looked so much like Rock my dirty mind immediately wondered if you'd be able to think of anything else when you climbed into bed with him. *Let's play* McMillan and Wife. *I'll be Susan Saint James. . . .*

Then I spotted a cardboard sign promoting the memorabilia show and noticed that they were running a celebrity lookalike contest. This Rock Hudson guy was going to win or there was no justice in the world. He looked over his shoulder at me with just the right mixture of pomposity and self-deprecation. I admitted to myself that he'd still probably lose to someone doing a ridiculous impersonation of Liza Minnelli. Along with Rock, I saw enough Marilyn lookalikes to gag a maggot, a pretty sorry Mae West, a downright tragic attempt at Lauren Bacall (why bother?), and one guy who apparently thought he was a shoo-in as Tim Allen. Oh, the unfabulousness of it all.

I showed a greasy lady my vendor card, but she insisted on stamping my hand. My life was becoming a series of disinterested women sitting at tables, controlling my admission to events I was reluctant to attend. I held my paw out, conscious of my chowed-down nails and excessively hairy knuckles. She held my hand gingerly and, with great concentration, pressed a small knob onto it. When she pulled it away, a four-pointed star was inked onto me, pitch black and unmissable. I guessed it would remain through about six regular showers unless I went at it with Ajax. She dutifully returned my hand to where she'd found it.

The show was as populated as a low-class wedding. There must've been ten thousand people there, which, yes, is an exaggeration. There *were* over sixty card tables draped in paper tablecloths and covered with about a ton of useless junk that, due to the sentimentality of Americans, was actually worth millions.

The patrons of the event seemed like normal nerds, garden variety, with choice, aggressively odd folks here and there. Fans of some of the most beautiful gods and goddesses in screen history, most of these people were too homely ever to be actors or models or famous at all. A lot of them were overweight, almost all the men were either visibly gay or visibly repressing it. Not to be ungenerous, but I sometimes think fandom does boil down to a Fat Ugly Faggot Convention. And I include myself in that equation to an extent, though even as a compulsively self-conscious individual, I felt head and shoulders above my fellow conventioneers.

I couldn't help being mildly interested in some of the stuff for sale. I'm always impressed to see an original Oscar with a price tag attached, considering they go on the auction block so rarely. Audrey's Oscar was likely to fetch a lot; I'd never understood her appeal, but she was one of those stars with a perversely obsessive following. She was an icon of class, which to me is the most self-loathing ideal to aspire to. Her Oscar was in good shape. Must have had her maid spit-shine it daily. I know she was legendarily kind and giving, but that's what made me suspicious of her.

Old movie posters were in abundance, with more than one calling me over telepathically so they could argue how appropriate they would be for one of the walls in my apartment. I longed to find a poster that would balance the fine line between brilliant art and high camp, but had been unable to locate it, and I'd be damned if I were going to be the next queen to overpay for a *Straitjacket* poster and hang it with unenlightened pride.

The table next to Carol's looked more like a Kmart threw up, a jumble of "collectible" trading cards devoted to everything from *M*A*S*H* to *The Dukes of Hazzard* to *The Man From U.N.C.L.E.* The little man who was running the table was stealing furtive glances at Carol, obviously unaware that she wasn't fond of sweat rings and guys selling Mrs. Beasley dolls mint in package.

Carol's table was, as usual, a cut above. It was still disturbing to see my cool friend haggling with maniacs over the price of Twiggy cover magazines, and yet I had to admire her fortitude, and her resourcefulness. I imagined that the shows must make her feel like those SoHo artists who spread their canvases out on the sidewalks and who endure the disinterest of all the passersby, always hoping that someone will approach with twenty dollars burning a hole in his pocket.

"You're so late it's *Sunday*," she scolded, stuffing some ones into her money belt. "I'm making a killing, too. Thank God you're here! I only need you until about three, but I was going to pass away if you blew me off." She hugged me with that genuine surge of feeling only women have. When men hug me in public, it always feels like a grudge or a matinee.

"Never," I reassured, not wanting to tell her I'd been on the verge. After taking off from Warren without having spilled the beans he was always hungry for, I had felt exhausted, in need of a brisk walk through the wilds of Manhattan. But Carol was the only person in the world who would never break a promise to me, and I hadn't wanted to let her down.

I came around the table, its surface delegated artfully, and sat next to Carol, surveying the loot I was going to have to help hawk. An inexplicably alluring headless Francie doll was available for *$1.* On the other hand, a *Battlestar Galactica* action figure stood nearest me on the table, its sticker demanding *$50.* Even Carol's handwritten numerals seemed chic.

"It's funny, because *Battlestar Galactica* was something I thought was the coolest thing in the universe when I was a kid, but now I realize it was just shit—no offense." Carol shrugged comically to dissociate herself from the art as opposed to the product. "Why would someone want to own a reminder of how gullible they were?" I was baiting her to see if she'd mention my *Charlie's Angels* fixation.

"It's the innocence they're buying, baby." Carol laughed, high on her so-far good luck. She sometimes enjoyed putting on her heartless hustler persona to mock her job, especially when she was raking in the dough. "They want to remember the innocence."

"Hmm."

"I'm glad to see you made it home alive," she said, scooting closer and pushing on my knee with her index finger. So it had taken only a minute or two to start rehashing the previous night's main event, to start tiptoeing around my unlikely crush, my betrayal of Warren.

"Yes, but I think I spent more time awake than asleep. I was just," stretching, *"unh."*

"Really? I slept like a log. All that dancing reminded me we aren't twenty anymore."

"Hmm."

"So have you told anyone about our sighting yet?" she asked, eyes wide and chummy. "I was dying to call everyone but didn't have an extra minute with all this stuff to get under control." She gestured to her high-class garage sale.

"No, who would I tell? My super? Maybe I'll write it to my mom."

"You know," she said, summoning up a seductive air, "he wanted you, David."

Ironically, we were interrupted by a girl looking for *Lifesavers* memorabilia. It was spooky, like the gods were teasing us. Carol didn't have anything much since most of the show's merchandising was too new to qualify as collectible and she didn't have an in at the network. That's how she got so much of her more current merchandise—an army of nebbishy PR goons who swiped all the press kits and promotions they could stash into their briefcases and under their overcoats and who would sell it all to Carol for a few days' worth of lunches.

Hoping that a *Lifesavers* fan would be a *Baywatch*er, too, Carol told the girl she *did* have an alarmingly genuine Polaroid of David Hasselhoff's bare-naked ass that a crew member had snagged for her on the set during a change of suit a few years back. The buyer seemed vaguely puked out by the offer, like Carol had leaned back and revealed a bag of kiddie porn between her legs.

"S'funny you mention *Lifesavers*—we just saw Alan Dillinger last night," Carol bragged, except it wasn't merely bragging. Carol was smart enough to know that such info might ensure a repeat buyer and at very least could lead to other contacts. She knew everything there was to know about pop memorabilia and its value to fanatics and yet had no *clue* what the appeal was. Carol was like an Egyptian kid moving to San Francisco who intuits enough about the culture to buy Alanis Morissette CDs, just to blend. She amused herself with the commerce, but Carol's real joy came from supplying what's in demand, satisfying a craving. And earning a living that way.

"*Really?*" the fan asked. She was just a toddler, a teenage girl with braces (the allegedly invisible kind, like Jordan Knight used to wear) and glasses and ratted hair and silly seventies flashback bell-bottoms. "You *know* him?"

"No," Carol preened. "We just met him. He's *very* cute in person. I'll be sure to let you know if we get any good stuff on him."

It took another half hour for the girl to completely evaporate from in front of our table. She had strained conversation with Carol as others came and went, bought and sold, until she finally just wandered off, frustrated that there was no more information to be had and no way of meeting Dillinger through us.

"That's why you get the big bucks," I observed, exhausted by the girl's persistence, drained by her need.

Carol shrugged. "You know, *you* could have had the best Alan Dillinger souvenir of all. I'm serious! He was hitting on you. If I hadn't been there and the moon had been right. . . ."

"And Alan had been drunk and high and desperate and gay. . . ."

"Oh, he's *gay*," Carol asserted. "Don't try to pretend you're the only gay man who doesn't think that, David. You said it yourself last night. Warren would be ballistic right now if he heard you saying that."

"Warren is likely to be ballistic at any given time." Losing interest in her line of questioning, I was tempted to make her give me the *I Dream of Jeannie* Halloween costume on the cheap, but decided my studio apartment just couldn't handle any more crap.

"Are you going to call him tonight and fill him in?" she asked, standing to rearrange her display to make it look fresher. "Warren would probably love to get some firsthand information on Alan Dillinger, how he looked, how he acted. . . ."

I paused. More strongly than ever, I felt the impulse in me to avoid telling Warren that we'd met Dillinger. I didn't want to tell Warren the story because I knew he'd side with Carol's interpretation and could feasibly write some snitty little nearsighted (if not out-and-out blind) item about our innocent meeting.

"I was at Warren's office today and I didn't tell him anything at all about Alan Dillinger," I blurted. I stated it as if it were the first step toward recovery.

Carol studied me while counting a stack of one-dollar bills, her lips contracting as she silently enumerated.

"Carol, do me a favor and don't tell Warren anything. He'll just get fixated and want to write something ridiculous and Dillinger will know it was us who fingered him."

"So?" she prompted, using the word as a beat in her counting.

"I can't exactly explain why it would bother me," I said, "but it would. I agree that Alan Dillinger seemed very, I don't know, *flirtatious* last night, I know he's gay, whatever. Just . . . just bear with me on this for a bit, okay?"

"Fine," Carol said, already thinking about something else or doing a great job of pretending to be. "I don't really understand why you care so much about a man you'll never see or speak to again," she said absently with no spite or censure, "but I'll keep my mouth shut."

She secured her ones with a rubberband and then looked over the table, puzzled. Where in the *fuck* had her original Superman Fan Club ring disappeared to? It had been on display. She had not sold it. It was gone.

I looked beyond Carol and my heart did a double beat when I spotted a familiar blond man in a tiny bikini slipping onto the podium at the head of the room. Faced away from me, he was Alan. When he turned and bent to speak into the microphone, he absolutely was *not*.

"Attention, one-two-three-four, attention. We're going to start the lookalike contest in exactly five minutes. We'd like to ask all contestants. . . ."

He was just one of the celebrity impersonators, and a pretty decent one until you squinted and saw that his bleached hair was a wig and that he didn't fill out his trunks with quite the same pizzazz.

And this guy's voice—a big *girl.*

CHAPTER 13

Enquiring Minds Want To Know!

David Greer — I walked into my apartment to the shrill call of my cordless, plucking it up frantically without thinking. I usually screened every call.

"Hello?"

"Hi, I'm not here right now. Please leave your name—" I punched the switch on my hair-trigger answering machine. "Sorry, hello?" I repeated.

"Do I still have to leave my name?"

Who in the fuck? This didn't sound like a salesperson reading haltingly from a prepared card about how great J.C. Penney's is, and it wasn't Warren. It was a man, so that let out Carol, plus she hadn't had enough time to get all the way to her pad in TriBeCa after the memorabilia show. It wasn't my brother or my father (though I had never actually heard my dad's voice on the phone; my mom was the caller in the family). An ex-boyfriend? A gay serial killer?

"Um, huh?"

Laughter. "It's Alan."

It didn't immediately occur to me to tack Dillinger to the end of that. Why would it? I ran through every Alan I'd ever known or met, not at all confident that Allen Stephenson from my high school home ec class was calling me after fifteen years. "Oh, hey," I bluffed.

"Aren't you surprised? Aren't you wondering how I got your number?" he asked. Then it clicked, it absolutely clicked. The precisely masculine voice recalled golden boy pumping my hand at the press party the night before and it became clear that the caller could only be Alan Dillinger. I silently prayed that my damn machine would discreetly, accidentally *still be taping*. I would need proof later for Carol to buy that this had ever happened.

"Oh, God, hi!" I blurted, on the verge of barely concealed hysteria. "Yes, you—how? How did you get my number?" *And* why *did you get my number?*

"Connections," he whispered in a bad, fake Italian accent, bursting with amusement. "You're in the book."

I was perplexed and had second thoughts about whether it was really him after all. I *was* in the book, but how could he have remembered my *name?* He'd heard Carol say it one time only, but it's not like I'd given him a card or anything, not like there was even one in existence to *give.*

"Oh, yes?"

"Yeah. Lucky for me, Shara never forgets a name." So it had been Shara with the steel-trap memory. But under what circumstances had they been discussing me?

Tight-lipped silence. *What do I say?*

"Listen," he said, pushing on, "sorry to spring this on you, but if you're free today I wanted to see if you wanted to come over, hang out, drink some brews."

Brews? Bruised, I felt a tear in the fabric as Alan's straightness sank in. What gay man said, "Yo, let's kick back some brews?" Call me a narrow-minded label queen, but I was just going on common sense. Could it be that all the gossip was bullshit? Carol was wrong? My own hopeful instincts sucked that bad? There's nothing more deflating than having a hard-on for a straight man. It's a kick-stomach situation with no true closure, especially if he's not violently homophobic, because you'll just go on pining over him. You'll never date, you'll never break up. You'll be in a perpetual state of expectancy, always waiting for the first kiss. It takes all your will power to push the crush away and move on to more receptive parties, if you're able to do it at all.

Straight or not, it was still a famous guy on the other end of the line, inviting me over to his apartment, it sounded like. I was hard-pressed to think of almost *any* famous person whose personal invite I would turn down. I mean, Dr. Joyce Brothers could ring me up for tea and I'd probably show up for the experience, even though I liked tea even less than the good doctor.

The silence on the line sizzled like bacon.

"Well, can you come over?"

"Where are you?" I asked, nervous to be entrusted with the address of Alan Dillinger's private residence. Would *Hard Copy* start tapping my line? Would I catch Tony Frost rifling through my trash? Would Carol steal my notepad and rub a pencil over the marks, retrieving the address for a private auction?

"I'm at this place I have in the meatpacking district," he said. As I scribbled down the address, I was amazed to find that he was living only about ten blocks away from my place at Twenty-second and Seventh. But then everyone I knew lived *about* ten blocks away from me; the beauty of living on an island.

"I didn't know anybody *lived* in the meatpacking district," I ventured. "I thought it was just clubs and warehouses."

"Yeah, for sure. Bette Midler lived across the street from me until . . . I don't know, recently. She looks like a Brahma bull out of her makeup. But she's okay. She sometimes acted like she thought I was stupid, though, which I'm not."

A whole new meaning to the term "celebrity gossip."

"No, what a bitch." I was at a loss, so decided to cut things short. The less time spent talking, the sooner I'd be at his place. "So should I come over right now?"

"Yeah, it's what? Two? Can you be here in half an hour?"

It was actually four o'clock. "Yes."

"Good, then we'll have some time and maybe we can have a bite before six. I have this, like, this *thing* at six I need to do. But I'm not trying to give you the rush or anything," he explained. I would have expected a star to have their personal assistant arrange meetings and dictate schedules with a lot more flourish, like Sly Stallone FedExing a Dear Joan letter. I expected a smooth power broker, but Alan sounded very natural, and somewhat embarrassed by his special requirements.

"Buzz twice," he informed me. "I've got a stalker."

I hung up and stared at the phone, my heart flip-flopping around on the floor next to me. "Why?" I shouted around maniacal laughter. "Why are you calling me? Why are you inviting me over? Why me? Why me?"

I heard my downstairs neighbor rapping his broom on the ceiling to shut me up, but I was too far gone, too immersed in all the questions anyone would be asking in my place, but that had seemed impossibly awkward to have voiced on the phone. Alan had just plain invited me over, allowing no drama, no room for astonishment. I rolled on the floor of my apartment, letting waves of giddiness infect me, talking out loud, as if to a special invisible friend.

It's rare that your circle of friends would ever include a star of any magnitude, one-in-a-million that you'd be asked on a date by one, but I'd just won the lottery.

"Why me? Why me?" I mouthed. Then, more seriously, "Why me?"

It was a question I would ask myself many more times in the following months, a question I'm only now beginning to feel comfortable leaving unanswered.

OFF THE LIST

BY WARREN JUNIOR

THE OBJECT OF HIS AFFLICTION

By now *everyone* claims to *know* somebody who *knows* somebody who was *in* the emergency room when Richard Gere arrived with a furry passenger down below. It's an urban legend with legs (four of them, actually), and one I'm sick of (and one, if you'll recall, I nervily disputed the moment I heard it sometime at the end of the last century). Anyway, regardless of Gere's full-page-ad sexuality, I've stumbled on a piece of info you'll find of interest: he has a male suitor who obviously believes those stories and is eager to feed the heiny HabiTrail.

Mr. Roboto—a fabulous Japanese import who's too unimportant for all but the most connected insiders to know his name—is a sleek little number with more fetishes than a Masters & Johnson index, and ever since he heard about Richard's alleged-and-highly-unlikely predilection, he's been pulling strings to get himself invited to an event where he can introduce himself to Mr. Gere in person. He's studied up on Tibet and has flushed the words *Cindy Crawford* from his vocabulary in preparation for their encounter, which will probably take place at an upcoming charity function that has invited both of them (and a score of other names, big 'n' little).

I think Mr. Roboto is barking up the wrong burrow, but it will be interesting to see how far he'll go in his attempts to seduce the silver-haired devil. Consider this fair warning, Richard Gere: Run, Dick, Run!

Believe me, I'm dead on with this one, dead on and "Off the List."

CHAPTER 14

Ed Anger's America!

David Greer — On the way to Alan's, I found my allergies kicking in. Summer in the city was ten times worse than my sneezy days in Iowa, when a couple of A.R.M.s had done the trick. My hay fever had started late, when I was ten or twelve, and had gotten steadily worse, until by the time I'd moved to New York I was regularly reduced to uncontrollable coughing and sneezing jags that left my eyes looking pink and glazed and the front of my shirt unsettlingly shiny. I think my body had grown progressively immune to the various pills I would buy, dropping six dollars for a package of twelve that would be consumed in a matter of days. Finally, I'd bolstered my pills with a number of extremely annoying ancillary tactics, like eating a lot of bananas and avoiding dairy products and drinking, *ugh,* eight glasses of water a day. Even on my personalized immunity-boosting diet, and even on a steady string of pills from March to November, I could sometimes be found scrunching up my face to fend off an attack or mopping out my eyes with tissue while desperately clinging to a pole on the subway.

Besides the usual pollen and dust, the things that aggravated my allergies were sleeplessness, tension, and cigarette smoke. I'd had a restless night replaying my handshake with Alan, was currently stressing out at the prospect of meeting him in the privacy of his own home, and was walking ten paces behind a cheesy Donald Trump wannabe puffing a Cuban. Damn all the Claudia Schiffers and damn all the Arnold Schwarzeneggers for embracing the resuscitation of the cigar as fad and friend. You might as well light up some dogshit.

I dodged into a bodega, avoiding the openly curious stares of the Indian guy running the place. He looked young enough to be my son, if I'd been seduced in late junior high by an aggressive South Asian woman. He stood at his register at the peak of awareness, apparently expecting an armed robbery to take place any second. Chelsea is a nice neighborhood, but Ninth Avenue heading toward the meatpacking district is a potential hotspot. Projects spawn some fairly hellacious teenagers, the most shameless of whom enjoy tormenting store owners with their presence, shoplifting or pretending to, in order to get a reaction.

I gave him a strained look to say silently, *I'm just some guy, don't mind me,* and found a tiny packet of generic pills to dry me out. In my glandular agony, I fumbled my wallet and stooped to scoop it back up, coming face to face with a lower-rack tabloid. Was it the *Enquirer?* The *Star?* The *Globe?* No, it was the lowly *Weekly World News,* a rag so ree-diculous it could safely print anything about any star in the world, since its legal defense was always that they printed lies for entertainment and couldn't be held responsible if any of their readers chose to believe everything they read.

"ALAN DILLINGER SAVED MY LIFE!" it screamed. A dodgy photo of Alan probably taken at a celebrity softball tournament (hence the cap and perforated shirt) was superimposed over the blotchy face of a teenage girl, whose mouth was cracked open as if she were muttering the headline. I grabbed the bloid and flipped through it. The story seemed to be about this crack-mouthed girl and how she had overcome kidney cancer after watching *Lifesavers* twenty-four hours a day. Her mother was quoted as saying that only Jesus and Alan Dillinger were responsible for her daughter's health, and not chemo or radiation.

"Seven eighty-nine," the clerk chirped.

"For two lousy pills?" I spat. Normally I cringe when people complain about the high cost of bodegas. It's like going to Arby's and bitching about the lack of vegetarian fare. But I knew the two-pack of pills couldn't cost that much.

"You were reading the magazine so long I am thinking you bought it," he replied curtly. He spent his days cowering at black teenagers after watching too many episodes of *Cops,* but he was taking a stand with the paunchy, thirty-two-year-old white faggot.

I paid for only the pills, dry-swallowing them and pausing to see if I could hope for any immediate effects. Pills work better with water, but I wasn't about to pay for a French-label bottle of H_2O that had secretly been filled in someone's kitchen sink. One of my next-door neighbors walked past me, looked at me, looked away, and kept walking—that's how unrecognizable I was under the influence of allergens. *Great,* I thought, *I will look awful, possibly even contagious, when I meet Hollywood's hottest hunk. At least I'm shower-fresh.*

I stumbled along Ninth Avenue toward the meatpacking district, the land of slaughtered cows, male-free lesbian clubs, prostitutes in drag with stories about Eddie Murphy, babbling addicts, rich artists wearing Buddy Holly glasses, the Divine Miss M, and Alan Dillinger.

CHAPTER 15

Symptoms

John Dewey—Another sheet-white day, no breaks, no relief. Just . . . emptiness.

John sat in his room in a ball, hunching forward as if to swallow himself whole. It was eating him alive, knowing about the movie, pondering Seattle, the urge for flight. He had to get there somehow.

If I wish hard enough, he reasoned desperately, *I can maybe do it.* But how?

Two days after receiving the old man's letter, John had written back, mustering all his care to craft an adultish reply on a low-rent postcard, recycling a stamp from a discarded letter he'd found down the street. He had removed the stamp with a surgeon's care, resticking it onto his postcard artfully. It hadn't been postmarked; surely it must have been a gift of fate, encouragement.

John had written his thanks to the old man, and had communicated his excitement over the fabled movie collection in a single muted sentence: *I hope to see them some day soon.* He left the note open-ended, promising to look up Truitt Connor if he were ever in Seattle.

In 1919, Jim Stepps had been flown to the West Coast to become a star rechristened Gil Romano. It had been a journey bought and paid for by a movie studio, which had been impressed with his photographs and with the mystical reviews his stage presence had conjured. Nobody would be paying for John's passage. He would just have to do it himself. It was not a perplexing concept—having to do on his own—but it was a large order to fill. If he succeeded, if he found himself on the streets of Seattle in his tennis shoes and clutching the old man's address, John knew it would be his greatest achievement so far. He tried to think of it as a goal, not an obstacle.

It wasn't raining outside, but it felt like it was. The interior of the trailer was stagnant with a closed-in quality that haunted John every night as he tried to sleep, the promise of suffocation in the event of a fire, of inevitable broken-bodied agony should a twister descend. The trailer was not a home to John, it was more like a waking tomb.

Granny staggered into view, propping her flaccid arm against his open door, leaning in to get a fix on his position in the corner.

"Man alive," he muttered, an expression of surprise he'd heard old men use, a rare flash of insolence. She hadn't startled him like she usually did—it was just the wrong time to be poking her face in.

Granny hadn't heard. "Why don't you get out of the house?" she asked him, relatively subdued. Intoxicated. "Why you're always around in here in your room? Go find some little friends . . , something." Her rheumy eyes struggled to focus, her sight failing to truly connect with him. To her, he was so cloudy he probably looked like a chair. Or her footstool, the one on which she would prop up her legs when demanding a shoulder rub.

"I want to stay in," he mumbled, shaking his head.

"Are ya sick?" The word stung him: *sick*. It didn't mean the same thing to John as it did to other people. To everyone else, it just meant a queasy stomach or a mild throbbing at the temples or a bad case of the blahs. But to John, especially as voiced by Granny, the word took on an almost supernatural air. It was like invoking a demon. It reminded him of his condition, of his awful headaches, the crushing weakness he carried around in his skull.

His migraines were so severe they had taken on their own personalities. He'd named them by their severity, giving them the black-hearted monikers of legendary villains. A Jesse James was the kind that seemed to send shooting pains from the pit of his noggin to the edges of his eyeballs. A Bonnie and Clyde was tumultuous, with flareups at different parts of his head and even other parts of his body. The worst was a Capone. Whenever he was felled by one of these—and they tended only to happen about once a year—John felt he was going to die. They would hit suddenly, forcing him to close his eyes against icy agony, then would creep over his whole system, causing him to vomit uncontrollably for hours, making his limbs curl with submission and—worst— keeping him wide awake through it all.

Of course, his sickness had changed radically with his pills. The doctor had acted like these pills had been available all along, that Granny hadn't made it clear to him just how acute John's migraines had been. Regardless, John finally had the power to fortify himself against most oncoming migraines, resulting in only minor discomfort if they were caught early on. Still, a Capone was so invincible that the pills could only cut it in half, and that wasn't perfection.

Sometimes, if John were reminded of his headaches, one would crop up. Added to the stress he was wading in over his Seattle goal, John was nervous that Granny might egg one on.

Moreover, John had always felt different from everyone around him in some unnameable way. Sick. Sick with the fear that his father had been a pervert, that John might be a carrier.

"I am not *sick,*" he seethed, trying to control his impulse to rage against her. "I'm *fine.*"

She shrugged, almost losing her footing. How many times had he awoken to her whimpers for help? He would creep out of bed, numbed from halfhearted slumber to find her sprawled on the floor of her room or the living room, sometimes soaked in liquor from a bottle she'd been working on, or soaked in something worse.

"You know what?" she asked, laughing a little. Then she clammed up, raising her eyebrows and waiting for him to bite. He found her eyes so alien sometimes, particularly when they were gleaming with joy as they were then, surrounded by papery wrinkles.

"No," he replied grudgingly, "what?"

She looked like she was about to laugh, then her expression drifted into slack-jawed confusion. The silence was uncomfortable, embarrassing.

Granny stayed there for several minutes, seemingly lost in her own mind. John watched her, unafraid. She was too far gone to pose a threat, and anything he said would likely be forgotten in the aftermath of her drunk. She just stood there, hanging on his door frame, hovering almost. For a flash, he felt sorry for her, she was so frail, like she might blow away. But then he recalled that she was no wilting flower. She was steely inside, in her heart, where it mattered most.

Before lurching away toward her bedroom, she asked in a high, little-girl voice, "Are ya sick, Johnny?" She was asking it aloud but not of him, like these were the lyrics to an old song she used to know. " 'Cause I think you're sick."

He sat there, his head beginning to drum as if on cue, cold in his pathology.

CHAPTER 16

The Untold Story!

David Greer —— Alan surprised me and opened his own door. I guess I'd envisioned a maid, but then maids were behind a lot of the stories that had circulated about Michael Jackson, so maybe celebrities had started downsizing their trusted staffs in the nineties.

He looked as good, if not better, than he had the night before. He was in what appeared to be a favorite old T-shirt and sweatshorts, and though the clothes certainly weren't new or exotic, they lent Alan the too-perfectly-worn appearance of a high-paid accountant at the gym.

He had inched the door open to confirm it was really me, then swung it wide and welcomed me into his enclave with open arms. The only thing that separated the world from one of its current favorite stars was a sloppy-fat doorman, an intercom system, and one last secured elevator that required a buzz-in on Alan's floor. He owned the whole floor, and later assured me that there were several diabolical security systems in place even though he appeared relatively unprotected.

"The best ones are the invisible ones," he'd said, though for my money I'd have rather had a very obvious laser or attack dog to ward off intruders, rather than a cleverly concealed security cam that would capture every frame of my bloody murder for easier conviction of my remorseless killer.

"Just checking to make sure you weren't the stalker," he said, self-conscious about having peeked at me to begin with. He looked me up and down without a trace of invasion, and without giving away his impression of the results of his inventory.

"I understand," I croaked unconvincingly. The closest thing I'd ever had to a stalker had been a creditor. They were persistent and all, but they didn't want to marry you and didn't carry handguns.

"She's this little girl with a grown-up face," he said of his illegal suitor. "Probably no more than nineteen or twenty, but a very good actress. Good because she's so plain you'd never question her. She's all about the Midwest, you know? She looks . . . normal. Doesn't act normal, though. I mean, she *acts* normal, but she *behaves* like a lunatic. Talked her way all the way up to my front door once. I thought it must be one of my security guys knocking, but it was this plain girl."

We came to the end of a long entry hall and into the main room, which was a piece of 3-D art. Whole books on New York interiors had been published around rooms like the one I entered.

In the center of it all was a massive sofa with a low, all-glass coffee table in front of it, on top of which were piled about forty expensive art folios on everyone from Georgia O'Keefe to Tina Modotti to Pierre et Gilles and Gilbert & George. The far wall was an immense window affording a Cinemascopic river view through a bank of tiny glass panes reinforced with metal frames, probably granting the same impenetrability of bars with none of the foreboding or claustrophobia. The largest single painting I'd ever seen covered the right wall, a huge, simplistic canvas with faint, summery colors.

There were several low, blond-wood bookcases that crept around the entire perimeter of the room, with most of the books' titles communicating a connection to art, architecture, or popular culture (yes, there was the infamous best-selling picture book of *Lifesavers,* the one that had inadvertently included a shot of Alan with his briefs riding a touch too low to warrant acceptance into high school libraries). The bookshelves had taffy-orange lucite sideboards that I later remarked on and that he identified as being by Charlotte someone, a French surname that sounded doubly foreign in Alan's subtly California-accented mouth. There was an unseen stereo system that continually pumped a disjointed mixture of forties jazz, organ music, and electronica.

It was maybe a touch too designed, but it was nonetheless a real apartment, a no-expenses-spared personal statement, the kind of "space" in which every New Yorker dreamed to be able to indulge. I sort of sighed as I took it all in.

Alan continued with his stalker story as I wobbled into the now-*this*-is-living room behind him.

"I expected to give her an autograph and got *this* instead." Alan offered me the underside of his arm, where a pink, smiley-faced scar grinned from just below his elbow, sexy as hell. I sucked air in surprise. I hadn't read anything about him getting attacked, though I did have a sudden memory of seeing footage of Alan in court, testifying against a persistent fan. It had been a report on male stars with stalkers, and had mentioned Alan, Stallone, and Todd Oldham. Warren once had a stalker, a weasely paralegal from Queens, but then the guy had disappeared. I had nightmares that Warren had bumped him off, dismembering him before flushing him down the toilet in an acidic stew.

I longed to run the pad of my fingertip along the unnatural smoothness of Alan's scar.

"She was trying to stab me but I deflected her and got the door closed. She went to some loony bin and then got released, all in less than a year. Good lawyers, I guess. Now I have a *real* security team. Gavin de Becker is in my corner. He protects people like, well, Dolly Parton and Madonna, whoever. With him around, no way some loony girl is gonna surprise me. Plus, I think she's in Germany or something now."

Alan was standing with his mighty arms folded over his chest, almost like a shy, topless actress on a crowded movie set. He was considerably underdressed compared to me, and I was only in jeans and a halfway decent Eddie Bauer short-sleever. I had been hoping he'd dress down, but had no idea he'd let me see him in an outfit he might have slept in. I couldn't help taking quick looks at his fleecy legs, so pumped and so graceful. I tried looking into his face while we chatted but failed at first, too overwhelmed by the big picture.

He was so famous that I found myself checking every word he said against his image, against what few things the press seemed to know about him. Considered something of an airhead, Alan's directness and his ability to speak freely and unselfconsciously threw me. Considered difficult, his easygoing manner as a regular person was also at odds.

Considered a possible closet homo, Alan was right on target. The reason we were so compatible, I decided right off, had to be connected to gayness, brewskis or no. *If he were straight, I'd be staring at him and he'd be clueless, but this guy is letting me check him out. He's ingratiating himself.* He *had* invited me over to his place, after all.

Alan directed me to the yellow, U-shaped leather sofa that punctuated the room. A sextet of beers sat on the table in front of us, the obviously frigid bottles sweating up a storm, beads of moisture rolling over their labels. Neither of us made a move for the alcohol; I later discovered he didn't even drink.

We sat down next to each other, then Alan sort of bounced until he was facing me. I'm sure I was cemented into place, staring straight ahead, hoping I wouldn't sweat all over his priceless furniture. It would be a few hours before I could totally relax.

"So why did you call me?" I asked, trying my best to pretend I was dealing with some exceptionally cute guy I'd met in a bar, trying to inject some of the control I usually maintained in dating and quasi-dating situations.

Alan laughed. "You're not comfortable, are you? I shouldn't have talked about the stalker." He kept laughing, apparently enjoying this harmless awestruck phase of any new friendship he cultivated.

"No," I said, though it occurred to me that in some ways he *might* have been showing off about the whole stalker episode. I could think of a lot of gay men I knew who would have been impressed rather than scared by that story. "No, I'm fine, I'm glad you called, but I'm just a little . . . weirded out. I mean, imagine yourself as me. We just met last night, very briefly, and suddenly you've singled me out to come over to your house. I realize you're just a normal person, but most people in your position are a little more reserved about making new friends, right? I mean, right?"

"Oh," Alan said, looking a little shy that I'd pointed out the obvious. "Don't feel strange about me being who I am. Famous people have nonfamous friends, too. You have to. If you only hung out with stars you'd want to end it all. I know we met in a weird way, or at least meeting now is kind of weird, but I've learned in the last three years that you meet a million people but it's very hard to connect with any you'd like to get to know better. It's hard making friends when there's all these fans around and agents and things. So if you meet someone cool, you have to take charge, because they never will. They have no choice. It's not like I'm reachable."

We looked at each other as we spoke, gauging reactions. He wasn't nervous at all, but seemed concerned with my own blindingly apparent discomfort. I could feel myself *shaking*.

"It's just that I'm nervous because I know so much about you, but we haven't exchanged a hundred words. It's an odd feeling, knowing someone but not knowing them."

"I know what you mean," he said, "but you just have to forget about some of the stuff you've heard, because most gossip or whatever is completely made up. You think you know me, but you don't, really. Not at all. It's going to be harder for you than for me for us to be good friends. You have more work to do. But I hope you'll give it a try. I'm going nutso without a good buddy around here."

He explained that he had moved his home base to Manhattan after living for almost ten years in L.A., where he'd gone from struggling, starving refugee to working actor to household name during that impossibly short period of time. What had I done in the previous ten years? I'd gone from senior Xeroxing drone to pornographer. I'd gained twenty or twenty-five pounds. I'd gotten my left ear pierced and had let it grow over. I had learned that sex was an urge like hunger that needed to be satisfied—but that should be ignored unless the rumblings were audible. I had fallen in serious like several times, had gotten my heart broken, and broken a few hearts. I'd watched approximately six hundred movies.

There was an unsettling silence as we studied each other further during a pause in the preliminaries. In that space, I again felt the spark of a potential attraction, like I had the night before. I frequently questioned my physical attractiveness, and yet I was willing to give myself the benefit of the doubt when the chips were down. I wasn't flawless like he was, but I knew I was appealing in some ways. I knew we were clicking—I was there and couldn't deny that.

I also wondered how long he would pretend to be straight, if he would play the pronoun game, start talking about the chick on his arm the night before.

I'd met quite a few closet cases in my time, and wasn't interested in knowing another. I can't honestly say I would've walked out of Alan's life then and there if our conversation hadn't taken the startling U-turn that it did.

"Look," he started, as if he were going to say the exact opposite of what he was about to say, "I *am* gay, David. I'm sure that's the main thing you're talking about when you say you feel you know me and yet don't know me, right? And you were probably nervous that you weren't supposed to bring it up, so let's get that out of the way."

I sat looking at him and he sat looking at me. He was smiling, pleased. I was nonplussed. What sort of cat-and-mouse game he was playing, I didn't know, but I felt that with any closet case who announced himself so readily, there had to be a catch. *Is this what it's like at Nathan Lane's house?*

I laughed nervously and made a there-you-have-it face, the accompanying gesture arriving a beat later. I became aware that his knee was touching mine as we sat beside one another, tentatively starting the dialogue that would fuel our first weeks together.

"That's so bizarre," I choked out. "I mean, I've heard the rumors, but I thought you . . . denied them." I was talking to him almost like a reporter might, concerned not to ask the wrong question for fear the star interview would grab my tape recorder and hurl it against the wall.

Alan didn't seem thrilled with the direction the subject was taking. I think he'd hoped I would accept the revelation and proceed without much analysis. When he spoke, he seemed to be repeating things he'd had to say a thousand times before. "Well, my publicist *has* said that it wasn't true, but that was just to protect my box office. And I *did* have her add that even though I'm not gay, I'm not against gay people and I appreciate all my gay fans."

It was weak, and he was talking agent talk. It wasn't hard to squint and see a certain rat-faced redhead saying the same stuff. Shara's style was all over this doublespeak.

"I'm not saying you're evil, or anything," I said, clearing my throat, "and I don't know you well enough to criticize you, but I'm just saying that it would be nice to have more gay actors, you know, out and about. I guess I don't know what it's like, but—"

"That's politics," Alan said, waving me off. "I'm openly gay in my personal life. I always have been and always will be. I'm here with you now, aren't I? It never takes more than ten minutes for me to come out to people I meet on a personal level. Producers and directors know I'm gay from the minute they meet with me, and I don't think that's stopped me from getting a part. But since so many of them think that being out wouldn't sit right with the public, I have to protect myself. Being quiet isn't that hard to do."

"That's probably why you get so much flack from the activists, the gossip columnists," I began, the potential turn-off of my connection to Warren Junior and *Island Rage* omnipresent in my mind. "The, um, ease with which you keep quiet. Of *course* it's easier to keep quiet. Maybe it's idealistic, but maybe it's more ethical, more honest, to *not* keep quiet. To just, you know, to just acknowledge it. Do you think it would be the end of your career or something if you just confirmed who you are without necessarily becoming an activist? Isn't there a happy medium between Lily Tomlin and Amanda Bearse?" I was wishing I had some coffee to sip or a cigarette to hold and not smoke, anything to keep me occupied.

"They're both women," he shot back.

"Well, follow their example and be a man," I said. It had just slipped out.

Alan was appraising me with a steely concentration, studying my mouth while I blew bubbles from my soapbox. I didn't want to piss him off, but I didn't know what it would get me to swallow my opinions. *Maybe,* I thought, *one reason he's never come out is because there's no one in his life to argue in favor of it, or even to bring the subject up.*

"Look, David," Alan said, skooching even closer, dropping a layer of reserve and becoming more straightforward. I half-expected him to whisper all the secrets of his life into my hot ear. "The thing is, you're wasting your breath. I'm not *against* coming out. I'm just explaining why I haven't done it *yet*. It's always been my plan to come out, and I will do it. I will. I just think that I could accomplish a lot more as an openly gay superstar than as just another gay actor. I need time."

"How much more famous can you get?" I asked. It was starting to feel like a combative debate, and yet he didn't throw up his guard, but instead became increasingly frank. The more I challenged him, the more he gave. I could see an earnest kid inside him, just beyond the impressive facade. I felt like I was having one of my late-night, defenses-down rap sessions with Warren, who would have me killed if he found out I was double-dealing him like this.

"Well, actually I'm getting close to putting my plan into action. I just want to wait until the network renews *Lifesavers* officially and my contract is re-upped for the long run, and I want to see if I can make the big announcement after the opening weekend of my, of this, my first movie I did. Have you heard about it? It's a romantic comedy and I thought it would be good timing. Maybe you can come to the premiere with me next month as my, uh, date—that'd be a great way to make an announcement, huh?"

I'd read he was doing a sort of sexed-up date movie, like a *While You Were Sleeping for 9½ Weeks*. I'd heard his leading lady was Linda Hamilton, who was thought to be trying to do some positive damage to her action-star image by appearing in a tastefully erotic role that would allow her to show off her toned body *and* feminine wiles. The movie had gone through more titles than *G.I. Jane*, everything from *Me + You = Us* to *Soul Collision*. Considering the casting, maybe they should have settled on *Mission: Impossible*. The movie also had the bimbo quotient of Sara Pasquale in a supporting role, or rather supported—she was a former *Juggs* starlet who'd made the transition to disrespected mainstream movies, TV, and pay-per-view.

Whether or not he was gay, confirmed or denied, Alan Dillinger was the last stud I'd pair with Linda Hamilton. The combination made me a little queasy, and also made me feel sorry for Alan. Were his big-screen dreams tied to *Moment by Moment: The Sequel?*

Again, in exact opposition to my best guess, Alan had blurted out the truth instantly, had treated it like no big deal, had confirmed he was openly gay (at least in his private life) and even seemed serious about coming out to the press at a very specific moment in the relatively near future. He wasn't an issue to argue, he was a flesh-and-blood human being in a moral dilemma, and he seemed keenly aware of it, in touch with the real world. Just being grounded was something I had to give him credit for—who knows what I'd be like if I lived in a showroom and had a shameless agent to cater to my every stray desire?

There are so many issues I feel are black-and-white, and I'd always included outing as one of them. I'd never felt sympathy for the careerists who denied their identities for the sake of stardom, and had never bought the underestimation that being gay was only one small part of their lives so they didn't want to be branded, labeled. To me, it was about honesty. I had no expectations that any gay celebrity should be forced to do gay-themed roles, appear at lesbian fundraisers, or wear pink triangles to the Oscars. My only expectation was for the truth.

Before meeting him, I would've placed Alan in that equation. I remembered clearly thinking he had no excuse not to be out. But sitting with him, I could understand his motives as less self-serving and self-delusional than they would have seemed in print.

I realized that another expectation I'd had of Alan had been that he was far too classically good-looking and gym-fit and blond to be very interested in kissing a regular joe like me. I hoped that he would continue to defy the odds.

"I accept the invitation," I joked, not joking at all. *Will he really take me to a premiere?*

"You're on," he said quickly, with an air of finality. "Now, please, David, just forget what you've read and take it from here and now."

"That's a plan," I said. "I'm sorry, I owe you an apology. I guess I'm just cynical—"

"And like everyone you probably believe a lot of what you read," he offered.

Believe it? My friend writes it. "Yes, too much, I guess."

"I just want to be sure we understand each other. Everyone *hears* things, and no matter how smart you are, you can't help absorbing some of it, even some of the least believable shit." He was forcing a smile, uncertain of whether or not he was making a good impression. That uncertainty saved him from ever being an asshole; he was too concerned to let himself run roughshod over anybody.

"Like you probably heard the rumor I was dating Cher," Dillinger said. It sounded like he was used to being asked about that particular piece of disinformation, but I'm sure my eyes immediately broadcast that I was not used to sitting next to Cher's walkers.

"Um, no. Actually, I'd never heard that one," I replied calmly.

Dillinger made a small O with his mouth and raised his unbleached eyebrows. "Oh. Hmm." I tried to focus on the sexy dark of his brow against his tanned skin, blond-white hair, the darting blue eyes too spectacular to stare at for too long.

After a pause, though, I felt I had to bite. "Well?"

"Well what?"

"Well, *did* you? Date Cher?" I thought I was making a funny since the guy *had* just come out to me.

Dillinger laughed and closed his eyes like he was blocking out a vision of the end of the world, feigning a heart attack. "No way! I mean, I'd probably go out on a *date* with her just to, you know, say I'd *done it.* Just for fun."

I know what you mean.

"But I mean, see, that's the kind of ridiculous rumor you get from Day One in this business."

I had trouble accepting that *that* particular rumor would be so personally devastating. At least he wasn't linked to, I don't know, Celine Dion, or someone even worse. I figured it was probably just the frustration of having someone tell a lie about you, and the inability to correct it believably. *Think of all the gay men frustrated that they know the truth about you, but who are unable to assert it believably.*

"I mean, I hardly even *know* Cher," Dillinger continued.

Things were starting to get surreal.

"Enough about Cher. Let's talk about me," I offered, my nerves discarded, replaced by my desire to explore the possibilities of dating a gay man who didn't identify as famous, who, well, who just happened to be a star.

He turned toward me and we stared into each other for a beat before starting to babble about our lives in ways that avoided the star trip as much as possible. It wasn't so much a decision as it was a conclusion that Alan was going to miss his six o'clock appointment.

Our conversation lasted twenty-one hours.

CHAPTER 17

Floating

John Dewey — Shelly was probably the only person in whom John could confide—to an extent. She was the only person he ever really spent time with outside of Granny, and definitely the only fellow Romaniac in his vicinity. Shelly hadn't come to Gil Romano like most of his fans, as an avid silent buff. She'd been turned on to him by a very weird source: Cyndi Lauper.

"I was reading this biography of Cyndi and they list all the kooky things that have inspired her and they say that she was really into Yma Sumac and Gil Romano, and I was all like, 'Gil *what?*' " She laughed like she coughed, every tooth revealed as she stooped in glee. "So I looked him up in *Halliwell's* and here I am."

This had been her how-I-became-a-Gil-Romano-fan speech when John had first discovered her. Shelly lived a couple of towns over, in Mahwah, where her widowed mother was a bowling alley attendant and part-time waitress.

Even though Shelly was his friend, it was Shelly's mother who John was more drawn to. She was a mysterious adult. Shelly's mom was extremely young to have a sixteen-year-old daughter, a pale woman, resilient but limp. He thought of her as pretty, but recognized that she was old beyond her years. She always kept her mouth tightly shut and seemed to defer to Shelly's whims, like when daughter had company, mother made herself scarce out back in the ramshackle garden, her knees planted in the soil.

John considered Shelly's mother alone in the world, just like himself.

Both had immediate blood kin, but both seemed to exist within solitary membranes, detached, zoning. John could hate Shelly very easily, and had at times.

"What are you *doing* here?" Shelly hissed through the screen on her window. John had scratched at the wire, alarming the half-sleeping girl, then whispered her name, which had sent her almost into shouts. Shelly had turned on her bedside lamp and awkwardly aimed it toward the window, John's haunted face reflecting the light spookily through the screened-off squares. She had stared at him speechless, too deeply afraid to make a peep, then had recognized him with a start and darted to the window for an explanation.

Shelly was in a very short nightgown, the opaque, cottony, pink bunny-specked sleepwear of a girl six years younger than herself. There was no telling whether Shelly, who considered herself a soft punk, was wearing the nightgown to be absurd, or if she had been caught wearing something treasured that contrasted ridiculously with her image. She had recently shaved one side of her head into a grid, just like her idol Cyndi Lauper had . . . three years previously.

"What are you *doing* here?" she repeated, and her red hair glowed in the amber light.

"I don't know," John blubbered. "I mean, I need some help." Taking a deep breath, "I need your help."

It was after midnight on a school night, and a weird guy who lived at least two hours away was at her window. Shelly couldn't calculate her next move, because no boys paid her any attention. She was considered a lesbian freakazoid in school, and though she desperately hoped for a boyfriend, she'd made her bed and would lie in it. She'd chosen to be unusual, and she wouldn't give it up, not ever. She would just have to find an equally unusual boyfriend.

Not John Dewey, though. The thought mortified her. He wasn't completely, disgustingly ugly, but he was so unkempt and gawky and so distracted all the time, and quiet. Creepy. And even though she thought it was wrong to assume anything about a person just because of their appearance (having been on the receiving end of more than one off-the-mark, staggering rumor at school), Shelly had always just assumed John was a fag.

Could she risk letting him into her house? Was he a threat?

"Come around to the back," she finally said reluctantly.

Behind the house, on the decrepit concrete patio, John and Shelly lounged in expatriate pool chairs, flimsy metal contraptions with slender vinyl strips supporting their weight, furniture without purpose. There was no pool here anymore. It had been filled with cement and buried ten years earlier, after Shelly's father had drowned in it while drinking.

Shelly shivered under her robe, slightly nervous her mother would catch them and get the wrong idea. Mostly, she feared her father's ghost, an apparition she was convinced she'd once seen roaming the yard when she was ten years old. But over time, the steadiness of her memory had shifted, and she could never really be sure that she had seen anything at all that night, so she'd stopped telling people about the ghost of her father.

"I'm trying to run away," John muttered, knowing how lame it sounded.

"Run away?" she parroted. "How? You don't have any money. Where are you gonna go? Do you think you won't be caught?" She had a thousand more questions, but the first few seemed adequately insurmountable.

John sank into his chair. He was miles away from home in the middle of the night. It was a high to him, a liberation. But it also felt like he had lost control. He had a sensation like he was wetting his pants.

"I have to get to Seattle," he said, "for a very important reason. I can't tell you why, but it's got to do with Gil."

"You sound like a crazy person," she accused. "Do you know the difference between being a *fan* and being *insane?*" She pointed to herself, then to him. "Fan, insane. Fan, insane." She laughed.

John looked over at the curly-haired loser with the patch of bald. He saw her clearly as a version of himself—a misfit, one who was attempting to make her outcast status into something cool, something chosen. He recognized it so perfectly it was alarming. He rarely felt insightful, and yet he believed he could write a book on Shelly, explaining every part of her and getting everything right. Instead, it was enough to say they were both Gil Romano fanatics.

"I need money," he blurted. Then, to soften it, "Please. I really need it. I never asked you before and you'll get it back."

She studied him skeptically. The sky was the deepest, blackest blue she'd ever seen, the crescent moon a dull gray in the night. John Dewey was begging her for money in her backyard, a few feet away from where her father had slipped off his raft and under the crystal surface of their pool, the middle-income family's showpiece for bragging rights.

If Shelly asked, her mother would tell her never to give money away, especially now that they needed it. But no matter how hard her mother seemed to work, and no matter how many frivolous items Shelly demanded and got, there always seemed to be cash. Shelly couldn't imagine cutting back on extravagances, let alone going hungry. Giving money away didn't seem an impossibility.

"Sell off your collection," she suggested simply. John looked shocked.

"Never," he whispered solemnly. "That's part of why I'm going. You just don't get me. . . ."

"But you can't carry it all with you."

"I want you to keep it for me," he said, hating the words on his tongue. He didn't know if he could trust Shelly to watch his collection, let alone to return it safely later, once he got himself set up in Seattle. But he had no choice. He couldn't afford storage, and he'd heard that storage facilities would auction off stuff that wasn't paid for on time. Once he left Granny, he knew she'd happily shovel it all right out to the curb.

"Yeah, I can keep it in my room," Shelly said immediately, enjoying the idea of having John's brilliant objects under her roof. She was not a resourceful person, so her collection paled. By the time she'd thought of ransacking libraries for old publications featuring Romano, she'd found that John had beaten her to the punch, all the images X-actoed out with his trusty blade.

The money. Though she felt uncomfortable around Dewey, even resented him for his impeccable knowledge of their mutual idol's cloudy career, even though she felt that John Dewey was the kind of human being you knew for a while when you were sixteen and who then slipped under the surface at some point and was missed by no one, there was something about him she couldn't say no to.

John was pathetic. She knew his story, the hateful grandmother and the elusive family tree. She knew that he was probably even more of a pariah at school than she was, that his only friends besides her were sixty-year-old books and magazines and posters and mementos. But more than pathetic, he was a good person. She tried to imagine herself living John's life, and all she could picture was her hand wrapped around a knife, stabbing her grandmother to death. Shelly knew she couldn't put up with mental torture the way John could, the way her own mom could, first with her father and then, later, with Shelly herself. And knowing that John could put up with things made him seem good in her eyes, better, better than herself. He seemed almost saintly, in a way. Shelly disliked him, but she admired him.

"I don't think it's good for you to run away," she said carefully, "because you *will* be caught. And I don't think it's good also because if you're not caught, you're gonna get into trouble somehow, like getting picked up by some crazy person. And how are you gonna eat? How are you gonna make money to live off of? Where are you gonna sleep? Blah, blah, blah." She took a deep breath. "But since you seem like your mind is made up, I don't know, I have some money I can give you. I can give you, like, a hundred?"

Two months later, one hundred dollars in cash hidden in the pre-Eisenhower encyclopedia in his room, it didn't look like John was ever going to follow through on his plan to emigrate to Seattle.

He had gotten the necessary funds, or at least a good chunk of them, from Shelly, he had phoned the bus company for rates, he had Truitt Connor's address, he was tormented by every spare minute he spent in Jersey—and yet John was gripped by fear of the unknown, and by the sickening realization that he might be apprehended by the authorities if he made a move. He remembered a movie he'd once seen on TV when he was too little to have been watching without parental discretion, something like *Portrait of a Runaway*. Wasn't Shelly right that most kids who ran away either got raped and killed, or at least dragged back home by the cops?

John was in his room again, pressed up against the wall his bed hugged, flat against the vintage Gil Romano poster that was one of his favorites. He sometimes talked out loud to the poster, to Gil, asking for advice, using the time to sort out his thoughts. When the sun was setting in the summer and the horizon went purple and blurred with the heat, John would cut the lights and watch the shadows on Gil's chalky-smooth face, studying the strength in his features, practically expecting the black lips to part and sage advice to rumble forth in the deep, masculine basso he presumed Gil would possess, not the airy whisper that he was rumored to have had.

He was rubbing his cheek against the poster, too distraught to consider the possible smudging. "Gil, tell me what to do," he begged.

OFF THE LIST

BY WARREN JUNIOR

$APPHO WAS A RIGHT-ON WOMAN

Missy Superstar is known for her temper tantrums and her need to be snuggled after long days on the set of her latest not-quite-blockbuster.

Everyone assumes it's her strapping, longtime "boyfriend" who does the consoling. The truth is that this strong, silent type keeps his trap shut because his voice is *so high* it makes *all* the collies go wild. This girlish he-man is a professional beard—he's even indiscreetly on his famous employer's weekly payroll! And in fact there's nothing Missy about his Superstar sidekick. This chick is a lipstick lesbian from even before the term was invented, a marquee attraction thought of as the perfect jiggle quotient opposite the serious actors she's costarred with for the past 15-plus summers. In retrospect, looking at her early poster poses, she was like an adult version of JonBenet, forced smile and ultra lashes.

Now that her bankability is falling with her chest, I'm predicting it's only a matter of time before she gives up the charade and announces to the world that her best girlfriend is a bosom buddy indeed. I hear both of these lifelong sellouts are interested in telling all to the right media outlet— if they can figure how to make as much cash as possible.

And as for the soprano beard? As a beard, he's so thin you could pour milk on him and let a kitty lick him off. My advice to this good-looker is to prepare for a close shave, full of—um—nicks.

When stars are party to a conspiracy, I'm happy to be "Off the List."

CHAPTER 18

Pizzazz on Parade!

David Greer — Parts of my marathon conversation with Alan Dillinger were so moving I regret not having made notes; there are whole pieces of dialogue between us that seemed to my ear like collaborative poetry. He'd said things I'd been wanting to hear, made confessions to opinions that echoed my own. It was like a pair of lovers communing, except we hadn't even kissed until it was ending.

One thing I was sure of was that Alan Dillinger was absolutely for real. He explained to me his conflicted feelings toward his celebrity like he'd given them great thought, but hadn't yet found an appropriate partner on which to dump them. It amazed me that he could latch onto me so quickly and with such trust. It was like his life had a massive hole in it and he instantaneously perceived me as locking into that space. For Alan, I discovered, I was his first love at first sight, though he wouldn't admit it until much later.

"Why don't people know anything about you?" I'd asked, flat on my back on the dull, smooth leather, sipping warm beer and nibbling on some fat-free caramel corn we'd dug out of the back of his fridge. "I mean, from the way I understand it, nobody knows your birthday or your hometown or any of your childhood friends. I thought that was impossible in this century."

Alan was on his stomach behind me. If I tensed my shoulders, I could peek back at him, his head just above me out of sight. "It's partly a gimmick," he'd said, munching on the corn, "and partly good luck. It started by accident. See, whenever I got jobs before I was acting, I never filled out any of the personal stuff in any applications, and I'm from a military family, so we moved around a lot. So there's not a lot of proof of who I am, and my professional name is completely random—my real middle name isn't Alan or anything." I thought better of asking his real name. "I'm also not extremely recognizable from my early years, with the blond hair and all. So it seems like fate made it hard for reporters to dig up my true history." Munch. "Although, I do keep it going on purpose, because I have a father who's kind of in his golden years and I don't want him to have to deal with Barbara Walters knocking on his door every time I run a red light. He raised me after my mom died, and he's, I don't know, I guess you could say he's religious. I don't think he likes me running around in a bikini and having sex on TV."

"So you're in touch with him?"

"Mmm, yeah. Oh, sure. All the time."

I digested this information, avoiding thinking about how I was suddenly privy to news that could fetch a year's salary from certain mercenary publications. Not *Island Rage;* Warren didn't trust gossip that was bought and paid for. "So how does your dad feel about you being gay? Does he know?"

Alan ignored my question. "You know, I just want to tell you that I've never told any of this to anybody. I know I can't keep my private life completely private forever, but I like trying to keep the reporters stumped for as long as possible. It would really bother me if they ever found out about my dad and went after him."

"I won't tell," I said, believing it.

"No, no, let me finish. I'm not trying to say I think you'll rat me out," he said, "I just want to make sure you know that I'm telling you this because I like you and I want to be closer to you."

"Alan—"

"I know. Too fast."

"No, it's just . . ." I looked back over my head. "It's just, I'm not really used to knowing guys who are so open and honest. Especially not in New York. So thanks for talking to me like this. I won't let you down." I became very depressed when I said this, because there was something so touching about Alan's need for it to be true. Whether or not I ever blabbed about our conversation, I knew he would eventually be found out. Some enterprising reporter was bound to stumble onto a clue, or someone from his past would recognize him, blond hair or no.

But also, it was romantically mysterious to me that he was so resolute about nobody knowing where he was born, when, who his family was. Was there something reckless he was hiding, even from me? Was he an escaped convict or the product of incest or the son of a sheik? A platinum blond sheik? Conditioned by the kind of melodramatic schlock he was becoming famous for starring in, my mind was presuming every outlandish possibility.

I wished I could have done the same thing—obscure my past. Aren't most of us ashamed of our origins? I could pretend I was not the son of two boring suburbanites from Iowa, of all places. Why Iowa? Out of fifty states and numerous provinces, I had to be born in the whitest, nerdiest space in the country. I could pretend I'd been born in France and had been raised by multilingual artists, writers. I could say my real name was Etienne—no surnames, please—and that I was part Asian (a very small part, just enough to seem exotic). I would let it be known that I was an heir, and that my parents had once met the real Anastasia, but only briefly. If I could erase my nondescript past, I knew I'd go whole hog. There'd be no end to my creativity, even though when presented with a blank sheet of paper that hoped to become one page of a novel, my creative side seemed quite limited indeed. Much as I would like to have laid my shortcomings at the feet of my parents, I don't think they were to blame for my inability.

"I know you won't let me down, David," Alan said contentedly. "That's why I picked you. I knew you'd be the one."

I sat up, battling an unexpected attack of shyness. Alan was offering me a chance to live up to an expectation.

He was moving quickly, saying things better left unsaid until much later in a relationship. I'd done that once—met a guy who seemed so perfectly tailored to me that I'd jumped to conclusions and had started proclaiming true love.

He'd been a lawyer, and there was something sexual about lawyers for me, something predatory. I'd always fallen for egomaniacal assholes, straight men, unattainables. And this guy had seemed perfect, in that he was cocky but civilized, dating someone but not seriously, and unequivocally gay. Abe had seemed like the best of all possible worlds, sexually appealing but good for me.

We'd met at a friend's birthday bash at a small bar in SoHo. He'd singled me out and had kept the drinks flowing between us. He was Jewish, another bonus for me. My exposure to Judaica in Iowa had been limited to Woody Allen rentals, and yet I'd always found a sexual core to anyone or anything outside the norm. My earliest sexual fantasies—pre-Hexum—had involved black men because, to my sheltered mentality, they had represented a pure form of lust that existed well outside accepted standards. Blackness was an emblem of positive volatility, an innately held belief that I would later be able to shake before I'd allowed myself to develop a fetish that would at its root have been racist.

Jewish men fascinated me as I became more aware of the Jewish influence in the arts and in entertainment, intrigued by the concept of Jewish men controlling Hollywood. I was impressed by the educated mind, especially since my own college experience had been so limited and undistinguished, and I came to think of Jewish men as cultured and sophisticated, blinded to all but the New York stereotype of the elite gay Jewish man: sensitive, well rounded, moral, outwardly repressed. All of these made Jewishness an aphrodisiac, all before discovering that Jews can be assholes, too. There are no guarantees.

Abe had been good-looking, smart-talking, aggressive, masculine, and hung. He'd been a dick-centered man, loving anything I did to help him get off, insisting that I yield to his every erotic ambition.

After our first one-on-one date, he'd held me and kissed my mouth in the lobby of my building, the tonicky scent of his aftershave in my nose as we dared the jaunty doormen to acknowledge us. "God, I love you," I'd said inaudibly into his ear. Then, "I feel like I have the deepest connection to you."

"Me, too," he'd said back quickly, conservatively, and without conviction. We'd gone upstairs and slept together and he'd spent the next two months navigating my body while I'd spent it realizing how wrong he was for me, a red herring who'd snuck under my waste-of-time net.

I'd spent almost every night we were together accommodating his penis, giving him my all to help him achieve a temporary peace, to sate his restless craving. It was more sex than I really wanted, and not much of it was any good. Abe had fucked me hard, but never at the time I wanted to get fucked hard. He was never in touch with what I wanted, and resistant to anything I wanted more than he did. It was out of the question that I should fuck him back. His selfish attitude was like that of a horny brother-in-law from the pages of the porn mags I wrote: "I'll *let you* suck me off."

He'd been fucking me once from above and behind, pounding me in a way that few men I'd found would have the energy or stamina for. I was thinking, *Will the condom break? Will he remember to pull out before he comes, like I asked? Will I be able to stand much more? Will a yawn annoy him?* I'd grunted in boredom and disgust before I could censor myself.

His sweat had trickled over my back and he'd gruffly asked me if I loved his cock fucking me that way, spurred on by the noise I'd made.

"No," I'd said, "I don't." He'd stopped and I'd squirmed away, had gotten up and pulled on my underwear. Sat on the futon beside him while he kept barking at me, "What? What? What?" half out of concern and half defensively.

"Nothing," I'd said. "It's not you." I'd meant that he wasn't the right person after all, that our stubby relationship had been a case of mistaken identity, but he'd taken it to mean that he wasn't to blame. Both sentiments were true, and I'd regretted all the things I'd said to him when we'd first met, like having said them once and wasted them meant I'd never get the opportunity to say them again.

But I didn't have that feeling with Alan, that feeling that we were moving too fast or connecting too intensely too early on. I didn't feel like Alan was blurting out that he'd chosen me just because he yearned to be able to say so and was using me for my proximity. Instead, I felt a tremor of anxiety when he told me extravagant things like "You're the one," but it was a nervousness rooted in the fact that I sensed he was right. I felt the same way about him as he did about me, this illogical welling up of emotion like I'd found the twin I'd never known, or, to resuscitate a sarcastic joke later made by Carol, a soulmate in a Speedo.

"I feel like I could fall in love with you so easily," he'd told me during that twenty-one hours.

"I know what you mean," I'd said, and had felt his large hand cover mine for the rest of our long, long talk.

When it was over, as I was about to walk out the door, Alan had looked at me, placed that same hand on my shoulder and pulled me into him for a brief, affectionate peck on the lips. Burned out after all the talking, I think it was like a dream for both of us. Did it happen or didn't it? It did. And the best part was that it felt like a promise of much more.

CHAPTER 19

Lifestyles of the Rich and Famous!

David Greer — The day after I'd chastely bonded with Alan Dillinger, I was on my way to having a new boyfriend, who just happened to be a little more famous than David Charvet and a little less famous than Brad Pitt and about twice as cute as both, plus smart, plus fun and funny. I kept hoping that I wouldn't wake up if it was just a stupid dream, but I had woken up at 6:01 P.M., Sunday almost over already, emerging from an hour-long nap/catatonic lull after that first marathon conversation. I'd woken up and looked around my room for clues that my night with Alan on his couch hadn't really happened, a sign that I'd simply dreamed the event. What I'd found had been a notepad by my phone with Alan Dillinger's home address, and a card in my pocket with his phone number, pager, and fax.

Such valuables transcended their position in my meager apartment, my body box.

I'd mastered bare-bones survival in New York, something everyone here has to do or be banished to the wilds of Brooklyn or Hoboken or, gulp, *Weehawken,* or some similarly Third World place. Basically, in order to live on my obscenely low porno salary, I had to sacrifice. I bought generic corn flakes, generic detergent, generic mayo; colorless boxes with stark lettering that stood in contrast to the whimsy of Count Chocula, Bold, and Miracle Whip. I wore the same clothing—mothy sweaters, the same old Eurythmics concert T from '86, jeans so distressed they were inconsolable—until I received requests *not* to.

I could no longer, as I'd done during my illegal-scholarship-skimming college days, go to dinner *and* a movie. In fact, I couldn't *go* to dinner at all, instead preparing all my own meals myself in my "cute, charming, and cozy" minuscule studio. I was so into forty-nine-cent noodles that I thought of myself as living what I called the Ramen Life, a deceptively neospiritual phrase that begged for a Chinese gong sound to follow it and that conjured the image of a spartan monk, persecuted by the government and yet among the only whole human beings alive. But it was just about curly, twig-crisp noodles inhabiting Styrofoam cups, reinvigorated by boiling water.

Most people have to make food in the kitchen and then walk over to the dining room to eat. Some have EIKs, or eat-in-kitchens. I had what was known as an EILR, an inscrutable abbreviation that had leapt out at me from the pages of the *Voice* as I'd searched for apartments. I had known that whatever an EILR was, it was the difference between paying over one thousand dollars a month to live alone in a shoebox in Chelsea and paying $865 a month for the same privilege.

An EILR, for anyone considering such a thing sight unseen, is an eat-in-living-room. I had a gas oven and a sink and a baby fridge *and* a tiny dining table in my living room, so that I could basically toast some bread, make BLTs, and then clean the dishes, all without ever having to leave my teacup futon. After sundown, my living room became my bedroom. Don't worry, there *was* a separate cube that served as the bathroom, a hair-split misnomer since there was no actual bath*tub,* just a columnar shower and a rather finicky toilet that demanded two flushes for a sneezed-out Kleenex. But at least I had a bay window in my apartment, which served as one wall of my shower, a moldy towel strung over it to block my soaking body from the prying eyes of rooftop sunbathers and anyone with binoculars or twenty-twenty vision in any of the shorter buildings around me. Perhaps the only good things about my pad, besides the indisputably low rent, were that I had a "high floor," a "quaint view," and fabulous air circulation, the latter of which was more valuable than money in August.

Returning from my overnighter at Alan Dillinger's, I had felt sort of like I had a fresh outer skin of grease that needed to be stripped away. Sitting in various positions on a leather sofa for almost a whole day-night cycle will do that to you. I'd smelled a tad ripe and had felt the unbearable burning in my eyes that meant my sleepless, talky night was going to be converted into a day or two of seriously agitated allergies. But I'd felt exhilarated, having connected with just about the cutest guy who'd ever looked twice at *men,* having just connected with anyone at *all.* It wasn't only rare, it was practically unheard of, and the fact that we hadn't had sex somehow made the new bond seem pure as well as fortuitous.

Our elevator was old and sterile, glowing white from sanitary walls bouncing light from an overhead O of fluorescence. There was a tiny vent in the corner that hummed just a *bit* louder than the diabolical bulb, and which I often fantasized was concealing a security camera whose tapes—dating back for years—would contain proof that when not in use the elevator was filled to the ceiling with swarming roaches, that seemingly tight-assed neighbors regularly sucked each other off between floors, that the fat kid on six was the one who was pushing the buttons for all the floors and sending the car on an all-building spree. In reality, there was probably just an antique fan humming beyond the grate, a prize that could go for twenty dollars at a flea market.

I had always avoided contact with my fellow co-opers, the ruthless, Republican owners, and the frazzled, disoriented, unclean, certifiable rent controllers. There were only a precious few spaces in our building that had fallen between the cracks, that hadn't been aggressively and yet inexpertly rehabbed and sold off, and mine was one of them. I was one of about six people in the building paying the high cost of living. The rest were paying what you might have expected to pay in the sixties, or even less—just paying the interest on airspace they "owned," whatever that meant.

I don't know if I can express the sinking I had experienced as the door to my apartment had swung open and I'd faced my existence, still fresh from an all-nighter at Alan's, a private residence that really—legally—should have been some sort of shelter to house up to forty needy families.

As I'd stood there on the outside looking in, deciding if I could make myself take that first step, my elderly, bowlegged neighbor Mrs. Simpson had emerged from her shabby flat amidst the metallic chug of several locks defused. She wore an unapologetic dressing gown with tiny pink flowers that had been red when I'd first moved in.

She was in the process of being dragged by her wheezing little Chinese pug, Winnie. Mrs. Simpson was actually on her sixth Winnie, having given away the first four because they barked too much, didn't get potty-trained quickly enough, snapped at her, or just didn't have the right disposition to suit her. This Winnie, Winnie VI, was relatively new; about five months. The fifth Winnie had slipped her collar during a once-a-day walk and run away, never to be heard from again. Mrs. Simpson had been apoplectic. Ironic that she'd feel so stung by the dog's display of disloyalty.

All of them paled in comparison to the love of her pet-owning life, Ampersand, a pre-Winnie miniature doberman who had survived a miraculous eighteen years in Mrs. Simpson's care, only to take a suicide leap out the window of our tenth-floor vantage.

"David," she had exclaimed softly, her voice too tiny ever to achieve more than a firm chirp. "What's wrong? Why are you just standing here?"

I didn't have *that* much against Mrs. Simpson, the veteran's widow with rent control, a lonely soul, and possibly inhumane expectations of doggies. She was sweet to me and I enjoyed rifling through her recycling for free, recent issues of the tabloids and *Mademoiselle*. It was just that it was such a chore being nice to everyone anymore, so much of a nuisance that I felt compelled to respond and be friendly, such an imperative. Other people I knew were able to brush off all their unwanteds, and yet I felt guilty for even entertaining the idea of being curt with the old woman. It's the disease of a good upbringing.

"Oh, I'm just lost in a moment," I'd replied, knowing immediately that it's never good to throw something so vague out there when you're dealing with such a nosy talker.

"Well, I guess that's better than being lost in the supermarket."

I'd choked out an unexpected laugh, but she had seemed meditatively serious. Winnie VI was showing swelling about the eyes as she tugged on her leash, threatening to topple her tiny owner with her need to make it onto that elevator, down to the ground floor, and out into the streets. I went outside to escape my rentable prison, but Winnie VI viewed the world as one big toilet. She may have had something there.

"Yes, well," Mrs. Simpson had said as she'd been swept onto the elevator by the enthusiasm of her dog. "You should come over for my famous chicken soup sometime soon. That's a promise."

I'd been over once the second week I'd moved in, just to be nice, no sense in riling up a possible lifelong neighbor. She'd served chicken soup that might have been famous but certainly not for its taste. Her refrigerator didn't even seem plugged in to me when I'd gone for some water. The water was in a pitcher but had obviously come from the tap, a distinct no-no in NYC. I'd gone for the milk but was turned off by the expiration date, which was so overdue it made me nostalgic. *What was I doing way back when?*

I'd lived through the meal, reasoning that the chicken was fresh (I'd seen her arrive from the store with it) and the broth had simmered long enough to wipe out anything too dangerous. *Does lead evaporate when you boil water?* I'd feigned an allergy bit to avoid the rice pudding she'd made by hand, fearing any dessert that could so naturally disguise so many unappetizing defects.

I'd had a lot to absorb after talking with Alan and needed to sleep, so I'd nodded to Mrs. Simpson and had gone into my apartment, instantly succumbing to the drill: coat off, watch into pocket, shoes off, wallet into shoes, strip naked, shower, deodorant, baggy shirt and shorts (wash them on Thursdays when no one is in the laundry room), collapse on the bed. Except that routine was usually for after work, and in this case it was a weekend evening, a Sunday.

After singing, as I lay in bed, I kept replaying the day before, and kept thinking of what would happen the second time we got together. Alan was jetting to the West Coast—probably in midair over the midsection of the country at the same moment I was lying there wide awake in bed—but when he returned, we were going to meet the following Friday and attempt to have dinner out in the real world, see how discreet we could be. I had to be careful not to be spotted by anyone who would rat me out to Warren, but Alan didn't know that. All he knew was that he didn't want to be photographed or even seen in too romantic a situation with another fella. That, on top of his usual struggle to do something normal in public without getting swamped by fans and the curious.

Probably the most important exchange we'd had had been about me. I had deftly avoided talking about my day job, but had told Alan what I told everyone: I was an aspiring writer.

"Why aspiring?" he'd asked.

"Well, I just mean I haven't been published yet."

"David," he'd said earnestly, "being published doesn't mean you're a writer. If you can write, you can write. It's a talent not many people have and, and that you don't need some corporation to tell you you're good at."

Idealistic, yes, and usually I am so resistant to idealists' pluck. But Alan felt strongly about what he was saying, and that moved me.

"Are you a good writer?" he'd asked.

I thought about it. "I think I'm good," I'd said. "I'm just really bad at motivating myself—"

"Stop—because that's important, too, but it's a different issue. First, you have to have the talent. And I'm sure you've got that if you think you do—you don't seem like someone who would overestimate himself, have a big head."

Bingo.

"So it's really just a matter of acquiring discipline," he'd stated simply, as if it were something you could buy. But something in his voice was so genuinely encouraging I almost believed that I'd start writing again as a direct result of his pep talk.

Much as I enjoyed replaying the bits of our conversation that were sweet and warm, I also had to keep in mind the unromantic practical chatter at the end, when Alan had looked so uncomfortable, like he was performing a chore he'd rather not.

"Listen, if we're going to do this—if we're going to start dating, and I want to—you have to remember that we will always be watched. There's always going to be a photographer close by, maybe hanging over a doorway like our friend Chip or maybe they'll just walk right up and shove a camera in your face and start taking pictures." He'd monitored my reaction, which was even—I was in denial that this would ever really happen. "We can't be . . . demonstrative in public, David. No PDAs, okay? We have to make sure we aren't perceived to be dating, at least not right away. After I come out, all of that will change. . . ." Where had I heard that before? Oh, yeah—from like every guy I dated at the end of high school and all through college.

I was ten-plus years past all that bullshit, past the idea of hiding out and fretting that I might be caught and exposed as a homo, and yet I was ready to plunge back into it with Alan. At least, I told myself, as long as it was absolutely necessary.

I can't explain why going back into the closet was an attraction for me, except to say that Alan Dillinger, with his rules and paranoia and silence, made being gay dangerous again. I felt like I'd recaptured a hot, sneaky rebellion from my youth, when I would feel like a sex criminal for staring at another boy for too long.

Alan Dillinger returned homosexuality to the realm of the forbidden for me.

CHAPTER 20

Caught on Tape!

David Greer — I woke up with a phone in my hand. It was like a dream at first, because I'd been dreaming of Alan's call on Friday. "I'll call you on Friday," he'd promised, and I was banking on it.

Except this wasn't Alan calling. And it wasn't Friday. It was only Monday. Monday at . . . *6:45 A.M.?*

"H'lo?"

"Hi, did I catch you sleeping?"

"No," I mumbled, automatically falling into that belligerent state of denial when you're torn from slumber. "Nope. Who is this?"

"Gerald. This is my wake-up call to remind you that your presence is anticipated tonight at my apartment for a party to which you RSVPed three weeks ago."

I'd gone to a glitzy bash a couple of nights earlier, and here was a massive housewarming, but it's not like my life was one big party. I'd been to two in the previous year, and that included a christening that I'd done to mollify a dateless friend. But I've since watered down my hatred for parties upon realizing that your whole life can change based on which invitations you accept, which phone calls you answer, which letters are safely delivered by the post office, which smiles you return.

It was galling that Gerald would dare to call a person so early, but he remembered I'd said I always set my alarm at seven to get up for work. Gerald was one of those annoying people who remembers absolutely everything you say and acts on it, sometimes inconveniently.

I dreaded the get-together, slipping into cold sweats whenever Warren's smiling face popped into my mind. Warren would be there, off duty since Gerald was just one of our pals and didn't know any stars to invite. Gerald was a starving literary agent with a few talented clients and lots of longshots. He seemed to be friendly with a lot of writers, which I'd found so intriguing at first, hoping to meet them and pick their brains for blueprints on how to succeed. Instead, I'd wound up meeting some really insufferable characters. People in publishing are the worst. Even my porn-biz pals were more likable.

I had managed to pull the wool over Warren's eyes for the weekend, but didn't want to risk seeing him and having him read my amateurish poker face. Nobody in the world knew I had met Alan in his apartment—I hadn't even told Carol yet—but Warren was good, very good, at picking out the truth. I hadn't seen him since I'd been to Alan's, so I wasn't at all sure I could keep my mouth shut without giving off hint spores.

I didn't shave, showering only because I craved the warmth and steam and not because I was expected at work by nine. I took a thirty-minute dousing, as long or longer as when I'd practically lived in the shower in high school, when I was first becoming acquainted with my orifices and appendages in a golly-gosh kind of way.

I walked around my room in a robe, drifting into imagined scenarios where Alan was coming up behind me, reaching around and loosing the sash, running the flats of his hands over my body and nuzzling my ear. The giddiness of the attraction was something I wanted to bottle and save, like I'd done with my first partner's semen, a curiosity-fueled mistake that had led to a shattering discovery by a roommate several years later.

I was listening to music, a venerable tape my best friend from high school had made me. I think I'd known Aaron was gay, too, the day he'd handed me a tape and said, "Hey, I made this for you. It's just some songs I like." I'd kept that tape, and the dozens of others he'd "produced and arranged" (selected and duped) and sent to me after I took off from Iowa. The successive tapes were progressively more elaborate, going from sixty to one hundred twenty minutes, suddenly sporting home-made sleeves with photos pirated from magazines and pasted with care into colorful arrangements. Still, I had a soft spot for the first tape, the one from when we were eighteen and addicted to loneliness and gay and celibate and probably, the more I considered it, kind of in love.

I grew morose thinking of Aaron with his bright brown eyes and earnest, studious air, imagining him in his room at home choosing music he wanted to use to communicate with me, carefully selecting the order in which the songs would appear, crafting the phony sleeve. I could still envision his face somewhat accurately, but the rest of him was brittle and opaque, like an image from a yard-sale Etch-A-Sketch. I was losing him from my permanent memory banks already, and he'd been so important to me. I was grateful for the tape to help me remember, and also for the dopey senior pics of him that were housed in my yearbook, two poses, one in sweater and one in suit, hair center-parted, fluffy and backlit: AARON WELLES, C/O '84

I liked to relive the past whenever something major happened to me; there didn't seem to be any question in my mind that Alan was major, and that he had happened to me.

My day at work was a blur, a series of disks inserted into noisy drives, masochistic coworkers (no, *literally*), irate phone calls. I talked to a Falcon star about the meaning of life and dutifully noted his sparse offerings. *Who cares what you think when you're hung?*

The party that night was like one big, staged bummer.

I had hoped Carol would keep her promise to attend, but she'd begged off, all partied out. The party was a block west of the Roxy, a sucky place to live. The street was beyond industrial with buildings that at night looked like bombed-out warehouses. On the way over, I'd had the treat of being informed I was a punk by a kid too young to remember a world before Oprah in the afternoon.

Gerald's building looked like it was about to sigh and collapse, but had a secured entrance and from the inside was livable.

The second I walked into the housewarming I got the chills. There was just something impenetrable about it, the well-wishers crowded into semiexpensive clothes and dipped in sweet-smelling fragrances and rubbing against each other while making small talk and getting steadily drunk. I spotted the hostess (one of them, the female one, Gerald's roommate Suzan), the shameless DKNY on her shirt providing a New York–style compass, NSEW. I made for her and hugged her and fabricated an excuse for not having been in touch and in response was cheerfully steered toward the cheese, left to examine the depth and vitality of all of these shallow but beneficent friendships I'd allowed to flower and even nourished with my attention and attendance.

I saw a very sexy guy I'd once longed to be seduced by, tallish with thick hair and a solid build and a blank expression, overwhelmingly attractive to me. I think I'd been most turned on by his always-open shirts and the five o'clock shadow on his broad jaw. He'd served as a decent infatuation for a couple of weeks until I'd asked Warren about him and found out he was a publicist. It was like meeting a guy with a "Timothy McVeigh Was Framed" T-shirt, or someone who begins a conversation with "I just read this incredible book called *Dianetics.*" Publicists, I had learned after many years of repetitive mistakes, are people too stupid to realize how unpleasant they are.

Warren was upon me like a hawk with a roadmap. He was laying into me before I knew he was in the room.

"How could you not tell me?" he asked, stony.

The jig is up. I smiled.

"Hi, Warren," I said in a daze. All my well-practiced excuses fucked up. "Did Carol tell you?"

"Yes, she told me. She told me because she's my *friend.* She told me because she knows my column closes on Fridays and because she knows I'm always hurting for tidbits." He wasn't genuinely mad or heartlessly attitudinous, just miffed that I had exploited his invite and then not coughed up a thank-you to use in print.

"I don't know, I just choked," I squeaked. "When Dillinger came over and talked to us, I have to admit I thought he was nice and I was—"

Warren bugged his eyes with shock. " 'When Dillinger came over and talked to us!' 'When Dillinger came over and talked to us!' "

Apparently, Carol had *not* let slip that piece of information, had *not* betrayed me in the least. Now I had gotten *her* into trouble, too.

"I was just going to ask about the bimbo he brought as his date," Warren said sternly.

Like the star of a porn video I'd recently reviewed, I had just screwed myself.

"It's not what you think, there wasn't anything to report. He looked really cute and he was schmoozing us because he thought we ran some little media outlet. He thought we were advantageous."

Warren seemed unconvinced, his penetrating eyes riveted to me for more. He often admitted to me that he felt he was a little psychic, or that he possessed a particularly acute skill for reading people that even he himself didn't understand. It was part of what had made him interested in gossip. He'd figured out as a kid that he saw TV news shows and read parts of the newspaper a different way than most people. After one brief TV news segment of a crying mother, he had sensed that she knew something about her daughter's disappearance or that she had even committed the murder herself—and she *had*. He had known from a few cagey words and a set of cow eyes which politicians were liars (admittedly not all that difficult considering the odds) and which controversial convicts were wrongly accused.

Most personally thrilling to little Warren was that he felt he was able to sense a connection between himself and some celebrities. Other closeted boys his age were gaga over the biggest, most overexposed chunks of teen meat being pushed in all the youth magazines, but Warren was gravitating to unlikelier dreamboats, convinced they shared a hard-to-pin-down secret with him, an otherness that the Bay City Rollers just didn't exude.

Warren began reading *Modern Screen* and *Jet* and his aunt Georgia's *National Enquirer*s to see what all the gossip was, fascinated by the immense gap between projected perfection and base truth. Reading about suicide tries covered up, noses bobbed, tempestuous loves lost, arrests unreported elsewhere, Warren began to document—in his mind— bits of information that only bolstered his natural gift for soothsaying. A lengthy fascination with Marilyn Monroe, with all the cover-ups and presidential espionage, had only exacerbated his knack for the ugly truth. He knew when explanations were hokey, and he knew that celebrities, desperate to maintain their calculated images (even if that image was one of not caring about one's image), were not above flat-out treating the public like a gang of imbeciles, lying with gusto and without even really trying to placate credibility.

Aunt Georgia and little Warren would talk at her kitchen table about the comings and goings of the elite, convinced they knew what made them tick. Georgia's fanatic devotion to soap operas was partially to blame, since they'd conditioned her to trust no one, that assuming the worst was always for the best.

More than anyone I'd ever met, Warren was born to do the job he eventually landed. He was a congenital gossip.

Warren looked at me and said, "You're a liar." It wasn't as stinging as it may sound; we were close enough to push the boundaries of acceptable banter. And Warren called everyone a liar. He felt that he was the only honest person around, which made him loathed by anyone unfortunate enough to have deserved his unvarnished opinion.

"I know." I shrugged. "But not this time."

Warren narrowed his eyes to slits and acted like he'd enjoy hitting me.

"Warren," I teased, "who are you kidding? Underneath it all, you're just a big pussycat." A woman standing within earshot did a double take. She resembled Eleanor Mondale from E!, but seemed less appalling.

"Let me tell you a story to remember," Warren replied with eerie focus. "Kitty cats are cute and adorable and warm and they'll be your best friend and they'll cuddle with you and lick your finger and purr. But kitties will *bite*. No explanations, no apologies."

We held the moment and then laughed. He was going to let it drop for the time being, but I knew I had a pushy reporter onto me. I knew I would have to tell Warren I'd met Alan . . . eventually. But at that point, I'd only *met* Alan. We hadn't gone out in public yet. I knew as soon as Alan and I left his apartment together, we were open to paparazzi photos which might seem innocent to the bulk of the planet—just a coupla guys hanging out—but which would catapult Warren onto my face.

The party was getting overcrowded and bodies kept arriving. Warren cut through them to get us some booze.

"I haven't read your book yet," I heard a woman gasping in a self-parodying, kooky way. "Do you recommend it?" Saccharine.

"No." The voice was familiar.

Stunned silence. "Well—*why?*"

"Because I've heard it's awful."

Warren laughed loudly at the man's response and I turned, shocked to see him in the company of a well-known author, an older, nearly blue-haired queer who always wrote bestsellers about coded gay subjects but who steadfastly refused to comment on his "private life." And yet in social settings, he could never seem to resist dumping the most embarrassingly personal information on the unsuspecting. At one event, with Warren standing six inches away, he'd fairly bragged that he had just gotten over hepatitis and that he'd infected his lover and two of his favorite tricks. Why don't people just talk about movies if they're at a loss for what to say? I don't know, but Warren had reported the story in a savage blind item called "Hepatitis: Easy As A, B, C." I couldn't figure out how the writer could have gotten over such a stinging piece, how he could stand to chat so amiably with Warren. It had to be the publicity. Maybe even nasty remarks are welcomed by true PR addicts.

The last thing I heard the writer snicker before I lost track of the conversation was, "It's who ya know and who ya blow."

Warren gravitated back to me and we saw a couple that we'd known since our days at the copy center. We privately referred to them as The Twins because they were a pair of men who couldn't have looked more alike, two fine-physiqued Chelsea boys with matching buzz cuts and smiles and tan lines and personalities . . . fingerprints? They were like shorter, less bulky versions of Bob and Rod Jackson-Paris, except still together.

That was the only truly impressive thing about The Twins: They'd been together since *college,* over a *decade,* which probably explained how they'd come to resemble each other with their close-cropped hair, slim, athletic builds, and even their clothes, which friends swore they swapped from day to day.

They seemed to be an almost perfect couple, but that wouldn't last, I'd always told myself. No two gay men could overcome all the normal speed bumps of an adult relationship *on top of* all the extremes that confronted gay companionship in New York, right?

"They're cracking," Warren said under his breath, pointing indiscreetly as he returned to his spot next to me. He'd brought me a lame papaya cooler.

Encouraged, and then appropriately shamed for feeling so competitive, I asked what he meant.

"They are no longer *faith*ful," Warren whisper-sang, keeping his lips perfectly still. Warren always felt that he could say anything in the world about a person standing right next to him, and as long as he adjusted his voice to a low-volume singsong, they'd never catch a bit of what he was saying, or that he was even talking about them. Or that he was even *talking!*

I gave him a question-mark face (I'm too loud to ever get away with gossiping at close range), and Warren turned to face me so he could speak a little more freely, even though The Twins were only five feet away.

"They called me to tell me that they had *added a person to their relationship,*" Warren said, eyes widened to take the place of the shocked reaction I was unable to register. One of The Twins had caught sight of me and was giving me a half-wave, obviously intending to come over to chat as soon as he could tear himself away from the hostess.

"No," I muttered.

"Yes," Warren confirmed. "They have added a twenty-two-year-old Gay Games boxer named Perry who is said to also be a model and a hustler." He could barely mouth the words *boxer, model,* or *hustler,* knowing that any one of them could trigger recognition if heard by The Twins. "They are now in what they are calling a 'trouple.' "

One letter away from trouble, I immediately thought, and knew that Warren was thinking the same. Warren was a true wildcat, a partier who had woken up with persons unknown in his day, and who believed in backrooms as therapy. He shouldn't have been so scandalized by the birth of The Triplets. I wasn't *My Little Margie,* either, and yet I was floored by the audacity of the concept. Everyone knew that long-term gay couples were prone to cheating or to adjusting the rules so that infidelity wasn't cheating in the first place, a depressing reality I hoped to avoid in my own future. And yet there was something truly anarchic about claiming to be in a three-way *relationship.* It was revolutionary, possibly even evolutionary, except something about it made me sick to my stomach.

I didn't have even *one* boyfriend, and here these clowns were reeling in their *second* apiece. Plus, there was something sort of retro-tawdry about sleeping with a hustler. Who wants that aggravation? That inconvenience? That clap? It was hard for me to picture these guys with a third, harder for me to imagine them explaining the situation to me with a straight face. Where was this third man? This home-stretcher?

I wondered if I was about to nail down Alan, to get that steady boyfriend I craved. It dawned on me that this sort of party would be virtually impossible if I were dating Dillinger. How could I expect him to attend a boring little gathering of my nothing friends, one I didn't even relish myself? How could I ask him to risk the stares and nervous inquiries that he'd already confided were unhinging him mentally? But that made me conceive of the difficulty we would have in just about any "normal" situation. Could I really envision spending Xmas at home with Mom, Dad, and Movie Star? Or going to the Chelsea Cineplex with him in tow? It wouldn't be like the time I saw Julianne Moore at a matinee of *Addicted to Love* and was the only one to recognize her, or my close encounter (and near shoving match) with Lee Grant over an empty seat at *Romy & Michele's High School Reunion.* It would be more like escorting a salmon into a grizzly den.

And yet, no matter how many quirky or downright flabbergasting possibilities I idly dreamt up, I kept returning to the idea that I wanted to grab Alan and make it work. I was too interested in the person I'd talked with to dismiss him out of fear.

As I heard Warren begin a loud conversation with The Twins, asking nonchalantly where Perry was, the door opened and Michael Musto slipped in, hovering by the coat rack almost as if he were having second thoughts about actually staying. *This is going to be good,* I thought, envisioning Warren's reaction when he spotted his arch rival.

But I never got to see it. I suddenly had a pinprick of recognition as I clearly heard Alan's name spoken. It had come from the TV, around which six or seven partiers had gathered, shooting the shit while downing the cutely childlike party snacks: Ho-Hos, King Dons, Twinkies.

The TV was tuned in to *Entertainment Tonight,* Chris Wragge's gleaming face a charming talking head as he narrated a brief segment on Hollywood couples. Chortling like the sexy, all-American ex-jock that he was, he was laundry-listing the latest hot pairs and had just uttered "Alan Dillinger," right before "Sara Pasquale." It was a disembodying experience, hearing Alan romantically linked with a woman to whom, I felt sure for that moment, he had no connection. My eyes welled up with suppressed pride, I was so giddy to debunk the report, to step into the circle of Ho-Ho hos and announce, *"That* isn't true. In fact, *I'm* the woman in Alan Dillinger's life."

But then, as they used to say on *This Is Your Life,* tragedy struck: To back up the assertion, *ET* ran some paparazzi video footage that probably lasted only about four seconds. For four excruciating seconds, I watched buxom Sara Pasquale straddling Alan at a Tavern on the Green promotional party for their movie, *No One in Here But Us Lovers,* or whatever it was currently called. Her erotically chunky thighs were parted by a discreet blur, an obvious censorship of the fact that she had been sitting in Alan's lap without the benefit of panties under her short, short skirt. Of course, it's not like they were having sex, but Alan wasn't standing off, appalled. Instead, he was embracing her, his eager fingers cinched around her waist, his face enmeshed in hers, both of them shining from the corner of the dark room. They were kissing with a passion I had only been dreaming about with him up to that point, and from the looks of things, they didn't kiss goodnight and go their separate ways afterward.

What could I think? I went from gleeful to mortified, equally unable to speak. I know I looked weird because one of the girls at the TV had shoved a golden snack into my face and was urging, "Twinkie? Twinkie?" She sounded French.

There's something about Twinkies that makes you happy to kill yourself. They're loaded with every tasty poison humans have ever devised, and yet you can't help smiling when you tear into that cheap cellophane.

I scarfed down one and then another. Warren watched me from across the room, pitying me for being so clearly disturbed by his news about The Twins, completely unaware that those two were not the couple preoccupying me. I grabbed my coat and left.

The last thing I heard was Warren's shrill, phony, embittered greeting: "*Michael!* So *fab* to *see* you!"

CHAPTER 21

Departure

John Dewey — Most of the summer wasted on self-doubts and second-guessing, it took a disaster to actually motivate John to depart for Seattle.

"John!"

Granny's voice had sounded shriller than usual that Saturday morning, but had given no indication of the scene John would encounter in the living room. He had bolted upright in bed, sweating in his T-shirt and yesterday's underwear. He'd fallen asleep reading a travel guide he'd lifted from a Barnes & Noble in Passaic. It listed all the touristy sites in Seattle and also showed clearly all the bus lines. It would fit neatly into his worn backpack on the trip. If he ever left.

John sprinted down the hall and into the living room, not caring if Granny saw him in his underwear. She didn't seem to have a strong sense of propriety at all, and could be counted on either to ignore him or call him a lard-ass, the latter of which hardly hurt his feelings anymore.

When he saw the floor of the living room, he later remembered having thought: *She finally died. She's dead. She's dead.*

Granny was on the floor, like she had been so many times before. She'd spent the lion's share of her old age on that shag, struggling to right herself after a boozy misstep or dozing in alcoholic unconsciousness.

But right away, John knew there was something different about this fall. She wasn't all spread out like she usually was, wasn't squirming like an old turtle, wasn't moving at all. *She's not breathing.* She was on her belly. Her leg was folded under her in an impossible contortion that turned his stomach. It was broken for sure, but that didn't seem to matter.

She was wearing her old robe, the garish, flowered housecoat he'd grown so used to, the one he'd found her wearing even in old photographs, pictures older than he was himself. Her one visible foot was bare, and as white as their porcelain tub. Her hands were palm up, slack, her arms close to her sides like she hadn't even attempted to break her fall. Granny's chin was propped up so that her face was perpendicular to the floor. It was her face that made him know.

Granny's eyes were wider than they'd ever been, like she'd just had a great scare and needed time to recover. Her mouth was slumped on the left, like the muscles inside had been removed and the wounds healed perfectly. Her chin was bright red, probably from the impact. Her bared lower dentures were pink with a wash of blood. She looked like a growling dog, fierce, fanged. But she was still. She seemed about to burst into laughter, but didn't.

The enormity of the event shocked John, took his legs out from under him. He came down with a hard thud next to the body of his grandmother, unable to process the big picture. He worked himself up into a painful stoop, squatting there like an infant.

"Granny?" he asked, his voice high and girlish from awe, tinny like from a vintage movie reel. His own voice scared him, and saying the old woman's name—or what passed for her name—seemed ridiculous, absurd. She wasn't even in the room. He didn't know if it had been a heart attack, a stroke—*what* it had been. But it was over.

An hour later, the phone was ringing while he was in Granny's bedroom, fishing around under her bed. He found a stocking, the remains of a newspaper—and the shoebox that he was looking for. *Ignore the ringing, nobody calling knows what happened yet.*

John worked mechanically, punching coins from cheap cardboard display folders, harvesting his grandmother's puny collection of pennies, nickels, dimes, quarters, half-dollars, silver dollars, none of them worth much more than face value. Still, they were money, about thirty dollars' worth, too much to sniff at. He added to them several dollars' worth of bicentennial quarters he himself had been hoarding. Ten years earlier, he'd imagined they'd be worth hundreds of dollars by 1986, but they were still worth only twenty-five cents.

All of his Romano memorabilia was secured in the furthest corner of Shelly's closet, all except the poster on his wall. It was a duplicate, so he'd have to sacrifice this one. He took the Seattle guide, a wax-papered unit of Graham crackers, some pens and paper, some postage stamps, the two handfuls of coins, all the underwear, socks, T-shirts, and jeans he could manage, and stuffed it all into his backpack. It sagged low, bouncing against his ass as he left the trailer. He reminded himself aloud to take the coin cases and shoebox with him to dump along the way. No reason to leave any sign that his grandmother had been robbed. She had, but not of very much, and certainly her death had not been planned. Just wished.

He left the trailer, unconcerned about being seen. None of the neighbors ever seemed to notice John, or else they felt too bad for him to look him in the eye.

It took a long while for his bus to make it to the Port Authority in New York, a mythical city he lived only a few hours from and which he'd only visited twice, both on school field trips to museums. Port Authority was large, crowded, loud, smelly. There were magazine kiosks and greasy spoons at every turn, weary travelers, men who looked as if they'd like to kill him, suited men who practically walked through him, whores. He staggered to the Greyhound counter and requested a one-way ticket to Seattle. It cost ninety-eight dollars, eight more than he'd been told on the phone, representing most of what he had. He would have to hope the old man could feed him on his arrival, scheduled for three days later.

Granny.

I've prayed for this was all John could admit to himself. He didn't allow himself any elation at the turn of events, he just put himself on autopilot and took off, huddling into a backseat on the enormous bus, hoping no one would sit by him, satisfied and relieved to have navigated from one state to its neighbor, through a terminal, and onto a big-city bus with no major problems.

He didn't cry.

When the police arrived, alerted by a nosy neighbor who'd become suspicious at all the lights being on for two days straight, they made the grisly find: A drunken old woman had died alone, probably a heart attack or stroke, and was busy rotting in her living room with nobody around to notice or care. The scene was typical in every regard. There was no sign of a break-in, no reason to suspect foul play, nothing removed from the premises—clearly, this elderly lady hadn't possessed anything worth stealing. The first cop there was silently thankful she hadn't had a little dog around the house for company, like so many lonely old ladies did. Starving dogs cooped up with corpses led to scenes that haunted him nights, much more disturbing than even the one time he'd been forced to fire his gun.

The only thing that bothered his partner, a rookie still convinced he would be living *Hill Street Blues* as a policeman, was the room next to hers. The second bedroom suggested she'd had a boarder of some kind, who was nowhere in sight. It was later confirmed by neighbors that the old woman had raised a boy in the trailer, the son—they said—of her daughter, a woman thought to have passed away years before. She had been a drug addict and the source of some neighborhood speculation, had given birth, had disappeared, and then had died. No romance, just an unoriginal, factual life and death.

"I *believe* I heard that he was going away to live with relatives. I'm almost *sure* of that," Mrs. Stevens told the police, not sure at all. She was confusing reality with a storyline from one of her programs. She didn't like answering questions for the police; the last time she'd done it, she'd been talking about her husband's disappearance, and that had ended with positive identification of his body in the Philadelphia morgue.

The boy, John Dewey, hadn't attended school in two weeks, leading the authorities to assume he had left well in advance of his grandmother's death.

"May be what killed her," one cop said. "Some people just can't live alone."

There was no evidence in the trailer of any living relatives, but since the old woman had not been killed or robbed, there was no driving interest in pursuing the absent boy. He was thought to have been seventeen or eighteen, old enough not to be of much concern. Left with no leads and no real reason to suspect anyone was technically *missing,* the case was closed and the boy presumed to be living out of the area, unaware his grandmother was dead.

"He won't miss her if he don't know she's gone," reasoned the officer in charge. The post office was alerted to forward all her mail to the police station in case the mysterious boy wrote from his new home, but all that turned up was a few bills, collection agency threats, local circulars, then nothing.

Shelly heard about the old woman's death in school and assumed John had run away and that he'd be found without her having to speak up. But when there was no word by the end of the school year, she started to forget about him, and instead focused on life with her mother, who was becoming increasingly dotty—Shelly's mother was separating herself from reality as if from a perforated edge.

Shelly wound up storing John's treasure for years.

She remained intrigued by Gil Romano long after she'd started to find Cyndi Lauper laughable, and as a former aficionado she knew better than simply to discard the ancient souvenirs.

If anything, she decided a decade later, *I should sell these.*

She placed several ads in local papers and a few more in collectors' publications, even resorting to a costly blurb at the back of *Movieline.* Just when Shelly was about to give up completely, a guy finally wrote her with an insultingly low bid for the whole kit and kaboodle. She spent her Thursday off boxing it all up and waiting around for UPS to collect it. She hadn't charged the buyer nearly enough for shipping, so she wound up only pocketing about three hundred dollars on the deal. She knew this amounted to highway robbery—what had John Dewey told her his stuff had been worth a decade earlier? Five times that amount? But what good is market value when there's no discernible market? She was just happy to be rid of it after so long, and to have recouped the hundred bucks she'd lent its owner when she'd still been a teenager.

Selling John Dewey's belongings left Shelly with a nagging feeling of doom, like she'd made an unforgivable mistake. She knew he was unlikely to call her up ten years after the fact and demand the return of his collection. Circumstances made it highly unlikely that he'd ever make contact with her again—if he were even alive.

Shelly didn't like not knowing whatever had become of John Dewey, disliked even more the possibility that the one hundred dollars she'd let him borrow had provided a convenient passage to an early death. Worst, she'd never felt right about keeping her mouth shut when the old woman had died and John had gone missing. It was a secret she'd kept for no good reason, just on instinct.

Smoking a cigarette in her bedroom, staring at the newly barren closet where she'd stored his things, thinking about her dead father, Shelly hoped she was doing the right thing in profiting from John Dewey's possessions. She'd already used the three-hundred-dollar money order to absorb a month's worth of student loan payments, and was looking forward to getting ahead for June.

OFF THE LIST

BY WARREN JUNIOR

YOUNG, DUMB & FULL OF GLUM

They're growin' 'em mighty young these days. I've always felt that as time goes by, each Hollywood generation gets closer and closer to being upfront about homosexuality—even shrugging their shoulders at it—though I'm not sure *that's* my ideal, either.

Case in point: Boy Wonder is a mere 15–17 (lawyers have forbidden an exact age since he's *way* easy to guess already, *dude*) and already has four medium hits and one monster smash under his pubescent belt. Most of these movies owe a part of their success to his impishly grinning mug and amusingly airheaded delivery. I hate movies like this, but then I aborted my inner child long ago.

Boy Wonder will grow up to be a real heartbreaker, but he recently confided in some of his equally underaged friends that he apparently just couldn't wait!

Gay since age 8, Boy Wonder has just wrapped his first adult affair. His partner? Mr. Glum, a rather unappealing, never-smiling former costar who should've known better—at 31—than to have frolicked with a rugrat young enough to be his "Go Directly to Jail" card. Sure, Brad and Juliette were hot and heavy when she'd barely had her period yet (she was 16, he 27), but everyone knows queer parallels to potentially risky situations are *that* much *riskier.*

The affair drew to a close when Boy Wonder's Alkie Mommy noticed her lanky son's attachment to the lower-billed and older Mr. Glum and put the kibosh on any further contact, thinking she had helped avert any blossoming romance. *Wrong!* All she did was cut things off well *after* the fact, depriving Boy Wonder of his lessons in "love" and Mr. Glum of his daily forbidden nookie.

Don't look for any smiles on Mr. Glum's face when he starts shooting that big western with You-Know-Who, and *speaking* of *lessons,* don't look for the now-gloomy Boy Wonder at all—to flex his muscle with Alkie Mommy, he's taking a potentially permanent break from Tinseltown to actually *attend* school for the first time in his home-tutored life. Of course, while he's readin', 'ritin' and 'rithmetickin', that means *no* Hollywood paydays. Believe me, Alkie Mommy will drink to that.

What were *you* doing at 16-or-so? Homework? Blow-jobs? Retirement?

When I was 16, I was on a list of underprivileged colored boys waiting to get into fat camp at a reduced rate. Thanks to my wasp waist, I'm now "Off the List."

CHAPTER 22
Crash-Scene Photos!

David Greer — The next day was Tuesday, *Island Rage* day. The paper hit newsstands at noon. I was dying to know if Warren had written anything about Alan before I'd copped to having spoken with him. I turned each page momentously, hunting for where in the paper they'd placed Warren's star column that week. Opposite one of those new Camel ads. Perfect—a two-page spread of stuff that kills people.

His blind item of the day was a strangely elusive story about a famous kid who was being diddled by a less-famous costar. As blatantly obvious as such a description should be (how many people could fit these profiles?), I had not a clue. I made a mental note to call Warren and ask him later. Warren always blabbed his blind items to me. Word of mouth wasn't legally actionable. Yet.

The main body of his nonblind column opened with a prototypical innocuous, nonnewsworthy envelope-pusher, a couple of lines that cashed in on sex and stardom and camp, the three things that made Warren's followers—and all of us, really—go wild:

> Does that out-of-work stud Andrew Stevens realize how much I'd love to suck his dick? I don't think so, because straight as he is he would *be here,* okay? Unemployed, my ass. *I'll* hire him.

Reading along with Warren's star encounters of the week, which plays he adored and which were shit, who was doing who, how unprintably hot the dish had been at his lunch with Paul Baresi, I skimmed for Alan's name or, worse, my own, and found nothing. I'd successfully tricked Warren into thinking that Alan Dillinger's presence at the party had been beneath chronicling. Thank God Carol didn't have a column.

I'd succeeded. And yet now I was reconsidering my deceit in the face of Alan's performance with Sara Pasquale. I considered calling Warren and blowing the whistle, but I couldn't do it. I just didn't want to be the unfamous part of some blind item. Thousands of people would jump at the chance at being Kelsey Grammer's latest talky bimbo or Dick Morris's informative whore or Joan Lunden's tattletale or Kato Kaelin. But I wasn't interested in notoriety just for attention's sake, not even for revenge.

I was in my cubicle at Whole Man, squinting at chromes of naked men, deciding which ones to use next to my review of the latest Catalina fuck flick, *Prickteasers*. The video box was adorned with the ultra-tanned Teddy, an Alan Dillinger clone starring in a porno take-off of *Lifesavers*. Teddy was a low-rent version of Alan, the hair a little over-fried, the body a little underpumped, though the law of averages led me to believe Teddy's horse dick probably compared favorably. I had watched this tape at home without one iota of sexual arousal, stunned to watch Teddy listing through his scenes like a zombie, emotionless even as he was screwed by two dicks at once, a feat that stretched credibility for me, even though it had been captured in full splendor by Chi Chi LaRue's unwavering videocam. Perhaps Chi Chi had received computer animation advice from Robert Zemeckis on this scene; how else to explain the ease with which both condomed schlongs coursed in and out of Teddy's overtaxed tunnel? And didn't the tops resemble Nixon and Clinton?

I think my dick had actually *shrunk* watching this pointless action, unhelped by the blank expression on Teddy's peeling face during the close-ups. "Pack my groceries," he'd mumbled at one point, forgetting the intended exclamation point at the end, incapable of commanding anything at all.

Not that I expected *Citizen Cock* from every release, not that I'd ever bought or rented a porn video in my life, but having to watch two or three dozen a week to review anonymously in *Pumped* had made me into a slight wank snob. I preferred the videos where the men were good at pretending to be excited, and disliked any overt signs of indentured servanthood, drug addiction, discomfort, disgust.

Teddy allowed both men to candy-coat his face with their loads, as we say in the industry. Afterward, he looked like a giant, blond, glazed doughnut from Krispy Kreme. I had leaned forward in suspense, hoping he would not open his eyes until after being toweled clean, but he had already dared one eye open and would show up with a nastily pink peeper in later scenes.

Of course, my review was a full-on rave, giving it eight boners out of ten. I was like the anti-Medved, praising films that pushed the boundaries of decency because it was my job. I was never allowed to offer even the most tactful criticism lest the big, cash-drenched studios pull their full-page ads from our pages. Good reviews = sales = expensive ads = continued publication. I thought this grotesquely unethical tit-for-tat practice was unique to porn mags, though I've since learned it exists in mainstream publications, too, though slightly more undercover.

And here was this video's box with its Alan Dillinger stand-in, the cute kid with the elastic anus and dead eyes, and I simultaneously missed the real thing and mourned the fact that he'd betrayed me.

I also wondered about Teddy's background and his future. I knew as much about Teddy as I did about Alan, when it came down to it. In fact, I knew more, because I had a really bad Xerox of Teddy's driver's license and also of his military ID, representing the two pieces of official identification we were required to keep on file for each and every naked wonder we published. Teddy's real name was Alessandro Pieter. He had been born in Brazil eighteen years earlier, around the same time I was buying clothes for my first year in junior high—1980. Was it really possible that a baby brought into this world in 1980 was ready for double-fucking and semen facials already? Was anyone *ever* ready for that?

Teddy was much younger than I was, way cuter than I'd ever been, was already at the peak of his admittedly not very distinguished profession, and yet I had no doubt he'd have left the planet before I blew out thirty-five candles. Unlike old soldiers, old porn stars *always* die, one way or another. Unless they do some miraculous sort of turnaround, as had that seventies het favorite Harry Reems, who'd saved his life by becoming born-again. So, they either die or you wish they were dead, take your pick.

I wondered how different Alan and Teddy really were, how close Alan had come to pulling a Teddy, to settling on porn and prostitution as ways out of poverty and directionlessness. Alan had told me he'd arrived in L.A. utterly alone at twenty. Warren had repeated rumors that Alan had turned tricks at some point in his life, something that gets said of just about everyone famous, true or false.

Alan's prosperity seemed all the more precious in light of his potential lot in life. Hadn't Sly Stallone done softcore? Arnie let guys ogle his muscled body and had posed nude—I had pictures of him in the same bed with another bodybuilder from an old *After Dark*. Weren't there loops of *The Rifleman* getting his dick sucked? Traci Lords, Vanessa Williams, Demi Moore, Madonna, Matthew McConaughey, Marilyn, Joan Crawford—how far back did it go? An endless parade of comers started out trading on their sexualities—just posing naked or renting their bodies—before being transformed into sex objects. How close had Alan come to winding up at the low end, among the ones who never progress *past* the phase of selling sex to make a splash, the ones whose names no one can list?

I was having second thoughts about Alan. I liked him a lot and the adventure seemed impossible to resist, but was it going to be worth putting up with the closet? The exposure? The inevitable alienation from Warren? And what about Sara Pasquale? Was she a publicity stunt, or was there something I didn't know about Alan? Oh, wait, there were a *million* things I didn't know about him.

"ITS GONNA BE A LONG-HOT SUMMER!" screamed the tag line on the *Prickteasers* box.

CHAPTER 23

Galpal Tells All!

David Greer — I finally broke down and told Carol the whole story. After work, I was propped up on the counter next to her vintage cash register at Gods & Goddesses, the one hiding the ultramodern digital model that kept her books balanced and the IRS at bay.

Carol snapped a wad of gum as I spoke. I'd impulsively brought her two Bazookas from the machine in the ATM lobby, and she'd been so wrapped up in my story she'd peeled them both, discarded the comics and started chewing the flavor out of them before I'd even gotten to the good parts.

I told her about the phone call, the meeting at Alan's apartment, the stalker, the run-on conversation, the kiss, the promised phone call on Friday and—of course—the footage of Alan orally impregnating Sara Pasquale. It's hard enough when you fear that your love interest is on the verge of being stolen by someone else, but somewhat worse when the other woman used to be in your best friend's favorite soap.

"But she was a *really* bad actress," Carol said sensitively. "I think they killed her off."

"So now you know." I sighed, my Alan Dillinger tryst laid out before her.

She tried to convince me that Sara Pasquale had probably just been a publicity stunt, that Alan would have a great explanation. Then she couldn't hold back.

Carol was suppressing laughter, her eyes twinkling at me as she chowed down on the sticky bubblegum. "You little *starfucker* you," she spat, talking around the wad. "And Warren—I can't believe you're not telling him. He's going to . . . I don't even *know!* I can't even *imagine* what he would do if he found this out. And he will."

"He won't," I said, "right *away*. And I was hoping that by the time he *did,* I'd have things sorted out more. I plan to tell him myself, I just need time."

"David, David," she uttered, lowering her voice as a lone customer came in, browsing among the 'zines and local bar flyers stacked by the door. She lunged forward and hugged me, laughing out loud. The customer was startled away by her outburst. "You're the *man,* David," she said, "You are the *man.* Way to go! I mean, I don't envy the Warren conflict, but it's so great that you met up with this guy. I can't believe he'd be so nice—good-looking guys are always such a pain in the ass, let alone *this* one. It's amazing. Well? What did his apartment look like? What did he say? What did you do? Tell me more, tell me more, did ya get very far?"

Carol brought me down to earth, making Alan seem like just another man I was dating and helping to normalize the situation. I felt like I'd let off some steam and that it had done me a world of good. I just hoped she wasn't going to ask me for souvenirs from Alan's home.

"You're so lucky, David," Carol said, beaming, but there seemed to be something darker just behind it. I had a sudden fear that I was a lousy friend, that I'd barged in and started yammering without noticing that *she* had had something to tell *me*.

"What? What's going on?" I asked.

Carol shook her head and retreated behind her register, fondling the ancient, oversized keys. "No, nothing. I don't really want to talk about anything tragic after talking about something so exciting. Believe me— you don't want me dumping on you now."

I pushed and she gave.

"Welllll," she started, laughing at herself, "it seems I've gone and done something rather lame. I answered one of those ads in the *Rage*—"

"You answered a personal ad?" This flew in the face of everything I knew about Carol. It didn't make sense. It was a moment of insight that rattled me, and that took courage on her part.

"Yes. I know what you're going to say, 'personal ads are for lunatics and psychopaths and losers,' but I just really needed to take this risk because I've been high and dry for so long and I felt like I needed to take some sort of action, even stupid action."

Carol had answered an ad in the back of *Island Rage* in the "Romance" section, as distinguished from the "Let's Get It On" section, which she admitted she'd glanced over but had never indulged in. The ad had been placed by someone claiming to be an attractive fortysomething businessman with graying temples and an appreciation for days in museums, backpacking in Europe, and reading novels that challenged one to think. Hearing Carol relate the contents of this ad was dispiriting, in that it effectively reduced my best friend to a grocery list of dating clichés. I couldn't believe she'd been attracted to such a bland ad, that she'd be attracted to *any* ad in the first place.

"So what happened?" I insisted.

"I let myself get *all excited,* David. I should never do that, and I rarely let it get this far, but I went out and bought a killer dress—full-price—and really made the effort to look good. I was turning heads on the way to that restaurant, David, and that's the main thing I got out of this, which is that maybe I shouldn't be so desperate if I'm still turning heads—"

"What happened?"

"Well." She screwed up her face, dreading telling me this. "You *can't tell anyone,* but, anyway. I showed up at Man Ray on Eighth, which is one of my favorites, as you know. I was shown back to our table, and he's sitting there waiting. There was a candle, there was a bunch of flowers in paper, he was wearing my favorite cologne, he had the gray temples and had worn this really nice suit."

"And?"

"And . . ." She rolled her eyes and spat it out, like it was the most distasteful thing she'd ever had to say in her life. "He was a fucking *woman,* David."

I couldn't help cracking up. She smiled, letting me know it was okay.

"I know, I know," Carol said. "I deserve this. I dee-zerve this. I should have known better. I never should have answered that ad. I'll never do it again, but I have to tell you something, David—I didn't expect perfection, I didn't even expect a love connection, but I damn well expected a man."

"Of course," I said, regaining my cool.

"And the worst thing was, she was just sitting there like she expected to get away with it, like taping down your breasts is going to work. I took one look and said, 'Uh, excuse me, but you are a *woman,*' and she said, 'Are you disappointed?' and I said, 'Are you nuts?' I guess she expected to fool me, we'd date for a year, get engaged, have sex, and I'd never figure out this was a woman, like all those stories you hear that come out every once in a while, 'Her Husband Was a She.' I told her I had nothing against lesbianism—and I don't. It's just, I don't know, if you're going to experiment with lesbianism, you might as well do it with another *female,* you know? Not, not . . . not Danny DeVito."

She was massaging her temples and I took over, trying to console her after her nightmare encounter.

"You poor thing," I whispered, soothing. "Carol, you're so far above personal ads you're in *orbit.* Can't you see that?"

"This is the only time I'm going to talk about this, but I have to say I have never felt more desperate in my life, David. I used to have to decide when I would schedule all the dates I was having—you remember?—and now I can go for six months with no possibilities.

"Part of it is age, I know. Guys, no matter how old they get themselves, they all want the perky twenty-year-old, not the ravishing forty-year-old. But Jesus Christ, every man I've looked at twice in recent memory has either been a complete fuckup or gay. This whole city is gay, which is great news for you but a disaster for me. I'm either out of the running or I'm secretly suspecting. How many guys I've dated have later turned out to be gay? Or bi? Like, thirty?"

I'd always felt that gay people had it the hardest, only able to meet up in bars, but it seemed my oldest straight pal was having a tough time of it, too. Where was she supposed to meet the man of her dreams? A *Star Trek* convention?

"Listen, Carol, I know you think I'm just saying this because I'm supposed to, but I sincerely mean it when I say that you are way too good to be answering personal ads and worrying about getting dates. You're gorgeous! You're the most interesting person I know, you've built your own business from scratch—you're a total catch. Maybe it's just a slump, but don't think about it too much, just relax and let things happen as they happen. Get out and socialize more. Look at me—I never would've met Alan if I hadn't gone to that party."

"Yes, David, but I was at that party, too."

"Yes," I said, "yes, you were, and I seem to remember dozens of execs checking you out. You probably would've been approached if you didn't have your fake date on your arm. You know, part of the problem is that whenever we're in social situations, straight men probably get scared off by me being around. They think you're taken."

"Not that you always get dates either, but how do you explain all the gay men who do approach you? Even when we're together?"

"Easy—gay guys know that gay guys hang out with women, and straight guys don't factor that in. Plus gay guys like a challenge, har-har-har."

She seemed mildly cheered. "You're right though, I do remember men noticing me at that party. I also remember a time in my life when worrying whether or not men noticed me was at the bottom of my list. I'm just being silly. Maybe I'm jealous that you got *the* Alan Dillinger."

"Please, I hardly 'got' him. Sara Pasquale went further with him than I did."

"Sorry!" She sucked air through her teeth at her faux pas. "But just in case you do get Alan Dillinger, promise to leave Harrison Ford for me, okay?"

"Deal." I think we both knew I had no shot at him. We also both knew that, given the chance, I'd break that promise.

"Thanks for listening, David," she said. "Hey, you want some leftovers? I have half a steak from Man Ray in the fridge." She started toward her back room and I stepped aside as two teenage girls entered the store, agog at all the dated Hanson and Spice Girls posters on the walls.

"Leftovers? You actually *stayed* and *ate* with that woman from the ad?"

"Sure, David," she said, back to her business voice again. "It *was* free."

CHAPTER 24

Haven

John Dewey — It was almost midnight when Truitt Connor's eyes snapped open at the sound of a fist tapping on his front door. He could hear it distinctly, though a wave of doubt passed over him. He never had visitors, and any he'd have would call on him at a more humane hour.

Didn't matter. He wasn't a sleeper.

Pulling himself up took longer than it would've taken him to get all the way to the door just a few years earlier.

Bette Davis had a pillow in her home embroidered with the legend: "Old age isn't for sissies." In the fifties, in his fifties, Truitt might have admired such a cheeky statement. But in his seventies, when he'd heard about it, it had made him profoundly sad, like a death sentence. Or a life sentence, since he was, if nothing else, still alive. Truitt had felt his seventies were unsurvivable, one long, humbling lesson in the limits of the human body, or at least of his own. He'd gotten so frail after bypass surgery, had lost most of his sexual abilities, gotten lazy, slow.

Now, recently into his eighties, Truitt actively hoped he would die soon. Life was full of too many tiny pains, great labors, and stretches of aloneness. The year sounded impossibly high: *1986!* It gave him comfort to know it was virtually unthinkable that he'd hang around to see 2000. He felt like he was killing time and vice versa.

Truitt made it to the door long after it had been answered by his live-in nurse, Strella, a commanding woman who took her job to be that of his babysitter, even though he paid her himself. He had no ungrateful adult children instructing her to run roughshod over him, one distinct advantage of being a homosexual.

Strella was a home tyrant, but she was effective and loyal. There was affection deep underneath layers of concrete efficiency.

"You—back to bed," she snapped, her words slurred with impatience. Her eyes were trained on Truitt with unmercy, daring him to defy her. She wore her hair close to her skull, so it wasn't askew, even in the middle of the night. Her robe was the only giveaway of the hour.

"What is it? Who's there?" he asked, not recognizing the rusty tinge in his midnight voice. Truitt angled to get a peek out the door as his hired help tried to fend him off.

"Now, now, you go on back to *bed,*" she said firmly, making each word its own, overenunciated sentence. When he'd hired her, she'd claimed to be from the Philippines, but in recent years had admitted she was not sure of her ancestry. She'd been abandoned to an orphanage in the middle of Montana and raised by nuns, a tiny brown dot on a field of white. She'd made her way to Seattle as a young woman, vowing never to allow any men into her life. A few helped her break that promise. She had raised a son under Truitt Connor's roof, an insolent and unimaginative hooligan now moved into his own apartment in sunny California, much to the relief of her employer.

Truitt shrugged off Strella's insistent directives and looked out at the figure planted on his doorstep. It was pouring down rain, a condition he computed when he heard a distant thundercrack and smelled ozone in the air, before realizing water was everywhere. The boy standing outside his home was soaking wet, a river of rainwater streaming off the point of his chin, his mouth open with the shock of the cool water in the cool night.

Truitt assesed the boy as round, uninteresting, no beautiful angles to his build. He was unused to dealing with homely boys, only handsome ones, bodybuilders who would come to his home and smile and pump his hand and talk about their girlfriends as they removed their clothes to stand stock-still for his cameras. Letting him point his lenses at their cocks and asses and backs and biceps and simple grins and oiled hair.

But he hadn't worked as a photographer for over twenty years, not since the last and worst time he'd been raided.

"Who is it? Who's there?" he asked, alarmed, although the chubby boy was right before his eyes, not hunched in the far-off darkness.

"Mr. Connor?" the kid asked, eyes beseeching.

"Who *are* you?" Truitt repeated, shivering at the open door. Strella threw her hands up behind him, telling herself out loud that the old man would invite the devil himself into his home at any hour.

"My name is John Dewey. I wrote you before," John said, trying to put the words together delicately, to receive the desired response. "I'm the one who wrote you about the movies?" Blankness in reply. "About *Midsummer Night's Dream*? About Gil Romano?"

"Oh! *Yes!*" Truitt exclaimed, desperately pleased to have made the connection. He belatedly welcomed the boy inside and sent a reluctant Strella off to find clean towels from the upstairs bath. As he entered, John shrank from Truitt's feather-light touch on the outsides of his arms, his immediate presumption of ownership.

"*You,*" Truitt said accusingly, merrily, "are the young man who shares my appreciation for Gil Romano. You wrote me a letter after you read about my *Midsummer Night's Dream.*"

"Yes," John said, relieved, terrified. "Yes, that's right. That's me. I'm really sorry it's so late, but I"—searching—"I just came from the bus station, my bus got here way later than it was supposed to, and I don't have a, uh, hotel. I was planning to find one if my bus got here on time, and I really didn't have anyplace I could . . ." He trailed off, catching his breath, distracted by the wrinkles in Truitt Connor's face.

John had known his correspondent—who, after all, had been a projectionist from practically the silent era—would be old. But knowing that a man is over eighty and seeing a man over eighty, a man who has not been blessed with the unnatural preservation common among movie stars, are two different things. John was silenced by his host's unmistakable decrepitude, his profound fragility. John felt like he was embarrassing the old man just by looking at him. Granny had left him shy of the aged.

"Nonsense!" Truitt exclaimed, too pleased to have company to worry that he was in a state of disrepair, to obsess over the fall of his white hairs, the position of his pajamas, the heft of his expanded belly.

As a young man, Truitt Connor had had a dreamy quality in his dark eyes, a glossy, unmasculine beauty that had been his pride. He'd embraced his vanity, indulging in fine clothes and spending more time in front of a mirror than any of his female friends. He'd enjoyed the looks he'd gotten from men, had used his attractive appearance like a muscle.

Even in decline, he'd struggled to look handsome and fit, stylish. But eventually, he'd retreated into sloppy comfort, realizing that nobody was around to notice whether or not he was appropriately attired or slender or pleasing to the eye. Not long after, he'd stopped taking satisfaction from his own appearance in any way unless an outsider encroached on his inner sanctum, and even then—as with the midnight boy—he rarely bothered. He forgot to care, a current phrase he'd been using a lot when talking with Strella, a canned line lifted from a bawdy television show.

Escorted into a dim kitchen, seated at a groaning chair before a well-worn table, John couldn't help looking around the place uncomfortably, unconvinced he had the right man. How could someone living nearly as econonically as he had with Granny have a collection of movie treasures? Maybe John had guessed wrong—maybe Truitt Connor was a phony.

Strella was toweling John's head brusquely, continuing with her monologue about trust and late hours and pneumonia as if she were preaching a sermon. The kitchen had the sharp, permanent odor of spiced food boiled into the paint.

Truitt examined the boy and deduced that he was probably only sixteen or seventeen years old, and that the story of his arrival had to be an untruth. He probably wasn't supposed to be there at all, which could only create problems for the aging sex offender. That's exactly what he was to the police, no better than a common rapist or pedophile, all for taking lovely photographs of naked, willing, adult men. *Decades ago.*

Truitt smiled with effort to cover his thoughts, a nervous tic. He looked eerily intent as he circled John, baring his teeth, speechless.

His voice startled John after such a long lull.

"Mr. Dewey," he began diplomatically, "it's a pleasure to have you here. I'm always thrilled to have guests, no matter the hour. And don't take this question in the wrong spirit, but do your parents know you have made this trip?"

Strella stopped drying him to hear the answer.

"No," John replied truthfully. "They're dead. I'm on my own. I'm eighteen, so I can be wherever I want to be with nobody knowing where I am."

"Eighteen." Strella harrumphed. There was no fooling her, John sensed dimly, but would it matter?

"You're eighteen?" Truitt asked, brightening at the phrase he knew he needed to hear, the phrase he'd hunted for in the old days, whenever a prospective model showed up, referred to him by some past subject. "Well, then forgive my asking. I just wanted to be sure you weren't running away from anyone who might come looking for you and might not appreciate my housing you. You should feel welcome to stay the night here, and in the morning we'll start digging around for what Gil Romano items I may have. What about Valentino? Are you a fan of the Great Lover's?"

John blushed deeply. "No, I prefer Gil Romano," he muttered, suddenly shy after all the necessary talk was out of the way. Instinctively, it felt funny discussing male stars in front of a woman. "I like, um, Gil Romano more than his competition."

"E-*nough*," proclaimed Strella, clearing the table's corner and coming to Truitt's side to guide him away. "I'm getting this one into bed right this second before he's awake one minute longer." She whisked Truitt away at the fastest pace he could accommodate.

"You may have the couch," Truitt managed to say over his shoulder. "I'm sure you'll find it beats all that mess outside. Good night, eh— *John*."

John sat in the kitchen awaiting Strella's return, her icy rebuffing, her assistance with his bed for the night.

I'm here, he thought giddily, *I'm here. It was easy. I made it. I'm going to see the movie. I'm going to see it.*

CHAPTER 25

Suddenly Single!

David Greer — Finally, it was Friday. I woke up at six in the morning with no help from my alarm, showered, had some grapes, and sat next to the phone like it was a dying aunt requiring comfort in her hour of need.

Alan had promised to call that day in the wee hours before I left for work. I hadn't given him my work number.

My guy may have swapped spit with Sara Pasquale on national television, but I was relying on him to call me as planned. I *needed* him to follow through with this much, at least. If the call ended in a shouting match and I never heard from him again, and no one but Carol ever believed I'd met him in the first place, so be it. But *please call me, Alan. Please call.*

At 7:45, when I'd almost lost hope, the phone rang.

"Hello?"

"Hold for Alan Dillinger," came a teensy little voice, the voice of an underling with three cups of coffee in her. She was probably an assistant of Alan's, or perhaps a sort of *Lifesavers* gofer.

It wasn't even five in the morning in L.A., and yet Alan was already awake and prepared for a day of filming on the beach. He must have used a bottle of sunscreen a day to avoid third-degree burns. I could imagine his body roasting in the rays.

"Hello, David?" Alan sounded more focused and formal than I had been expecting, like he was checking my name off a list of things to do before shooting commenced.

I held my nose and did my best Brooklynese. "Hold for David Gree-ah, please." I waited twenty seconds and then came on.

"So, you have your flunkies calling me?" I asked, confrontational from the get-go. I'd tried to be funny, but it had come out as hurt and angry. I hate when my emotions win.

Alan seemed blindsided. "Look, I have to be on the set like ten minutes ago. I have to make every second count, okay? What's your problem?" Then, quickly and quietly, "I *missed* you."

"I missed you, too," I replied coldly, "but then I had footage of you to remember you by. I saw you on TV with Sara Pasquale. At first I thought I was seeing things, but they tastefully blurred her things out."

Leaden. "Oh, you saw it?"

"Oh, I saw it. What's going on? What were you doing with her? Are you into girls?"

"It happened before I even met you. It's just a PR thing," Alan said dismissively. "Truthfully, I can't stand her, but she's itching for some attention and Shara pushed me to put on a little show. There was this guy there with a video camera. He thought he was getting away with murder, but it was all planned." Alan laughed hollowly, forcing it. He was trying to lighten the incident. "Don't you see how funny that is?"

I didn't. "And how does this relate to your *plan* to come out when the movie's released? This is such *bullshit*."

"David," he said, his voice deepening. I sensed someone had stepped into the room with him. "Gotta go, man. I'm due on the set *right now*. I'll call you tonight when I get to New York." Then, he whispered, "Just so you know, Shara is telling people you're my New York assistant."

You can tell the public anything you want, I thought. *But the question will be if anyone with a brain* believes *it*. Does anyone really believe that "Gomer Pyle" got hepatitis after cutting himself with a straight razor while shaving in India? And if he did, then whose asshole was he trimming?

"I have to run—honestly, David."

"Yeah, okay," I said bitterly. "I'm really sorry to keep you, Mr. Dillinger. I'm sure you have things to deny that you do." I slammed the phone down and didn't pick it up when it rang three times a few seconds later. It echoed around me, shrill and distorted, sounding submerged, leaving the room weirdly expectant when I refused to answer and it ceased midring.

The phone call hadn't gone at all like I'd hoped. I'd wanted Alan to apologize for the footage, to come up with a perfectly sound reason why it existed. I wanted him to tell me he was dying to see me, that he was coming over to my apartment that night, that he didn't care who saw him enter at 9 P.M. and exit the next morning at 10:30 A.M. I wanted, it seemed, way too much.

I called in sick. I needed the time to be alone and to do something I almost never did and that I had no business doing at that point in my life—I had to bawl my eyes out, eating chocolate and watching *Leeza*.

CHAPTER 26

Hollywood Whodunit!

David Greer—I was recovered from my minibreakdown, I was dressed, I was lying on my stomach on the floor absently watching Lifetime, "Television for Women," when my doorbell buzzed. It startled me—one good thing about my building was having a doorman, and though he always let food bearers in unchecked, I hadn't ordered takeout. Who had come up to see me? Who could it be except for the one person I couldn't believe it *would* be?

I stood up and peered through the eyehole, hoping to see Alan Dillinger and not the next Andrew Cunanan. Jackpot.

I opened the door. Alan was standing there with a flower for me, a weary-looking pansy with a ribbon tied around it rather hastily. He was disheveled, obviously fresh from a plane. He hadn't shaved, the dark stubble of his natural beard contrasting with the sunny glow of his hair, the brightness in his eyes. I softened immediately, an unexpected wave of relief rolling over me—he'd come through. I was pissed off at him, but he'd come through.

"I missed you," he said, stepping forward and taking hold of me, hugging me tightly. "And I'm so sorry. I almost screwed things up, didn't I?" He whispered in my ear, apologizing over and over, saying my name. It was like we hadn't seen each other in years, but it hadn't even been a week. I let him apologize without saying anything myself, too caught up to respond.

Mrs. Simpson chose this moment to emerge from her apartment, the noises of her sudden progress making us jump in place. There was no chance that Tabloid Tess wouldn't recognize Alan on the spot, so I grabbed his head and buried his face in my chest just as she poked her head out.

"Oh!" she gasped. "I heard voices. Is anything the matter?"

"No," I whispered over Alan's shoulder, "my friend just had some bad news." I rocked Alan maternally. "Please just—" I nodded her back toward her apartment, and she complied, the look of concern on her face so solemn it seemed to hover in the air after she'd pulled her head back into her rooms and secured the door.

Knowing she was bound to be staring through the eyehole, I awkwardly hugged Alan toward me and into my apartment. He pulled the door shut with his foot, hopping the rest of the way in. Concealed, we broke into giggles, trying to keep quiet so Mrs. Simpson wouldn't hear our merriment through the walls.

Alan looked around at my apartment, marveling at the kitsch. If I hadn't seen *his* place already, I might have believed he was impressed with where I lived. At most, he must have been amused. But hadn't he lived in a small place once, not so many years before? Hadn't I heard he'd once lived on the street, that he'd been an extra in *My Own Private Idaho?*

"Your place is great," Alan said simply, handling my Boy George doll, my Gay Bob, my brand-new Billy with the obscenely bloated prick and pride necklace. I kept Wonder Woman intertwined with the much bigger Xena, and the male dolls always seemed to be positioned in front of or behind each other in meaningful ways.

I realized at that moment that thirty-two might be a good age to get over dolls.

"I'm surprised you're here," I replied. I was always good at moving things in the direction I wanted them to go because I never minded being obvious. I liked being direct when I could. Alan didn't.

"Let's just forget everything, okay?" he suggested, mugging with the earnest cuteness of a child star. "I just want to start over." He employed his charm like a semiautomatic.

I sat down on my futon, looking up at him, wishing I hadn't worn my by-then dated T-shirt that said "p*o*r*n*s*t*a*r" in lowercase letters across the chest. Every kid in the Village had bought and worn the same shirt over the past year. I used to be good at finding shirts and other personal statements that nobody else discovered, relishing the annoying attention when strangers would stop me and compliment me or react to my opinionated garment. But there in my apartment, I felt like nothing so much as an aging hipster. It didn't help my discomfort that Alan could practically extend his arms straight out and touch the opposite walls of my human cage.

"Well, I don't think we can start *over*," I said, "but I would like to get past this . . . argument. I just don't want to feel like a business contact, you know? I want to be called when you say you'll call me, and I want to hear from *you*, not your assistant. I know you're busier than I'll ever be, but, I don't know, I just want to make this . . . *normal*." It sounded like wishful thinking even as I said it.

Alan sat beside me, finally dropping his crammed-full carry-on, and grasped my hands. His own hands, younger, were nonetheless paternal as I stared at their rugged skin, their size, felt their assurance. His long, thick fingers moved in unexpected patterns over my palms, turned me on with their contact. I imagined a finger from one hand thrust inside me as I sucked a finger from the other.

"I know, I'll try not to let the star trip interfere. It's not me, David," he said insistently, "I'm not Mr. Superstar, you know? I'm a regular person doing some very irregular things. I mean, I was in California today, shooting a scene on the beach with Debbie Reynolds."

I laughed. "Hardly the nymphet I would've imagined."

"Yeah, she's a guest star playing my character's grandma."

I wanted him, but I pushed it anyway, self-sabotaging. "What about Sara Pasquale? What's she playing?"

Alan looked guiltily away from me. "*That*—was a mistake. I just . . . I know it may seem manipulative and weird to, you know, to plant a story like this. And I know it makes you think that I'm bullshitting about coming out at some point." Yes, I did think that. "But—*how can I make you understand?*—when I first started doing interviews and photographers started popping up out of the bushes, it was a very strange feeling. It was like, even though I was in total control of my acting and of what jobs I took and of all these businessy aspects of my life, even though all that was coming together, I was losing control in my personal life. I started having to make time to give people autographs, I had to spend hours on the phone giving stupid interviews to magazines that would print these stories about me being a fucking prostitute or something—it was like I was losing my grip on the real me even though the fake me, the actor part of me, was falling into place."

I noted his implicit denial of the prostitution rumors and softened, wondering if even someone as skeptical as I could have been taken in by factless gossip, sleazy speculation that nonetheless was drenched in romance: Massively popular star sleeps his way to the top. Still, you should never rely totally on an informed denial—they're so often hair-trigger damage control.

"Go on," I urged. "It helps hearing this stuff because I can't—I can't really *relate* to it."

"Well, I feel like I have no control, and reporters and the paparazzi can sometimes take over your life. Like, if I go out to eat, not only do I get a steady stream of people saying they're sorry to interrupt but could they please kiss my cheek? I also get minipress conferences springing up around me. It's more than an inconvenience, David, it's like you have no private life sometimes, unless you're at some asshole's mansion with guards posted outside, and what kind of life is that?"

He struggled to pull off his heavy boots, untucked his shirt, and lay down on what for a normal person would have been his belly. I couldn't help shifting closer to him, drawn.

"So, I started to do little things to get revenge on them," he blurted, as if the new comfort had freed up his thought processes.

"Revenge?"

"Yeah," he said. "Instead of bending over backwards for everybody, I put a lid on the interviews except for when they were to promote something important. I stopped posing for pictures unless it was necessary to plug the show, or unless Shara made the photographers sign all these guarantees that they couldn't be sold to the tabloids, that they couldn't be sold to anybody *we* didn't approve of. I started talking back when the producers wanted me to tour the malls and judge Miss Universe and shit. But the best thing of all is to fool the reporters and the paparazzi, make them write some strange shit about you or take misleading photos." He smiled at remembered antics, stealthy hits.

"Like what?" We started eating the chocolate-covered peanuts I'd been numbly scarfing before he'd arrived.

"Like making everyone believe I was sitting there making out with Sara Pasquale for real, when everybody with brains has heard I'm a three-dollar bill. Or telling people fake stories about my life, lying about my age, telling them I was in movies that I really *wasn't,* just to see how many times the titles turn up in filmographies."

"*My Own Private Idaho?*" I asked.

"Please—even Gus Van *Sant* thinks I was in that," he said. "The best thing ever was last year, when I got drunk and stayed over at Kathy Najimy's place—we did a dog food commercial together years ago. We had this girlie slumber party and these photographers took pictures of me leaving in the morning. Everyone on the outside thinks we did it, but we didn't. It's just fun sometimes to lie and to make the press believe you."

"But see, I like honesty," I said. "I don't want you lying to *me* about things, too, you know? And besides, why couldn't you get drunk and sleep over at Rupert Everett's house and have fun making the press think you did it with *him?*"

He shook his head. "Aw, you take me too seriously, too, David. It's just a game for now. I promised I'd take you to my movie premiere. I'll be good and come out. You gotta believe me on that. Just let me do it my way, on my terms, man."

I believed he wanted to be out, but suspected it wouldn't be as easy as he thought. He didn't seem to have a game plan after all, only a game.

His impish streak made him cute, his body sexual. I couldn't help the warmth in my chest when I thought about him.

"Besides," he said slowly, "most of the papers wouldn't print a story about me fucking a guy. It just isn't done."

Along the way, we'd jettisoned the political overtones of what we were saying, so that all that really connected from his last sentence was "me fucking a guy."

I lay on my side, peeking up at him, willing him to push things further than friendship.

Alan was on his elbows, the closeness a hot thrill. Erotic geography. I could feel his breath on my forehead. I could smell his body, the musk after a cross-country flight, sweat, oil, the aroma of privacy. I was hard in my jeans and aware that if he were looking at my crotch—and what gay man wouldn't be monitoring a close-range, unguarded crotch?—he could probably tell.

Suddenly, I felt Alan's hand at my side, digging into my jeans and tugging my shirt up. I sort of lost control for an instant, swept up in his undressing me, wanting me. I looked straight up into the unfathomable blue of his eyes and studied the surprising wonder in his face, apparent even upside down.

He stopped when my shirt was bunched under my arms, my entire torso bared, my chest hairs tingling, nipples hard as fingertips. I was aroused, and yet fighting second guesses—it was hard to lie there with my problem areas exposed to his gaze. But Alan wasn't a critical person like me, didn't analyze anything, just accepted it.

"I like your chest," he said. His own chest was like sculpture.

"Thanks," I mumbled. "It's not . . . I'm not very—"

"No, it's sexy," he said, running those smooth fingers through the hairs, avoiding contact with my nipples, not taking it to that level yet. "I like your hairy chest. It's natural. I think mine is kind of plain and boring, but everyone likes chests to look this way on TV."

We laughed and I convinced myself he wasn't just being astonishingly kind. After the chuckle, we were more relaxed, more prepared.

"Yeah, well, I appreciate hearing that. I'm a little self-conscious about my body," I admitted, ashamed and yet also proud to be as forthcoming as he had been. My secrets couldn't be sold, but they were just as valuable to me as Alan's were to him. "I've porked out a bit since my peak."

Alan ran his hands down my sides, touching the small love handles that vexed me to no end. "You mean this?" he asked, grasping them like he was back doing the Special K commercials that had first gotten him noticed by TV brass. "This is nothing," he said almost contemptuously. "I was an ugly kid—once you're self-conscious, you always will be. You never forget it, and it makes you immune to small imperfections. Once you've been there, you can appreciate it," he said.

"But you're not fat. I know because I was kinda fat for a long time. You're just real," he said approvingly. His hands came back up to my chest and grasped my pecs, his palms pressing my nipples. "I love that."

I moaned a little, arching my back, wanting to fit entirely under the scorching flatness of his outstretched palms. He ran his hands back down my belly, his fingers sliding under my jeans to lodge just beneath the waistband of my underwear, just above the hairs that surrounded my swollen cock. His face was in my neck, his lips kissing me lightly behind my ear. I was ecstatic, leaking with need.

"Is it okay?" he asked, like a teenager having sex for the first time. I nodded. "Yeah . . ."

He fumbled with my zipper, undoing it slowly so I could watch my own helpless striptease. My cock was pushing my cheap black briefs up and out obscenely. I could only stare at it dumbly, surprised to be seeing myself from that angle, his hands controlling me every step of the way. He mumbled something else in my ear, too close and wet to hear, but I could feel his breath sputtering.

Pulling himself further into me, he gained enough slack to push my jeans down and then to grip the elastic at the top of each leg. It was an exquisite unveiling, a prolonged, agonizing pleasure—I didn't feel like I could take his orchestrated sex for long without direct, brutal stimulation.

Finally, he tugged my briefs down, over and away from my erection, the material burning over the sensitive ridge of the head. My cock stood straight up in the firmest hard-on of my life. It looked so sexily displaced there, a dick out on the futon when it was my couch instead of when it was my bed.

Alan reached over and enveloped my cock between his hot hands, the sensation dousing me in pleasure, security. He held my cock with the familiarity of holding his own, stroked me knowledgeably and without hesitation.

"Oh, God," I breathed.

"I know," Alan whispered. "I know."

His tongue darted in and out of my ear, teasing me as one hand caressed me below and the other rose to taunt my nipple. I'd never experienced a more loving barrage of stimuli, a more unselfish sexual encounter with any man, let alone one famous for his star ego. You don't typically think of studs like Jean-Claude Van Damme as being especially giving in bed and yet Alan Dillinger seemed almost selfless the first time we made love, almost lost in his discovery of my body.

Cupping the fullness of my testicles in his hand and kneading them to the brink of pain, he continued to flick his fingers over my chest, stroking the hair and pinching my nipples. I felt like a spoiled pet.

"I could almost come this way," I remember saying after long minutes of his milking my balls, nudging my tits.

"Then why don't you?" he directed, increasing the touch of his hands and fingers and mouth and of his broad shoulders against me and behind me. I felt overloaded, bogged down by feeling good. I couldn't focus on any one part of my body as he managed to concentrate on provoking every part at once. He knew exactly where to touch me, when, and how. He was able to predict each body craving just before it dawned on me.

He slipped the tip of his finger inside my clenched ass, stretching, then suddenly stroked my hard cock. He pumped and prodded me until I lost myself and heard a low moan as I felt my semen coating me, raining onto my chest, his arms, his hands. I couldn't catch my breath as his fingers insisted on infinitesimal kisses all over my tingling body.

I felt momentarily exhausted by the enormity of my orgasm. It was rare that someone could push every button as perfectly as he had, and only with his hands. He'd timed my release as if I were jerking myself off; I sat up in shock.

Alan sat up next to me, nuzzling me and nibbling my chin. When I opened my eyes, he was pressing his lips against mine, and our tongues met in our first legitimate kiss.

"I wanna show you," he said, taking my hands and unbuttoning his shirt. He stripped his clothes away and pulled me down on top of him, guiding me as if I might be too afraid to touch him. When he erased his shorts, I saw something that one hundred million fans worldwide knew for certain they'd never see—I saw Alan Dillinger's tan line and beyond.

Alan guided my hands over his brown, smooth, firm body, instructing me on the places to touch, to pinch, to grasp. There's an unreality in having sex with a perfectly developed body. Bodies like Alan's are the Holy Grail for some men, even for men like me who've resisted succumbing to the stale idea of Greek proportions as the ideal, of gym fitness as the ultimate. I had decided that physical perfection was not the highest goal in life, and yet faced with Alan's I was reduced to excitement and wonder—a child with the asked-for toy at Christmas.

It didn't take long for Alan to throw his arms back over his head and allow me to take over. I buried my face in his body, nipping and licking his salty skin from shoulder to pec to ab to thigh. I allowed his erection to roll under my cheek as I sucked each of his heavy testicles, pulling them away from his body with my hungry mouth. He spread his legs and allowed me to eat him alive, to smother his flesh with my hunger.

My hands, my tongue, touched every part of him, and I wound up behind him, my arms wrapped around him, his ass pressed against my still-hard cock as I jerked him off. The whiteness of his pelvis kept me as hard as if I hadn't come already. His white ass sandwiched between the planes of brown was a new preference for me, the kind of sexual discovery that gets rarer with each person you sleep with, each possibility experienced. His sun-stained skin made his cock and ass into magnets, or, no, targets—they drew my eyes and made me want to keep my mouth all over them, to grasp his ass while my own darker cock split it in measured thrusts.

I knew we wouldn't fuck with no condoms on hand—I'd recently ditched my aging supply rather than rely on them only to one day tear them open and find them in dust, way past their expiration. But I didn't need to actually fuck Alan for the idea to charge our bond.

He was extremely energized as I brought him closer and closer, squirming against me, rubbing his ass against me animalistically, communicating how far he'd be willing to go with me—as far as he was capable. Under other circumstances, I'd have been inside him when he came, but it was a small sacrifice and didn't lessen the rush when he shouted my name and decorated the futon under us, my hand glued to his prick and my cock safely embedded between his buttocks but well away from the most sensitive spot.

I held him as he came down from it, our bodies smoldering in repose.

It was the kind of sex stars aren't supposed to have, not really. There were no tabloid headlines or sleazy rumors, no gossips clucking, their tongues firmly in cheek. It was visceral, drowned in scent and sensation.

"I'll bring condoms next time," he murmured. "I want you to fuck me. I want to fuck you." We were still close enough to the sex to be able to speak frankly.

"I know," I said. "I know."

We spent the rest of that first night kissing and exploring, but there was the promise that we were only breaking the surface.

CHAPTER 27

Found

John Dewey — There was no doubt about the smell. It was the same whiff of aging that had always wafted from under Granny's tattered tank tops, the scent of the elderly, of infrequent trips to a risky bathtub. It was present in Truitt Connor's home—everywhere but the kitchen— but not nearly as severely as it had been in John's, thanks to Granny.

But aside from Strella's cooking and Truitt's decay, the home had other smells. There was the unmissable odor of photography, of developer fluid, the high, heady stink of film, though he shouldn't have been able to smell any of that so many years after they'd been in active use. He remembered the scents from a trip to the film archive of a local TV station back home. He'd gone on a class trip and had blocked out all the kiddie tour information, preoccupied with the reels of film stored just out of reach.

He was nestled into the small, comfortably broken-down sofa, wrapped in a mothy afghan, warm as grilled cheese. It had been so late his hosts hadn't considered that John might be hungry. In truth, he'd been starving. He'd long ago crunched through all of his Graham crackers, and had only indulged in a couple of Marathon bars obtained at gas stops along the way, savoring the tough, resistant caramel, too afraid to spring for anything more expensive until he was safely on Truitt's step.

It was the middle of the night and he was an official if unexpected houseguest—he was going to have to eat immediately. His stomach felt twisted into knots, like it was about to give up.

John slowly extricated himself from the fuzzy afghan and crept blindly through the dark toward the kitchen, retracing his steps. The sensation was uncanny, wandering in the darkness of a strange home three thousand miles away from the drama of Granny's death. It was like walking a tightrope.

The linoleum was still damp, with pools of water marking the spots where he'd stood earlier draining off the wet the skies had dumped on him; it seeped through his socks as he made his way to the refrigerator, chilling his toes.

Expecting nothing more elaborate than a peanut butter and jelly sandwich, John was elated to see the icebox packed to the gills with not only an abundance of food, but an inexplicable variety. There were sardines in tin cans painted with colorful mascots—teensy, comic-eyed, yellow fishes dressed in tunics, offering ruby-red grins; half a baked ham steeped in gelled-over juices under a hastily torn sheet of aluminum foil; an ornate if aged platter of cheeses and chips and dips and some sort of meaty spread; several unopened boxes of King Dons, Little Debbies, Hostess Fruit Pies; industrial-sized plastic gallon-jugs of condiments, white, yellow, green, and tabasco red; two large loaves of bread, one white and one rye; more plastic baggies bursting with fruits and vegetables than he could readily take in.

John felt a string of saliva pour from his mouth before he could catch himself, felt his stomach wrench with impatience. Checking to see that his movements and the soft glow from the fridge's interior hadn't brought footsteps from above, he dove into the ham, grabbing out fatty chunks and stuffing his face with his bare hands. He went through two apple pie snacks before seizing into painful hiccups that slowed him, allowing him to wait until his first pig-out had hit the bottom of his stomach. Then he removed ingredients and made himself a large ham sandwich to be eaten alongside several snack cakes. Even after he'd removed so many items and silently toweled off the counter to make his pillaging undetectable at best, politely necessary at worst, the hoard of food appeared unchanged, undiminished. John sat at the kitchen table in the pitch black, slowly sucking down each coveted bite until he felt his bowels tug.

He knew there was an upstairs bath, but if he used it, he'd risk waking Strella and having to deal with her. Instead, he wondered if he could find a bathroom downstairs, anxious for an excuse to at least *peek* down there, see if it housed a massive screening theater or a safe full of movies. He didn't know exactly what to expect.

John wasn't afraid of the dark at all. He'd never allowed himself luxurious fears, fears based on what-ifs and nonsensical fantasies. He wasn't scared of monsters, dragons, the bogeyman, the dark. He was afraid of starvation, death, being attacked, robbery. Reality.

He felt his way down the stairs, apprehensive that they might be creaking as a prelude to snapping, but deciding logically that Truitt Connor's girth would have brought them down long before if they were anywhere near collapse. At the foot, he could see that he was in a large cellar, but that it appeared to be jammed with tall bookshelves that aisled off its space. It wasn't just cool down there, it was *freezing*. Before he could decide whether he thought it was natural, he became aware of the low, even hum of a machine somewhere; there was a cooling system in place, a sign that there was film nearby.

Other things he noticed about the basement: It didn't seem musty and there were no visible water heaters or other household mechanics. It felt more like a small convention hall than a cellar.

There was a small, doorless bathroom opposite the noisy stairs, and John bolted into it, dropping his pants, sitting on the toilet, and releasing almost out of control. He was shaken by the idea of shitting with the door open, even if there was no light to illuminate his shame and certainly nobody nearby to witness it. He was grateful for the flaky rolls of toilet paper he found stacked on the floor, an afterthought. Now there was another odor in the house, his own stench.

There was a metal door inside the bathroom, behind which John could faintly hear a boiler, where he imagined a sump pump and other more common cellar implements were housed. He listened to their mechanical pace as he wiped himself and flushed the toilet, holding the lid shut to suffocate the noise.

After he'd pulled up his pants, he spotted a dangling bare bulb in the cellar a few feet away. John figured that the bulb would give off enough light to make the bookshelves visible and yet not enough to attract anyone's attention in case Truitt or Strella happened into the kitchen in search of a glass of water or a 3 A.M. snack.

He shuffled to the light, almost stumbling over two folding chairs leaned against the side of the stairwell. The bulb clicked to a glow when he tugged the chain, and all John could do was stare at the discovery of his lifetime.

The cellar was not full of bookshelves, it was full of stacked film canisters, reel upon reel in lopsided columns in row after row, reaching as high as six feet in some places. The canisters were metal, a thousand different shades of gray, with titles inked on in a crisp hand. The one closest to him was *THE HEIRESS ('49)*, an Olivia de Havilland movie he'd never seen but which he had read about in his Oscars book. He thought he'd read that parts of it were considered lost, victimized by impulsive theater owners and the nonexistent preservation considerations of the late forties. But he knew he'd be jumping the gun to guess that this could be a complete, original reel. Surely not *all* of these films would be one-of-a-kind, or even rare. Bearing that out, *GONE W. T. WIND ('39)* rested in three large installments under *THE HEIRESS ('49)*, and under that, *ABBOTT & COSTELLO MT. FRANKENSTEIN ('48)*.

As John moved from stack to stack, timidly reading the titles, he realized that the first few stacks nearest the steps were the more recent titles, from the forties and later, mostly big-name films that would be familiar to anyone, not just buffs. But beyond these, the titles became obscure to him, the dates more distant. John loved old movies, of course, and read about them every chance he got, but he knew that he wasn't an absolute expert, couldn't be expected to know every single title. Just because he didn't recall *GINGER TALES ('19)*, didn't mean it wasn't a famous film, or that it was a last surviving copy. Just because the old man had owned a one-of-a-kind movie didn't mean he owned any others.

John was shivering as he ran his fingers over the icy metal canisters, his damp feet frozen beyond feeling. He crept further and further into the stacks, gradually losing his trepidation that one of them might top-

ple and set off a chain reaction, burying him, suffocating him with celluloid. *The perfect way to die,* he thought half-seriously, unbreathing
amid the towering tin.

The basement had the cleanliness of a cellar that had never seen children or family pets cooped up while their masters and mistresses took
off on vacation. The floors were gray and cold and shiny from lack of
use. Even as John worked his way progressively further back, toward
the wall, he didn't feel dust clotting his nose. There didn't seem to be
any danger of a migraine coming on, even though he had tempted fate
by doing so many aggravating things at once—he was sleepy, he had
been starving and had then gorged, he was nervous, he was excited. He
had about thirty pills before his supply petered out, and hoped to make
it last at least six months.

SGT. YORK ('41)
THE INFORMER ('35)
LAST COMMAND ('28)
THE GOLD RUSH ('25)
MOON BEAMS ('14?)

The titles left John's head swimming, the exact opposite of the con-
stricted aches he feared. Some were classics, some probably unheard of,
all precious and all preserved in the brisk storeroom by the old man with
the fat fridge who was sleeping two floors above.

John lifted the lid off only one canister, on the shortest pile he found.
The film was called *NEW YORK '08* and the film stock looked quite
fragile when exposed, and yet it was remarkable that it existed at all
considering the notation as to its year of origin—*('08)*. Too mesmerized
to be overly concerned, John touched the coiled film lightly with his finger, to have contact with history. It felt dry, like he imagined a snake's
skin would feel, and firm, like the blade of a fan.

Feeling like he was being watched, John carefully closed the canister, turned, and spotted a dilapidated projector hunched on a steel filing
cabinet at the end of the makeshift aisle, its empty reels silent, hungry.

He longed for the knowledge of how to make the thing work, as if he'd get away with stringing up a series of old movies to watch without waking the house.

As he had this thought, two things happened: One, he spotted a reel at the very bottom of a stack with a title that he recognized as being a rare—but not missing—Gil Romano picture, *SO YOUNG SO SWEET* (*'25*). Two, he heard the steady pat of stockinged feet on the basement stairwell, and the discombobulated heavings of his elderly host.

Panicking, John didn't know what to do but sit down. He sat at the end of his narrow aisle, cowering under the projector, his chubby legs bunched together, heart racing. Like clockwork, the fluidity in his brain seized and he felt the unmistakable surge of a migraine's head start. *I'll never be able to sit here with it aching,* he thought, then, separately, *I can't let him see me.*

Truitt's progress halted, his breaths dissolving in the chill air for a moment as he surveyed the lighted cellar. He knew he must seem like a troll under a bridge, or a wizened dragon protecting his lair. He wasn't used to anyone being in his sanctuary. If the interloper had been Strella he would have been angered, but knowing that it was the unassuming boy made it seem acceptable somehow.

"You there?" he asked, and immediately John regretted hiding; it was the voice of someone who understood.

"Yes," John said bravely, struggling to right himself without sending any canisters into orbit. "Yes, I'm here. I—fell asleep here. I'm real sorry."

He walked toward Truitt, grateful that it was he and not Strella who'd happened upon him. She didn't seem like she would have tiptoed around this invasion.

Truitt was in a bathrobe, spilling out in spots, unable to hold himself together and to hold onto a cane at the same time. John's face flushed red at the sight, wanting to help the old man.

"What in blazes are you doing down here *now,* son? It's practically the break of dawn."

John couldn't really answer, so he shrugged, but he was way too old to get away with such a childish gesture.

"Well?"

"I'm sorry," he repeated, "I was hungry so I ate some ham from your refrigerator"—now he realized he was confessing to a crime undiscovered—"and I came down to use the bathroom. I never, I've never seen so many old movies like I knew you'd have so I couldn't help coming down here." As Truitt looked him over, John involuntarily stuttered, "I couldn't help it." His temples blazed.

"You look sick," Truitt observed. "Are you ill?"

"I'm *not* sick," John snapped. "I get headaches. I need to find my medicine."

"Go on up, then," Truitt said quickly, "and when you're ready, if you're not too tired, come back down and I'll show you some things you'll like." He smiled broadly again, back to his harmless old self in John's eyes. Approvingly, he said to John, "You're just a rabid cinema buff. Rabid."

John smiled gratefully and bolted past Truitt, up the stairs in search of relief.

CHAPTER 28

Star Tracks!

David Greer — I woke up with Alan's underwear on my face, his naked body stretched across most of my cramped futon. *This would warrant a full page in* Paris-Match, I thought idly, trying to keep myself from waking up.

"*Ugh,*" Alan said, snapping an eyelid open and focusing on me where I lay across from him. "I didn't think you were *ever* gonna wake up." He stood and started dressing, chattering about going to get an indulgent, fatty breakfast at a diner as if bacon were a once-in-a-lifetime event for him. Did I mention I'm not a morning person?

"I can't help it, I just need a stack of silver-dollar pancakes and some animal meat," he said, beseeching. "Why question that?"

He was adorable in the morning, peppery and quick and pleasantly rumpled, padding around the room in a pair of my boxers. They made me look like Walter Matthau. They made him look like an Abercrombie & Fitch ad. But I knew a small part of him belonged to me, that we'd started something it would take a wall to stop, so I was content. And in my magnanimous morning-after mood, I felt *I* could even afford a pair of eggs lousy with butter alongside about forty greasy sausages.

Wait—something didn't make sense.

"Where are we going to go so you won't wind up running down the street with little girls chasing you?"

He rolled his eyes. "*That* extreme only happens in the movies. Besides, I'm not worried about who sees me. I'm turning over a new leaf. You're going to be my first step. You'll see."

The progress was too easy. It was bound not to stick.

We didn't even shower, just donned baseball caps and sweatshirts and shorts and elevatored down to the ground, to the real world. Anyone seeing us would logically assume we'd just woken up together. I was incredibly tense, my chest and arms tightening as we passed each floor. *What if someone gets on and recognizes him?* I thought. *What will happen?*

Nobody did and we made it to the sidewalk feeling like cat burglars with full knapsacks. It was an incredible day, completely sunny and clear—Chelsea looked clean and crisp and defined and colorful under a cloudless sky. It was the brilliant natural lighting that did us in.

Overwhelmed by the fresh air and instinctively trying to ease my concern, Alan smiled and gave me a fast peck on my cheek.

"Bea-*u*-tiful . . ." I heard from behind us. We turned to find the source and were confronted with the long, black, phallic tube of a camera lens winking at us, balanced by a professionally steady hand. The photographer was not Chip this time. This was a much older guy, paunchy around the middle, what looked like a bald pate hidden by a porkpie hat. His longish hair retreated from his spherical head in curls, growing increasingly gray toward the ends, which were white with age. The effect was like he'd dyed his hair white and it had grown back in its natural chestnut brown. He vaguely resembled Jerry Garcia, and had probably shot the rocker for thirty years or so, beginning around the time I was born and ending around the time Jerry died.

Standing at the other end of a camera, having had no chummy warning to say "cheese," I would've been grateful to have been *dead*. It was creepy, it was unexpected, and seeing the lens clicking like a mechanical sphincter left me feeling choked off—there was something final. The man must have taken a dozen perfect shots—including a possible snap of Alan planting a chaste dry one on my cheek—before we could even react.

"Hey, Alan," the man said from around the devouring camera. It dawned on me that I still hadn't seen his eyes. "Just need a few shots and I'll bug off."

"Yeah, fuck you," Alan growled, turning and stalking away from the victor. I followed, feeling uncomforably unprotected from the rear as the man kept advancing, even with our faces out of the line of fire.

"Come on, pussy boy," the man said in an even voice with no obvious malice. It was disorienting to hear a call to arms that carried no passion. This guy wasn't angry, coolly using fighting words. "Why don't you show off your new friend, you miserable butt pirate—"

Alan spun around and made a grab for the camera, tearing the strap off it in one clean jerk. The paparazzo fumbled his prized tool in midair, catching it before it struck the ground, then sprinted nimbly out of immediate danger. Where is George Clooney when you really need him?

"Fuckin' pansy," he accused glibly, hailing a taxi. "Come on, take a shot at me—I need a couple *million* in my account."

Completely unused to fistfights, to confrontation and violence, I was pulling Alan around the corner and away. The photos had been snapped—the only way to erase them would be to destroy the film, which would constitute Alan having to pound the photographer and then wreck the camera. Deserved as it would have been for the lensman, I wasn't about to witness that.

"It's not worth it," I begged Alan, "come on, don't let that sick fuck run your life."

The photographer blew us kisses as he shambled into a cab, speeding off to have the shots developed so he could hustle them globally. I didn't think he had anything all *that* scandalous, just photos of Alan with his new personal assistant, possibly—if he'd been quick enough—one of Alan kissing me in a nonsexual way. If anything, Alan's objections might make the photos seem suspicious. As far as I could tell, Alan had nothing to worry about—but as for me, I was going to have to confess to Warren much sooner than I'd hoped. Alan didn't know it, was incapable of fathoming it, but *I* was the one who would probably suffer more from those particular candids.

That's when it sank in that all these deceptions were no way to start a relationship.

"Did you hear that motherfucker?" Alan seethed, desperate for someone else to know what he'd known for years—that paparazzi routinely taunted their subjects to provoke visual responses, to create events, to fatten their market. Though I'd obviously never witnessed it firsthand, I knew all about the evil ways of the paparazzi, having seen a tongue-clucking report on the subject filed by Leanza Cornett a few years back, a documentary called *Blast 'Em,* and about a month's worth of Di coverage. And yet I cherished those photos from the tabs, the ones of Tori airing out her implants, Liz on a stretcher, Janet's big, fat ass—I knew it wasn't nice to take invasive photos, but I also knew that made them twice as fun to look at. Until, of course, it was *my* guilty-as-shit face in the frame.

"Yeah, just forget it," I said. "It's just more pictures that'll show up somewhere. Let it go." I didn't sound convincing.

"Let it *go?*" he said, incredulous. I had a feeling he was pondering the phrase a little too deeply, still reeling over the control the photographer had just tapped from him.

"Come on, just relax. You have to be used to this shit by now. I'm the one whose heart is about to go on strike." I clutched my chest comically, but actually felt the pounding in sync with the banging in my temples. I took a few deep breaths as we made our way jerkily toward the diner. People were openly staring at us, Alan's identity beginning to dawn on them. Streams of good-looking Chelsea queens were beginning to do head-turns as Alan passed.

"I'm sorry," he said. "I'm sorry you had to put up with that. It's gonna happen again. These, these *lunatics* will stop at *nothing* to get a juicy shot, man, *nothing.* That should be *illegal.* Everyone thinks Sean Penn is a madman, but to me, it's a lot more understandable to beat the shit out of one of those little monsters than it is to smile real big and pose and help them make a fucking living off you. It doesn't end until they get the last snaps before the coffin lid goes down."

In the restaurant, I was still shaken. Making me fidget even more, I noticed that a few of the passersby who'd recognized my breakfast date were lingering outside the windows, pretending to walk back and forth as they double-checked their first glances. I had to call Alan's attention to them; otherwise, they wouldn't have even registered for him.

I wondered what would likely come of the photos. Surely this couldn't have been the first time he'd ever been shot with a romantic interest at hand.

"No, they've gotten me millions of times," he said, tearing off half a piece of toast and stuffing it between his lips. Our waitress never took her eyes off Alan, and never closed her mouth. "Like I said, I don't date much, but they've gotten shots of me with every guy I've ever seen. It's not like they can run a picture of me just standing next to some guy and use a story saying, 'Look, here's proof he sucks big dicks.' " An elderly woman at the next table feigned shock at our conversation, then studied Alan's profile intently as we ate. *Who is that boy?* she must've been thinking. *I've seen him on the television.*

"I guess it just feels more violating because I'm with you, and not with, I don't know, Dean Cain or whoever." He smiled a *little,* wary of abandoning the dark mood.

"You *dated* Dean Cain?" The old woman watching us raised her eyebrows with an expression that said *I knew it.*

"No, no," he laughed, "Just an example. You know what I mean."

"I never get why they don't treat stars better," I said, using the word *stars* in a whisper, like it was a profanity. "I mean, wouldn't they be smarter to be nice so they can get more cooperative pictures?"

"Nah," Alan said, seeming like a jaded old-timer when discussing the industry. "They get more flamboyant shit this way, and they know no matter how pissed off an actor gets, they're always gonna be able to weasel into his next premiere or stand outside his house and get the pictures they want."

As previously predicted, seven different people came up to our table with napkins and various other paper goods for Alan to sign, everyone from a little girl under ten to a man so old it was surprising he'd know Alan's name. "I'm a big fan," the man crowed, "big fan." The stocky manager of the diner arrived with a Polaroid and convinced Alan to pose for three shots with her, the two of them grinning in the booth, photographs that would later be taped for all eternity in the window, where the neighborhood would watch them fade to blue.

"Who are *you?*" one woman asked me nervously as Alan scrawled his name on a crisp dollar bill for her.

"I'm David," I said, sticking out my hand.

"No," she said, turning her nose up at my proffered paw. "I mean, who are you on the *show?* Are you an actor? On *Lifesavers?*"

"No, no . . . I'm just, I mean, I write. I'm a writer."

There followed a pause that could've drained the water from our glasses. "Oh," she said flatly, then left. Maybe if I'd starred in a dinner theater rendition of *Forty Carats,* she'd have let me initial a penny for her or something.

It should have been hilarious, and I guess it was, to somebody. But being so blatantly put in my place depressed me. It made me aware I was sitting on a sticky vinyl seat in the same diner in which I'd eaten weekend breakfasts for the past five years. In that same stretch of time, the younger man across from me, for whom I felt such unexpected tenderness, had made his first five or ten million. Alan sipped his coffee and peered over the cup at me, oblivious to the slight I'd experienced, never truly focused on anything when chattering fans were in the area.

"Sorry, did I miss something?" he asked. "I'm paying attention, I promise. It's just that sometimes they sort of tap all my energy. I get distracted."

"No," I said, "I'm sorry I brought you here. I'm sorry it got so annoying."

"Doesn't matter." He shrugged. "It's the same wherever." He smiled, attempting to pull himself back together again.

"I thought you said it only happened in the movies."

He smiled indulgently. "Well, sometimes wherever I go becomes like a movie. I don't get chased, exactly, but I always have an audience. You will, too." He'd reminded himself of the photographer and I could see very clearly what he was thinking: *Did he get a shot of me kissing this guy?*

The rest of our meal was what passed for our quality time: We enjoyed about five minutes' worth of disjointed conversation before Alan paid the bill and we took off. He'd insisted, saying, "Don't be crazy. I have way too much for just me. I used to be a leech so I like to pay for everybody now. You pay when you make a million writing your novel."

It was nice not to have to pay, nice that he was taking me at my word that I'd amount to something someday, but devastating to understand I had no chance of duplicating his success. It wasn't jealousy I was feeling, exactly. Disappointment.

He hopped into a cab to avoid a small crowd gathering outside the diner, leaving me with a promise that he'd call later. He hugged me and maybe even gave me a good-bye kiss—with his eyes. If he had been a regular person, like I was a regular person, we were in the right area of New York to have done some open same-sex kissing and cuddling. I told myself that if Alan Dillinger had been Joe Blow, he would've kissed me again, with feeling. But I had to settle for a meaningful wink.

As the cab pulled away, three or four guys with cameras took pic after pic, none of which could've possibly turned out. Still, they aimed and they shot—click, click, click.

As soon as Alan disappeared into traffic, everyone scattered and I was left alone on the curb.

CHAPTER 29

Feature

Truitt Connor and John Dewey — *I can't go back to jail,* Truitt Connor thought. The concepts were so clear as to almost appear as block writing in his head. **I CAN'T GO THROUGH THIS AGAIN.** No, more like title cards, *The elderly gentleman knew he must not return—to jail!*

The scraggly teenager who'd written him about *Midsummer Night's Dream* and Gil Romano was upstairs getting some kind of pills for a headache, and Truitt was left standing alone in his cellar, looking at his treasured collection of original nitrate films but remembering a time when the cellar had housed . . . *more.*

When he remembered, Truitt did it in terms of film, endlessly editing and reediting an internal silent biopic, complete with emotive piano accompaniment.

Except he'd lived in color, not black-and-white.

FADE IN

OPENING MONTAGE: For years, this cellar (and, prior to it, one in New York) had been a makeshift dark room, where as an expressive and fearless photographer Truitt had spent days on end producing beautiful, colorless portraits of men, nude or close to it. He could vividly recall sifting a sheet of film through a chemical bath and watching a nearly perfect male form bubble to visibility under the red light. Was it a hallucination of the substances, a testament to his talent or to the model's beauty? He could never decide. It was the debate that pushed him forward.

He would shoot a different man every few hours during a peak time. The summer was the busiest, with all the easy sailors in town, all the aggressively sexy local boys in dungarees and grubby T-shirts, shirts he'd coax up and over their pretty faces. Many of them posed for free, tickled to be considered worth asking. Others required copies of Truitt's work for themselves and their girlfriends and, sometimes, for their boyfriends. So few of them were actually gay, so few identified with Truitt. The gay men bought the pictures, the straight men posed.

Occasionally, with a little beer, a hetero-inclined model would not flinch as Truitt closed in with his camera, setting it down to unfasten the posing strap that shielded only what was absolutely necessary legally. Truitt would hold and admire the model's hard cock, lick his testicles, and then swallow him, the skilled photographer bringing him off with a parallel expertise. Some of the models were up for more, and at one point Truitt had installed a cot in the cellar, for those times he felt like raising his legs onto a pair of broad shoulders he'd just memorialized in black-and-white, the real colors of their flesh so much more visceral and thrilling, the difference between his art and his life.

He had shot thousands of young men, white, black, some Mexicans and Europeans, whoever looked —to Truitt's eye—to be in the proximity of perfection. He didn't have a type outside of masculine, but he felt he had a strong sense of beauty and of the ideal. He had been beautiful himself, and had taken idyllic self-portraits—clothed and not—that rivaled his most erotic work with other models.

But those photos no longer existed. Nor did most of his work, save for the later stuff, and save for the few odd pieces he had been able to retrieve from acquaintances, gifts ungiven, or which had been willed back to him by friendly customers passing into oblivion.

CUT TO: The only photo Truitt had of himself as a young man was a darkly romantic image. He posed in a very stiff white shirt,

211

black breeches, shining shoes. He lay on his stomach, face up to the lens, concealing in his hand the device that would trigger his bulky camera to record his youthful face that day, at twenty-two, when he'd felt he'd been about to take the world by surprise.

CLOSEUP: Instead, the world had surprised him.

(Noises upstairs as John fumbled to swallow a pill dry, tripping and falling to one knee. Truitt had no clue his guest was in such pain, and worried that the noises would attract Strella, who wouldn't understand their dawn conference in the cellar. Strella didn't understand anything about that basement, or about obsession, or even about creation—ironic since she professed to be a devout Catholic.)

CUT TO: A devoted fan of images, Truitt had purchased his first Kodak camera at sixteen with money earned working the counter of the dime store in his hometown in Maine. He'd begun by mimicking the avant garde works he'd seen in an article about art photography, stark, eclectic—then had progressed to doing interpretive portraits of his family, photos that shocked his subjects with their underexposed, ghostly quality, and the inorganic found objects whose diaphanous forms had been juxtaposed over their faces. His mother had fretted that a crucifix on her forehead was blasphemous, when all Truitt had been trying to do was state that she was a saintly woman, an opinion he changed when she stole his camera and told him he would go to hell if he kept at his hobby.

When he left for New York City in 1926, he had no reason to believe he'd make it as a photographer, and no money to convince him he'd make it as anything at *all.*

Truitt worked for an Italian green-grocer who instructed him on sex between men and the bond that could go along with it. The grocer bought the young man another camera. Soon, his close-knit, initially suspicious group of homosexual friends began seeking Truitt out for the privilege of posing. It was risky to pose in such a way that left little imagination as to one's preferences, but Truitt captured his subjects' true personalities, telling them to remain relaxed instead of aping the stiff poses popular in portraiture at the time. He snapped two men holding hands, two more kissing—when he saw the latter appear in his darkroom he wept at the newness of it, at having preserved the contact. He believed he was the only person alive to have photographed a male kiss.

Truitt took photographs of men dressed as women, feline creatures he'd met on the rowdy Bowery and who made themselves available around the clock to sit, until he finally realized *he* should charge *them* for posing and not the other way around. He started to earn steadily by taking lovely, flattering, sometimes illusory photos of haughty drag queens, the fees provided by their cock-whipped patrons. He was completely unaware of what a maverick he was, satisfied to be honing his talent and making a living at it.

At the same time, the daring shutterbug began a job as a projectionist for the Shelby Theatre on West Twentieth Street, satisfying a need for a stable paycheck and his love for the cinema at once. The Shelby was one of the oldest in the city, and it had a vast underground storage cellar that housed both stockpiles of concessions and carelessly stored one- and two-reels that went straight back to the turn of the century, thirty years before Truitt helmed the bill. The films were kept in metal cans, the subterranean basement making these shells painful to touch, so cold they almost felt burning hot.

From his earliest training as a projectionist, Truitt was coached to be exceedingly careful with film, since the nitrate stock was known to be extremely volatile, its elements working against each other, patiently waiting for the smallest spark to combust. Small fires were common in movie houses, deadly explosions not unheard of. But Truitt loved the movies too much ever to allow accidents, handling the black, shining feed like Indian cobras tamed to his touch.

Defying the parameters of his job, he would sometimes give free midnight screenings of the basement's forgotten commodities to friends, some of them his models, who appreciated the obscure serials and loopy, arty early efforts. These forgotten reels combined city street scenes with weight lifters at their task, soundlessly barking dogs and galloping horses—otherworldly to watch without any piano accompaniment. There were even some awkward "pornographic" loops, showing topless dancers and one of a man swallowing another man's soft cock, a reel Truitt and his friends watched until it was too worn to bother. The theater's owner turned a blind eye to all the free shows and denied knowing where the obscene loops had come from.

One of Truitt's fondest memories was of watching *The Divine Woman* with a dozing Dutch sailor, almost frightened by the intensity of Garbo's beauty and the absence of any sound at all, except when the film had snapped and ticked loudly against the reel, necessitating a fast patch job.

Slowly, instead of veering into fine art photography or even into moviemaking, Truitt had been seduced by the commerce of persuading muscular men to shuck most of their clothes, flexing their bodies for pay. Despite his attraction to film, he never made a moving picture, but he had been inspired by the industry's principles of distribution and supply-and-demand, and by that magical cocksucking loop that had made something forbidden available for impulsive viewing.

Signing his erotic photography "Truitt of Chelsea," he sold small sets of six erotic snaps disguised as mementos for fans of athletes, eventually printing hundreds of thousands over the years. By the late thirties, he'd worked up to a list of almost one thousand regular buyers, men who would sound awestruck on the phone when discussing a new set of a favored model, a beloved idol. Local weight lifters from Coney Island, reluctant mechanics, anonymous sailors, gym dandies with wives and children—these became more essential than Garbo to the buyers, or more appropriately, more essential than Valentino or Romano or Novarro, because the models' near-nudity put them one step further from the dream and one step closer to the attainable.

(Truitt didn't like to ponder the enormity of his output since so little of it survived. Surely some of his work existed in the hands of collectors, but he could rarely afford to buy any back—the artist had been outpriced in the market for his own work. Ironically, though he'd saved a cellarful of movies, the material that had meant the most to him had been the only he couldn't hold onto— his own output, his own creations.)

CUT TO: From the beginning, cops had come around pestering Truitt of Chelsea with accusations of homosexuality, prostitution, pornography. Aside from the occasional chaste kissing portrait for well-heeled boyfriends, Truitt only ever took solo photos of men with their privates tastefully concealed, so he refused to consider it obscene. It was like art to him, like ancient Greek statues except the molds were flesh and the models still living. And their bodies were touchable and embraceable and they perspired on top of him if the mood was right for both.

It had been his attraction to his burly models that had led to his first arrest. A sexy Irishman, all too willing to strip beyond the traditional posing strap, vocal as Truitt swallowed his hard cock and toyed with his dangling testicles, fingering him, always adept at milking semen. Later, the Irishman had mounted him from behind on the steps, had penetrated him for long minutes, taking the sex to a new level of enthusiasm. Truitt could hardly recall certain friends he'd had in his life for spaces of ten or twenty years, but he would never forget the danger, the urgency of that hour-long encounter.

Immediately after the Irishman had ejaculated inside Truitt, he'd slapped his conquest with cuffs, arresting him for soliciting. He convinced his buddies on the force to disbelieve Truitt's indignant account of the way the afternoon had really been spent.

The cop was a family man and Truitt was a homosexual pornographer, as incomprehensible in the thirties as a unicorn and dark as the devil.

Bailed out by his old boss, the grocer, Truitt had returned to his apartment to find his photographs missing and many negatives shredded on the floor, including the portraits he'd taken years earlier of his family, all of whom were by then dead or dying. Seeing the devastation, he'd felt the oxygen leave his chest, had felt the cold floor connect hard with his knees, had lain down abruptly in the spaghetti-thin negatives, unable to accept the loss.

It had happened in varying ways many more times over the years, with the final, in the sixties, being the worst, when his name and photograph had made page two of the *Seattle Intelligencer*. Moving cross-country to escape the oppressive expenses of living in New York, he'd been unfamiliar with Seattle and vice versa, and the sharp reaction of the local authorities had shocked the defiant artist. A kangaroo court had sentenced him to three years for taking explicit photographs of a totally naked youth who'd signed a waiver that he was eighteen when in reality he'd been six months shy.

If Truitt hadn't succumbed to the consumer demand for more sex, if he hadn't artfully photographed the young man's climax, he might have wriggled out from under any punishment. Instead, he was branded a sex offender and spent part of his life incarcerated. In jail, he'd found himself surrounded by the kind of men he photographed, some of whom tended to protect him. One, a former subject, lashed out at him, identifying him as an opportunist who'd profited by his naked need, the faggot. It was a banquet of violence and aggression and anticipation, and it lasted for three years.

The last time Truitt had had sex had been in prison. After that, he'd lost interest. He didn't learn until almost ten years later, at the end of the seventies, that what had actually happened had been rape.

His photography, which had led to incarceration and abuse, was considered groundbreaking art or harmless camp by 1986.

FADE TO BLACK

"I'm ready," John said, startling the old man. Truitt shuffled in a semicircle and stepped down into the basement completely, sweating in the unnaturally frosty air. He was wearing his effortful smile again, covering up.

"So you are," he replied, attempting to sound bright. He was filled with the sadness of knowing he had so much to tell but no idea of where to begin. He knew that he had a film the young man would thrill at seeing, even more so than *Gay Was the Hero*. It was a historic document he'd often wanted to unveil to the planet—but something had always held him back. At first, he'd mostly felt protective of the legendary actor, Gil Romano, not believing in exposing a man's homosexuality since it was nobody's business. But ultimately, it was both a contempt for the world that imprisoned him and a desire to exist happily, invisibly, that had convinced Truitt to keep most of his treasures—and his greatest possession—to himself. "So you are."

"I didn't know you had so many," John said, glancing around again, his awe restored, his head swimming as the medicine flowed through his system.

"No," Truitt said. "I didn't tell the press that I have this many films and I don't expect you to, either. Is that clear?" It was an unexpected moment of Strella-like firmness and John promised, warmed at being party to a secret.

"You see, I don't want just *anyone* to know what I'm sitting on here. I don't need the government getting involved."

John was confused. "The government?"

"Yes," Truitt said, stepping over to the chair and lowering himself to a sitting position, his gnarled hands propped on top of his cane. "It's *illegal* to own a copy of any film that's still under copyright. So Warner or MGM could, in theory, get a whiff that I might be in possession of some of their product and turn me in. The older stuff—the gold, the stuff you and I like best—isn't illegal to have, since it's too old to be protected. But those would kick up even more of a to-do because then all the preservationists would be knocking on my door, begging me to hand it all over. The American Film Institute even has a ten-most-wanted list, like the FBI."

John absorbed the idea of the harmless man as a movie outlaw, a western antihero in black, shooting blanks and pulling on the curled ends of a mustache.

"I have two of the ten they're after," Truitt said mischievously, wiggling his eyebrows. John laughed out loud and spooked himself with the sound. He was already shivering again in the refrigeration.

John was itching to start rifling through cans, to ask the paramount question: *Do you really have any Gil Romano? Do you have the ultimate Gil Romano? Do you have* Gay Was the Hero? He held his tongue, sensing Truitt needed him to work up to it. "But if you're so worried about being caught, how come you let them have *Midsummer Night's Dream?*"

"Mainly I did that just as a taste. I wanted to see how they would be about such a donation, how they would react. I told them it was the only film I owned, which I doubt they'll believe forever. I told them I've kept it in my icebox ever since the thirties, just because I liked it and didn't want it to perish. They can't raid my home unless they come up with evidence that I'm sitting on copyrighted objects. But if they figure me out, they'll do it, believe me. They went into Roddy McDowall's home and grabbed back a lot of film, and he's a star—of sorts."

John felt totally at ease as the drug continued to work its magic, totally loose and totally relaxed.

"How did you get all these movies?" John asked. He knew they were probably on original nitrate stock, which he knew was potentially dangerous. It was also fragile and tended to erode even at room temperature, and it was the reason that so many of Gil Romano's movies were extinct—the reason that so many movies of the thirties and twenties no longer existed. He'd read many books on the subject, sickened to read that movie studios had treated films as one-time attractions for years, never foreseeing a future use or understanding their intrinsic value. Movies had been routinely dumped, their most impressive background scenes hacked out and redistributed, or even torched to help make menacing fires to be filmed for other epics. Cannibalism. Waste. Common belief held that Gil Romano barely existed on film anymore, but John had a good feeling that Truitt Connor might be about to prove that theory wrong.

"I was given most of them," Truitt said. "I used to be a projectionist—but then you read that in the article, yes? yes—and I worked at a lovely old cinema in Manhattan that was a strange sort of elephant's graveyard for movies. We didn't get the big hits until well after their first splash; we'd get everything later and screen it cheaper, and so after we'd run something, there was nobody else who needed the movies, not even the studios. So the owner just stuck it all in the basement. Terrible fire hazard, but he didn't seem to care. I started working for him a few years after sound, and when the talkies arrived, believe me, those old silents were considered garbage.

"When I moved out here to Seattle some time later, I offered to buy some of the silents, but the owner told me, 'Take whatever you want.' I rented a truck and piled it high. Also dangerous as hell. Took me two weeks, but I made it here in one piece. They've been here ever since."

Truitt thought of all the time he'd lavished on the old reels, ever since he'd noticed that some of them were rotting. Even in the cool of the theater's basement, several of the tins had contained bubbling liquid or sandy ash when he'd dug around them in search of treasures to relocate to Seattle in the late fifties. He'd lost *The Divine Woman* that way, or most of it. He still had part of one reel, and it was among his most prized possessions. He'd had an original nitrate of *Wee Willie Winkie* with Shirley Temple but had allowed it to congeal into a toxic stew rather than waste his time—he'd always hated that brat. He'd also lost two Gil Romano films to neglect, to the physical impossibility of getting to all five hundred films on a regular basis, but wouldn't tell that to the boy. Why rub salt? Especially when he had at least two items that were much more interesting.

"It's been," he stroked his jaw thoughtfully, "a *chore,* John. It's been a real *chore* looking after these movies, keeping them free of rot, snipping out segments that are too far gone. If I thought an archive could do any better than I, I'd give them over in a jiff. But the fact is that no amount of attention can stave off obliteration forever."

"Are most of them as rare as *Midsummer Night's Dream*?" John asked.

"Of the five hundred or so I've saved, I'd say that at least seventy or eighty would be completely nonexistent but for me."

John thought of what it would be like to own anything—anything at all—that could truly be considered one of a kind. He thought of his own hard-won collection sitting in Shelly's closet back in New Jersey, suddenly seeing it as ordinary and plain, like the mother of the girl guarding it.

"I've spent so much time caring for this nitrate. Also the few films I've paid to have transferred to safety stock, which are the only ones I can actually *watch*. The rest won't be seen again until after I've died."

Unexpectedly, John thought of his grandmother, dead and probably buried. A panic seized him that the police might be looking for him.

"Do you have many Gil Romanos?" he blurted. "Do you have *Gay Was the Hero*?" That was the money question, that was the lure that had tempted him across the country on no food.

Truitt looked at him for a long moment, at the pleading in John's eyes. He could see himself in there somewhere, though he'd never been so desperate, just dazzled by images—pictures, moving and still.

"No sense in beating the bush." He winked. "Yes, I have it. I am happy to tell you that I have it."

John grinned sloppily, unable to control the confines of the gesture, feeling like he'd start drooling and crying if he couldn't calm down. He said a silent prayer that the pills would last. He wasn't supposed to take more than one a day.

"I can't believe it," he gasped. "I knew it. I never expected it. Where is it? Can we see it?"

Strella called down from upstairs. "What in *hell* are you two doing down *there*? Mr. Truitt? You okay?"

Truitt rolled his eyes and made a face, a broad, Keystone Kop gesture that made John giggle, so tickled already.

"Yes, Strella," he said, putting on airs. "Yes, my dear, we are just— as they say—*having a moment.* Please make us some breakfast."

There was the sound of Strella's indignant movements about the kitchen, but she did not respond. Only later, when they smelled grease frying, did they know that she had chosen to comply.

OFF THE LIST

BY WARREN JUNIOR

BUTT-INSKY

Plenty O'Peroxide, an elegant blond sitcommer, hides a *shocking* secret behind her toothsome (capsome?) grin—her cute boyfriend, Remember Me?, who used to be so big on that '80s medical drama, demands to use the back door *exclusively* during sex. Is that written tastefully enough for a family paper? This *isn't* a family paper? Oh, okay—let me rephrase that. Remember Me? only wants sex if he can fuck Plenty O'Peroxide up the ass.

What's the problem? She doesn't *like* it. Believe it or not, this is a common reaction. (I don't understand it, either!)

Frankly, this is one blind item I question *myself* considering that this skinny creature doesn't seem to have any *ass* to *fuck*.

More of a shocker, or perhaps I'm just going soft in my old age, is the fact that Remember Me?—who, give it up for the boy, *is* still extremely handsome, fit, and (I hear) hung (sorry, Plenty)—posed nude years before his big TV break, and those photos have yet to surface. The problem is that the photog who lucked into snatching him in the buff croaked aeons ago and his widow bitterly tossed all the negatives of naked male mods. The photos were published in a really, *really* small-scale local mag (circ. 100?), and only recently has a collector put two and two together. He may own the only copy in the world, thanks to that damned recycling craze.

I would *love* to just name Remember Me?, but haven't seen the photos myself and he is litigious, baby, litigious.

When it comes to the lineup of defendants in a lawsuit, I'm only too happy to be "Off the List."

CHAPTER 30

The Insider!

David Greer — Our morning-after breakfast had been followed up by a harried call from a salon. Alan was having his body waxed and his head trimmed by an apparently famous stylist, after-hours in the Fashion District. I couldn't remember feeling any stubble on his assets, and certainly his hair had looked immaculate. Alan told me he was groomed in that way every other week.

"It's a pain, but the producers like everyone to, um, 'maintain.' It's a small price to pay, I guess." He'd laughed. "Besides, it's environmentally sound to be hairless since you're using less soap." He had not been thrilled by my questions: "Does it hurt?" "Why do they wax you in places the camera can't see?" "Do they have this sort of thing in your contract?" "Can they wax a friend for free?"

But what was distressing was that even on a month-long break from filming, even though Alan was in the same city I was, he was immersed in business. He would sound half-asleep when he'd call at nine o'clock in the evening, inviting me over to talk, unwind, make love. I couldn't believe that such a young, healthy guy would be ready for bed by eleven. It helped me understand when he ticked off the list of things he did on a given day:

✓ Read and respond to select pieces of fan mail.
✓ Confer with Shara.
✓ Confer with legal team.
✓ Read incoming faxes and letters regarding acting jobs.

✓ Return phone calls.

✓ Read two to four scripts previously approved by assistant.

✓ Work out (three hours).

✓ Lunch with potential producer, director, costar, or corporate shill (Alan only did TV commercials and print ads in Japan and other places that, apparently, "didn't count" like America would).

✓ Continue reading scripts.

✓ Read new *Lifesavers* materials.

✓ Do itinerary with assistant/go over press clippings.

✓ Fitting for TV movie with Kirstie Alley.

✓ Photo shoot with Francesco Scavullo for *YM*.

✓ Photo shoot with Greg Gorman for unspecified celebrity portrait project.

✓ Charity dinner at Laura Belle for Special Olympics/photo op with the Lawrence Brothers.

✓ Return phone calls/phoner with radio station in Australia.

✓ Call boyfriend.

Oh, that's me.

Once, I was cradling him, enjoying the feel of his broad shoulders curled into my lap, and I watched Alan fall asleep before the news even came on. I just sat there with him, watching his face, uncomposed and boyishly open with his eyes lightly closed. There was so much happening behind that handsome mask, but there was so much happening in front of it that I could only feel a pang of loss knowing that I'd never get a chance to meet the kid Alan had been before he'd become famous. I knew that in a very real way, he was inaccessible to me, almost like I was just another fan standing patiently outside his high-rise, hoping to see him for thirty seconds as he sprinted from lobby to limo.

During our first week, we passed up a number of opportunities to push our sex life ahead. We deliberately "forgot" to buy condoms, staving off the penetration level that we both professed to want very badly. I think, in retrospect, we might have been using the condom issue as a barrier against that next stage of intimacy. We'd felt such a tremendous rush of feeling, it was almost unthinkable that it might be magnified if we were *inside* each other. We limited ourselves to fingers and tongues and the results were already wildly exhausting.

Still, each time we became lost in the sex, I could tell when one of us or the other was ready, *ready,* to get fucked—and each time that opportunity was lost, it made me feel it was less and less likely it would ever be taken at all. And why? What final test were we waiting for each other to pass before giving in completely?

But within a week of our first night together, we had more serious things to contend with than just our disconnection or Alan's breakneck schedule or the lingering, implied emotional mistrust.

I had bought several magazines on my lunch hour that Friday, and all I'd wanted to do the minute I got home was settle in to read them, a quiet evening at the homestead. Alan had said he'd be too tired to see me that night, so I'd planned to use it to rest my brain.

I decided *Details* and *In Style* could wait. I wanted to read the *People* cover story on Prince William. I opened it up and noticed something unusual.

My debut in *People* was fairly inauspicious.

After two decades' worth of loyal subscribership, after thousands of hours spent consuming its spongy contents as you might a box of Mallomars, I was repaid by being accidentally published, a background figure in a dazzling candid of my boyfriend, Alan Dillinger.

"The yummiest *Lifesaver* flavor is Alan Dillinger, seen here stepping out for a midmorning stroll after a hard day's night."

What the hell was *that* supposed to mean? Why didn't they identify me? I was standing right there, my face only half obscured by Alan's decidedly unromantic-looking kiss, and the photographer was quite aware of who I was to Alan, probably even knew my name if he knew where I lived. I was right there, in the frame, a shockingly obvious omission in the caption. Even if I weren't me, I would have read that page and thought, *But who is the schmuck he's snogging?*

It was at first galling to have been so heavy-handedly slighted—I could only hope an angry, nosy housewife would write in to the Letters column demanding to know the identity of Alan Dillinger's even cuter friend. But after the insult came the kick—I was in *People* magazine! I'd gone national.

I went to the junk drawer for scissors and carefully excised my likeness from the pages, liberating Alan and myself from our spot wedged between Dyan Cannon on one side (I disagreed with the assertion that she didn't look sixty-plus) and Kathie Lee Gifford and her clan on the other (What would happen if Cody grew up to be an infamous clod? Would his name be removed from all those cancer wards and charitable facilities?). Then I did the only thing I'd ever learned to do with good news: I stuck it on my fridge with a magnet that had been crafted to look like a realistic Oreo cookie.

As I admired my handiwork, reality punched me in the guts. Seeing the picture out of place like that on the dead-white surface triggered other considerations: If I was in *People,* how long would it take for Warren to lick his pointer, turn the page and see his best buddy caught up in the tail of Dillinger's comet? How long would it take for my cover to be blown? *Oh, my God—it looks fraternal but the fact remains that he is kissing me.*

I realized my answering machine was flashing—I had messages. I started talking to myself out loud, like people do in the movies. "Okay, just take it easy. It's probably not going to be Warren. He's way too busy to have looked at this magazine as soon as it arrived on his desk. It's going to be oh-kay."

I pressed Play.

"David? David? It's Mom. Guess you're not there. I just wanted to say hi and remind you I love you." *You see? You have time. Warren won't pick up on it right away, if ever. You're not as recognizable to others as you are to yourself.* "I also wanted to tell you that there's a photograph in *People* magazine that looks just like you. It's a hoot! It's right on page, let's see, page eight. It's a photograph of that *Lifesavers* actor, Dillinger, with this fella who's your spitting image. I'm going to cut it out and send it to you. Thought you'd get a chuckle from it. Bye, now."

I sat there with my arms folded, staring at the machine, waiting for the second message to play.

It *was* Warren. "Hello, David, I'm leaving this message since you are probably at Jones Beach hangin' with, oh, I don't know—maybe Chris O'Donnell? No, maybe not, since he's straight. Now, let's see . . . who might you be spending your day with? Maybe . . . ALAN FUCKING DILLINGER? David, this is *war.* I have never felt so betrayed in my *life.* I have gotten completely unprofessional leads from personal physicians and IRS agents, and yet my friend—who I had *assumed* to be, anyway—can't pick up a phone and tell me he is FUCKING ALAN DILLINGER! Are you on *crack?*"

I was shaking from the sonic boom of Warren's voice and the sinking feeling that there was no turning back.

Or was there?

CHAPTER 31

Diary of a Mad Marriage!

David Greer — Though I was tempted to call 911, I instead called Alan at home. I left a brief message, always nervous that if I talked too long it would eat up space reserved for David Geffen calling with a three-picture deal. Alan returned my call almost immediately, like he'd been screening. He sounded like he might be calling from the space shuttle, staticky and uneven.

"Where are you?" I asked, stalling.

"I'm in a car going north on Eighth Avenue," he said playfully. "I just got done with a reading for the next *Batman* and I think it went really well."

"Didn't they stop making those?" I thought aloud.

"Well, Joel Schumacher wouldn't have had me over and wooed me with a wonderful home-cooked meal if they weren't at least *considering* doing number . . . what? Six?"

I didn't reply.

"So what's up? I'm gonna stop by and surprise you." Whispering, "I had my assistant pick me up some condoms."

Romance at the fin de siècle.

Jaded or not, it made me lose my breath in anticipation. Or in fear that I was about to blow it. His proposal made me see clearly how ready I was to dig in deeper with him.

"Um, nothing's up," I said, wishing I could take back my message, pretend I'd never seen *People*. But I couldn't. "Well, I actually have bad, or weird, news. Maybe I should just show it to you. . . ." I was holding the phone in place with my jaw, my hands buried in my pockets. Across the room on the fridge, I could see the paparazzo's photo of us. I looked kinda good.

"What is it?" he urged, punching buttons on his cellular for a better frequency. As a sitting duck, he was very good at picking up on signs of danger, rustling in the reeds.

"Don't panic," I said. "because it's not a big deal, it's just something you won't like." It felt like a bigger and bigger deal the more I stalled.

I could hear Alan instructing his driver to hang a right on Twenty-second—they were only a block away. The absurdity of our phone call hit me; were we going to hang up when he walked through my door, or would we keep talking into the receivers, even when we were standing next to each other?

"What is it? *What?*"

"Remember that paparazzo?" I said. I could hear Alan stop breathing. "Well, he sold one of the pictures to *People*. It doesn't look too weird or anything—"

"*People?* As in *People* magazine?" He was quiet for a second. I bit down on my lip, hoping he wouldn't be too upset. I could almost sense him calculating the circulation of an average *People*.

"You're sort of kissing my cheek, but it doesn't look at *all* sexual—"

"I can't fucking believe it," he said. *What's not to believe?* I thought. He'd known the photos would show up *somewhere*. He'd also known they weren't particularly incriminating. This wasn't Di and Dodi in a premortem clinch on a yacht, it was just two guys with beard growth walking out of a building side by side, one playfully kissing the other like two jocks might as a joke. At worst, the photo would just be more circumstantial evidence for everyone who already thought they knew Alan was gay. "This is why I had fifty messages from Shara today. I just thought she was trying to look busy."

"It's not that bad—" I started.

"That's easy for you to say," Alan said sharply. "You're not losing anything. I'm the one who's—look, this is really too much for me right now. The last thing I need is a hundred reporters calling up Shara or, or, a hundred photographers camped out at your apartment."

"You're acting like this is my fault," I interjected. "Besides, you haven't even seen the picture."

"I don't *have* to *see* the picture, David. I was *in* the picture, David."

I crossed the room and peered out the window. I didn't notice anyone loitering, waiting to pounce on us. I looked across the street at the silhouettes of people leaning out their windows, having a smoke or just watching the traffic on the sidewalk. Could any of them be preparing to photograph me hugging Alan as he entered my apartment? Kissing him in the doorway? Fumbling with a condom as he raised two brown legs sky high?

I didn't see Alan's car anywhere, either.

"Well, what about the premiere? You're going to be seen with me there, and there *will* be a lot more than just one paparazzo at the premiere. Have you thought about that?" In the second it took him to respond, I realized I had zero chance of going to any premieres with Alan Dillinger. I'd just heard on *Extra* that his movie had been retitled *My Best Friend's Engagement.*

"Jesus Christ, why are you fighting me on this?" he insisted. "Can't you just get that I am not *you,* I am not as comfortable as *you* are, that this is something I need to *ease into?*"

I felt freezing cold suddenly, and knew Alan was not going to stop by after all. If he were, he would have already been at my door by then. The street was eerily vacant, no cars at all. As if everyone in New York knew my heart was breaking and wanted to avoid driving past my building out of respect.

"Yeah," I said, dejected. "I can get it, Alan. I know exactly what your position is on this. You don't want to lose anything, you just want to keep on gaining. I understand that. But listen, I may not have a movie career to lose or millions of dollars or even just my Q rating, but I feel like I'm already losing something important. Or at least something . . ."

"David."

"Something that had the *potential* to be important . . ."

"David."

"Something I really wanted so much to happen that's *not* going to happen—"

"David, listen, I have to regroup and think about all of this." To his driver, I heard Alan give directions to a newsstand on Seventh Avenue, a few blocks in the opposite direction from me. "You can't expect me to just throw all caution to the wind and say, 'fuck the media.' I have too much invested in this, and it's not just money, David, it's emotional, it's an emotional thing to decide to be an actor and to be working for it and to get a shot at, at succeeding to a point so few actors ever get to, you know?"

"You need to make more time for your emotional life outside of acting. Not every emotion should be staged, Alan. You shouldn't have to act full-time in order to act for a living."

He kept rolling. "For me to put in jeopardy everything I've worked for . . . I can't. I can't risk throwing it all away. I can't just do that without a lot of thought first. You're asking me to just *come out of the closet*"—he said the phrase so awkwardly, like it was a complete joke, or something so terrifying he couldn't even bear to discuss it—"at the drop of a hat."

I sat down on my futon. "Nobody's asking you to do that," I said quietly.

"No, David, you aren't asking me directly, but it's been there from the beginning. Our first conversation was about whether or not I would be coming out."

"Alan," I replied, not arguing anymore, just reacting, "that wasn't all we talked about that night."

We were both quiet, remembering our first words to each other, our candor and our attraction.

"Risk, Alan," I said. "You've got to risk in order to gain."

He didn't reply immediately, but when he did, he surprised me. "I could say the same thing to you," he said.

We were at loggerheads and his car was already retreating from his cellular's radius. *I know, I know: "I'm losing you, babe."*

"Da—id," he said, his voice breaking up, "I —ust need —ome ti— to th—nk."

I hung up as I heard him saying "—bye."

CHAPTER 32

Named

Truitt Connor and John Dewey — "Oh, God," John muttered, the first time he'd heard himself take the Lord's name in vain out loud. Granny had never allowed it.

Truitt Connor was pointing to a canister almost at the very bottom of a stack towards the back, closest to the cooler. It was darker than the others, its title jumping more clearly from the decayed masking tape barely adhering to the tin.

"Damn labels are even harder to keep up with," Truitt cursed impatiently. "Masking tape lasts about a year."

Truitt knew he'd been horribly behind in his rounds of late, and couldn't recall the last time he'd inspected the original print of *Gay Was the Hero*. He owned what was certainly the only copy ever struck. He'd had the original camera negative at one point as well, rescued along with this pristine nitrate print by a belligerent employee even though the studio head had demanded it torched. The negative and print had later been given to Truitt after a romantic interlude and during the beginning stages of a friendship.

"It's the only, only, only," the young man—Eric—had told him in the forties, when Romano had still been alive. Eric had been immensely pleased to be able to give something of value to his new friend. "Truitt, you can't ever tell anyone I took this. I could get blackballed. The head honcho would choke me personally. But you seem like the best person I know to have this."

Truitt had had many boyfriends, many friends, countless acquaintances. He'd lived to socialize, to meet, to mix. He'd loved his private screenings and the trust placed in him by his comrades, the same sort of trust he'd placed in them. They'd been gay before it was a word. They'd kept each other's secrets without question, shunning the less reliable queers, the ones who would rat you out at the first sign of trouble, or who were too unhinged to be anything but destructive, unable to accept their reality.

Though he'd loved being with his buddies and had loved having sex, "making romance," Truitt had never had one special, long-lasting bond with a man, nor had he ever felt that was his ideal. But of all of them, Eric had been the one who'd come closest. They'd spent five years of their lives enmeshed, then had separated during World War Two, when Truitt had been a flat-footed reject and Eric a healthy enlistee and immediate casualty. The negative of *Gay Was the Hero* had been decaying already by the time it had come to Truitt, and it had passed the point of no return when he first began routine cleaning of his films. The nitrate was all that remained, an impressive print he'd screened only three or four times before retiring it, knowing its value.

Truitt hadn't thought of Eric in years. The boy was a wonderful catalyst for him. Maybe, in time, John Dewey would become another of his life's buddies. The rest were dead.

John was scrambling to remove the canister. Truitt laughed. "Be careful—that should go without saying."

John removed the films above it, tin by tin, placing them in an equally neat stack.

"You know," Truitt said, *"Gay Was the Hero* isn't half bad, not compared to most of those first talkies. You'd like it. And let me tell you, a more appropriate title there never was."

John halted his job and looked up at the grinning man. The implication was unmissable, as sharp as a slap. "Are you saying you believe Gil Romano was like *that?"* he asked, angry. It was just like when his childhood classmates had branded his father queer.

Truitt was baffled. *Can this little fairy be serious?* For a moment, he had the dreadful feeling he'd gotten himself deeply involved with the wrong person after all. It confused him that this Romano fan could be in denial of something so . . . true. People had *always* known Gil Romano was gay, even in the twenties. The confusion annoyed him. He would not be made a fool of in his own home.

"If you mean do I think Gil Romano was not fond of women, I can tell you I don't think it, I *know* it. As a fan, you must be aware of that. Does that bother you?"

John didn't know how to respond to the older man's authority on the subject. It was crossing his mind that Truitt Connor was probably queer, too. Though he'd always rejected it in the past, John realized he felt strangely unopposed to the idea of his idol's sexuality, like a scientist peering into a microscope, seeing things as they were and not as he'd hoped they were.

"I'm . . . not sure," John said. "I mean, his biographies say it was probably true that he was, but I think sometimes things are made up just out of . . . jealousy."

"You *do* know how he died?" Truitt said, alluding to the suicide, to the gay hustlers rumored to have staged it. "You've heard the stories?"

"So? Lots of people . . . do that," John replied, clearing his throat. "People kill themselves all the time."

Regaining a sharpened sense of control, Truitt let John's comment hang in the air long enough to give his response a weighty dismissiveness. "*Nonsense,*" he asserted. "You know perfectly *well* that Gil Romano was a *homosexual,* regardless of whether he took his own life or had it taken. He did not advertise his sex life as some people do today, nor was he able to, but was quite open about it. I'm *not* a Gay Liberationist, John, but I am not *about* to conceal the truth from someone, even an eighteen-year-old. I'm too old for rubbish."

John felt stung and resumed unstacking and stacking, nearing the tin with *Gay Was the Hero.* He wanted to cry thinking of Gil as a queer, but instead felt like he was falling out of love. It wasn't a loss of his intense feeling for Gil, it was a loss of illusion, not a disappointment that Gil had been gay, but that he had been *real.* He'd been just a man, an actor, a homo with a job that had been filmed. He'd been a human being, just like John, just like Truitt Connor—if he were alive, Gil Romano would be even *older* than Truitt Connor.

John felt Gil slipping away from him on some level, and in his wake felt a lonely longing. He'd obsessed over Gil Romano, deftly avoiding thinking of it as a kind of, well, *love*. As John felt Gil retreating into the shadows, the love remained, in need of a new object. John shuddered as his fingers numbly handled the frigid canisters, realizing in the basement that he was gay, too, and had been all along.

Why is it so hard to think about?

Because it's not your missing father who was a homo, it was you. All along it was you.

He stacked a movie called *PURITY* (*'16*) on top of one called *DUMPLING* (*'18*), on top of Claudette Colbert's *CLEOPATRA* (*'17*).

"I have the original Theda Bara version of *Cleopatra*, too," Truitt piped up clumsily, to help divert attention from the flare-up. "I have all of it except the title cards. Did you know that the title cards start up a lot of the decay in the first place? I got rid of many of those long ago. Do you know Theda Bara?"

"Yeah," John said, "Of course I do. She was fat and wore opera outfits. I've never seen any of her movies, though."

"Most of them are probably ashes," Truitt said. "I think *Cleopatra* is probably one of my top five favorite possessions, and it's probably the most important. Except for a certain film I'm going to show you after breakfast."

John looked up instantly, slapped. *"After?"* He had just reached the can neatly marked *GAY W. T. HERO* (*'27/'28*). "But can't we see *Gay Was the Hero* now?"

"We'll talk about that after. We have time. This film has waited sixty-odd years to be seen. It can wait another thirty minutes."

John held the can in his hand, shaking it and delighting in the shifting of the contents, heavy and mobile. Not liquid, not dust, but a chubby reel of film he had made it his life's goal to discover, and that nobody else but he and his host were going to watch.

OFF THE LIST

BY WARREN JUNIOR

HIT & RUN: BITE-SIZED BLIND ITEMS FOR THE ATTENTION SPAN–IMPAIRED

He's rich, he's famous, he's over 60, he's a screaming queen and he's a director du jour. He's F.X. Galore, and he should either come out of the closet or build an addition—it's, ahem, *stuffy* in there. . . .

Miss Grunt is not good-looking, was never slender, has never had a romantic part and yet has starred—*starred*—in a dozen good, bad and ugly feature films. She would like to confirm her Sappishm but is afraid she'll be asked to do gay benefits every day of the week. Makes good sense. After all, turning them down would just be so *uncomfortable*. It's *much* easier to live apart from your lover of 16 years, hire dates for awards shows, and chatter about how your love for your pets keeps you from settling down with the "right man". . . .

Lucy Legend is *going* to die within this calendar year, an assertion that's been made many times before but that is indisputable as of this writing. She's definitely loved men, but she's loved women even more—and more often. She's one of my all-time cinematic faves and yet she ticks me off because she still sends checks to "protect the family" anti-gay causes. The last face she'll see before she drifts off for the last time will likely be that of her lesbian niece, or possibly her longtime female confidante, who was also once her sexual savior. . . .

If gay marriage were legal, I'd be picking out china and stemware with this cuddly Latin ball of energy. He's not classically handsome, but is as hot as a cookie sheet left out in the sun, a gifted, rubber-bodied clown *and* dramatic actor who's making it big on TV (using a Jewish-sounding stage name) with a dumbed-down kiddie show. He recently had a one-night stand with the very married Suzy Shutterbug, and said Shutterbug would like to know why the stand couldn't have been extended a bit? Fear or loathing? Which is it, Sr. Gymnastic? I just love acting as a go-between for heterosexuals. . . .

Hey, Ass of Steel—your action-adventure movies are not setting the box office on fire, but that's no reason to kill yourself with crystal meth. Take it easy, and stop using the names of your more famous rivals when you check into rehab. Nobody is fooled and Mr. Seagal—who's *never* been hooked on airplane glue—is said to be sizing you up for a lawsuit. . . .

I *always* rag on Miz Biz, the ultimate gay icon with *loads* of lesbigay fans (even a few trannies buy her albums and see her unspectacular flix and read her periodic mem-wahrz). Well, let's keep the tradition rolling: Miz Biz, if you're out there reading this, nashing your expensive teeth, I challenge you—*challenge* you, I say—to pick up the phone and call me to tell me off or to deny the things I write about you, albeit blindly. Don't worry, I don't have caller ID, and I would never *dream* of doing a trace and then selling your private number on Christopher Street. I just want to know why you refuse to sing love songs for ladies, why you have bald-face lied in asserting you're hopelessly heterosexual, and why, oh, why, you recently helped eulogize *Sonny Bono?* We'll never forgive Cher for her involvement with him, but at least her indefensible marriage was before the Defense of Marriage Act, Miz Biz. Or are you even less politically astute than you claim? Perhaps you have forgotten that you are, underneath three layers of MAC, spackle, and sealant, a *bulldyke?* If that's the case, please take my frequent malsmots as friendly reminders. *Toro! Toro!.* . . .

Next week, I promise a blind item that will open a few eyes as to the real nature of Beach Boy (and I don't mean

Brian Wilson). It will be the ultimate blind item, the juiciest I've ever written, because I will provide the key to the item in the issue after the one in which it appears. And just in case anyone is rolling his eyes, expecting it to be something lame about famous toes stepped upon or Oscar-caliber roles fumbled, guess again: Next week's column is going to be *an outing to remember.*

In your face, *out* of control, and "Off the List."

CHAPTER 33

David's Brave Fight for Life—
"It's Up to God Now!"

David Greer— The day was Saturday, just one week after Alan and I had slept together—or, rather, stayed awake together. I found myself sitting with Warren in his East Village apartment. As always, it looked like it contained all the unclaimed objects from a storage facility somewhere in Indiana.

Warren Junior's personal HQ was a fairly spacious two-bedroom apartment, and yet he owned no bed, instead preferring to fold out his sofa sleeper and crash after a full day on the phone and on the computer. Warren rarely received guests, unwilling to reveal the fact that he didn't live someplace outrageously kitsch, glamorous, or at least *unique.*

Warren lived in what could have been mistaken for a solitary old woman's final apartment, except for the gigantic, yellowing Diana Ross in the Park poster tacked to one wall. She was his guilty pleasure, a woman he knew deserved his ridicule but who was instead the only celebrity of any repute who'd *never* received an unkind word in "Off the List"—and never would.

He had been open to my coming over when I'd called the night before. Warren Junior was obviously more curious than furious, relaxing the brittle—then volatile—demeanor he'd communicated on his message to me, after he'd seen the picture of me with Alan.

It was an unspoken fact that Warren's weekly deadline was Friday at noon, so anything I told him that morning would not show up until a week from the following Tuesday—but he'd probably already written *something* about Alan for Tuesday, something that had been dashed off in a rage at the zero-hour.

As soon as I sat down next to him, Warren clicked into reporter mode. He plopped a tape recorder on the table between us and matter-of-factly informed me what he expected. "You sit there and tell me everything—*everything*—about why the hell you and Alan Dillinger were photographed leaving your building at nine o'clock in the morning, his lips on your face no less."

I angrily turned the recorder off. "Come on, Warren, go easy here. I'm not some asshole you dug up for your column. You know me. You know I'm not here to blow any whistles. I'm your *friend*—I'm not going to become one of your *scoops*."

He had put on a closed expression, eyes tightly lidded, jaw forward, daring me to impress him. He'd crossed his legs and further crossed his arms in front of them, completely shut off from me even though I was sitting right next to him on his ratty couch, the same couch on which we'd sat and comforted each other over lost boyfriends, dwindled finances, life's little setbacks, the rise to prominence of Mariah Carey. We were old friends, but the basis of our friendship was being put to the test—were we intimates or just pop companions, too lazy to extricate ourselves from a stagnant relationship?

This nagging question was probably at the root of why I hadn't confided in Warren about Alan in the first place.

"David, do not start getting melodramatic," he snapped. "Do not try to turn this around on *me*. If you want to approach this as friends, it's going to be a lot worse than approaching this as two fags dishing a closeted actor. Because if we approach this as friends, I'm not just going to be cold, I'm going to be in your *face*." I rolled my eyes and started to get up. He reached over and held me down, stared me down. "If you want to, we can talk about how you have lied to me and mistrusted me and how you have *apparently* started going out with one of the most famous men on the fucking planet and yet I have to figure it out from a picture in a *People* magazine. Jesus Christ, it's worse than going to

Musto, it's so, so *mainstream.* What's that *about,* David? What is *that* about?"

He let go and I stayed put. I had expected fireworks, but Warren was slow-roasting me. I felt guilty looking at him, faced with the deception. I'd once been annoyed that he'd gotten free passes to see *The Brady Bunch Movie* and had gone without inviting me, and yet I had shut him out of the kind of event around which Dove Audio Books memoirs are formed. I was angry at Alan for refusing to give up his privacy, and yet I had not managed to tell him I was a pornographer whose close friend Warren Junior wrote one of the most star-hungry columns in the country.

"Warren," I started shakily, "it's not like that. It's not like that at all. It's just—"

"What is it like, David?" he spat, standing up and waving his fists in the air. "Is it like opening up a magazine and seeing *your* face next to Alan Dillinger's? Do you know that I almost convinced myself it wasn't really you? It was so outrageous that even though I was staring right at you—*right at you*—I thought, 'No, it can't be him,' and was gonna turn the page. I'm staring at you right now, too, David. Is it you? You tell me. Because you don't look a whole lot like you to me right now."

He was trying to be witty, to confront me in the same way he'd write a column. I stood up and faced him, absorbing the menace. *We'd never hit each other. Right?*

"Oh, come down off your column for a minute, Warren, and get over yourself. You're not that clever. Just because you did time for sodomy, that doesn't make you Oscar Wilde."

The pupils in his wild brown eyes diminished to pinheads and he opened his mouth. I was equally surprised—I'd just said something almost unforgivable to him, had brought up the one incident that, if he were a movie star, would have Warren paying the tabloids to leave unreported. As much as Warren demanded the truth of everyone in the world, there was one incident from his own past that he sought to forget, to brush under the rug.

He'd been arrested in a Penn Station men's room at age eighteen, accused not of sodomy, exactly, but of soliciting an undercover agent.

Warren had told me the story only after we'd been friends for years, and only because it haunted him. He'd been set up, he told me, and had been unable to convince anyone. Even his Legal Aid lawyer had defended him skeptically. He'd gotten off with probation, but had been permanently scarred by the idea that telling the truth hadn't saved him from punishment and humiliation.

"Warren, I'm sorry," I said quickly, ineffectually.

He sat down and looked away from me, devastated.

"So basically, even though I trusted you with . . . that story," he said, "you couldn't trust me with the information that you were dating Alan Dillinger. We were both wrong."

I hated lashing out at Warren with all my heart, but couldn't convince him I hadn't meant it, that I was just cracking under the strain.

"You don't understand," I said, emotional. "You don't know what it's like. It's like I've always said, whenever you trash somebody in print, I was always the one who would say, 'Hey, maybe this guy deserves to be trashed but maybe he doesn't,' and asked how would you know who deserved it and who didn't. You always said that everybody deserved it."

I pictured Alan speeding away from my neighborhood, snug in his armored limo.

"If that's true, then you deserve it, too," I cried, "and so do I, and so does Alan."

Warren turned to me and studied my face. "Tell me," he said evenly, "everything."

CHAPTER 34

Sources Close to the Investigation Reveal ...!

David Greer — Almost immediately, I second-guessed my decision to talk to Warren on the record. Even though Alan had behaved like a shit, I knew I was exposing him. It really wasn't bitterness that drove me to sing like a bird, it was disillusionment. I felt like I'd fallen in love with half a man, and that the other half was sapping me of my capacity to love. I didn't see why I should idly allow Alan Dillinger to put over his hoax, or why I should let him continue to deny himself his personal sanity in order to bank a few more million or get cast in a cheesy movie.

Yes, there was probably resentment behind my talking to Warren. Revenge, even. But I wasn't nasty, didn't lie or exaggerate, and didn't tell Warren the things that I felt should be kept private.

I told him Alan Dillinger was gay, that we'd met at the party and had dated since then. I told him how Alan had been dogged by the paparazzi, that he was in danger of having no personal life at all. I told him that Alan Dillinger was the hardest working person I'd ever encountered, that he was talented and driven and that—when he wasn't being squashed like a tennis ball by the pressures of fame—he was a sensitive and giving human being. I told him that Alan wanted very much to come out, but that he probably needed to be nudged. I was hanging onto that idea, hoping I was nudging him and not booting him rudely out of the closet.

Off the record, I told Warren that I'd been falling in love with Alan, and that Alan had seemed to be getting there with me.

Warren, once he'd gotten over my stinging attack, received my story with equal parts friendship and professionalism. He recorded everything I said and we went over the facts to double-check that he had everything right, and to make sure there wasn't anything I wanted him to delete.

Though I'd spilled Alan's guts to Warren, it's not like his column was literally going to out Alan Dillinger. The lawyers at *Island Rage* had been over it a thousand times with Warren: No way they were going to ever, ever let him call anybody gay who hadn't already said, "I am gay" in print or on tape. The only way around that was through blind items. I wouldn't have let Warren print everything about my time with Alan. I wanted the story to be blind so that people would figure out who was being discussed while still giving Alan a buffer, plenty of room to ignore or deny the story. It wasn't less of a betrayal on my part, but the results would be far less absolute.

"Of course, now I've already printed that I'm going to out somebody's ass," Warren said when we were through, showing me his next column, "when in reality I'm just going to do another blind item. I'm going to have to figure out a loophole or just—oh, fuck it. I guess I can just say, 'Sorry to disappoint you but there is no outing after all.' "

"Whichever," I said. "I'm sure you'll find a way to do it with style."

"Natch, natch." He cracked a smile and I knew everything could be all right between us again, with effort.

Warren let me out and the first thing I saw in the hallway was Carol backed against the far wall, distractedly chewing sugar trinkets off a candy necklace she was wearing. She must've bought it at the confectioner's store on the ground level and had the air of a caught girl.

"Mmpf," she said. "I thought you were never going to finish. I was getting ready to call the morgue or the FBI."

"What are you doing here?"

"I called her," Warren said behind me. "I told her what you were coming over here to do and suggested she show up for moral support."

"You need to come with me and sit in Central Park," she said firmly, "and watch Rollerbladers and lay in the grass like an old dog."

"But what about Gods?" I asked, knowing her store hadn't missed a regular business day in its history except for when her mom had died.

She shrugged. "I could use a day off."

That's when I knew something major had happened. I started to cry, believing that—good intentions or no—I had probably lost Alan forever. Carol's concerned face dissolved to tears simultaneously, so quickly and with such alacrity of emotion it made me laugh, then she laughed, and then Warren allowed a rare group hug before Carol and I headed down and out and up Second Avenue, navigating our city until we dropped, exhausted, in the middle of the park.

CHAPTER 35

Draw Me and Win a $1,000 Scholarship!

David Greer — It was a cool evening, but I had the window open, listening to the cars on Twenty-second careening past in waves, sounding like the shore, the displaced noise of churning water in a conch you hold to your ear, natural ventriloquism.

After confronting Warren—and myself—Carol had held my hand in the park and reminded me of every ditzy boyfriend I'd shed, the exact opposite therapy a less-informed friend might have tried. True to her instincts, the ploy had made me laugh until I was crying, had lost control of the muscles in my face—our hilarity drove away the towel people around us, the sunbathers and picnickers and the men who cruised me, unaware that the last dick I'd handled had belonged to a household name.

Sprawled on the grass, I'd held Carol's hand and had asked her a few questions.

"Will I ever be a writer?" was first. "No, I mean a real writer, with something . . . finished?" It was supposed to be rhetorical.

She'd squeezed my hand three times sharply—I love you—and said, "David, you will never be *anything* if you keep wasting time asking what you'll be. But if you're asking me, really asking me, if I think you're talented, look at me," propping herself up on her elbows, staring at me, "*yes,* David, you are one of the most intelligent people I know, you're sensitive, and you have a natural facility with words. Yes, you could be a real writer, David. The question is whether you're ever going to apply yourself and do it."

Where had I heard that before?

I considered her words. "I know that," I heard myself saying, incredibly. I'd felt so much self-doubt in the previous few years I'd thought I was on the verge of giving up completely, not rededicating myself. "I know I can do it, and I think, honestly, that I've figured that out in part due to . . . Alan."

She'd settled onto her back, staring into blue. "He *is* a hard worker. A regular James Brown."

I watched her watching the sky. "I don't know if I could handle all the pressure he's got, but I would love to know I'd achieved as much as he has."

"You know, he probably envies you in a lot of ways, too," Carol said.

"Until he reads 'Off the List' this week," I replied.

"No," she said, "maybe even after."

The park was like a gigantic quilt of people, their dogs, rolling lawns, trees that whenever I was on a plane always looked so out of place tucked among the concrete superstructures. Sometimes I felt like an alien in New York City myself, a place where almost every citizen was constantly busy maximizing their time, and where I spent so *much* time *wasting* time.

After a sleepless night, I'd spent another lazy Sunday putting off the editing I'd brought home to do—*I am a fugitive from a porn gang.* One hundred thousand *Pumped* fans were going to be stroking air if I didn't get back into work mode, start building the next issue. But I really needed the time and couldn't imagine presiding over anything erotic. All the readers' letters I'd fake would be about blond television stars, closeted studs, sexual surveillance.

I'd sat around my apartment moping, and yet I'd also used the hours to sketch a few scenes for my novel. *Even if it's never published,* I thought, *I'm going to finish this motherfucker.* No matter how many times I started, I kept gravitating to a main character strikingly similar to Alan Dillinger, filling in his mysterious background with elaborate, romantic details.

By not telling the world anything about his past, Alan had unwittingly created a fertile field for speculation. He was Keyser Soze in a thong, and after all, weren't even sexy, shiny heartthrobs capable of having a mesmerizing past?

When I wrote, Alan was a prodigy, an orphan, the illegitimate son of Alain Delon. So many possibilities. I had no idea which one I'd eventually pick, so many that they eventually led me away from writing about Alan figures, into different stories, my own.

When someone knocked, I expected it to be the Chinese I'd ordered. I picked up my wallet and hurried to open the door, not hungry at all, my stomach already anticipating grease.

I opened up and it was Alan. I almost collapsed.

"Alan . . ." I whispered. My eyes teared up and I didn't know what to think or say. I was immediately recalling the horrible yearning I'd felt when his car had sped away from me two days earlier, and also the confusion that had blanketed my confrontational confession with Warren. I'd thought I'd never see Alan again—at least in person.

"Hey," he said softly. He looked a little different than I was used to seeing him, radically different than the world was used to seeing him, unshaven and dressed down, a baseball cap backwards on his head, covering his platinum hair. He looked like one of those fleet-bodied teenagers who shot hoops on the Houston Street courts, his body shifting gracefully and with measured movement.

"What are you doing here?" I asked blankly.

"Take a walk with me," he said, his eyes embracing me. "I want to talk."

We walked down Seventh Avenue to Fourteenth Street, turned west until we hit Eighth Avenue, and followed it to Bleecker. It wasn't an out-of-the-way route; it wasn't *possible* that not even *one* person would recognize Alan Dillinger strolling with a buddy, and yet nobody seemed to look twice. As we walked, the lack of attention built and our expectation of intrusion diminished until we felt like we were sealed in an invisible cocoon, protected in some flimsy way, easy to rupture, like we had to hold our breath to make it last.

"How you been?" he asked tenderly.

"I've been . . . sort of lost," I admitted. "I didn't know how much it would hurt when you freaked out over the picture of us. I guess I took it to heart, like *I* was something to be ashamed of."

"That's not what it was, you know," he said. "I guess that no matter how comfortable I am on a personal level with being, you know, gay, until I can be cool with it on a professional level, I'm never gonna really be comfortable. I told you from the beginning that I've always wanted to be a famous homo." We laughed. "Well, maybe it's time I got off my ass and did it. So I'll lose a few roles. I might gain a few. I can do a movie with Ellen, for sure, that's a gimme." He smiled and I watched him from the corner of my eye, enjoying my private peek at his handsome face curling up in the moonlight.

We came to the wooded playground at Bleecker and Eighth, all the climbing structures silent and unused, the gate chained. There were several pairs of wooden benches in the tiny park next to the gates, distributed evenly over a redbrick walk. I could see dark figures stretched across two benches on the Hudson Street side, homeless sleepers. We picked a bench and sat down, both of us straddling the wood, facing each other. The darkness was like a blanket we'd pulled over our heads.

"David, I don't know if I can forgive you for talking to the press . . ." he started, looking down.

Shara had gotten ahold of Warren's column, since she turned out to be a close friend of Dot Hiawatha's. Apparently, Shara had once been a performance artist herself, not so surprising since she was still doing basically the same thing.

Alan had read Warren's bold promise of outing "Beach Boy," and he had assumed I must've contacted the press. But he had no idea that Warren wasn't really going to out him, that the lawyers would never let him. He didn't know I'd made Warren promise to do nothing more than a blind item, didn't know Warren Junior, gossip columnist, was really Warren, Jr., my friend.

I lost my breath, thinking I'd destroyed everything. "Wait—I haven't been as honest with you as you've been with me."

He looked confused.

"I didn't just talk to Warren Junior, he's one of my best friends."

Alan was clearly taken aback. "What are you saying?" he choked, looking around as if fearing our whole conversation were being filmed.

"Warren was the reason I got into the *Lifesavers* party in the first place. I used his press credentials to get myself in. When I met you, my first thought was, of course, that I'd call Warren up and report all my impressions. But after you and I talked, after the incident with the photographer, I knew I was going to put off talking to Warren. I didn't tell him about you at all, ever, while we were seeing each other. I kept it from him because I wanted to protect you. I knew how important your privacy was, and how important it was for you to control it. I didn't talk about you, Alan. I waited."

"David—"

"No, wait. Listen, I know I can't understand about sacrificing since I don't really have anything to lose. Not even a job. You know what I do for a living? I work for *Pumped* magazine. Your ex- is a pornographer. And a liar, too. And eventually, I *did* rat you out to Warren, because I felt betrayed by you and also because I felt like I was doing you a favor. I convinced myself that by giving Warren enough information for a strong blind item, the story might force your hand, or at least make you see it wasn't worth it to keep trying to cover up."

"*You* write for *Pumped*?" he asked me.

"Yes," I said, defensive. "Is it that strange? Don't tell me you've never looked at porn."

"No." He laughed, but quietly. We both felt the urge to be silent, like we were sitting in the bedroom of the homeless men dozing within earshot. The entire area was dead quiet, with only a trickle of foot traffic and the omnipresent but smooth and stealthy whir of cars down Eighth. "No, I like that magazine. I've seen it before. I mean, let's face it, *Lifesavers* is sort of like the TV version of it except without the nudity, right? I just mean . . . *you?*"

I felt my face flush. "Yes, *me*. What, do you think I'm a prude or just asexual?"

He smiled and leaned closer until our noses were separated by only about an inch. His eyes were wild in the intimate shadows, searching my face, suppressing a grin, excited and won back, just like I was. "Neither. I know you're *not* a prude and I know you *are* sexual—for a fact. I'm just surprised because I'm sure your writing is a little overqualified for a sex magazine. People don't actually *read* them, right? I haven't read anything you've written, but I just think, you know, that if someone as interesting and perceptive as you is going to spend time writing something down, it should be available to a wider circle of readers than, you know, the horny masses."

He was so close I was anticipating a kiss, and would have accepted it, even in public. I was always reserved when there were people—or *People*—around, but right then, I didn't give a flying fuck.

We were interrupted by one of the men who'd been sleeping in the park. He had stumbled over during our conversation. I'd thought he'd been headed for the playground, but he'd stopped right next to us. *Please don't panhandle me now,* I begged inside. *This is the worst timing ever.*

We looked up at him. He had the severe, strong features of a Native American, his skin leathered by exposure, his clothes secondhand (though recently so, like he'd spent some time in a shelter). He reeked of alcohol, but his expression was benevolent.

"I just wanted to tell you guys that you two are beautiful," he said through a wide smile in a gravelly voice. He was beaming.

It was like we were being granted some sort of approval by the cosmos. He immediately took off toward Bleecker, moving with uncertain steps. The moment had passed but had somehow stamped me with a feeling that Alan and I were trapped in a fairy tale, where the sun never came up and you never missed it because the cool moon was so magnificently silvered and bright, where Alan's fame could be switched on and off, where drunken vagabonds didn't make you angry or sick or guilty but handed out compliments for free, where you could kiss another man in public and not worry about hecklers or about being attacked.

We faced each other again, so close our noses brushed, and then our lips fell into place and we were kissing. It was all lips at first, just feeling the softness of pressing our mouths together, gently pecking away the discord of the week before. Then we moved into a deeper kiss, our tongues sliding in and out and against, our arms grasping each other and pulling closer until we were sharing a passionate, cautionless expression of love.

Then a flash went off.

It's disorienting to have a brilliant light strobe over you from the darkness of a deserted park, especially when your tongue is in another man's mouth. I'm sure that explains why we nearly cannibalized each other. The sinking feeling was immediate and deep: *The fantasy is over. A paparazzo has just stolen the single most romantic and emotional moment of my life.*

But it was just a tourist, a blonde in a running suit posing with her arms outstretched at the entrance to the park. Her husband or lover or boyfriend or beard was snapping her picture.

"Listen," I said, turning back to Alan, "are we okay? Can we fix this?"

"Yes," Alan offered immediately. "But, David, I have an idea. It involves your friend the columnist."

I was again eyeing the couple with the camera, untrusting.

They were oblivious to us. We were invisible still. For the moment.

OFF THE LIST

BY WARREN JUNIOR

COURTING DISASTER

This volatile, charming, strawberry-blond tennis type—
U.S. Open Wide—spent a recent January in drug rehab,
where he wrote indiscreet love-to-suck-your-dick letters to
an action star so famous they know his name on Mars. The
98% straight Action Jackin' prefers impersonal hand jobs
from the boys he likes to collect (none over 20, please), but
always feels uncomfortable receiving a blowjob or—
heaven forbid—anything *more* from a man. Something
about it is just too "faggoty" for Action Jackin'. I think it's
safe to say that U.S. Open Wide will settle for such unchal-
lenging volleying rather than rushing the net and risking
the match.

But on to more important matters.

LOVE IS BLIND

The promised blind item is not going to happen in *quite* the
way I promised.

I'm going to lay it on you *without* providing a key next
week, because I have it on good authority that by this time
next week, the already ve-HERR-y famous name of this
Beach Boy ("but I play one on TV") will be on everyone's
lips, so there will be no need to reveal anything at all. I just
love that for once I'm doing a blind item knowing that the
subject will be grateful upon reading it, instead of fretting
that the damn fool might slash a wrist over an insignificant
tumble told.

Here goes:

Beach Boy isn't just hot, he's *HOT*. He's everywhere
right now: on TV, in the movies (soon, kittens, soon), on al-

most every magazine cover, certainly in all our collective wet dreams. He's the inescapable face of the '90s, the blond god with the eyes that really complement his sea-blue schlong (oh, sorry—didn't realize there was a *swimsuit* painted on).

Beach Boy has been linked with every actress in town, some of whom have been the sources behind those rumors, most recently Sara Pasquale. As if.

Beach Boy has long been rumored to be gay—and is. Point-blank.

In fact, Beach Boy has met Prince Charming, someone with whom to build sand castles, a dashing young man who scooped him up at a skanky (or did he say "swanky"?) party for Beach Boy's dippy TV show (sorry, Prince C, at *least* give me *that*). This seductive 32-year-old saved Beach Boy from a—*boo! hiss!* . . . except I sort of *like* them— paparazzo, and the new couple later spent quality time at the more famous half's fortified bachelor pad in the—unh!— meatpacking district of the city that never *zzzzz*. The lovebirds quickly became a red-hot (blind) item.

Now, weeks later (hey, Ellen 'n' Anne were married on their first *date,* remember?), these two guys seem to be headed toward the legendarily elusive Happily Ever After.

Beach Boy is not about to keep lying about matters of the heart. Don't believe me? ASK HIM. And say hi for me, because it turns out his Prince Charming is my Bosom Buddy, so I will be a regular part of Beach Boy's posse. Yes, queer reader, I am—if only this one time—most definitely "On the List."

(P.S. He-mail to Noah Wyle: If Beach Boy's outcoming inspires a new fad in Hollywood and you decide you really *are* gay after all, please stop by my apartment because I just really need to have you in a little cage by my bed. I'll even scrub before we play, Doctor!!!)

CHAPTER 36
Voices

John Dewey, Truitt Connor, and Jim Stepps — The two film buffs were seated in tattered folding chairs that had been allowed to go to pot even as the hundred thousand feet of nitrate film in the room had been kept artificially alive. The rickety projector, also neglected, was propped on phonebooks between them, the aging master and the novitiate preparing to experience a unique event.

Strella was washing dishes upstairs. John realized that listening to Strella's movements must have taken up a lot of Truitt's time as he'd worked on his collection in the arctic cellar.

"Now, I haven't seen this thing in *years,*" Truitt prefaced, suppressing his dread at having to disappoint. "And remember, this is not the absolute original, of course. But this safety reel was struck from the original negative, so the quality should be pretty fine even now. It may break off here and there—"

"I don't care," John said. "I just want to see this movie—it means everything to me."

Truitt paused. "John . . . you *will* see *Gay Was the Hero* . . . someday. But we can't now. It's on the original nitrate—we can't just string it up and hope for the best without risking the reel."

John couldn't believe what the old man was telling him. "What do you mean?" He was holding in his hand the canister with the elusive nitrate, the film nobody knew existed, the film *he had found.*

"John, we can't see the movie immediately, but there is something else we *can* see, something small I was able to afford converting to safety stock, to, eh, *acetate.*"

Feeling his hope evaporate, John lifted the lid and breathed deeply at the sight of an intact reel of film. It looked rattled, a bit disheveled, and had obviously come apart and been reaffixed in places. Directly underneath was another reel, separated by some sort of clear plexiglass.

"Ah, I see everything's tip-top, pat-on-the-back for me—but even with breaks, this is going to look good to you, John, very good indeed."

"What is it?" John asked, pointing to the other reel.

"The top reel should be *Gay*—it's not a short feature, as I recall. The bottom reel is what I thought you would want to see, but I'm having second thoughts about that." Truitt sounded very grim, very serious, his voice lowering an octave. "After our conversation about Gil Romano, I'm not sure you're ready."

John was annoyed with the tease, with all the buildup. "What is it? Is it Gil Romano? Then I want to see it."

"Yes, it's Gil Romano, but it's not one of his features."

John couldn't guess what the safety reel contained. He started feeling feverish from anticipation. Here he had been about to see *Gay Was the Hero,* and suddenly he was being distracted by a different film, something that by the look in Truitt Connor's eyes promised to be even more important.

"What?" John begged. *"What?"*

"You know I told you that I knew Gil Romano to be homosexual," Truitt began.

John stiffened. He didn't want to return to that topic, not so soon. He hated the way the term exited Truitt's mouth. Ho-mo-*sex*-you-all. "Yes."

"Well," Truitt continued, "anyone who cared to know, knew. It was knowledge we didn't have to question. But more than rumors, I later knew that Gil Romano was a homosexual because of that second reel."

John was mortified. A dirty movie? Impossible. "They didn't make those kind of movies in those days," he finally stuttered weakly. "And Gil would never—"

"On the contrary," Truitt interjected. "They did *indeed* make, as you call them, *those kind of movies*. I used to have some, but they were made on film of such degraded quality, they disintegrated before I was even aware of the short life of nitrate. I only have a few now, and this one I only have because once I saw it and once I determined what it was, what it meant, I knew I had to preserve it at all costs. To me, and to a lot of people, it's probably more important than *Gay Was the Hero,* John. In fact, just in artistic terms, it's more important than most of the pulp I've saved for nostalgic or historic reasons. And though I'm sure it still has the power to titillate, it is most certainly more than just a dirty movie."

John stood up and stepped over to the nearest stack of films, time bombs in cans. He started to feel very strange, very isolated. He felt like he was in the presence of something greater than the facts argued, like sitting at a Ouija board and peaking into the future—or the past. All these movies, all these objects that should be history, but which had been saved like survivors of the *Titanic.* So many unique items, so many things the rest of the world would never believe existed, never knew existed in the first place.

And Gil. Gil Romano, the icon of his teenage years, the man he'd spent so many hours thinking about, dreaming about. Fantasizing. What else had he been but in love? With a man? Even if "Gil Romano" was only what remained of Jim Stepps, a man who had once been real, but who had returned to ashes long before John's debut on the planet, what had he been but in love with Gil Romano? He was hard thinking about how much he desired Gil Romano, scared at what Truitt was offering. Proof that Gil Romano had been—gay?

"John," Truitt said, surrounded by the tiny scraping noises of the film being removed, being mounted in the projector. "John, I think you have to watch this. You may be the one person in this world for which this piece of film will have the most impact. It's going to change your mind about a lot of things, I feel. It's—aside from anything else, it's an extraordinary film. It's a film they risked everything to make. It's . . . art."

John turned around, his eyes avoiding Truitt's penetrating stare. "Go ahead," he said quietly, sitting down and looking up only to focus on the small, inadequate screen across from them. "I want to see."

Truitt immediately started the projector. John reached up automatically and tugged the bulb's chain, extinguishing all light.

The screen was an unearthly white, then exploded with images. The film had no beginning, no titles at first, just a crazed juxtaposition of image upon image. The first thing John remembered being aware of was a closeup of a man's back, the small of a man's back, smooth and pale in a lustrous black-and-white. He was shocked to see a few hairs sprouting along the lower part of the spine, natural as today and yet unseen in any black-and-white oldie. Projected shirtlessness seemed out of place in the absence of color.

Next was a series of shots that simulated a dense, magical forest; dense due to a rich overlapping of blackest leaves and veinlike branches, magical due to the lighting that made it glow and shimmer. Points of light appeared and disappeared across the onyx forest, artificially recreated fireflies, patternless and serene.

A stark, unreasonable close-up of a stern-faced young man, his concentration illustrated with flickering jump cuts between his searching expression and suffocatingly canned shots of the mysterious, manmade forest.

It was Gil Romano.

Slack-jawed, John digested the beauty of the image, of Gil Romano's face, younger than he'd ever seen it in motion. The shot held at times for almost a minute, another strange departure from the usual style of moviemaking in the—when had this picture been made? the late teens? Younger, smoother, more boyish, Romano's hair was fuller and thicker and shinier and unkempt, rakish. But it was unquestionably Gil Romano.

No, it was Jim Stepps. Before he'd become Gil Romano.

Slowly, John connected Gil's inky hair to the texture of the forest. "He's thinking of the forest," John said, pleased to have puzzled it out, as if he were playing silent charades with the screen.

A sudden cut transported them to a white, antiseptic room. Gil was standing in the center of it, his whole form captured. He wore a loose shirt that seemed old-fashioned even for the early part of the century, high pants, walking boots. A cut stripped him to nothing at all, and in that instant, John felt himself seize with shock at the nakedness of the man whose enigma dominated his life, at the pleasure he took from seeing him. The desire swept over him even as the scene cut swiftly to another man.

John could hear himself breathing over the noise of the projector. He held back from crying for Truitt to replay the brief segment—he hadn't seen any detail, only Gil's alabaster body, the black around his crotch, the impression of nudity.

The new actor on the screen was much older and more darkly photographed, though he was in a similarly white room. "It's the same place," John ventured, his face hot and red over the flash of skin.

"Yes," Truitt murmured, watching his guest with concern.

"It's his—it's his father," John blurted, guessing.

The film's older man, the paternal figure, was wrapping something with twine. The twine filled the screen in a series of oddly angled shots, the coarse fiber perfectly communicated, making John feel itchy. The man was wrapping a small animal in twine, a dog, a puppy. It was a live puppy, white and alert, playful as it attempted to tear the twine from its captor's grip. The image was charged with a disturbing sense of doom, the implication that the man would continue wrapping the puppy until it was helpless, then dead.

The projector banged loudly like it would give, but John never looked away, catching a fragment of film so brief it couldn't have made up more than a few frames, and yet it was clearly a close-up of Gil's sobbing face, a realistic anguish foreign to melodramatic silents. John's own eyes were already moist, his heart beating, annoying him.

Then a lingering shot of Gil Romano, future screen idol, fully nude, reclining on a bed, his legs demurely locked at the knees, his flaccid penis flopped back against his small, fleshy belly. His body was smooth and still radiating white light, obviously overexposed by powerful Kliegs. His chest was broad and flat, the nipples painted as black as his lips would later be in one of his sheik epics.

John was transfixed by the nudity, the vulnerability. A close-up of Gil Romano's face, emotionless, defiant. An even tighter close-up of his bare neck, the most erotic thing John could imagine. It was an image he would never forget.

The first title card emerged, but it wasn't a true title card, more a filmed shot of one. It was handwritten, not rendered in the affected script so common in silent screen titles. It was crudely crafted, the single word: *voices*

" 'Voices'," John repeated.

The screen filled with a pan across the night sky, intercut with frenzied images of Gil running, naked, through the phony forest. They were clearly the same shot looped over and over; the forest was a finite, interior creation in a studio, or more likely someone's home, so there had probably been only a few feet for the actor to run before he'd reach the edge. Compensating, the film reused the initial take repeatedly, which made it seem like he was running for a long stretch, but never getting anywhere.

When he stopped, a brief segment showed the paternal figure walking uncertainly in the woods, at the edge of it, it seemed, soundlessly calling out. A close-up showed his frightening face twisted with rage; he was screaming, howling. There was the very real sense that if he found his son, he would kill him.

Gil's journey through the forest ran again, superimposed over the enraged father's face, a technique John had never seen in a silent movie.

The next scenes were more lightning-fast shots that piled on top of each other so quickly there was no time to reason them out. John found himself laundry-listing the objects rendered in shaky close-up.

"A hammer," he said. "A screwdriver? What is that . . . ? A wrench. A broom—broom handle. A stick, walking stick. A book . . ."

A scene clearly meant to approximate a flashback showed the paternal figure holding a large book in a very showy manner, as if reading it. He sat in a cozy, familial room that seemed in stark contrast to the rest of the film, a traditional scene. Gil entered in exaggerated schoolboy clothing and the man hurled the book at him, striking him in a way that seemed realistically painful. A close-up of Gil on the floor, cowering in abject fear, blood running down his face, obviously black ink or paint due to the richness of its void.

"They're all things his father hit him with," John said, frightened, remembering Granny, mentally superimposing her over the film, over the cleverly disguised implements of torture.

"Right," Truitt echoed.

"They're all things he hit him with. . . ."

John watched in wonder as the screen filled with Gil Romano's nude body, walking languidly in a bright field, outdoors, a location—it could have been somewhere near Jim Stepps's hometown in New Jersey. Tightly rounded clouds charged overhead, the sky full of so many undulating grays its original blue seemed unmistakable. John couldn't take his eyes off Gil's naked body, off his sinewy form, his unaffected sense of movement, and his skin, always the skin.

The camera unashamedly watched Gil from behind, capturing almost accidentally the emergence of another nude man from the side, a man close to Gil's size, only stockier, with fairer hair. The man's penis played against his thighs as his progress intersected Gil's. When they met, the film cut to a close-up of the two gazing into each other's eyes. John was choked by their gaze, by their eyes, their faces.

The other man was handsome, devilish, a blond imp with an initiating grin at the corners of his lips. After several long moments of staring, Gil's face moved closer until they were almost touching at the nose. And then Gil tilted his head and the man moved in closer still. They kissed, their lips sealing and their hands rising into frame to hold each other's faces. It was a long, leisurely kiss—more real than the traditional Hollywood smack performed between two mannequinlike stars with lips firm and immobile. John felt himself dizzying, had forgotten to breathe.

When the two men pulled apart, two close-ups revealed the imp's expression, infused with desire, like he meant to kiss again, and Gil Romano breaking into a delighted and embarrassed grin, the whites of his teeth glaring on the film.

Everything John was seeing completely contradicted what audiences of the twenties had known about Gil Romano onscreen. He'd always played the vanquishing lover, the Romeo, and here—here it seemed clear that Gil was the vanquished. Gil Romano had never smiled on-screen, keeping his allure and his distance, the untouchable.

Here was Gil Romano, smiling and blushing with obvious enjoyment over the romantic exchange, the act that John knew so many people would consider the embodiment of the profane. And yet he couldn't help feeling—perhaps ushered into it since the actor was his idol—that he'd seen something of unsurpassing beauty, something momentous that he couldn't comprehend or put into words, but that warmed him through and made his heart break. He felt he had seen the core of Gil Romano, had seen the actor playing no role but himself.

It wasn't a part, it wasn't even Gil Romano, it was Jim Stepps reaching across time and exposing his soul, the soul of a man who loved men.

It was the first time John had ever seen two men kiss. He felt his hard cock release, closing his eyelids against the buzz of ejaculation.

He became aware that the film had ended, just as abruptly as it had begun. The screen was back to dead white after a series of noises, the sound of the end of the reel flickering around and around and around the projector. It had lasted less than five minutes.

The lights came on, Truitt Connor holding the chain.

"Thank you," John said in his smallest voice, crying, smiling, the words hard to form.

John wondered if he'd ever get over the movie, like he'd once wondered if he'd ever get over Gil Romano, whether or not his obsession would ever end.

It did.

Life with Truitt Connor and his controller, Strella, was completely un-like life with Granny, unlike any life John had experienced. The three spent their time domestically, with Strella on an endless campaign to keep the house clean, John assisting and eventually taking over from Truitt the chores of maintaining his beloved nitrate.

John was introduced to the neighborhood as John Connor, a distant relative's young son. Nobody wondered too hard at the veracity of the story since John was seventeen and still beneath notice.

John's reinvention was really an emergence, a new birth.

He spent hours poring over Truitt's diaries of gay life in the thirties, forties, and beyond, helped to catalog what remained of his host's exquisite beefcake photographs, and arranged in his mind the complexities of the person he would become. He never gave a second thought to his friend back home minding his Gil Romano collection. He owned a part of Gil Romano that was more rare than any movie magazine or play program or autograph.

When Truitt died the following year, John helped Strella organize for the liquidation of the film collection. The one-of-a-kind or best-existing material was grudgingly handed over to the American Film Institute and other agencies, with assurances that the films would be kept intact and eventually transferred to acetate. Budget allowing.

The duplicate films were sold to collectors and raised enough money to ensure that Strella had a modest retirement fund. She'd been shocked, never having had faith that the old movies on which Truitt had lavished so much attention were worth anything at *all.*

The house was sold.

John kept *voices,* the fragment that had once been part of a gay experimental film, from a time when film itself had been an experiment. There was no evidence of who had directed *voices,* how long it had been originally, how many people had ever seen it. It had probably been made in 1917 or 1918, before Jim Stepps had become a stage actor, a movie star, an icon, Gil Romano.

The only interesting piece of information Truitt had was unconfirmable—the other actor, unknown, had been identified as a New Jersey native named Alan. Alan what? Nobody knew. In some ways, he was even more a mystery than Gil Romano.

That safety reel was sticking with John; let the American Film Institute and others bicker over Colleen Moore, Theda Bara, Greta Garbo—John had Gil Romano. John had Jim Stepps.

Strella had recognized the renewed vitality John had given her boss, her companion. She knew him to be an honest and sensitive boy—queer, yes, but a good, decent person. She gave him some money whenever he needed it, paid for the cold storage required for *voices*. Strella gave her blessing when he moved to Los Angeles. When he'd sent her a picture three years later, she couldn't recognize him at all. His hair was yellow, he was so brown all over, he had muscles like the men in Mr. Truitt's old pictures.

She had been the last person to see him as John Connor, and the only person alive who knew that the boy who had arrived at her door at seventeen in a rainstorm was the same person as the beautiful actor on TV, the blond beach hunk who had been on the cover of her *TV Guide* three times already in only a couple of years. She'd canceled her *National Enquirer* subscription over rude remarks they'd made about her John—she *liked* the way he dressed.

Always entranced by the screen, it had been natural for John to transfer his enthusiasm to acting. Acting was the legacy of his obsession, the way in which it was salvaged, put to use. He felt like an impostor at times as he watched himself in the mirrors at the gym, saw his body changing, narrowing, widening. The blond had been a suggestion of his first boyfriend, the first man he'd been with and the first to disappoint him. He'd gone for the traditional nose bob and had had his teeth fixed, straightened, relieved that not everything was set in stone, that things could change, or be changed, that no exterior part of a person was determinate.

He'd chosen his professional name—his third—from his migraines. Dillinger had been a term he'd used for a migraine that emerged from nowhere, with no warning, and which disappeared with the same suddenness. John wanted to take the world by surprise.

Alan he'd chosen for the other man in *voices*. There was a magnetism in that man's eyes, in his playful expression, something so powerful it had even toppled the most legendary silent-screen Casanova, had drawn Gil Romano into his kiss. That was also what John wanted to mimic, that was his dream: to seduce the world and to do it on his own terms.

And when I am famous, he'd thought idealistically, enduring his hundredth dismal audition, *I'll do what Jim Stepps never could. I'll be honest. I'll be real.*

John Dewey, John Connor, Alan Dillinger. All the same man, but three different people, with different dreams; when he became famous, it was going to take time to decide which to be true to, whose dream to follow.

John Dewey couldn't conceive of coming out to the world, John Connor couldn't conceive of staying in.

Alan Dillinger couldn't decide *what* was best—he needed to be nudged.

CHAPTER 37

Breaking News!

David Greer — The Tuesday that Warren's next column came out, Alan and I were plunked in front of my TV. We could have been sprawling on his fits-six luxury bed watching fucking Imax, but we'd thought it might be less taxing to hang out in my humble burrow. We had all the news shows on, switching back and forth to monitor the coverage.

I watched as Alan pressed a small plastic digit to his forearm, compressing it until the tiny needle inside broke free enough to stick him. *I* winced, but he didn't. With the dispassionate professionalism of a nurse, he wrapped the used needle in a plastic disposable container and held sterile gauze to the bloodless wound. Alan had told me he'd suffered from sensational migraine headaches his whole life, and though they'd gotten far less frequent every year, he still needed to medicate himself against them. Whenever one came on—always at times of stress—he innoculated himself with a kit he'd been using for the past few years. The medicine provided near instantaneous relief, and its administration was probably behind those pesky heroin whispers.

"Are you that stressed out about all this?" I asked, wondering if maybe I had pushed him into something he wasn't ready to do.

He was already feeling some relief from the shot. "No," he said firmly, "it's not the column, it's just that after all this is all over, I have some things I want to talk to you about. Some . . . surprises."

I was full of surprises myself.

The day before had been the best day I'd ever had at Whole Man. I'd accomplished more in my first *10* minutes of the day than I had in five years on the job. I'd quit.

The faces had been priceless. My co-workers had either been in frantic disbelief (knowing Sandra would probably take her time in replacing me, meanwhile dumping my workload on them without dumping any of my salary on anybody at all), or they'd looked smug: *He'll be back.*

Nobody knew why I was leaving or anything about Alan. Nobody had noticed me in *People,* but I knew that they would notice us the next day.

I left my desk untouched, only removing a picture of Carol and Warren and myself from my bulletin board and deleting the personal files from my computer. After poking my head into her office to tell her I was out of there, I was escorted from the premises by Larajane, who performed her task with an air of military duty. She straightened her suit and patted her hair as we strolled down the long, long hall back toward the elevator, with people poking their heads up over their cubicles to watch our procession.

"You really could have been decent and given the company two weeks' notice," she sniffed, not turning her head to look at me as she muttered.

"Yes, shockingly inappropriate on my part. Surprising there aren't more stand-up kinda guys in pornography," I said.

"We won't be able to give you a reference," she said curtly, as if I hadn't spoken.

We reached the door, the elevator. "That's okay," I said, anticipating the snoopy press calls she'd be fielding once reporters identified me as Beach Boy's Prince Charming, accessed my tax records, and showed up at Whole Man. "I'd be only too happy if you didn't refer to me at all."

I got on the elevator and she stood facing me, as if deciding whether she should hop on with me to watch me physically leave the premises. "There's no need to be so vulgar about this," she hissed, losing her composure around the edges. She was such a human pinch.

"You're right," I replied, the door almost cutting me short. "And suck my dick."

It's always a good thing to leave an unwanted job, but I'd had the rare privilege of leaving with a flourish, and I didn't take it for granted. I didn't take anything for granted, least of all my life with Alan.

We were at the beginning of something that felt like it had roots, like it might outlast most other unions, but we knew we couldn't be sure for a long time—months or years.

As a start, he and I were going to keep living apart, though I imagined I'd probably crash at his place a little more frequently than vice versa. I had quit my day job and had pledged to try writing for a year with Alan's generous patronage. *It's who ya know and who ya blow.* I knew I'd have plenty of alone-time to devote to the writing, since Alan was committed to a few more seasons of *Lifesavers* and its Left Coast shooting schedule, not to mention all the other demands of his career—presuming Warren's column didn't end all that.

I'd be taking baby steps toward realizing my dream, but Alan was already at full sprint in the middle of his, and that was more an inspiration to me than a drag. I would want to see him more than I was able, but we were together in spirit, already a team.

The *Island Rage* with Warren's column hit the New York streets at noon and it took about ten seconds for Cindy Adams to reach Shara in L.A. The "dealmaker" had been briefed and was probably three sheets to the wind in preparation for the calls, the press release, The Event.

After that first inquiry, calls, faxes, and e-mails began to deluge Shara's offices, each one receiving a simple press release in response, a release with no precedent and with no predictable reception.

Were the producers going to buy Alan out of *Lifesavers*? Were his girl fans going to throw up, or decide that they loved him all the more? Would he ever be hired again to play a romantic lead? What would the reviews for his movie be like (especially since its final title had been chosen: *Boy Meets Girl*)? Would he be boycotted by the Baptists? Would other actors follow suit?

I *was* fascinated to see what would happen, but I was more concerned with what would happen between Alan and me. We had so much to learn about each other, and it would start later that week when I found he'd converted his living room into a temporary screening room, complete with ancient projector and makeshift screen.

Shaky and raw and vulnerable, Alan said, "This is where we talk about the, uh, surprises. I've lied to you about most of my life history, David. I can't take the lying away, but I want to tell you everything there is to know about me."

He started threading a movie into the projector. "First, I have something I want to show you."

— FOR IMMEDIATE RELEASE —

CONTACT: SHARA QUINCY/FRESH MEAT TALENT
(818) 555-3452

IT HAS COME TO OUR ATTENTION THAT A BLIND ITEM IN WARREN JUNIOR'S "OFF THE LIST" COLUMN IN *ISLAND RAGE WEEKLY* NEWSPAPER REFERS TO A GAY ACTOR BY THE PSEUDONYM "BEACH BOY."

WE HAVE RECEIVED NUMEROUS REQUESTS FROM THE MEDIA TO CONFIRM OR DENY WHETHER "BEACH BOY" IS ALAN DILLINGER OF THE HIT TELEVISION SHOW *LIFE-SAVERS* AND THE EXCITING NEW ROMANTIC COMEDY *BOY MEETS GIRL*.

ALAN DILLINGER WILL *NOT* DISCUSS THE INTIMATE DE-TAILS OF HIS PRIVATE LIFE, INCLUDING HIS FAMILY HIS-TORY, AS IT IS IRRELEVANT AND PERSONAL. *HE WILL REJECT ALL REQUESTS FOR INAPPROPRIATE OR INTRUSIVE INFOR-MATION.*

HOWEVER, MR. DILLINGER WOULD LIKE TO SAY THAT:

"AFTER SEVERAL YEARS' WORTH OF THOUGHT ON THE SUBJECT, I'VE DECIDED I DON'T THINK DISCLOSING WHETHER OR NOT YOU'RE GAY IS OVERLY INTIMATE IN-FORMATION. IT'S LIKE ACKNOWLEDGING WHETHER YOU'RE REALLY A BRUNETTE, IF YOUR TAN IS REAL OR FAKE, OR IF YOU'RE A MAN.

"I WOULD LIKE TO CONFIRM THAT MY HAIR WAS ORIGI-NALLY BROWN, THAT MY TAN IS MOSTLY FAKE, THAT I AM A MAN, AND THAT I AM HAPPY TO BE GAY.

271

"I WOULD LIKE TO THANK MY FANS FOR ALL THEIR LOVE AND SUPPORT UP TO THIS POINT, AND WOULD LIKE TO SAY THAT I HOPE THEY'LL CONTINUE TO SUPPORT MY WORK AS AN ACTOR AND MY DECISION TO BE HONEST. I COULDN'T HAVE DONE IT WITHOUT YOU.

"FINALLY, I WOULD LIKE TO SAY THAT ANYONE WHO IS GAY BUT FEELS UNABLE TO BE HONEST ABOUT IT SHOULD CONSIDER HIS OR HER DECISION TO BE CLOSETED VERY CLOSELY—YOU DON'T KNOW WHAT—OR WHO—YOU'RE MISSING."

Gnats – 12, 15, 96, 129, 198
241